GW01157730

Hello Kerry,
997 people entered
and you were the one Sele-
Talk about An Act of F
I just hope my book
to the promise of
the contest. Hope to
back from you in the Fut-

[signature]

The Poe
Consequence

KEITH STEINBAUM

THE POE CONSEQUENCE
Copyright 2014© Keith Steinbaum

Library of Congress Control Number:	2014952764
ISBN 13: Paperback:	978-1-942296-01-0
PDF:	978-1-942296-02-7
ePub:	978-1-942296-04-1
Kindle:	978-1-942296-04-1
Hardcover:	978-1-942296-05-8

All rights reserved. No part of this publication may be
reproduced, distributed, or transmitted in any form or by any means,
including photocopying, recording, or other electronic or mechanical
methods, without the prior written permission of the publisher or author,
except in the case of brief quotations embodied in critical reviews and
certain other noncommercial uses permitted by copyright law.

Although every precaution has been taken to verify the accuracy
of the information contained herein, the author and publisher assume no
responsibility for any errors or omissions. No liability is assumed for
damages that may result from the use of information
contained within.

Printed in the United States of America

ACKNOWLEDGMENTS

In order of appearance, I want to thank my wife, Danielle, for her understanding of the vast quantity of time I needed to spend alone with my story and the many occasions where my mind was elsewhere. To my daughter, Adrienne, who was the first person I told about my desire to write a book, and who encouraged me to, "do it, Daddy." To my son, Justin, who showed his interest by making a habit of sneaking a peak over my shoulder to read lines off the computer screen. I also want to thank my two writing group cohorts, Isabella and Peter, for the numerous hours spent together at our homes, helping to strengthen each of our stories while simultaneously developing close friendships.

And a special debt of gratitude to Krista Michaels, my educator and literary lifeline, whose tough-love editing turned out to be just what the story needed. Thank you for giving me the encouragement to stick with it, and to "carry enough provisions to make the journey through the desert."

CONTENTS

Thy soul shall find itself alone

'Mid dark thoughts of the grey tomb-stone;

Not one, of all the crowd, to pry

Into thine hour of secrecy.

Be silent in that solitude,

Which is not loneliness - for then

The spirits of the dead, who stood

In life before thee, are again

In death around thee, and their will

Shall overshadow thee; be still.

From 'Spirits of the Dead' by Edgar Allan Poe

ONE

THE BOND BETWEEN THE BROTHERS commenced in the bunk bed of their mother's womb. Now an ominous future loomed, destined to rip them apart in a world of prophecies, horror, and death.

"Still plan on getting your fortune read tonight?" Kevin asked, reaching for his coffee.

"Hell, yes," Warren exclaimed. Returning the credit card to his wallet, he added, "A woman at the wedding party told me the best place to go."

"I see USC in your future," Kevin said, waving his hands over an imaginary crystal ball.

"Make fun of me all you want," Warren replied. "But the chance of finding someone credible is a lot better here in New Orleans than back home in L.A. Mysticism permeates this city. Stories of voodoo and magic are woven into its history. How could I not seek that out?"

Kevin stared at him, his blue eyes twinkling in apparent amusement. "It's unusual how we were born minutes apart, but in certain ways remain miles apart. Your belief in that psychic nonsense is another example of how different we are."

"There will always be con artists, I know that," Warren admitted. "But that doesn't mean clairvoyance isn't real." Placing his arms on the table, he leaned forward and gazed into the disbelieving eyes of his brother. His face, like Kevin's, was square jawed, with a slightly sloping nose that extended to a narrow tip bordered by long, thin nostrils. Their sandy brown hair hadn't yet shown any signs of receding, with the one difference being the shorter style preferred by Warren contrasted to the medium length curls that Kevin favored. Jutting his chin slightly upward, Warren continued his argument.

"There are two friends of mine, neither of whom know each other,

1

who both recently told me about a sudden feeling they got that something was wrong with one of their parents. One called home and was told that her father had just died. My other friend found out his mother was on her way to the hospital. She'd had a stroke. How could they have known that?"

"Lack of sleep and too much imagination," Kevin shot back. "The perfect recipe for delirium."

"These friends aren't flakes," Warren countered, annoyed over his brother's sarcasm. "We're still just scratching the surface of what our brains are capable of. Having inner visions and prophesying things is like an extra sense, that's all. True psychics are able to cultivate it."

Kevin looked at Warren with one of those "that's nice, are you finished now?" expressions that had pissed Warren off for years. "Truly mesmerizing, Professor Palmer," he said. "But your course in *Bullshit 101* will have to continue another day. I've got a plane to catch."

Rising simultaneously from the seats, their six-foot two-inch frames stood at least a half foot taller than a passing waitress who slowed her walk, angled her head upwards, and looked back and forth at the both of them before smiling and moving on.

"Even after thirty-five years, I sometimes forget you're almost Carbon to my Copy," Kevin remarked.

Warren nodded. "A dated analogy, but no less accurate." Approaching the exit, he placed his arm around Kevin's shoulders and said, *"I looked upon my future felicity as secured."*

"What?"

"It's a line from Edgar Allan Poe," he answered. "*The Black Cat.*"

Kevin closed his eyes and nodded. "Poe, of course. Silly of me to ask."

"A line of optimism, Kevin, as my fortune tonight will affirm."

Omnipresent Bourbon Street jazz provided the soundtrack as Warren advanced towards a man operating a mobile souvenir stand on the corner of Bourbon and Orleans. "Excuse me," he said, "I need directions to Jackson Square Park."

The vendor pointed his finger toward Orleans Street. "Keep heading that way," he said. "Go past Royale 'til you see the back of St. Louis Cathedral. There's an alley on either side that'll take you there."

As Warren approached the cathedral, he spotted a cardboard figure of a serious looking woman in a pink dress near the front of the alley on the left. A beige-colored sign covering the lower half of the dress read, "Madame Genevieve, spiritual reader." Behind the cutout was a street level window framed by lighted figures of moons and stars. Warren reached for the knob... and stopped. A feeling in his gut told him Madame Genevieve wasn't the one for him. He couldn't pinpoint the reason for his hesitation, but he knew that bypassing her was the correct thing to do.

Warren turned around and walked toward the alley on the opposite side. When he arrived at the narrow, semi-darkened entrance, he looked up at the side of the building and saw a black and white street sign that read, "Pirate's Alley." He looked at his watch and saw that almost forty minutes had passed. He hadn't expected to take that long finding a reader, but his instincts told him he'd soon come across the right one. As he exited the alley he stood facing the park at Jackson Square. Bright lights offered a view of several colorfully garbed individuals sitting at separate tables.

"*Now I can see why I was told to come here,*" he said to himself.

Warren chose the closest open table, sitting across from a woman who called herself Madame Irene, a sultry, raven-haired woman with wild eyes and a piercing, laser beam gaze. As he settled in his chair preparing to begin, he encountered that same sense of doubt he experienced about Madame Genevieve. "I'm sorry," he told her, rising from his chair. "Maybe another time."

Warren walked past the six other psychics without stopping. He couldn't understand the reason for his sudden selectivity, feeling like a kid who couldn't decide which flavored ice cream he wanted. He crossed the street and returned to Pirate's Alley. "Maybe I should just forget the whole thing," he said out loud. A few steps in, the sight of another alley branching off to the left startled him. "*How did I miss that?*" he whispered.

Warren stopped at the entrance, peering down a passageway that appeared devoid of anything other than an unusual looking structure about halfway down. "*I can't stop now,*" he told himself. "*This might be the way.*" As he drew closer, he observed the strange shape and realized it was a large awning tilting so far down it almost touched the ground. He sidestepped the fallen canopy to get a closer look. "*The High Seas,*" he said quietly, peering at the sign above the door. "*I wonder what kind of place this was?*"

Warren continued walking, sensing he was now on the right path. The distant sound of jazz music had morphed into an eerie silence that seemed a strange contrast to the festive atmosphere a few blocks away. As he looked around, he realized he stood in complete isolation. Now that he thought about it, there hadn't been anyone in sight for a while.

Within the shadows, concealed by leafy trees in man-sized terra cotta pots, a small entranceway appeared. He turned and moved towards it, feeling *drawn* there, like those stories of lost animals that somehow find their way home. He saw an open door leading to a garden courtyard no more than twenty feet away. And there, in the window of what appeared to be part of someone's home, shone a bright blue neon sign in an upstairs window that read, "Madame Sibilia- Psychic."

He clutched the cold wrought-iron railing and ascended the narrow stairs. A solitary gas lamp illuminated the checkerboard stonework and abundance of potted plants. Warren tugged at the creases on his jacket, took a deep breath, and discovered that the door stood slightly ajar. He looked for a doorbell and when he didn't locate one, knocked twice before peeking inside.

"Hello?" he called out. "Hello? Anyone here?" Standing with a foot inside the doorway, Warren scanned the tiny room. Yellow pillar candles placed in tall, antique holders provided a dull light. A small glass table with two chairs was situated near the center of a drawn, shiny gold curtain. "Hello?" he repeated, knocking again.

The curtain moved as someone entered the room. He readied himself to explain why he was there, but found himself staring into the chocolate eyes of a beautiful, silk-skinned black woman. She appeared to be in her mid thirties, tall and shapely, and she wore a maroon-colored floor-length caftan with a matching headdress that exposed her face like a jeweled amulet.

"Are you Madame Sibilia?" he asked.

"You have come for a reading."

The intonation of her French-hued accent seemed unusual, as if she was telling him about his visit rather than asking him.

"Is it all right?"

"We will begin in a few moments," she said. "Please, sit down. I would like to talk with you before we proceed to the other room."

The subtle aroma of incense created a pleasant addition to Warren's anticipation. He took his seat and noticed a single business card in a plastic holder at the edge of the desk.

"Mind if I take your last card?" he asked, grasping it in his fingers. "A souvenir for my brother."

He studied the bland design of several stars and moons against the white background. He turned the card over, revealing the same white setting with black letters across the center reading, "Madame Sibilia,

Psychic." She had her phone number in smaller type at the bottom, but no address listed. He contemplated the different turns and alleyways required to find her. *Why no address?* he wondered, unzipping his jacket pocket and depositing the card inside.

"You are prepared to seek the truth?" she asked.

"I'm eager to find something out," he replied, "about a teaching job I'm hoping to get."

"Let me see your palm."

Warren reached out and rested his right forearm across her desk. Placing his hand in hers, Madame Sibilia remained silent as her head moved in inconspicuous nods.

"I see something that must be explained," she said, her voice a loud whisper. "The Tarot is a source of enlightenment and self-knowledge, and you will hear much about your life. Not just the past and the present, but also what lies ahead."

"Great," he said, "the future. That's the reason I came."

"Please understand," she replied, her tone a bit too serious for his liking, "you will be told all that is revealed. Nothing shall remain a secret."

"That's fine... fine, no problem," he replied, anxious to get started. She gazed into his eyes and nodded. Placing her hands flat on the desk, she rose from her chair. "The reading room is through the curtain," she told him. "Please go inside."

Warren entered a larger room filled with a continuance of similar candles. To his right stood a table with two wooden chairs placed across from each other, each facing a bulky gray handkerchief covering something in the center of the table. In the middle of the room, an old-fashioned avocado green couch with matching chairs brought back memories of early photos of his parents in their younger days. Long strands of hippy beads dangled from an open doorway and a dark blue lava lamp glowed from the opposite corner. He walked over to watch the hypnotic spectacle of the lamp, perplexed by the unplugged cord lying on the floor.

"Let us begin," she said, standing near the curtain. He followed her to the table and settled in the closest chair. Madame Sibilia slid the handkerchief off the unknown object, exposing a pack of Tarot cards. Raising her eyes to Warren's she said, "There are seventy-eight cards in the Tarot. We will use ten."

She eased the cards over to Warren and asked him to shuffle them, making sure to keep the pictures of each card face down. "By shuffling the cards, your conscious and subconscious mind will be made one with the Tarot," she explained. "Now divide the cards into three piles. These will represent your past, present, and future."

"Which pile is which?" he asked.

"Your own intuition will determine that answer," she told him.

Enjoying the sense of mystery, Warren brought the cards together and shuffled them one more time upon her request.

"The cards are ready to be revealed," she announced.

"Let's do it," he told her, rubbing his hands on his knees.

"There will be ten cards chosen, each representing a life force. I will place them in a spread called, 'The Celtic Cross'. They will explain what is behind you, show your present position, and reveal your future. The final card will determine the outcome. Its meaning will be communicated to us by the influences of the other nine cards."

Madame Sibilia placed the first six cards, face up, on the table. With the exception of a single card lying horizontally across another, the other five were separated from each other and placed in vertical positions. Warren couldn't help noticing how her eyes started blinking and her eyebrows narrow with each card she set on the table. She reminded him of someone playing a high stakes game in Vegas and showing distress over the hand they'd been dealt. He also perceived the increased time she took with each successive card, as if she didn't want to see what came next. All the silence and solemnity made him uncomfortable.

"That bad, huh?" Warren said, hoping to lighten the mood.

Madame Sibilia held up her hand in an unspoken request for quiet and selected the final four cards from the deck. These were placed face down, in contrast to the others whose identity was exposed. Taking her fingers and grasping the left side of each one, she turned the last four cards over from left to right. When the final card revealed itself, Warren was sure he heard a groan.

He didn't want to believe that her mannerisms were just part of an act, and that he was the audience watching a performance, yet he wasn't sure what to make of her reactions. There was something about her expression that made him feel uneasy and fidget in his seat.

"Why are some of the cards backwards?" he asked.

"Those cards are reversed," she answered. "Their direction affects how they're interpreted."

"Six of the cards are black and four are red. Does that mean anything?"

"Everything has meaning."

As Warren lifted his gaze from the cards she unnerved him by her intense stare.

"Something wrong?" he asked.

"Your future disturbs me greatly."

Warren's stomach tightened. "What... what do you mean?"

"The answers are coming," she said. "We'll begin with the first card."

Card number one, a red one, was called a Ten of Cups.

"This is your present position," she said. "You have contentment in your life. You are surrounded by an aura of love."

"That sounds good, doesn't it? Why were you so troubled before?"

"My concern begins with the next card," she replied, a strange edge to her voice.

"Go on," he muttered. "I'm listening."

Madame Sibilia placed her hand on the one horizontal card, an Eight of Swords, lying across the Ten of Cups.

"The second card shows an immediate influence of something that exists in your near future," she said. "By crossing the Ten of Cups, it will affect your life's path."

"What does the Eight of Swords mean?"

Madame Sibilia's demeanor remained somber. "When a black Eight of Swords reveals itself in this manner, there is serious difficulty ahead. Perhaps an accident of some kind." She appeared ready to say something else, then her shoulders sagged and she fell silent.

Warren sat up in his chair. "What kind of accident?"

"Let us continue," she said, "so that we may understand."

When Madame Sibilia pointed in the direction of another black-suited card, he recognized the character immediately.

"The third card is called The Devil. It represents your destiny."

Warren swallowed hard.

"You seem like a nice man, Mr. Palmer. But I see violence in your future. And evil. A strong attraction to evil."

Warren shook his head, flustered, unable to recall when he had told her his name.

"That's ridiculous!" he cried. He took a deep breath to regain his composure. "I didn't come here to listen to this doom and gloom nonsense, all right? The person you're talking about sure as hell isn't me."

"I told you before, Mr. Palmer, I was going to tell you all that I see," she said.

"And you see evil and violence, for me, huh? Do you scare everybody like this? I came here to see about a job opening I hope to get. But this has been very depressing and I'm damn upset about it."

"Do you wish to continue?" she asked.

"Let's hurry through the remaining cards, all right?"

Madame Sibilia proceeded to the fourth card, a red-suited Six of Cups.

"This card represents past influences that affect present events," she said. "You grew up in a home with strict morals. You've taken on those same characteristics in your own life and in your family. You resent what you see as a moral breakdown in society. You long for what's referred to as 'the good old days'."

"Now that's more like it," Warren exclaimed. He looked down at the black-suited card that came next. "Please continue."

"The fifth card is a reversed Four of Wands. In this situation, it stands for recent past events. There's a dark cloud here, sadness of some kind, over someone very close to you. A health problem, perhaps, or a disappointment with someone in your family."

"My wife, Michelle, died of cancer last October," he replied.

Madame Sibilia closed her eyes for a few moments, nodding her head. She advanced to the next black-suited card. "The sixth card is a reversed Nine of Swords," she said. Pausing, she glanced at Warren with an expression that seemed almost sorrowful, reminding him of her earlier warning about his future. "I see isolation. Wandering and despair in the after-life. An angry restlessness."

"Here we go again," he complained. "Wandering and despair in the after-life? What the hell does that mean, anyway? That I'm destined to become some sort of ghost? A restless, wandering ghost? Is that what you're saying?"

Madame Sibilia gazed into Warren's eyes. "Death doesn't always bring a peaceful conclusion, Mr. Palmer." Her voice was calm, yet her message, terrifying. "There are some who believe when a person dies they are given a choice of two pathways into the next world. They take the form of separate lights, and they are quite different from each other."

Warren remained silent, too numb to respond.

Madame Sibilia continued. "When someone's soul is disturbed, when it's unsettled, there is another light that veers away from Heaven, a darker entrance, that one may choose to take."

"And where does that lead?" he asked. "Hell?"

"Not Hell," she answered. "But a place where one may wander

forever. If these spirits finally achieve serenity, they can find their way back to the light of eternal peace."

"Is that what a ghost is?" he asked.

"Some of these restless spirits, or ghosts as you call them, remain in one place where their souls are secure, like a house, or an area of land. They are often harmless. Others... others may attempt to violate. These are the dangerous ones."

Warren didn't understand. "What do you mean, 'violate'?"

"Invade the sanctity of someone's mind and body," she replied. "Poison their emotions. Control what they see, and hear... and think. Some even have the power to kill."

"For what purpose?" he asked.

Madame Sibilia's expression was calm, but her eyes blazed with an unnerving power.

"Revenge."

He stared in silence, wondering, again, what he had to do with any of this.

"Even good people are familiar with evil deeds, Mr. Palmer. Our lives present many opportunities to learn of such things and use this awareness on others from the after-world I've described. These acts of evil can be nurtured from knowledge that is real or imagined. It doesn't matter."

Warren leaned back in his chair. Edgar Allan Poe had written about such evil. "You said before there are some who believe in different pathways to the next world. Are you one of them?"

Madame Sibilia's hardened visage displayed a trace of a smile. "I'm quite sure of it."

"And this might happen to me?" he asked. "An angry ghost entering someone's soul? Intent on doom and destruction?"

She waited several moments before answering. "Yes," she whispered.

Warren stared down at the cards. "Let's go to the next one," he said, looking at another black-suited card.

"The seventh card is a reversed Wheel of Fortune. It describes your present position with personal things like job and family."

"I've applied for a teaching job at U.S.C. Can you tell me anything about that?"

"I'm sorry, but in this card I see bad luck."

Warren's shoulders sagged. Without a punch being thrown, he felt beat up. He knew he shouldn't believe her frightening scenarios, but the constant barrage of troubling news was upsetting nonetheless. He stared with a feeling of emptiness at the red-suited card that came next.

"The eighth card is the Sun card," she said. "This can be interpreted as a symbol of love, devotion, contentment from others."

"Thank you, Sun card," he said. "I welcome you like a long, lost friend."

"It also shows you to have a positive influence on other people." Madame Sibilia raised her head and looked at him. "People like... Bill and Joanne."

Warren's eyes widened at the mention of Michelle's parents, who he'd be meeting tomorrow in Phoenix before returning home. A frightening realization occurred to him, transcending any lingering doubt. *She's for real.*

"How do you know about them? Are they all right?"

"Yes, Mr. Palmer," she answered. "They're fine.

Warren looked at the next black-suited card, and, still wary, wondered what this female purveyor of darkness would say next.

"The ninth card is a reversed Star. This represents your troubled emotions, like bad dreams, or anxiety in situations you have yet to face."

Warren bolted out of his chair. "Enough!" he shouted. "I'm out of here!"

"Please wait, Mr. Palmer," she said, her expression maddeningly calm. "The tenth card is vital to understand."

Warren looked at Madame Sibilia for several seconds before glancing downward. His eyes grew wide and he had difficulty pulling them away. A red-suited card, entitled "Judgment," contained an image of an angel blowing a horn over a man, a woman, and a child-like figure in an open tomb. The picture felt like a dagger to the heart. The woman and child reminded him of Michelle, and their son, Seth. and seeing them in a tomb with a man, who he feared was himself, gave Warren a sickening feeling of claustrophobia.

"I don't want to know about that card!" he roared, backing towards the door. "I don't want to know!"

Madame Sibilia following him to the open doorway as he hurried down the stairs.

"A new beginning, Mr. Palmer!" she cried. "The Judgment card shows a new beginning! You were directed here to learn this!"

At the bottom of the steps, Warren looked back and saw Madame Sibilia standing just inside the doorway, looking down at him. For a brief moment he thought about asking her what she meant by "a new beginning," but he was too upset. *Directed here to learn this?* The woman was a nut-case.

Warren rushed past the open gate into the obscurity of the darkened, soundless alley. He hesitated, unsure which direction to take, then turned left and broke into a jog through the unfamiliar landscape. He wanted to reattach himself to civilization again, to see a face and hear a voice. As he ran from one alleyway into another, the welcome sound of a spirited saxophone seemed to appear out of nowhere, causing him to stop in his tracks and close his eyes in gratitude. Turning his face upwards, he inhaled the air as if he'd been a drowning swimmer rescued from an unforgiving sea. His throat felt devoid of any moisture and his damp shirt clung to his body. His head ached, throbbing to a steady rhythm of pain. He wasn't sure what street he was on or how he got there, but he knew what he needed; a good, stiff, drink. He resumed running, heading towards the music.

♪♪♪ ♪♪♪ ♪♪♪

"A Hurricane," he managed to say, his voice rendered weak and raspy.

Warren's eyes never left the hotel bartender until she placed the magical rum concoction within reach of his unsteady hands.

"If you don't mind me asking sir," she said, "are you all right?"

Warren closed his eyes and guzzled the drink for several moments, relishing the cool rush of liquid salvation sliding down his throat in search of a direct route to his brain.

"Now that I'm here, I'll be okay," he replied, continuing to clutch his drink. "Why do you ask?"

She looked at him, offering a slight, hesitant smile. "I was wondering if you had the flu or something," she said. "You're as white as a ghost."

TWO

*H*E HAD NEVER SEEN a forest, but in the neighborhood where he was from, his imagination was no less inspired by the wonder of those telephone poles.

"*Like rifles to the sky,*" he whispered to himself. "*Ready to shoot down some motherfucker's ass.*"

"Who ya talkin' at, Face?" Hawk asked, sitting on the ground to his left. "Weed got you seein' shit, homie?"

Alejandro Torres, born twenty-one years earlier in East L.A., acquired the gang name '2Face', because his natural angelic expression turned into a vicious snarl during those early fights arranged to test his manhood. As the years passed, and his boyish appearance matured into a dark, rugged handsomeness, the "2" was dropped in favor of just "Face." His eyes, however, highlighted the most memorable aspect of his appearance, resembling a pair of mysterious black coins that portrayed a different side to each gender. For the foxy women, *las mamacitas,* his gaze caused them to turn their heads a second and third time, searing them with his animalistic sexuality. For men, his penetrating stare instilled an uneasy intimidation, a sense that those two dark searchlights could see right through you.

Face kept his attention on the overhead view. "Just chillin', Hawk," he answered, after a long moment of silence. "Look at that sky up there. It's beautiful, man. Ain't seen a friendly sky for a long time."

Hawk laughed as he reached into his shirt pocket. "What the fuck you talkin' 'bout, 'a friendly sky'?" he asked, striking a match to another

13

joint. "Have some more of Hawk's *kick-ass mota, vato.* You'll be flyin' the friendly skies, man!" After a few minutes Hawk rose to his feet. "I need a fuckin' beer. You comin'?"

Face took another deep, satisfying drag. After exhaling, he watched the smoke drift away before answering. "Be there soon."

Face returned his attention to the sky. Through the lens of his marijuana haze, he no longer visualized the telephone poles as rifles, but as giant stiff-armed stick figures lined up and down the street. Tilting his head at another angle, he imagined them to be dark wooden pillars supporting the weight of the city sky. The beautiful *L.A.* sky. From May to March he'd spent ten long months at a detention camp somewhere in the mountains. He had missed those telephone poles, and the cable wires, too, criss-crossing above his head like Etch-a Sketch designs.

Etch-a-Sketch. He remembered that little red toy. Fuck, yeah, he remembered. The way he grew up, it was easy to recall the few things he got when getting nothing was a way of life. The only thing he got regular was his old man's fist. He was real good at giving when it came to that. Face took another deep hit, hoping to block out any thoughts of his father. Instead, a distant memory resurfaced as he fingered an old scar, reminding him of the day he paid a painful price for the discovery of a distinctive power he inherited, his gift, that he wouldn't come to understand until later.

Glancing back at the deepening purple sky, Face approached the comforting sound of broken glass echoing through the abandoned, outdoor parking lot as another empty beer bottle shattered against the graffiti-tagged wall. All that was left of the old structure were numerous areas of chipped blacktop and an assortment of straw-colored weeds jutting from the cracks. Without any nearby streetlights, this darkened, out-of-the-way section of the neighborhood acted as a favorite hangout for the Diablos to plan war strategy or just get high. Tonight was a cause for both.

"Got more beer, Kush?" Face asked, joining the others.

"Got your gold mama's milk right there, *vato,*" he said, pointing to a large cooler on the ground. "All that time away, you forget who's got your back?" Kush adjusted the angle on his baseball cap, pushed his hands down low into his deep, baggy pockets, and swaggered his way over to the cooler.

"Tonight's the night, man," Cat remarked, loud enough for the other six to hear.

"What other way to show respect for our *comarada*?" Cherry said. "Apache was killed a year ago, man. We gonna honor him right."

"Payback!" Kush shouted, handing Face his beer.

"Payback!" Player repeated.

"Payback gonna be a *bitch*!" Swat added, pretending to fire an assault rifle.

"To Apache!" Face yelled, raising his beer bottle high.

"To Apache!" everyone shouted back.

"We ain't through gettin' our heads right," Hawk said, removing a folded paper from his pocket. "Get your motherfuckin' asses over here."

"You got what I think you got?" Face asked, smiling.

Hawk chuckled. "Hell, yeah, Face," he answered. "Gonna speed you to those friendly skies you was talkin' 'bout."

On that April evening, as darkness settled in, the next order of business pertained to the memorial for Apache on the sidewalk outside the yard.

Cherry's trembling hands lighted the saint-covered candle. "*Te estraño*, Apache," he said, his voice a balancing act between solemnity and anger.

"We all miss him, Cherry," Swat added.

"*Vaya con Dios,*" Kush whispered, placing a beer bottle next to the flickering glass encasing.

Player set a handful of flowers next to the other items. "We ain't never gonna forget you, Apache," he said.

In the cool, reflective silence, as the six other Diablos surrounded the candle's meditative flame, Face turned around to contemplate the ultimate legacy to Apache's artistic gift. Extending more than half the length of the yard, at a height close to seven feet, the old, white cinder block wall had been transformed into a masterpiece: a self-portrait of Apache, set in the time of the Old West. Wearing nothing but a moccasin-colored cloth around his waist, and a green and red-featheredheadband encircling his wavy, black hair, the muscular warrior-artist sat atop a mighty stallion charging into battle. As several bloodied cowboys fell victim to his bow and arrow mastery, the smiling, confident face of Carlos "Apache" Diaz represented victory over the enemy.

"We got the Indian warrior in us now, *vato*," he told Apache at the painting's completion. "Protectin' our yard for all the homeboys."

"You gotta believe it always, Face," Apache replied. "The wall represents what we're about. Courage and strength, man."

"For every goddamn battle we fight, Apache. Courage and strength."

The passing of a year's time did nothing to calm Face's uneasiness over Apache's death, as he contemplated how that indestructible feeling he inherited over the completion of the painting had eroded into an unsteady footing. None of the others would have believed that Face felt vulnerable, but he did. Tonight, as he gazed upon Apache's work, the painting not only seemed less protective than before, but an eerie feeling of hostility seemed to have emerged. He wondered if there might be a bigger battle in store, even more significant than the ones fought against their sworn enemy, the North Rampart Lobos. Apache's soul was forceful and present, but Face didn't believe that was enough to defend them. He sensed the possibility of another spirit. A different kind of warrior. An uncommon type of war.

ⵝⵝⵝ ⵝⵝⵝ ⵝⵝⵝ

A separate gathering, less noble in purpose yet just as meaningful to the different gang members involved, occurred later that evening a mile away.

"Hey, *pendejo,*" King snarled. "Two fuckin' sixpacks? That's all you took off with? Hell, that ain't no party, stupid. You got shit for brains, or somethin'?"

"Gimme a fuckin' break, man," T-Moe replied. "That 7/11 asshole didn't take his eyes off me."

"This ain't gonna gimme no goddamn buzz," King complained. "Bud's like water to me, man."

"You drink more of that shit than anybody I know," Bone said, laughing as he passed a joint. "That's why you're 'King', man. Always drinkin' The 'King of Beers'."

King responded with a loud belch. "God damn right, *vato.*"

Standing near a bench in Lafayette Park with a group of Lobo homeboys, King guzzled the last of another can before squashing it with his foot and hurling the flattened metal towards an overhanging light. The sun had long set, and people who were concerned for their safety had already gone home to hide behind locked doors and barred windows.

King walked over to some nearby bushes to urinate. When he returned looking for another beer, he saw just one can remaining.

"We need more *pinchi* suds, man," he said. "And we get what we goddamn want, ain't that right, Ghoul?"

16

Tall, thin, pockmarked and pale, Ghoul laughed his crazy laugh before taking a hit from the joint. Ghoul laughed his crazy laugh a lot, even when there wasn't anything to laugh at. Slice was there too, throwing his knife against a tree, showing King's eleven-year-old kid brother, Luis, the proper release point.

"Sure you don't want no weed, Slice?" Ghoul said, offering him the joint. "I ain't never seen you smoke the shit."

Slice tilted his head, offering Ghoul a serious look. "There's a reason for that, *cabron,*" he said. "Watch and learn." Slice approached the tree and proceeded to carve a head-sized circle at the same level of his own. Walking away, he didn't stop until he passed a lamplight that stood no less than twenty-five from the target. He tucked the handle under his belt, allowing half the blade to be exposed. Standing in trance-like silence for several moments, he reached down for the blade with a sudden motion, clutched both sides of the metal between his fingers, and sent the knife streaking toward the tree.

Luis was the first to hurry over and confirm what everyone could see from a distance. The knife had hit the inside portion of the circle.

"Right in the fuckin' center!" he shouted.

After the others inspected the result themselves, Slice pulled the knife from the tree, slid the handle back into his pants, and sauntered over to Ghoul. "No booze, no drugs," he told him. "Just me and my knife. Understand, *cabron*?"

Ghoul cackled as he took several steps backward. "Yeah," he replied, looking away.

"Your old lady give you beer money, Bone?" King asked.

Bone reached down into the pockets of his sagging pants, pulling out a couple of crumbled bills. "Six dollars," he said.

"*God damn!*" King spit a large wad of saliva onto the ground. "Is that all you fuckin' got? That ain't enough for shit! I thought your old lady worked, asshole! You're gonna make me lose it, man. *Seme va la onda!*

"I'll kick her fuckin' ass when I get home," Bone promised.

King turned away. "Don't fuck with me, man. *No me chinges!* I need to think."

Seizing the last can of Bud, King walked through the darkness to the other side of the park. From here, he had a better view of the street where he spent so much time. He took a cigarette from his jacket and used the last of the one he was smoking to light another. He inhaled until his lungs were full, letting the smoke seep out like a leak from a tire, drifting up past the nasty scar over his left eye where the brow had been replaced by overhanging skin that resembled chewed, flesh-colored gum. He began to feel *tranquilo*, at peace, scanning the familiar sights of his neighborhood: The *clínica medica* and *farmacia*, where his mother used to take him when he was sick from something other than a hangover. The *lavandería*, where they went to wash what little clothes he had. The auto shop, where his old man used to take his beat up piece-of-shit to get fixed. The *panadería*, where he used to go as a kid so he could smell the fresh bread baking, making him so hungry he'd cross the street to steal food from the fruit and vegetable *mercado*. The place he didn't want to look at was the *funeraria*. He'd been there enough through the years.

As a kid, his parents started giving him beer to get him drunk when they wanted a good laugh with their other drunken friends. When he danced or sang for them, they'd give him more. When they needed to fuck and scream without being disturbed they supplied him with enough to pass out, but that didn't always work. He still heard them sometimes.

His old man ran off with some bitch when his mother was pregnant with Luis, and she started drinking more after that. No one knew where his old man was anymore. His mother's cleaning jobs were just enough to pay the rent and live on canned food and beer. When the rent was due, or a bill had to be paid, his own efforts on the street helped them survive. His mother didn't ask any questions, but he knew she was grateful for whatever he could provide, however he did it. Luis understood the way things worked now and he'd start helping soon.

King had "checked in" the North Rampart Lobos when he was thirteen. His old neighborhood *camarada*, Viper, took him under his wing and showed him the life of a Lobo. He still couldn't bear to think about Viper's death in prison. When he heard that he took a knife in the neck he felt like he'd also been stabbed. Viper had made a lot of enemies through the years, but when King got the news an Alvarado Street Diablo had killed him, he knew the order had come from the outside. From that day, he promised himself he'd find the one responsible and kill him for taking the life of his blood brother and teacher.

From his first day in the gang, two things were made clear: You could die any day, so every moment you're alive, live it as a Lobo. And because you could die any day, if you wanted something bad enough, do whatever the fuck it takes to get it. At twenty-four years old, Miguel "King" Ruiz had learned his lessons well, and tonight he wanted to get drunk and party like a Lobo – no matter what it took.

They'd wait for their chance at the late-night store down the street. The lights weren't too good and he figured they'd find somebody around there to jump. King would make sure the asshole kept his mouth shut before they left. Shoving the barrel of his .38 into his balls while the others stomped on his head worked before and would work again. King couldn't wait to see the look of helplessness in his eyes. The look of *fear*.

And if it was a woman? His heart started pumping faster at the thought. Maybe she'd wanna go inside her car and get a look at a *real* man. King pictured the scene and smiled as his dick stiffened.

Either way, man or woman, somebody was gonna be his bitch tonight.

THREE

"RAUUUUUUL!" "RAUUUUUUL!" "RAUUUUUUL!"

The chant for Dodger third baseman Raul Hernandez thundered throughout the stadium as the Cincinnati pitcher stood on the mound, reading the signs from his catcher. With two men out, the bases loaded, and the Dodgers down by two runs, Seth Palmer, age eleven, covered his face with his glove, too afraid to look.

"Rauuuuuul!" "Rauuuuuul!" "Rauuuuuul!"

The next pitch was hit high and deep down the left field foul line. As Seth heard the roar of the crowd, he leaped up out of his seat screaming, "Home run! Home run!" Within seconds, however, he added his voice to the collective moan of forty thousand others when the umpire signaled a foul ball. Seth sat down and glove-shielded his face once again; his shoulders slumped in a sign of dismay. When the catcher turned to the umpire to signal a time out, Warren tapped his son on the shoulder. "Don't forget to breathe," he said, smiling. "It's okay, Seth," his Uncle Kevin added. "You're not the only one who's nervous around here."

"Rauuuuuul!" "Rauuuuuul!" "Rauuuuuul!"

On the next pitch, Hernandez popped-up to the third baseman and just like that, the game was over. Warren and Kevin started their trek up the crowded aisle, followed by a despondent Seth.

"Geez," Seth lamented, "if Langley hadn't stopped at third when Ruiz hit that double to right center in the eighth we would have only been down by one run instead of two, and then we could have tried a squeeze play when Baker came up. He's our best bunter, you know."

Warren pinched the bridge of his nose, trying to will away the headache that had cradled his forehead most of the game. "The word, 'if' doesn't do anybody any good, son," he told him. "What's done is done." Glancing at Kevin, Warren noted his look of disapproval.

"I want to get a souvenir," Seth said.

"Not tonight," Warren replied. "The longer we wait the longer it will take to get out of here."

"Please, Dad? I've been saving my allowance to buy something. I won't take long, I promise."

"All right," he snapped, "but make it quick."

"I will!" Seth shouted, dashing towards the stand.

"Go easy on him," Kevin said. "You're all he's got now."

Warren closed his eyes and massaged his temples. "I know," he said. "But these headaches come on without a warning and I admit I get irritable sometimes. You wouldn't have any aspirin on you, would you?"

"No, sorry," he answered.

"The latest rounds of budget cuts have all of us on edge," Kevin said. "We don't know from one day to the next what classes will be dropped or if we'll still have a job." Kevin shook his head. "I bet the U.S.C. profs aren't feeling the knife like us junior college teachers."

"They should have hired you," Kevin said.

Warren shrugged his shoulders and glanced at Seth, pleased to see that he had chosen something in the display case. "Do you remember the poem Dad wrote after his war buddy was murdered in a liquor store?"

"*A Victim's Time*, right?"

"Yes, that's it," Warren said. "A few days ago I was cleaning out a box of old poetry books I used for my classes. There it was, *A Victim's Time*, sticking out from the pages of *The Tell Tale Heart*. I had forgotten about it."

"*The Tell-Tale Heart?*" Kevin exclaimed, his eyebrows rising with an amused look. "You used to go around reciting lines from it all the time."

Warren stared at Kevin, his eyes squinting. "*True. Nervous. Very, very dreadfully nervous I had been and am! But why will you say that I am mad?*"

"Okay, okay," Kevin said. "If I don't stop you now you'll go on all night."

"When I read Dad's poem I realized it's just as relevant today as it was the day he wrote it."

"How so?"

"Because our military is still fighting and dying for the rest of us who attend baseball games and worry about three game losing streaks," Warren answered. "Listen to what he wrote.

> *"The valiant soldier's blood will spill*
> *On red-stained lands of sacrifice..."*

The recitation came to a halt as Seth hurried to his father. "I bought you something, Dad," he said, smiling and holding one hand behind his back. "Close your eyes."

"Are you serious?" Warren asked, doing as he was told.

"Okay, open 'em!"

Warren gazed at a gold-colored baseball in Seth's hand, with the Dodger logo written between the seams. "They had different colors, but I liked this one the best."

Warren's headache didn't prevent his appreciation for his son's gift, but he knew that Seth's delay at the concession stand meant he'd have to deal with the pain for an extended time now that so many people had already arrived at their cars.

"Seth, I love it," he said. "Thank you."

A few minutes later they arrived at Kevin's car first. "Maybe next time I won't have to work late and we can ride together," he told them. His face showed concern. "I can tell you're in pain, Warren. Maybe you should stop off at a market and take something for your headache now. You've got a long drive ahead of you."

"Not a bad idea," Warren said. "You know this neighborhood better than I do. Where's a market around here?"

Kevin looked towards his left at the nearest exit before removing a small notepad and pen from his inside coat pocket. "I'll write the directions for you," he said, leaning forward on the hood. Handing the paper to Warren, he pointed towards the Stadium Way exit. "You'll go out there and make a right at the bottom. Just follow the directions and you'll arrive at Alfredo's Market in about six or seven minutes. At this hour you'll be in and out in no time."

⚱ ⚱ ⚱

Warren started to navigate his way through the stadium traffic. He noticed Seth sitting motionless, staring out the window. In the solitude of that moment, Warren saw Michelle's face in his son's profile. Along with her identical dark brown wavy hair, he had the same wide forehead and small, slightly curved ears. Unlike his own narrow, sloped nose, Seth possessed a well-formed, delicately turned-up shape, complimenting his high cheekbones and bright, hazel eyes, brought to him, as well, courtesy of Michelle.

"Still upset Baker didn't get a chance for a squeeze play?" he asked.

"No," Seth replied, his voice vacant of emotion.

"Something wrong, son?"

Seth startled Warren when he saw tears filling his eyes.

"What's the matter?" he asked, glancing back and forth from his son to the cars ahead of him.

Seth swallowed hard. "Dad, is everything going to be all right with us? I mean, Mom's been gone for awhile now, but... I still don't know if..." Lowering his head, he added, "I... I really miss her."

Warren placed his hand on his son's shoulder. "I miss her, too," he said. "But we've been doing fine so far, don't you think?"

"Yeah, I guess." Seth wiped a tear away. "Do you think she's looking down on us?"

"Definitely," Warren said, knowing no amount of head pain could compare to the emotional trauma of their loss. "I picture Mom strolling through a warm, sunny garden, surrounded by beautiful and fragrant..."

"Roses!" Seth blurted out.

"Yep. Her favorite flower."

"The ones named 'Peace', for sure," Seth said.

"No doubt about it. Those roses were the ones she loved most. How many times did we hear her talk about 'those beautiful yellow and pink blooms'?"

"Remember when Uncle Kevin gave her that rose bush for her birthday, and he found that birthday card with somebody giving the 'peace' sign?"

Warren nodded then stopped, his pain rattling like ice cubes against the inside of his forehead. "Your mom loved that gift."

"Do you think everybody goes to Heaven when they die?" Seth asked.

"I don't know about everybody," Warren said, working his forehead with his fingertips. "I'd hate to think Hitler's up there sniffing roses with your mom, but I'm sure she's feeling right at home."

Neither one spoke for several minutes as Warren exited the stadium on Scott Avenue.

"Uncle Kevin told me you saw a fortune teller in New Orleans," Seth said.

"Damn it!" Warren snapped. "I just told him about it this morning. Why would he even mention it to you?"

Seth turned away. "Sorry," he muttered. "We were just talking about different stuff when you went to get some hot dogs. He asked me if I believed in psychics like you do. He said you told him about seeing one

24

when you were there."

Warren took a deep breath, regretting his outburst. "The woman I saw didn't tell me what I wanted to hear," he explained. "It was during the time I applied for that opening at U.S.C. I got caught up in the atmosphere of New Orleans, I guess."

"Did she have one of those crystal balls?"

"She read Tarot cards. They're like big playing cards with pictures on them."

"What was her name?"

"Madame Sibilia," Warren answered. "She called herself a psychic, but that's just a fancy name for a fortune teller."

"Was she for real or just a big faker?"

Warren remained silent for a few moments. "I don't know," he replied, his voice not much more than a whisper.

"What did she tell you?"

"I'll answer your question and then we change the subject, okay?"

"Okay."

"We talked about ghosts."

"Ghosts?" Seth repeated, his eyes opening wide. "Wow."

Warren made his body shake as if he were shivering from fright. "Ooooooh, I was scared."

Seth smiled. "Well, it serves you right."

"What's that supposed to mean?"

"You know that spooky story you read sometimes when my friends sleep over? Where the guy kills that other guy and hides his heart under the floor?"

"I'm surprised you don't know the title by now," he said. "You've heard it enough times. It's called, *The Tell-Tale Heart*. Written by Edgar Allan Poe, one of the greatest minds the literary world has ever known. All my students know it's my favorite Poe composition, his work that I quote the most."

"Yeah, whatever," Seth said. "Anyway, like I said, it serves you right. Don't you remember my birthday last year when Freddy and Mike slept over and you read us that poem? Freddy woke us up at four o'clock all scared and everything. And then he wanted to go home 'cause he was hearing heartbeat noises."

"As I recall, you wanted your friends to hear the story before you went to bed. *When I had made an end of these labors, it was four o'clock-still dark as midnight.*"

"Yeah, that's it, four o'clock," Seth said, "when the guy finished hiding the heart under the floor."

Nearing a darkened street corner, Warren spotted the market. "There it is," he said, pointing towards the neon sign with two letters unlit. He turned down a narrow side street and entered the empty parking lot. He didn't like the fact that they were alone at night in this neighborhood, but in a few minutes he'd have a pain reliever in his system and heading for home. "C'mon," he said, reaching for the door handle. "Let's make this quick."

The first thing Warren noticed was the abundance of scrawl on the side of the market. "*The signatures of scumbags*," he mumbled to himself. He wasn't too young to remember when graffiti wasn't the commonplace occurrence it had become; even in his own neighborhood. Hell, he could never read the stuff anyway, with all those illegible gyrations.

"What do you think 'NRL' means?" Seth asked.

"Probably someone's initials."

"He sure likes writing them a bunch of times, doesn't he?"

"He wants the world to know he's here, I guess," Warren said. "Maybe if his parents cared enough he wouldn't be here at all."

The elderly Latino man inside the store stared at them as they walked in.

"Hello, señor," he said. "May I help you?"

"I need a pain reliever and a bottled water."

Finding what he wanted, Warren paid the man and immediately swallowed three of the green gel caps.

"Are you Alfredo?" he asked.

"Yes, señor. Alfredo Valenzuela."

"How long has your store been around, Alfredo?"

"Over thirty years señor. But I don't know how much longer I can stay here. The area's gotten bad. People are afraid."

"Yeah, I noticed all that damn graffiti on your walls. Who's this 'NRL' character, anyway?"

"It's not a person, señor. It's a gang. They call themselves 'The North Rampart Lobos'. The police try to help, but..." The man shrugged his shoulders in an act of sad resignation.

At the mention of gangs, Warren felt an urgency to leave right away. As he neared his car, he heard a deep unfamiliar voice from behind.

"Hey, man, got a dollar?"

Warren's heartbeat accelerated the instant he gazed into the eyes of a tough looking Latino man. "Sure," he said, hoping the money paid their ticket out of there. "I think I got..."

A violent shove from behind sent him tumbling headfirst towards the ground. Breaking the fall with his hands, he prevented his forehead from hitting the rough blacktop of the parking lot. When he scrambled around to look up, a gang of menacing Latino men surrounded him, and one of them, pale and thin with long hair and a pockmarked face, held Seth with an arm around his neck.

"Let go of my son!" Warren shouted.

"Shut up, asshole!"

Warren whirled around. Behind him stood a frightening man who appeared to be in his early twenties with an obvious deformity, maybe a scar, over his left eye.

The man holding Seth cackled like a hyena. "I think the boy's gonna cry, King."

"Hey, little boy," King said, "you don't want to see your old man get hurt, do you?"

Tears filled Seth's eyes. "N-n-no. P-please... don't... don't hurt my Dad."

"Then follow my orders, you little shit. Bring me his wallet."

Warren handed the leather billfold to Seth. "Just do as he says, son," he whispered. "Everything will be okay."

King seized the cash and examined what he held. "*Fuck!*" he shouted, slamming the wallet to the ground. "*Twelve fuckin' dollars?*" His eyes bore a hole in Warren. "Change of plans, Rascal," he said, stuffing the cash in his pants. "You packin'?"

A small man wearing several necklaces and a Yankees cap reached into his jacket and flashed a gun.

"Good. Thanks to our poor white friend over here we maybe gotta hurt someone. Go inside and take care of business."

Warren hoped Alfredo had an overhead camera somewhere and had already called for help. The police were their one chance. Still, Warren appealed to them.

"We did as you asked," he said to King. "Now let us go."

King brandished an evil looking grin then turned and nodded at the same gang member holding Seth. "Show 'em how we let 'em go, Ghoul." Ghoul placed his foot against Seth's back and propelled him forward. Everyone laughed as he cried out and tumbled to the ground.

"*God damn you!*" Warren yelled, darting over to Seth. He felt him shaking as he wrapped his arms around him.

"Come on, Seth," he said, lifting his son off the ground. "We're leaving."

The circle remained closed, moving as a group with Warren's every step.

"We ain't done with you yet, asshole," King said.

"Yes…you…*are!*" Warren said, seething. "And don't you *fucking* touch my son again!"

The gang members started laughing and mimicking him, increasing their volume with each repetition. "*Don't you fucking touch my son again.*" "*Don't you fucking touch my son again.*" "*Don't you fucking touch my son again!*"

King approached him. Warren didn't say a word as he looked into the cold black caverns that passed for eyes.

"What are you thinkin', you white prick? Huh? I'm not good enough for you, or somethin'?"

"You got what you came for," Warren said, struggling to remain calm. "Let us go. Please."

King backhanded him hard across the face. "*Fuck you!*"

Seth started sobbing.

"Hey, Luis!" King shouted. "Look at the little mama's boy over here."

Luis walked towards Seth in the same determined manner that King had shown advancing towards Warren. Warren tried to pull Seth away but two of the men grabbed and held him from behind. Ghoul laughed as he wrapped his arm again around Seth's neck. This time, however, he grabbed Seth's hair with his other hand in an apparent attempt to hold his face still.

In a bold, mocking tone, Luis said, "Hello, little baby."

"Dad, help me!" Seth cried out, his eyes looking wild with his head unable to move.

Luis spit in his face. "You gonna cry again, little baby?"

Ripping himself free with all the strength he had, Warren stormed towards King. "*You sons of bitches feel like big men picking on a kid? Is that what you assholes do for fun?" Fuck you! Fuck all of you!*"

Someone hit Warren hard from behind. He felt a shot of pain in the back of his head that dropped him to his knees. As his focus began to clear, he saw King standing above him. King reached down and grabbed a clump of Warren's hair, forcing his head back into a painful, upward angle.

"Who the fuck you think you're talkin' to, you piece of shit? Nobody disses a Lobo like that, motherfucker! Nobody!"

"Take my car, okay," Warren said, fighting through the pain from his scalp. "Just let us go. Haven't you done enough?"

"You want me to take your car?" King asked, his anger rising again. "You think I'm a stupid Mexican, you fuckin' white prick? So you can call the *pinchi policía*? Tell 'em how to find us? I'll show you what I think of your fuckin' car!"

King pushed Warren's head away and turned towards a slim, bandana-wearing gang member dressed in baggy jeans and a Miami Heat jacket. Twirling a knife through his fingers, he handled the weapon with a proficiency that rattled Warren even further. "Hey, Slice," King bellowed, "give our friends here somethin' to remember us by."

Warren didn't know what to expect but feared the worst as this gang member with the knife rubbed his hands over the hood.

"Luis," the banger shouted, "*venga aquí, cholito!*"

"Get your ass over there, Luis," King said, laughing. "Slice wants your help."

"Watch this, little baby," he sneered, putting his face a few inches from Seth's.

Luis hurried over to the car. His face lit up like a kid on Christmas morning as Slice handed him the knife.

"Remember, man, put some *huevos* into it, like I showed you," Slice said, grabbing his crotch.

"I'll show you who's got *huevos*!" Luis shot back. He gripped the knife and raised his right arm, holding that position long enough to look back at Seth with a smile that nauseated Warren.

The harsh, banging noise of the knife's unyielding tip connected with the hood, followed by a shrill grating sound that seemed to rip through Warren's gut as well. After Luis handed the knife back to the banger they called Slice, the two Lobos on Warren's left and right grabbed his arms and pulled him over to the car to view Luis' terrible handiwork. In large initials, the letters, 'NRL' screamed their silent, mocking memento.

Warren's attention veered from the car to his son. Seth's head slumped to the side and the part of his face still visible appeared white and motionless. He wondered if his son had gone into shock.

"Seth!" he shouted. "Seth! Are you okay? Say something! Seth!"

At that instant, uncertainty vanished from his thoughts, replaced by an emboldening urgency of the matter at hand; his son needed him now more than ever before. He'd require courage, calm, and intelligence to get them both out of there. Or, if he got lucky, an act of fate.

FOUR

THE AK-47 LAY HIDDEN UNDER a tattered blanket on the floor behind the front seat. Player drove and Face sat next to him. Cherry and Swat occupied the back.

"Makes me feel right you puttin' in the work tonight, Swat," Cherry told him.

"I won't let Apache down, man" Swat said.

"You're not just honoring Apache, *vato*," Face said, "you're dignifyin' all of us."

The time neared 11:00 o'clock. The engine sounded steady, aided by Face's tune up earlier in the day. His knowledge of auto mechanics dated back to the days when he skipped school to hang out at the local Pep Boys with the store manager, Jessie, an ex-gang member who took a liking to the boy. With the exception of his sister, no one knew that Face stashed the money he earned from servicing cars in the neighborhood in order to make a deposit for a mechanic's shop one day.

"You sure they'll be at Lafayette tonight, Face?" Cherry asked.

"Sure as flies to shit," he answered.

"It's dark over there," Cherry said. "Will Swat see those assholes?"

"We ain't takin' the main road," Face told him. "We'll catch those motherfuckers by surprise. That side street past Alfredo's Market goes to back of the park. They got them dirt roads for the maintenance trucks. That's the way we're goin' in." Face turned towards Swat. "At the right moment, homeboy, you'll spray those *cabrones* down like fuckin' bug spray."

"Just tell me when to cut the lights," Player said.

Face's eyes moved everywhere as they headed south, surveying the darkened working class areas of Echo Park. His heart raced with a cold-blooded mixture of adrenaline and anticipation as he listened to Swat's fingers dance a rhythmic drumbeat on the barrel of the gun.

"*For you, Apache,*" he whispered.

"There's the market," Player said, slowing down to make his turn.

Face noticed something unusual before the others through the faded yellow lighting. "Look over there!"

"It's gotta be the fuckin' Lobos!" Player hissed. "What should I do, Face?"

"Don't turn! Go straight! Straight!"

Player accelerated, following Face's instructions.

"We wasn't ready, that's all," Face said, his tone calm again. "Find a place to turn around."

"What the fuck were they doin', man?" Cherry asked.

"Jackin' a car, maybe," Face replied. "Hard to tell."

"Fuckin' *pendejos*," spat Cherry. "How many assholes they need to jack a goddamn car?"

They drove another block before turning around. "I ain't gonna take long," Swat told them. Player turned his headlights off and started his right turn. "It's payback time," Face said, his voice cold and unwavering. "Get ready." Face prepared to flash Diablo hand signals when something unexpected caught him off guard; some Lobo punk ran out from the market, waving his arms and pointing to their car. He realized they'd been sighted, and watched in growing anger as the Lobos started scattering like cockroaches, blowing any chance for Swat to get clean shots. He glanced back and watched him move his rifle back and forth without firing a round, as if confused about what to do.

"Hurry!" yelled Player.

"You're gonna fuckin' lose 'em, man!" Cherry yelled. "Shoot! Shoot somebody!"

Face fell silent. A sudden rush of warmth circled inside his head like a speeding merry-go-round, causing a battle with dizziness that removed him from the action at hand. When that familiar sensation of increasing heat behind his eyes occurred, and flashes of light started streaming across his sight, he expected a vision to appear as it always had, one that would show approaching danger. But nothing came into view, just the split-second sound of a screaming voice followed by gunfire. Regaining his focus, he noticed something, someone, that seemed out of place. It was a white kid. A little *huero!* That changed everything. If that kid got hurt, or worse, killed, the police would have a real reason to care. His mind raced. He watched as someone dragged the boy with an arm around his neck, keeping the boy in front of him as a shield. Swat moved the rifle towards that direction.

"Not the fuckin' kid! *No!*"

Face lunged forward and yanked Swat's arm back. He didn't know if he caused the firearm to go off or if Swat pulled the trigger at that same instant, but the shouts that blared from the direction of the boy ended in abrupt silence. As Player sped away, Face realized that the screams and gunfire were the same sounds he'd heard in his head moments before Swat fired. His ability to foresee peril always started with the same kind of dizzy spell he experienced in the car, but the sounds never occurred without images. This time, he felt as if he'd listened to a recording of something that hadn't yet happened. Confusion dominated Face's every thought. *Where was the danger?*

FIVE

THE BLANKETED BODY OF WARREN Palmer lay lifeless in the parking lot of Alfredo's Market. Warren viewed his inanimate form, a phenomenon that seemed quite natural and real. He also observed the flashing red lights of three squad cars and an ambulance. He heard the police choppers circling in the sky, and saw their searchlights shining through the neighborhood. His main focus, however, centered on Seth. Watching his beautiful son, now a disheveled, lost little boy sobbing in the arms of a large, black policeman, Warren felt no peace in death. He had advanced within a few seconds of reaching Seth, his eyes shifting back and forth between the emotionless face of the gang member holding the rifle and his son entrapped in the arms of the one known as "King." He thought back to the last few moments leading up to his death.

As the car pulled up, the gangbanger who had gone into the market burst outside yelling about "Diablos" and "a drive-by." In an instant, Warren found himself standing alone. The two muscular gangbangers who had been sandwiching him ran off in different directions. Warren looked at Seth, then towards the car in the street. He saw the end of a rifle protruding from an open window in the back.

"*Dad! Dad! Help!*"

King dragged Seth across the parking lot, using him for cover, but Warren closed in fast. The recollection of a loud voice from inside the car, followed by the sound of a gunshot, preceded his world fading to black. After the bullets ripped through Warren's chest, his son's cries brought him back to a momentary state of clarity. As Seth cradled him, Warren sensed his final breath drawing near.

"*Seth,*" he whispered. Seth lowered his head, sobbing. "*Dad, don't die! Don't die!*" He looked into his son's eyes. "*I... love you, Seth.*" Warren offered a fading smile, determined to finish what he had to say. "*I promised... your mom... I'd... look after you. And... protect you.*" He fought to gain another breath, struggling through the pain and enveloping darkness. "*I... promise you I... will. Always.*"

Within the complete and silent blackness of death, a familiar sensation of his identity still remained. Detached from any perception of time, a sparkling light appeared, surrounding him at first, then transforming into a white, misty doorway mirroring his naked image. Warren watched the arms of his reflection reach out towards him, *inviting* him, and he instinctively knew that his wife, Michelle, waited on the other side. An all-encompassing serenity warmed his spirit, and he sensed a planned, peaceful finality.

As Warren drifted towards his radiant destination, and the sights and sounds of his life separated and floated away like the discarded parts of a spacecraft, he suddenly stopped, drawn back by the final, lingering fragments of his earthly conscience. Just as a single cancer cell splits and starts to spread, Warren felt himself succumbing to a malignant type of anger growing inside of him. He couldn't be there for Seth anymore, couldn't fulfill his promise to Michelle to raise and look out for him because of those worthless, cruel pieces of shit. Warren sensed he had some unfinished business. In his own way, he would make the world a better and safer place for his son. For both of the gangs responsible for his murder, there would be *consequences.*

The final traces of the sparkling light faded away. In its place, a different kind of light revealed itself; one that Warren anticipated. Visions of Madame Sibilia paraded like a montage through his thoughts as the dawning realization of her true psychic powers started to unfold. She had been correct, there *was* another light. Predictions were now reality, denial was now acceptance, and Warren welcomed this afterworld with curiosity and purpose.

A dark red glow drew him in and guided his way through a tunnel of translucent fog as individual strands of flashing light multiplied and twisted like a spider's web across his field of vision. Advancing towards the blood-colored beam, he heard a faint noise, solemn and repetitious, beckoning him to come forth. Floating shadows, resembling human faces, slithered above him like night clouds drifting across the moon. With the emerging clarity of a camera adjusting its lens, he recognized the images of those gang members named King, and Slice, and that freak they called, Ghoul, who wouldn't stop laughing. Warren's gaze held steady on another recognizable likeness, as his own killer's face hovered overhead like a poisonous balloon, inflated with the cold air of wickedness. A surrounding cluster of laughing faces soon engulfed his line of sight, dominating his direct and peripheral views and taunting him in a defiant challenge. He stared at them with revulsion and anger as the faces began to twist and stretch in violent, contorted motions, transforming into enlarged and monstrous creatures. He watched, trance-like, as the floating images departed in a sneering parade of ridicule and reminder, dissolving into nothingness. He continued to stare into the empty void, left with the visual echo of their recurring outline, sketched into the darkness of haunting recollection.

The muffled, drum-like beating that had continued as an audio backdrop intensified into a feverish pitch. The sound of a heartbeat, rhythmic and powerful, penetrated his spirit and prevailed over angry and urgent thoughts. Words from Poe's *The Tell-Tale Heart* took on a life, and a reality, of their own.

> *Meantime the hellish tattoo of the heart increased*
> *It grew quicker and quicker and louder and louder every*
> *instant.*

Was it mere coincidence that he found his father's poem, *A Victim's Time*, stuck inside the pages of *The Tell-Tale Heart*? Warren didn't believe so. He saw the poems as omens, as foreshadowing the events that were now destined, when the destruction of the heart is the only answer.

> *It increased my fury, as the beating of a drum stimulates*
> *the soldier into courage.*

Warren stood still and remained calm as darkness now enveloped him. From the insulating blackness, two eyes appeared, about the size of a man's fist. In chilling recognition, he stared in awe as one of the eyes transformed into a bluish hue, appearing diseased through a transparent layer of mucous-like fluid. He watched the eye enlarge and thicken until it covered the other like an apocalyptic eclipse. Warren now stared at the one large socket of decaying, blue horror directing its gaze at him. As he peered at the ocular spectacle, aware of the unspoken message before him, he deduced the meaning from a defining line of *The Tell Tale Heart*.

> *I think it was his eye! Yes, it was this! One of his eyes*

resembled that of a vulture - a pale blue eye, with a film over it.

Warren understood that this defining moment directed his judgment and guided his purpose. He thought of Seth. His anger surged forth with lava flow intensity, seeking a release through the cracks of his interior. Images of the gang faces encircled his thoughts in a nightmarish shell, stimulating his obsession for revenge against those who represented all that was vile.

Because Death, in approaching him, had stalked with his black shadow before him, and enveloped the victim.

Warren felt resurrected, baptized in the whirlpool of contempt and retribution. From here on, each murderer would pay for his deed with his own life, feeling Warren's frigid hand upon their heart until death announced the final beat. To learn appreciation for life, they, too, must die. And in their last moments, struggling through their final breaths, his recitation of *A Victim's Time* shall honor his father's message of heroic sacrifice by ending the life of those who honor none but themselves.

The appropriate time of death, of course, will honor Poe.

When I had made an end of these labors, it was four o'clock-still dark as midnight.

Four o'clock; when the beating stops and the silence proclaims victory of right over wrong.

There was an iciness, a sinking, a sickening of the heart.

Warren's own murderer would now be the first to die.

SIX

KEVIN STARED AT HIS DIGITAL desk clock, his eyes feeling as red as the numbers moving another minute ahead to 12:33 a.m. He sat alone in his office at *The Los Angeles Times* building, alternating between the taped interviews from the L.A. County Men's Central Jail and reviewing the data scribbled inside his notebook. His upcoming article detailed the modern day Mexican-American gangs of L.A., a subject of local historical interest stemming from their origins in the 1930's, decades before the more renowned Bloods and Crips existed. The information he accumulated on the violence and drug trafficking carved an emotion that had left him feeling hopeless and disheartened. The consistency of young people killing each other seemed without end. And for what? Drug profits, turf rights, evening scores, wearing the wrong colors. What these gangs considered important were the nuts and bolts of their existence; what they lived, killed and died for. Kevin viewed their entire way of life as a pitiful and misguided means to a dead end.

He stretched his arms and walked over to the window. At this time of night, with the multitude of lights shimmering through the blackness, everything seemed so peaceful. He knew better, however. He couldn't avoid thinking about the dichotomy that existed between the illusion from his vantage point and the harsh reality of the streets. The more time he spent on his research, the more cynical he grew about anyone's ability to prevent the mushrooming gang culture taking over the city. Running his hands over his face, he ruminated about how the facts of life could sometimes be so damn overwhelming, and how he used to depend on scotch, morning, noon, and night, to dull his senses and offer the coping mechanism he craved to sustain him. With a bit of effort, he banished the thought from his mind.

The sound of his cell phone startled him. He recognized the caller I.D. and answered; part curious, part cautious.

"Kevin, it's Carl Atkinson."

Lieutenant Atkinson had met and befriended Kevin at an L.A.P.D. community affairs event, and had been instrumental in working with the Sheriff's Department to arrange the interviews from Men's Central Jail. He'd been the necessary mediator for Kevin, coming from a background as a respected figure in two of the LAPD's successful anti-gang programs.

"It's an odd time to be hearing from you, Carl," Kevin said, feeling uneasy.

"I'm at the station with your nephew, Seth. You need to come down here right away."

Kevin's heart raced. "What is it? What happened? Where's Warren? Is he okay?"

More silence. "I'm sorry to tell you, Kevin... your brother's been killed."

Kevin mind went numb. For several seconds he couldn't speak. "What? What did you say?" he asked, struggling for his voice.

"Warren was murdered tonight in a drive-by shooting," Atkinson explained. "He got caught in the middle of a gang war. I'm very sorry."

Kevin somehow found his chair and sat down. His eyes burned with hot tears. "What...what about Seth? Is he all right?"

"He's unhurt, but we're concerned about his mental state. We've got people keeping a close eye on his condition."

"Does he know about Warren?"

"It seems your brother died trying to save Seth from a dangerous situation. He was killed a few feet in front of him."

"Oh... my... God," Kevin whispered. "Where did it happen?" Atkinson didn't answer for several moments. "Alfredo's Market," he replied.

"*I sent him there! Jesus Christ I sent him there!*"

"Damn it, Kevin, listen to me! Seth told us why you sent them there, but this wasn't your fault, you hear me? I tried to explain the same thing to him, too. That market's been around forever."

"You're wrong, Carl," Kevin replied, his thinned voice not sounding like his own. "I'm to blame. What the hell was I thinking?"

"Just get down here, all right? Seth's been traumatized pretty bad. He needs you."

Kevin closed his eyes, somehow hoping the stinging continued to worsen. "I'm on my way."

He dropped the phone on his lap, staring as if in a hypnotic trance towards the unlit part of the office. When he attempted to stand, he collapsed back into his chair, his legs wobbly and devoid of willpower. He lowered his head on his desk and sobbed uncontrollably, calling out to his brother.

"*Warren... Warren, I'm sorry... I'm so sorry... it's all my fault... How could I have done this to you?... I'm sorry, Warren... Oh, God, I'm so sorry.*"

SEVEN

*A*T A TIME BEFORE THE North Rampart Lobos killed his older brother and two uncles, Rafael 'Swat' Carranza showed much enthusiasm as a thirteen-year-old learning to shoot a gun from these three *veteranos*. First practicing with his uncle's hunting rifles, he acquired killing skills early, proving to be a quick study with various types of handguns. His father had promised to teach him, but that was before his murder conviction, his *187*, sent him away a week after Rafael's ninth birthday. From then on, his brother and uncles, more than his two-job-a-day mother, raised Rafael and molded him the Diablo way. They taught him how to think, fight, and shoot, all in preparation for the day when he would be "checked in," initiated, into the gang.

Before he reached his fifteenth birthday, two years after he started banging, Rafael's reputation for accuracy with a gun earned him the name 'Swat' in reference to the well-known police sharpshooters. In the next few years, his mastery of assault rifles solidified his standing and brought him the distinction as the most reliable Diablo for a drive-by.

Swat figured he had earned everyone's respect, so Face's interference at the market left him seething with anger. If that Lobo asshole, that *culero,* used some kid as protection, so what? Swat knew a split second more is all he needed to blow a hole through that motherfucker's head. Everyone would have been talking about that kill for months. But Face started yelling at him and throwing him off his game, and he settled instead for the Lobo running out from the shadows. Swat remained agitated, smoking cigarettes and staring into the darkness until he fell asleep around 2:30.

As the numbers on his clock glowed 3:43 a.m., Swat dreamed of a familiar vacated warehouse where donated produce had been stored and the ricocheting sounds of target practice rang unheard from the constant rush of the nearby freeway. The graffiti-coated door swung open to reveal his brother and two uncles standing at the entrance, laughing and beckoning him inside. He noticed their eyes changing shape as he approached, compressing from circles into the recognizable form of bullets. A yellowish white flash of light exploded from their sockets as they started blinking every few seconds, and within another minute the three of them disappeared in an instant.

Swat entered the warehouse feeling an intense excitement, almost sexual in nature, as he rejoiced in the beauty of a stash of weaponry he never imagined possible. Hundreds of shiny guns and rifles, gathered in a mountainous formation of destruction, arose with a peculiar heat that warmed his flesh like a summer sun. Admiring, probing, and stroking different selections from the extensive stockpile, Swat spotted the trigger-half of an AK-47 sticking out from the same old blanket he always used to hide his weapon on a drive-by.

Swat reached out towards the rifle with a steady hand, moving the jacket aside and lifting the gun into the air. He saw this as an omen, destiny's offering at killing the Lobo still holding that kid. Wasting no time, Swat clutched the rifle to his chest and swaggered out from the warehouse towards Alfredo's Market. He'd achieve his greatest accomplishment without the help of anyone else, and not even Face could stop him. He found it unusual that the light of day had turned black without his having noticed any transition, leading to a strange and disturbing sensation. His *machismo*, which empowered him earlier, felt shaken. His composure and determination had been eclipsed by an eerie echo to his footsteps, punctuated by the menacing stillness of a cold, gloomy night. Swat followed the sudden sound of a raspy, murmuring voice he couldn't quite distinguish. The pale blur of a lone street lamp offered nothing more than a foggy haze, making each step seem treacherous, and each moment, significant.

"*Swat... Swat, over here. Swat... Swat.*"

The repetition of the voice, weak yet urgent, drew him in, pulling him forward. He stopped. He stood outside the yard of the Alvarado Street Diablos. He recognized the wall, and then the voice. He peered through the stingy light at the bleary portrait of Apache. The spirit of his old friend called to him, summoning him. "*Swat,*" the whispering voice beckoned. "*Come closer.*" He bent down, touching the painted image with his hands. An unusual dampness grew thick and heavy, as small liquid streams descended from numerous cracks on the wall. Swat strained his eyes to peer closer at his fingers, startled at the recognition of blood, sticky and black red. He placed his hands on the dripping wall again, puzzled by the unsettling coolness of the blood. Within seconds, a violent freeze attacked his fingertips, shocking him into tearing his hands away. Without warning, the streetlamps flashed over and over, alternating between split seconds of intense light and complete blackness, as if in cadence to a soundless, frenzied drum roll. As Swat stumbled backwards into the street, Apache's whispers escalated into maddening screams.

"Swat! Help me! Help me!" Swat watched in disbelief as the ghastly skull that had been Apache's face turn and direct its hellish gaze on him. *"We're dead, Swat! Dead! All of us. Dead!"*

Now the pattern of the street lamps changed. They were no longer turning on and off in rapid sequence. The darkness had extended in duration, interspersed by two quick bursts of light, a pattern that kept repeating. An odd, rhythmic tom-tom now accompanied each blast of light, leaving him gripped by confusion and undeniable alarm. A sudden constriction in his chest intensified, and he now recognized that the rhythm of the drum he'd been hearing beat in direct time with his own heart. He started to panic, running through the infuriating street-lamp rhythm of light and dark. The pain worsened as the pounding sound increased. He continued running. Away from what? He didn't know. Where? He didn't care.

Swat bolted up in bed. His consciousness downshifted from relief into anger as soon as he realized that a stupid nightmare had left him in a cold sweat and short of breath. He looked at the clock.

"Shit," he muttered, "three fifty. What the fuck kind of dream was that?"

Swat rubbed his face and flinched in pain at the surprising swelling circling his right eye. In the darkness of his room, his fingers seemed to touch melted wax, and when he looked at the clock again, he felt disturbed by the gauze-like fuzziness of his vision. Swat started to reach for the lamp switch when he reeled back in bed, seized by the same sharp pains in his chest and drum-like pounding in his ears that haunted him in his nightmare.

"What's... happening... to... me?" he gasped.

Out of nowhere, a whispering voice answered him:

> *"I placed my hand upon the heart and held it there many minutes."*

The electro-shock reaction of Swat's jerking body resulted in nothing stronger than a faint cry of dismay and fear. He lay there, helpless, as the unrelenting pain in his chest continued to strike like a rhythmic hammer to the beating of the drum.

> *"There was an iciness, a sinking, a sickening of the*
> *heart."*

An intense chill forced him into a rage of violent shivers, making his blood feel like a frozen current beneath his tattooed skin. Whoever occupied his room seemed within reach when he spoke, so Swat started flailing his arms in a desperate attempt at capture. Overcome by the increased pain, he careened on his side, face to face with the numbers on his clock. At 3:54, unable to move, he wondered if he was dying. The quiet of his room changed into something sounding like an invasion of rats scampering close by on the floor. Swat cowered in his bed. The squealing was of an intensity he had never imagined.

> *"Looking to the floor, I saw several enormous rats*
> *traversing it. They came up in troops, hurriedly, with*
> *ravenous eyes, allured by the scent of the meat."*

A throng of frenzied rodents enshrouded Swat in a clawing, scratching body cast of agony. Throwing themselves at whatever exposed areas they could find, the pick-axe claws of the creatures dug in and held on through the hardened chill of his flesh, clinging to every inch of Swat's body in a ferocity of pain and purpose. As the numbers on the clock reached 3:59, Swat was neither aware of the length of time the rats had remained, nor their disappearance from his room. His ordeal had short-circuited his sanity and turned his mind into the cerebral equivalent of an empty gun.

The voice spoke again, echoing inside Swat's head like a death knell.

> *"The valiant soldier's blood will spill*
> *On red-stained lands of sacrifice*
> *The unknown stranger lies as still*
> *Apart from honor's noble price*
> *Two victims of a time to kill*
> *Beware the heart as cold as ice."*

Swat's heart clocked out with a final beat. The time was 4:00.

EIGHT

SETH SAT BY HIMSELF DURING lunch period, separated from his classmates behind a wall of green bushes, eating a peanut butter and jelly sandwich he'd made that morning. He had returned to school last Tuesday, so that now made five days out of seven eating peanut butter and jelly. Seth lived with his Uncle Kevin now, and there weren't the kinds of things like turkey or tuna fish or some good leftovers like before. *Before*. Nothing really mattered anymore. Once his mom died, lunches never tasted the same anyway. She was the best sandwich maker ever. He started making his own lunches when she got too sick to stand, with his dad helping out sometimes. Now his dad was gone, too.

Seth had been living with his uncle for almost two weeks, and most of the boxes from the move remained unopened. The two that were completely emptied had contained most of his clothes, but he still couldn't find his favorite pair of jeans and Tony Hawk tee-shirts. Dinners had been picked up ready-made from the market, but sometimes he ate at Burger King, or the pizza place down the street. Uncle Kevin claimed he'd been too busy with the funeral, and moving, or visiting Grandma, to have had time to put the house in order, but he still had time to go to the liquor store three times already. Seth never realized his uncle drank so much. After a couple of glasses he went from not having much to say to talking about all sorts of stuff. But Seth didn't pay much attention. Why should he listen to him? His dad listened to him and got killed. That's all Seth needed to know. His uncle's the reason his father got shot that night. The night of the *Mexicans*.

When he returned to school, he didn't feel like hanging out with anybody, not even his two best friends, Freddy and Mike. After awhile they started to stay away so they must have got the message. His teacher,

47

Mrs. Fisher, had met with him, telling him to come to her for any reason if he wanted to talk. She told him she still expected Seth to try his best. *Yeah, right.* He didn't feel like trying at all. He didn't want to listen in class, or take notes, or do his homework. He just didn't care anymore. A part of him knew he needed to go back to school, but he didn't want to deal with the pain that came with it, like watching the other kids dropped off and picked up by their parents. Or eating the homemade sandwiches that their moms made.

Seth resented Clearpoint Elementary School for another reason; they had Mexican kids there. He never knew a lot about them before, never gave them much thought. But he did now. They were mean people and killed his dad. The lesson he learned from that night, one he would never forget, is that he would always fight back - something he had already done once since his return to school.

On his second day back, Seth shot baskets by himself near the main court where a game took place.

"Hey, Palmer! Palmer!"

Seth turned and realized the group of boys from the basketball game were all looking his way. He felt a knot tighten in his stomach as he heard Lorenzo Gonzalez, a Mexican kid from the other sixth-grade class, calling out to him.

"Hey, Palmer," Lorenzo shouted again, "this ball sucks." Bouncing the ball several times to show Seth the problem, he said, "Let us use yours. C'mon, game's tied."

Seth took a deep breath and decided to refuse. Maybe if one of the other kids, someone who wasn't a Mexican, had been the one to ask, he would have agreed. But there was no favor granting for *Lorenzo Gonzalez!*

"No!" Seth answered in a firm voice.

"Oh, come on, Palmer!" Lorenzo shouted, followed by outcries from some of the other players.

"I said, no!" Seth repeated. Turning his back on them, he resumed shooting at his own basket.

"You suck, Palmer!" Lorenzo exclaimed. "You little baby!"

Seth stopped dribbling and stood motionless, squeezing the ball against his chest as if he were trying to pop it like a balloon. Lorenzo's insult shook him to the core, lifting him by the collar of his memory and slamming his emotions against the wall.

"Hello little baby." "Watch this, little baby." "Are you gonna cry again, little baby?"

That gangbanger, Luis, had called him "a little baby." He had taunted him and spit in his face. Lorenzo Gonzalez just called him a little baby, too. Seth felt his eyes burn. Tears of rage and frustration, rather than fear, moistened his vision as he ran, unforgiving and delirious, in a beeline towards Lorenzo.

Seth got off with a warning that day, but in his mind he delivered the message to Lorenzo Gonzalez and all the other Mexicans who thought they could intimidate him. They had better leave him alone or else.

From the other side of the shrubbery, he could hear the rest of the kids sitting at the lunch tables. In a sudden defensive gesture, Seth raised his right arm, reacting to something zooming down in his direction. After the mushy, wet substance made contact with his forehead, he looked down and realized someone had thrown a half-eaten tomato at him. Seth heard some boys laughing and leapt to his feet, running around to the other side. Two Mexican kids from his class stood next to the bushes, yelling and laughing some more about what they had done. Seth charged at them like a sprinter from his starting blocks, not caring which one he reached first.

"*I hate you*!" he screamed, slamming into one of the boys and knocking him backwards onto a table. He had never been in a real fight before, but his instincts took over as he balled his fists and flailed away at the Mexican's face.

A pair of strong hands grabbed him by the shoulders. "*Get off of him*!" Mr. Terrell shouted, yanking him back.

"Ha! Ha!" Seth shouted, triumphant tears of rage still welling in his eyes. "Serves you right, you stupid Mexican!"

"Shut up!" Mr. Terrell hollered. "And stay right there!"

Seth watched with satisfaction as Jaime Cardenas cried, covering his face with his hands. Mr. Terrell kneeled close to the boy. "Calm down, son, it's okay, you'll be okay," He stayed in that position until the boy sat up. Seth's happiness increased as a trickle of blood oozed from the Mexican's nose. Mr. Terrell sent Jaime's friend, Esteban, to get a wet paper towel. "What are you smiling at?" Mr. Terrell asked Seth in an angry tone. Seth hadn't been conscious of the grin on his face, but no amount of wet paper towels could have wiped that smile away.

In the outside waiting area of Principal Lee's office, Seth couldn't hear the conversation taking place inside, but he could see everything through her large window. The two Mexicans sat with Principal Lee and Mr. Terrell, probably making up stories, telling them that it was all *his* fault, that they didn't do anything wrong. Liars! Seth wondered if she had already talked with his Uncle Kevin, but what did *he* know? He wasn't there that night. He didn't know about Mexicans. He didn't know the *truth*. They were bad people, and nobody had the right to tell him he was wrong to do what he did. He was just sticking up for himself, and from now on that's the way he'd always handle the situation. *He* shouldn't be the one in trouble; it should be those two Mexican creeps. They were the ones who threw a mushy tomato at him and laughed about it, thinking he wouldn't strike back. They were wrong, weren't they? No matter what happened to him, Seth knew he had done the right thing. He also believed something else; his dad would have been proud of him. He had fought back. And he had won.

Principal Lee opened her door and stared at Seth with a look of seriousness that left him unconcerned. "Come in," she said.

Taking his time to rise from the chair, Seth shuffled into her office. He sat down in a chair next to Mr. Terrell, refusing to acknowledge Esteban and Jaime sitting on one side of the room. Principal Lee returned to her desk, leaned forward on her elbows, and eyed Seth.

"I called your uncle as soon as Mr. Terrell told me what happened," she said, her calm voice a surprise. "He's coming to take you home."

Seth stared back at her, unhappy about taking the blame.

"What you did is very serious," she said. "Do you understand that?"

"They started it!"

"Liar!" yelled Jaime.

"No, we didn't!" Esteban exclaimed.

"You say they started it, but that's not what I heard, son," Mr. Terrell said, glaring at Seth. "Apparently, you attacked Jaime for no reason."

Seth tensed at being called "son." "He threw a tomato at me!" he shouted. "I was just sitting there."

"One of the boys admitted he threw it over the bushes," Principal Lee said. "And that was wrong. But they were just playing a game, and they didn't know you were there."

"They're lying! They knew I was there! They just didn't think I'd do anything about it." Seth looked at the two boys. "They thought I'd be afraid," he sneered.

Principal Lee slammed her hand on the desk. "That's not it at all, Seth! You're taking this way too far."

Seth didn't want to hear any excuses for those two lying Mexicans. He knew he did the right thing, and nobody, not even Principal Lee or Mr. Terrell, could convince him otherwise. He even felt like crowing about it.

"Yeah," Seth said with a contented smile, "Jaime wasn't so brave when he was by himself, was he? When he wasn't protected by a bunch of his Mexican friends. He..."

"*That's enough, young man!*" Mr. Terrell shouted, standing up and walking over to the window. "I've heard all I want to hear," he muttered.

"These boys never teased you before," Principal Lee told him. "Why would they mean you any harm now?"

Seth continued chewing on his lower lip, looking down at the desk to avoid eye contact. Her words meant nothing, incapable of persuading him that she was right and he was wrong.

"All right, Mr. Terrell," she said, "go get them."

Seth wondered what Principal Lee had in mind.

"Jaime," she said, "when I was on the phone with your mother, she asked to have you call her after our meeting. Do you want her to come get you?"

"No, I'm okay," he replied.

Seth knew the Mexican looked at him when he answered.

"All right," she replied. "You can use the phone outside to call her. Esteban, go with Jaime. Please wait for me out there."

Seth's head remained down, his eyes staring at the floor.

"Stay here," she instructed. "Your uncle's arrived."

Seth watched through the window as she started talking to his uncle before pointing to Jaime and Esteban. He could tell by his expression that they repeated the same lies. When his uncle turned to look at him, Seth stared back, showing neither remorse nor fear. His confidence turned to confusion, however, when Mr. Terrell returned with Freddy and Mike. What were *they* doing here? Seth eyed Mr. Terrell as he approached the office where he waited.

"Come out here," he said.

Seth stood, quickly this time, and hurried to the front room. He ignored his uncle and stared at Freddy and Mike, troubled by their expression.

"Seth," Principal Lee said, "Mr. Terrell was told you attacked Jaime for no reason. If you thought Jaime and Esteban were the ones who told him, you were only half right." Turning to face Freddy and Mike, Principal Lee continued. "Boys, I know Seth's your friend and you would never do anything to hurt him. But there's an old expression you may have heard that says, 'A friend in need is a friend indeed', and right now Seth needs you. He needs you to explain that what happened today was all a great big misunderstanding. Please tell him that his classmates, *all* of his classmates, are his friends, not his enemies."

Mike spoke first. He cleared his throat, looked at Principal Lee, and then at Seth. "Me and Freddy were sitting next to those guys. They started throwing food around. Then we watched 'em get up and throw that tomato over the bushes. You can't see anything on the other side, Seth. Nobody knew you were there, okay?"

Seth's mouth tightened as he glared at Mike.

"That's what happened, Seth," Freddy said. "Mike's right. They didn't do it on purpose. Nobody knew you were there. Nobody!"

Seth stood there speechless, feeling betrayed, knowing he could never be friends with Freddy and Mike again.

"You boys can go back to your class now," Mr. Terrell said.

Before the door closed, Seth caught sight of Mike giving Freddy the 'he's crazy' sign with his finger circling the side of his head.

"I know things are difficult for you right now," Principal Lee told him. "But I don't tolerate fighting in our school, and a suspension is the usual punishment." She took a couple of steps toward Jaime, looked at him, and turned her attention back to Seth. "I'm going to make you deal. In return for getting off with nothing more than a warning, I want you, no, I *expect* you, to apologize to Jaime."

"*No! No way!*" he yelled, stamping his foot.

Uncle Kevin walked over to stand next to him. "You heard Principal Lee, Seth," he said. "You're lucky she's not going to suspend you. You hurt Jaime. You need to apologize to him."

Seth stared straight ahead as his eyes began to water. He could feel his face getting red, but he didn't say anything in response. "So, is it a deal, Seth?" Uncle Kevin asked.

Seth lowered his head as a moan escalated into a scream. "*No! No way! No way! I won't do it! No! No!*"

"Seth, calm down!" his uncle shouted.

"*You can't make me!*" Seth cried out, turning his back on his uncle. "*I won't do it! I won't!*"

"Mr. Palmer, perhaps I'm wrong," Principal Lee said. "Maybe what Seth needs is two weeks of after-school detention to think about things."

"*No!*" Seth shouted.

"Well then, Seth," she said, "is there something you'd like to say to

Jaime?"

Seth looked at all three adults observing him like a weird bug on a wall. He didn't want to be here anymore, and he knew he'd leave as soon as everyone got their stupid apology, even if it wasn't sincere. His mom used to call them "little white lies." Sometimes you say things you don't really mean if it makes the other person feel better. Sometimes you say them to get you out of a fix. Like when she would tell grandma how good her baked banana bread tasted even though she always overcooked it. That's what Seth would do now, tell a little white lie.

"I'm sorry," he said in a solemn voice, avoiding eye contact with Jaime.

"I don't believe you," Esteban blurted out.

"Esteban, this is between Jaime and Seth," Principal Lee said.

His uncle leaned in close. "Come on, Seth, do it right," he whispered. "Go over to him, shake his hand, and tell him you're sorry."

Seth closed his eyes and reminded himself what to do. *Little white lies.* He took a deep breath, hesitated a moment, then walked over to Jaime.

"I'm sorry," he said, struggling to raise his hand.

Jaime didn't acknowledge the attempted handshake, but after some prodding by Mr. Terrell, returned the gesture.

"Thank you, Seth. Thank you, Jaime," Principal Lee said. "Seth, your uncle's already here, so you may as well go home for the rest of the day. I don't expect anything like this to *ever* happen again. Is that clear?"

Seth felt everyone's eyes upon him, so he told them what they wanted to hear. "Yes," he said, remembering Grandma's banana bread.

NINE

*O*N A LATE WEDNESDAY NIGHT, Francisco "Ghoul" Martinez stood with King, Ram, Slice and several other Lobos in Lafayette Park.

They gathered around the same bushes where a maintenance worker had found Rascal's body weeks before. Their appetite for revenge had reached a fever pitch and everyone agreed the heart attack stories were lies. Some of the gang believed the police had commited the murders, but the majority felt the Diablos were responsible. There had been no explainable reasons for the strange deaths but none seemed necessary in the fire and brimstone fervor of Lobo hatred towards their sworn enemy.

"Next *pinchi* Diablo I see," Slice promised, "I swear I'll cut his *huevos* off and stick 'em down his motherfuckin' throat!"

The excited reaction of the others to Slice's remark gratified Ghoul, confirming his belief in the *familia*. He'd love to be there if Slice wanted some throat-stuffing company.

"Those chicken-shit Diablos are challenging our manhood," Ram yelled, grabbing his crotch. "They think we'll be afraid. That's fuckin' bullshit! They can all go to Hell, man. *Qué se vayan a la madre!*"

Everyone hooted their approval, with Ghoul's strange scream of a laugh rising above the rest.

King sauntered forward, then turned to face the crowd. "We've lost three *hermanos* in the last two weeks," he added. "The fuckin' Diablos wanna wipe us out, make us run like fuckin' pussies with our tails between our legs. Fuck 'em! We're the North Rampart Lobos, God damn it! Nobody fucks with us. We got a killin' party to throw for those Diablo motherfuckers. But we need more guns, man. How do Lobos honor murdered brothers without payback? What the fuck is takin' us so goddamn long? It's time! We're gonna smoke every one of those Diablo *puto* motherfuckers and turn their asses into cemetery shit!"

Ghoul walked home alone in the early morning darkness, wired from the meth he had snorted before he left. He chuckled as he thought about King's "cemetery shit" line. The chuckle elevated to a laugh when he recalled what Slice said at the meeting. Cutting off a Diablo's balls and stuffing them down his throat seemed like the perfect thing to do. So did blowing away that homeless piece of shit on the way to the meeting. He hated that motherfucker, always hanging out in the 'hood, talking to himself, and dissin' Ghoul with his stare. He deserved to die. By luck, Ghoul found the perfect moment when he caught the stupid ass taking a leak in a darkened alley near his house. *BAM. BAM.* Two shots from his .45. left him lying in his blood and piss. Fuck that homeless asshole.

Ghoul stopped to smoke a joint deep in the shadows of a deserted railroad yard. He liked to get stoned here and think back to the days when, as a young boy known as "little Frankie," he watched the trains come and go, imitating the "choo-choo" sounds for each arrival and departure. He smiled as he thought back on that loud, belching blast of the whistle. Ghoul couldn't resist the temptation to be that same kid, if only for a few seconds.

"*Choo-Chooooooo.*" "*Choo-Chooooooo.*"

In the responding silence, as the train that colored his childhood sped further down memory's track, Ghoul found comfort in another deep drag from his joint. His illiterate father held a job as a janitor and maintenance man there, cleaning floors and toilets, repairing seats and doors, and replacing overhead lights. On weekends and summer days, "little Frankie" went with his daddy to work. Whenever a train pulled into and out of the station, he fantasized about being the big-shot conductor. Those were the best times of his life, until the railroad station shut down and his daddy lost his job. At nine years old, Francisco's train fantasies came to a screeching halt. He didn't remember much thereafter, except that things were never the same. Especially Daddy.

Stoned, eyes closed, hearing the comforting noise of those distant engines once again, Ghoul enjoyed the return back to his own little Paradise. A faint, unusual tapping in his ears brought him back into the present. He first speculated the sound as drops of water somewhere nearby, but the pipes had been dry for years. He started feeling uneasy; some strange shit was going down with the Diablos and he was alone out here. The tapping intensified. He recognized a certain pattern, similar to a slow, steady drumbeat. He sensed his own heart pounding in time with the noise in his head. Ghoul ground the joint out on the ground. Still, the tapping, no, *beating*, grew louder as his heart thumped faster, knocking as a frantic fist against the inside door of his chest. His eyes shot back and forth but he saw nothing.

"*Was there PCP in that shit I smoked?*" he wondered. "*It didn't taste or smell like it but what else could explain this crazy fuckin' high?*"

That weird beating sound started freaking him out big time, scaring him, as the hammering of his heart grew painful and leaving him short of breath. Fighting a losing battle against fear, he just wanted to go home.

A sudden squealing from the gutted railroad building caused him to reach for his gun. Peering through the darkness, he spotted several large rats scurry across the open yard. He broke into a jog toward the street, but stopped in his tracks as the rhythmic beating sound in his head ceased, replaced by a voice from seemingly out of nowhere.

"Looking to the floor, I saw several enormous rats traversing it."

Ghoul cried out and spun around with his weapon ready to fire, but no one was there. *No one was there!* He struggled to control his shaking gun hand as he stood motionless, wanting to see something.

"Show your face, motherfucker!" he shouted, fighting to overcome his fear.

"I refrained and stood still."

Ghoul's eyes darted in multiple directions but were met with dark, empty space. He started to run. Beads of sweat grew heavy on his forehead and the back of his neck, rolling down like a heavy nosebleed. Scrambling towards the street, he stopped and ran back the other way when he heard the voice again.

"All in vain; because Death, in approaching him had stalked with his black shadow before him."

"I'll kill you!" Ghoul screamed. To his dismay, he now realized that the vision from his right eye had somehow become blurry to the point of near blindness. Ghoul placed his hand near the affected area and reeled from unexpected pain. The inside region felt inflated and heavy, and when he attempted to close his lid, a gummy, liquid-like thickness prevented him.

"And the old man sprang up in bed, crying out, 'Who's there?'"

Whirling around, yet still seeing no one, a surging tide of panic overwhelmed him, unraveling his sanity like used gauze. He looked around again, desperate to regain command of his senses. *"It must be the Diablos!"* he whispered to himself. Ghoul ran deeper into the shadows, keeping his ears and one good eye alert for any signs of danger. He reached a fence and grabbed the chain link to pull himself over to safety, but a crushing pain in his chest toppled him to the ground. Unable to move, Ghoul surrendered to the power of the voice.

"I placed my hand upon the heart and held it there many minutes."

Ghoul's breathing grew raspy and labored. The pain swam through his body like swarming piranha, but he forced himself to speak. "Help me... the pain... so... so cold. *Cold!* Ple-Please."

The unmistakable squeal of rats drew closer, reverberating through his skull, yet he remained anchored by the paralyzing pain in his heart. He felt the hostile clawed frenzy of rodents sliding up his body, enveloping his legs, his groin, his stomach, arms and chest, marching northward towards his neck and face.

"They writhed upon my throat; their cold lips sought my own; I was half stifled by their thronging pressure; disgust, for which the world has no name, swelled my bosom, and chilled, with a heavy clamminess, my heart."

The rats pressed against his face, barricading Ghoul's nose and mouth. His consciousness faded in and out. He tried to lift his arms and legs, but his powerless limbs didn't respond. Ghoul's head rolled to the side as the rats scurried away, leaving him cold and sedentary as a railroad track.

The voice spoke again.

*"The valiant soldier's blood will spill
On red stained lands of sacrifice..."*

The following morning, not long after sunrise, a cleanup crew beginning their rounds in the same yard where "little Frankie" used to play, discovered the pale, stringy-haired corpse of Francisco "Ghoul" Martinez. Based on the look of his face, it seemed apparent that several hungry rodents had found him first. Under a dreary sky, his body lay sprawled near the remains of the train station that once upon a time had given him the best years of his life.

TEN

*C*APTAIN SHERMAN DEAN OF THE LAPD toiled in the business of getting a front row look at man's inhumanity to his fellow man. Hatred and death made quite a formidable and unrelenting tag team opponent, and over the course of his career, perhaps the greatest example of this two-headed adversary was the insidious proliferation of the gang culture, which had spread like a horrible disease throughout the bloodstream of society. And, during the last couple of months, no other gangs commanded his attention as much as two vicious rivals: The North Rampart Lobos, and the Alvarado Street Diablos.

The street gangs he dealt with in Chicago during his first twenty-three years as a cop were no less ruthless than the ones he'd experienced in L.A., but at least when you froze your ass off in The Windy City you knew the icy temperature had a constraining effect on gang activity as well. He sought a change when he took that job offer in sunny Southern California six years ago, but as winter came and the sun kept shining, he discovered the deadly gang games in this town weren't forced to take a time-out due to harsh weather.

Dean had long ago accepted the general populace's ignorance concerning most of the depressing bullshit that cops see every day. Dean just wanted to do whatever he could to keep the lid on the ever-simmering cauldron of violence, but he hadn't been doing a good job of it in recent weeks. There had been a total of seventeen reported deaths between the Lobos and Diablos over the last two and a half months, and *eight* of them were diagnosed as heart failure. Eight massive heart attacks striking young men with no previous history of heart problems. His ongoing attempt to find additional heart attack victims from other gangs throughout the city had thus far produced a big, fat zero. In L.A.

County there were approximately eighty thousand gang members in over twelve hundred different gangs. *"So why is it only happening to these two?"* he kept asking himself. Several members of both gangs had been brought in for questioning, but their code of silence seemed as impenetrable as a castle fortress.

Dean's years of investigative work had taught him to suspect the unobvious, to notice dirt in areas that others saw unblemished, to read clues where others remained blind. After the autopsy from the first victim had been released he felt a genuine bewilderment, as nothing he'd ever experienced compared to it. When the report detailing the second victim's death revealed the same unusual outcome, the uncomfortable pangs of suspicion started gnawing at his gut. Stories of young, healthy athletes collapsing dead on a basketball court or a football field happened on occasion, but eight gang deaths, all from only two gangs, seemed too odd, too *unexplainable*, to be a coincidence. Now, two months beyond that second death, the proverbial shit had hit the fan, exploding into a modern day version of the Bubonic Plague, with gangbangers dropping like flies.

Logic dictated the culpability of these two murderous gangs, but Dean didn't believe they possessed the necessary degree of sophistication to perperpetrate these particular lethal acts. No amount of DNA analysis, including lab tests and autopsies, had produced any clues or evidence showing markings of a usual gang killing. No blood, fingerprints, or hair samples had been found, other than those of the victim. No clothing had been left behind, no tire tracks or shoe marks had been detected, and no use of any weapon could be identified.

Another finding that Dean found perplexing, considering the subject pertained to gang-related deaths, centered on the apparent lack of a *normal* struggle. There existed a numerous amount of tiny, bloody scratches all over the bodies, but each of the coroner's reports concluded, "rodent inflicted." *Rodent inflicted?* Maybe that made some sense for the victims found outside, but how do you explain the same scratches on the ones inside their bedroom?

Another unsolved issue concerned the bluish-hued swelling in one of the eyes of the victim. The lab results continued to report the same damn thing; no abnormalities found in the chemical structure of the eye fluid. *As if nothing was wrong at all.*

Devoid of any conclusive answers on the *"how"* of these killings, Captain Dean's focus turned to the *"when."* He recognized a consistent pattern of the time the murders occurred, and solving a puzzle starts with seeing the patterns. He needed to confer with a man who could help. Over the loudspeaker, Dean spoke. "Lieutenant Atkinson, come into my office."

When Atkinson's large, bald, black head leaned in through the doorway, Dean never looked up. "Hello, Carl," he said, scanning his report. "Please close the door and sit down." Atkinson sat in the chair across from Dean's desk, waiting to be addressed. "Another Diablo, found and identified an hour ago," he told him. Turning away from his paperwork, Dean continued. "Wilkerson and McBride are there now, combing everything in sight, but the kid looks like he died, stop me if you've heard this one, of natural causes. No bullets, no knives, no blood."

"Jesus Christ," the Lieutenant mumbled, shaking his head. "Where this time?"

"In some bushes near the Silver Lake offramp."

"You said he was identified?"

"Yeah. Name's Jaime Vasquez. They called him 'Player'. We knew him from the past. Illegal possession of a firearm, breaking and entering, couple of DUI's." Dean shook his head, furrowing his eyebrows in a manner that didn't quite show sincerity. "Just another misunderstood kid."

"Dammit!" Atkinson shouted. "What the *hell* is going on?"

"My question, too, Carl," Dean said, offering a tired smile. "I keep telling myself we just need more time."

"I'm sorry, Captain, but I just don't get what's happening. All these damn heart attacks make absolutely no sense."

"Are you more concerned with these heart attacks than the marked increase in drive-by shootings?" Dean asked.

"The drive-bys that really get to me are when innocent people get killed," Atkinson said. "For my own sanity I've learned to accept certain... *realities*. It's obvious that these guys want to keep massacring each other. It's just that..."

"It's just that we can accept the reality of gun violence," Dean exclaimed, "but we can't tolerate the unexplained deaths. Right?"

Atkinson nodded.

"Let me share something with you that *is* known, Carl. We've verified that five out of eight of these deaths occurred somewhere in the vicinity of four a.m. The others are harder to get a bead on. They died alone and their abnormal body temperatures make it difficult to be exact.

But within a four hour range, we know they were dead before sunrise. Around four a.m also? Maybe."

"Hmmm, that's interesting," the Lieutenant replied.

Dean continued. "We're beyond coincidence, don't you think? In my mind, we got us an early bird catching the worms."

Atkinson stared at Dean. "So you think one killer's behind all eight deaths?"

"I'll tell you what I *don't* think, Carl. Neither of those two gangs are causing the heart attacks."

Atkinson pursed his lips and nodded. "I guess eight identical deaths at around the same time tells us something, doesn't it?"

"Let me ask you a question," Dean said. "In all your years working the streets, dealing with major players like the Bloods and Crips, or smaller ones like the Diablos and Lobos, you've witnessed a lot of deaths, am I right?"

"Yes, sir," he answered. "Far too many."

"And in all of them, Carl, from guns to knives to drug o.d.'s, have you ever come across one whose cause of death couldn't be figured out?"

"Not until this latest round of bizarre bullshit, Captain."

Dean rose from his chair and came around to the front, sitting on the edge of the desk. Adjusting his shirt collar from the increasing tightness of his recent, cigarette-free weight gain, he lowered his frame to Atkinson's eye level and peered at him in silence for several moments. "There's no question they died of heart failure," he exclaimed. "Just look at the autopsies. But somebody has to explain to me the shit the coroner keeps reporting about those hearts. It just doesn't *happen!*"

"That's for damn sure," Atkinson muttered.

"I've been involved with gangs for a long time, Carl, just like you.

Most of these young men are tough, yes, but to know how to cause a heart to do that? No, I don't buy it."

"Which strengthens your argument about a third party."

Dean offered a sarcastic laugh. "Well, as far as the Lobos and Diablos are concerned, it's one hell of a party. *Somebody's* crashing it and causing lots of trouble." Dean chewed on his lip for a moment and narrowed his eyes, the dark brown hue highlighted by the matching horn-rimmed glasses. "That's another thing that's weird about all this. We got hundreds of gangs in this city but somebody out there has chosen these two as their own personal poster boys of evil." Dean stroked a hand across his mustache and refocused his gaze on Atkinson. "This is why I called you in here, Carl," he said. "I need you to do something."

Atkinson sat up in his chair. "Go ahead, Captain."

"You helped that *Times* reporter who's written those gang articles, right?"

"Yes, sir," he said. "I got him some interviews at Men's Central." Atkinson paused before adding, "Those meetings took place *before* his brother was killed in that drive-by a couple of months ago."

"What a fucking shame that was," Dean said. "That poor kid seeing his father killed like that. And the goddamn killer's still out there, unless he's one of the dead gang members."

"I've read every one of those articles," Atkinson said. "Reporters are supposed to be objective but his disgust was evident. No doubt it's at a whole new level, now."

"Enough to be considered a suspect?" Dean asked.

"Kevin?" Atkinson replied, his eyes opening wide. "No way, Captain. The man I know has a right to be enraged, hateful, any word you can think of, but he's no murderer. Not unless he's come up with a way to leave his nephew alone in the middle of the night to stalk and kill these guys twenty-five miles from home."

Dean smiled. "Unless his nephew acts as Robin to his Batman, I guess you're right," he acknowledged.

Atkinson offered a slight nod of his head and remained silent.

"The man interests me for another reason," Dean said. "I'm throwing caution to the wind here, but we need a goddamn lead and I'm thinking he might have heard something during those interviews. Do you think we can we trust him to keep things confidential? Reporter's are paid to report, you know what I mean?"

"I know what you're saying, but I believe he can be trusted under the circumstances," Atkinson answered. "Because of what happened to his brother, he's got a rooting interest in this case. I think he'll play it smart."

"Go see him," Dean said. "I trust your instincts, and logic, that we shouldn't consider him a suspect. So if we're dealing with an outside killer here, maybe those interviews from Central can help us. Maybe someone said something, or dropped a name. Maybe there's a dealer with a medical background *and* a reason for a grudge."

Atkinson stood up, put his hands in his pockets, and walked over to a corner window. "How much can I tell him, Captain? He's going to be curious about my sudden interest in his interviews."

"I'm pretty sure his opinion of gangs will blind him to the possibility of an outsider," Dean said. "I'm giving you the go-ahead to let him know, *off the record*, that there could be another reason for these deaths. Put it off as some bad shit selling on the street. That's nothing newsworthy, right?"

Atkinson turned towards Dean. "It's a good idea," he said, "considering we don't have anything else to go on."

Dean smiled at his trusted Lieutenant, whose wide-eyed, round-cheeked expression belied a tough, no-nonsense cop possessing a mountain range for shoulders and a neck the width of an ancient Oak. More importantly, his street smarts matched his brawn.

"I know it's just a shot in the dark," he said. "And the coroner would tell me nothing's been found to substantiate what I'm asking you to do. But somebody's out there doing something crazy, and he needs to be stopped." Dean removed his glasses and wiped the lenses one at a time against his shirtsleeve. "This is more than just heart attacks, Carl. It appears we got us a major league serial killer."

ELEVEN

"...Happy birthday, dear Margie
Happy birthday to you."

MARGARET PALMER CELEBRATED HER SIXTY-FOURTH birthday in the recreation room of Bromont Hills Senior Villas. Several gifts had already been opened, including the Barbara Streisand CD that played in the background. Margaret closed her eyes and started making a wish. "I don't know what *you're* wishing for, Margie," her friend, Lizzy, remarked, "but I think I know what Mack wants!" Everyone howled at Lizzy's not-so-subtle remark, including Mack Harris, who made no secret of his amorous feelings for Margie and his desire to follow Bromont Hills' slogan of "Active Living for Seniors."

Kevin's spirits received a boost by his mother's joy in the midst of the party. In the two and half months since Warren's murder, she seemed to be managing all right, a testament to the healing power of friends in times of need. Kevin got support from co-workers and received several calls from friends in the first few weeks after his brother's death, but his life had become a topsy-turvy ride of fractured emotions and altered considerations. He knew he had to appear strong for Seth's sake, but he couldn't evade his complete responsibility for the tragedy. The guilt suffocated him, making each day a struggle to endure.

After an earlier period of his life battling alcoholism and successfully overcoming the problem, he had now started drinking again, trying to suppress thoughts like his final conversation with Warren and his current situation with Seth. He'd initiate the day with a smuggled shot or two in the morning, some more at lunch time, another glass from a local bar before going home, some more before dinner, another one afterwards, and a final nightcap before bedtime to dull his mind so he could sleep.

Kevin's father had died, and now Warren, so the added burden of responsibility for his mother fell on his shoulders. She seemed happy where she lived, however, and today he enjoyed a rare moment of contentment attending her party. As she started unwrapping another gift, Kevin's cell phone rang. When he looked at his screen and read *Clearpoint Elementary School*, his mood plummeted like a bird shot in flight. Something bad must have happened with Seth, again. Kevin threw open the doors of the recreation room to step outside.

"This is Kevin," he said.

"Hello, Mr. Palmer. This is Eleanor Lee, principal of your nephew's school."

"Principal Lee," he blurted, "Seth's been going to grief counseling sessions for a few weeks now. He's in a program that helps children deal with anger management. He just needs some more time, okay? A little more time and I'm sure..."

She cut him off in mid-sentence. "Mr. Palmer, something happened to Seth today."

"What do you mean, 'something happened'?" Kevin asked. "Is he okay?"

"A little shaken up, but he's fine." she answered. "He's in my waiting room right now." Kevin closed his eyes, rubbing his face with his free hand. "So what happened?"

"Seth was threatened today by a few Latino students. I don't know if you remember the name, but Lorenzo Gonzalez was one of them. Seth had a confrontation with him awhile ago. They surrounded him on the playground and started taunting him."

"Damn it," Kevin muttered.

"I'm just grateful it didn't escalate into something worse," she said.

Kevin closed his eyes, pinching the bridge of his nose. "How's he doing?"

"Well, like I said, he's shaken up," she replied. "The taunting seems to have affected him more than that fight did."

Kevin pictured the ugly scene unfolding. The scenario gave him an overwhelming feeling of sadness. Sure, he felt anger towards those other boys, but he wasn't surprised. It was only a matter of time before one of those kids that Seth attacked decided to strike back. He's just lucky the confrontation wasn't physical. This time. "I had a feeling something like this might happen," he said.

"Once this type of situation starts, it's hard to stop," she replied. "I'm not excusing the bullying that occurred, but confrontations lead to grudges and grudges often lead to consequences."

Kevin knew she hit the nail on the head. "What's going to happen to those boys?" he asked.

"Detention for a week and a one day suspension for all of them. I've already talked with their parents to make sure we all understand each other."

"Well, do they understand you?"

After a few seconds of silence, her response sounded weary and laced with doubt. "I hope so," she said, "but we can't be sure, can we? When Seth attacked Lorenzo a few weeks ago, he made no secret of the fact he didn't like him because of his Mexican heritage. Lorenzo wasn't the only Mexican-American kid here to take offense at that."

"Can't say I blame them," he answered, too dispirited to offer a defense. "I'll be there as soon as I can. Thank you."

Kevin stood on the patio for a couple of minutes, staring at the cascading water of a nearby fountain and listening to the calming gurgle. How he wished he could stay here and revel in the tranquility of his surroundings. But he couldn't stop thinking about the principal's words, how "grudges often lead to consequences." Wasn't that the same theme he heard over and over during his discussions with gang members? Anger, hostility, resentment, persecution -a poisoned baton of hate passed on from one generation to the next. Grudges. Consequences. *How right you are, Principal Lee.*

Kevin walked towards a corner of the building where he knew he couldn't be spotted. He reached inside the pocket of his pants and extracted a small flask of scotch that he'd begun carrying around each day. He glanced in different directions before guzzling a few large gulps. He then removed a small box of breath mints from his other pocket. He placed two of them inside his mouth, repeating the same routine he'd been executing at work.

Kevin stood at the door and watched his mother dancing to a Barbara Streisand song with Mack. He waited for the song to finish before approaching her. "Mom, I'm sorry, but I have to leave. Seth isn't feeling well and wants to come home."

"Oh, poor thing," she said. "But can I see him soon, please? I miss my grandson!"

On the way to the parking lot his mother placed her arm around his waist. "You look tired, Kevin. Thinner, too. Are you all right?"

Kevin laughed; a cynical, self-pitying laugh. "That's a good one, Mom. *You're* the one we should all be concerned about. But look at you. You're laughing with your friends, dancing with Mack. What's your secret? How were you able to move on like this?"

His mother stood there in silence, staring at her son with a rigid jaw and troubled eyes that made him feel childish and uneasy. He felt ashamed for asking the question. His mother reached out towards him as her eyes misted over with a sadness Kevin didn't mean to summon. "You know better than that, Kevin."

"I'm sorry, I shouldn't..."

She held her hand up, indicating she had more to say. "I'll never be able to move on from what happened," she said. "Never. No parent can ever get over the pain of losing a child."

"Of course not. I only meant..."

"When your father died of cancer, at least we all had time to prepare for the inevitable. But this? Here and then gone at the snap of a finger?"

She covered her face with her hands as her shoulders trembled. Kevin felt a cold blade twist in the pit of his stomach. Warren had been sent to his death because of his brother's own stupidity. He wanted to scream, to beg her forgiveness, and to explain everything. But he couldn't. And wouldn't. It would just make things worse for the both of them.

"I'm just trying to make it through each day," she said. "You and Seth are what I live for now. But don't fool yourself. I often cry myself to sleep."

Kevin smiled at his mother. "You've always been my rock, you know that?"

"You lost your brother and now you're taking care of Seth," she said. "On top of that you work hard at your job. What you need is a woman in your life."

Kevin opened the car door and sat behind the wheel. "I promise you, you'll be the first to know when my dream girl comes calling."

"We aren't meant to live alone in this world, Kevin. Remember the words to that Streisand song? 'People who need people are the luckiest people in the world'. There's someone out there for everybody, including you. Just give yourself a chance to find her."

Kevin glanced at his watch. "I've got to go," he said. "I'll call you tonight."

As he drove off, he shook his head at his mother's apple pie bullshit and ridiculed her Streisand remark. "Yeah, I need someone Mom," he said, "and his name is Warren Palmer. So *don't* tell me I'm one of the luckiest people in the world."

TWELVE

K EVIN ALLOWED SETH A DAY away from school to help
him regain his composure, but he made sure his nephew returned
the second day after the taunting incident. Seth's grades had spiraled
downward to "C's" and "D's," and television privileges were now
curtailed. Kevin had hoped that by enrolling him in a grief counseling
program with other children who had lost a parent, Seth might realize he
wasn't alone in this kind of situation. But his grades continued getting
worse and his anger the evident cause. Kevin wanted some advice, so he
placed a call that morning to the man who ran the program, Dr. Stephen
Hobart.

Dr. Hobart had been kind enough to attend Warren's funeral,
introducing himself afterwards as the man in charge of the grief
counseling sessions Warren had attended after Michelle died. Through
Kevin's urging that his brother seek help, Warren discovered Dr. Hobart's
"Share and Care" group, where adults who had lost a spouse could find
solace through the support of others in similar positions. Warren had
spoken well of him, and when Kevin learned that children also had such
a service available, he approached Seth with the idea. After a couple of
heated arguments, (and a purchase of a new video game), Seth relented
and started attending the weekly meetings.

Dr. Hobart returned Kevin's call late that afternoon.

"Before I explain my main reason for calling," Kevin said, lowering
his scotch glass to the table, "I want to ask you if you've noticed any
progress these first four weeks because, frankly, I haven't."

"I'm not going to tell you anything you don't already know,"
Hobart said. "Seth's anger is unhealthy and misguided. We have a couple
of Latino kids in "Share and Care," so I have to monitor that situation

carefully. At this point in time, their own personal tragedies don't seem to have softened his feelings."

"Maybe it's just wishful thinking," Kevin replied, "but I keep hoping he's going to come around."

"Perhaps he's still in the observing and listening stage, Kevin. He doesn't volunteer much right now. Four weeks isn't enough time for certain kids to open up, and Seth's story is unique. To be terrorized by that gang would have been bad enough, but to witness your father's murder, well, that's pretty rough. He's dealing with a trauma that would bring an adult to his knees, let alone a young boy."

Kevin lifted his glass and gulped more of his drink before responding. "I can't believe that I used to feel pity for some of those guys," he said. "Now I hope they all walk a paper bridge to hell."

A brief silence followed. "What was the other reason for your call?"

"Seth's grades are slipping quite a bit. I've gotten notes from some of his teachers but I write my articles at night so I don't have much time to help him with his homework. Have you had other parents with the same problem?"

"Too many, unfortunately," Hobart said. "In Seth's case, he's a bright kid who's having a hard time focusing right now. Have you considered a tutor?"

"Not until you just mentioned it," Kevin replied, rubbing his thumb along the rim of his glass.

"There's a young woman who runs our child care center at the hospital. She's accredited and tutors some of these kids after work. I let her use one of our offices to provide a quiet atmosphere."

Kevin guzzled the last of his drink as he pictured the scenario. He'd drop Seth off with the tutor and find a local bar while he waited. "You really think she'll be able to handle Seth?" he asked.

"Well, certainly he has to do his part," Hobart told him. "But she's quite bright. A degree in Child Day Care Management as well as a teaching credential. She's tutored kids in everything from Math to English to Science." Hobart chuckled. "And, of course, Spanish."

"Why were you laughing?"

"At the irony, Kevin," Hobart said. "She's a Mexican-American."

Speechless at first, Kevin found it difficult responding to the idea of Seth receiving help from a woman whose nationality symbolized the fundamental problem. As he pondered the idea, however, he realized that a *Latina* tutor made a lot of sense. Seth's traumatic experience had been with Mexican men, so maybe she wouldn't present any of the familiar fears. In time, who knows? His views towards all Mexicans might soften.

"I don't know how Seth's going to react, but I'm all for it," Kevin said.

"Based on the reaction of grateful parents I've talked with, if he'll give her a chance, I think his grades will improve," Hobart replied. "Just call our office and ask to speak to Veronica."

When the conversation ended, Kevin stood and stretched, proud of himself for doing the right thing. This called for another drink.

THIRTEEN

*T*HE RISING SUN REAPPEARED WITHOUT a trace of mercy, inflaming the smothering air that lingered from the night, and signaling the return of summer's fiery yellow dictator. King sat propped up on the pillows of the sofa bed, sweating freely as he lit another cigarette. With puffy, bloodshot eyes serving as a reminder of heavy partying and too little sleep, he watched cartoons and flipped open the pop-top of another Budweiser. His caffeine-stained teeth exposed themselves in a self-satisfied smile as he relived the struggle, and eventual conquest, of the hot pussy, *la puta caliente,* from the night before. "*Bitch kept sayin' 'no', but I fucked her good. Just like she really wanted,*" he said to himself. He put the remaining matches on the nearby table, inhaled and closed his eyes, enjoying the sensation of his reawakening erection. King recalled the lesson Viper had taught him when it came to bitches: if they brought you far enough, "no" means "yes." Always.

Under normal circumstances after the night he had, King continued sleeping into the afternoon. But the past few months had been anything but normal. Too many comrades, *camaradas,* had died and he didn't know why. Heart attacks? For so many? No fuckin' way. The Diablos *had* to be behind these deaths. Who else could it be?

King hadn't slept much but he had no trouble recalling his weird, disturbing dream. Flash card images of his dead homies appeared and vanished over and over like zombies under a strobe light. They reached out for him, calling his name as he ran down a darkened alleyway into a deserted street. He awoke feeling drained, his throat sore and parched, his proud warrior's heart battering his chest as if in a frenzied need to escape.

King experienced nightmares as a kid, as little Miguel, but his parents gave him enough beer to help him sleep. He refused to admit he'd had a nightmare again because that kind of shit didn't happen to a tough motherfucker, a *chingon*, like him. When he stumbled into the apartment sometime in the early a.m., he kicked off his shoes and put his head down, figuring he'd sleep for hours. As the moaning of dead Lobos echoed in his head, he sat up with a jolt from the sledgehammer of his dream. He raced for the refrigerator, guzzled down most of a can of beer, and lit his first cigarette of the day.

When Fred and Barney broke for a commercial, King returned to the refrigerator to retrieve another beer. Hearing the sound of someone's keys in the lock, he cursed himself for leaving his gun under the mattress. Too late-the handle turned and the door opened. Appearing before him, disheveled and red-eyed, stood his mother.

"Shit, Mama!" King snapped. "Where the fuck you been? I thought you was here."

"*No me chinges*, Miguel," she said bitterly. "It's too damn early for your shit." She tossed her purse on the table by the door. "I gotta get ready for work. If I'm late again I'll be fired."

"You been out fuckin' Ernesto again?" King asked with disgust, sitting back on the bed. "*Pinchi cabron*. What about Luis? Remember him? My little brother? You left him alone?"

"Don't you talk to me like that," she protested. "I got me a life, too, baby, you understand? You think your *pinchi* father don't know what he's missin'? That *puta* bitch ain't got what I got, honey." She opened the refrigerator. "Damn it, Miguel," she shouted, slamming the door, "you been drinkin' all the beer again?" Approaching him, she sat on his bed.

"There's one more can in there and it's for me, you understand? Me! I'll drink it when I get home from work." She pointed to the two cans King opened earlier. "Anything left?"

"Yeah, some."

His mother grabbed the empty can first and threw it back on the bed before gulping down what remained of the other one. She walked into the kitchen, selected a dirty cup from an array of unwashed dishes in the sink, and prepared some instant coffee. "Luis told me he was going to a friend's house to watch a movie and not to wait up for him," she explained. "He said he'd be back in time to get some sleep before school. When he left, I was alone. I didn't feel like bein' alone, *okay*? I left him a note on his bed with Ernesto's phone number if he needed me. He never called. Everything's fine."

She sat on the bed for several minutes, watching the cartoon and sipping her coffee. "Here," she said, standing up and placing the coffee cup on the table, "finish the rest. I gotta shower and get ready." As she disappeared around the corner, she called out from her bedroom. "Do me a favor, baby. Wake Luis. Tell him to hurry up. I don't want his school callin' here again askin' me where he's at." When King pushed himself off the bed, he heard his mother's voice again. "And tell him to eat somethin'. We got some corn flakes, I think."

The moment King opened his brother's door a cold stream of panic surged through his gut. The bed hadn't been used and his mother's untouched note still lay on the pillow. He didn't know what to think. Was he overreacting? All he knew was Lobos were dying and his little thirteen-year-old brother didn't come home.

The dark ravine of King's concern deepened as he visualized the possibility of Luis lying dead somewhere. If anything happened to him there would be hell to pay like no one had ever seen. *"Pinchi Diablos!"* he growled to himself. The recent insanity had him believing the worst, and he forced himself to calm down in order to think straight. He knew he couldn't tell his mother the truth, preferring make up a story in order to buy some time. He didn't need her going crazy right now. After she left, he'd get Slice and they'd find him.

The urgency he felt rammed an elbow of clarity to his foggy head, and as he heard his mother turn off the shower, he darted into Luis' room, stuffed the note into his pocket, and yanked back the sheets. In the kitchen, he took a cereal bowl and a spoon and threw them in the sink, filling the bowl to the top with water. King kept a close eye in the direction of his mother's bedroom as he quietly opened the front door before slamming it closed. After a few moments his mother charged from the bedroom fumbling with her robe and looking upset. "What the hell are you doing?" she griped. "Why you slammin' doors?"

"That wasn't me, it was Luis," he said, standing rigid by the door. "He ate fast and ran out of here. Said there's a ride waitin' down the block."

"With who?"

"How the fuck should I know?" King snarled, hoping to change the subject. "What are you standin' there for? I thought you was in a hurry."

"Yeah, yeah, I gotta get movin'," she answered. "Hey, baby, can you help with dinner this week? The cupboard's pretty bare, know what I'm sayin'?"

King knew exactly what his mother meant. In the Ruiz household, just like in the North Rampart Lobos, the end always justified the means.

"Sure, Mama," he replied. "I'll see what I can do."

As soon as his mother left for work, King called Slice, who had to be awakened. They planned to meet at the AM/PM market down the street. He slid his hand under the mattress of the sofa bed and pulled out a .38. Returning to Luis' room, he opened the closet and took an old shoe box from the shelf, placing it on the bed. King opened the chamber of the gun, removed the lid to the box and grabbed a handful of cartridges. He started loading his gun when he again heard someone stick a key in the lock. Startled, he closed the bedroom door, leaving himself a small opening to peer. His breath caught in his throat as he watched Luis stumble and fall to the floor.

King rushed to his brother and stared for a few seconds at the sight of him lying on his stomach with his hands over his face, sobbing in a soft, steady rhythm. He dropped to his knees and eased Luis over onto his back. He gained relief at the realization that Luis hadn't been shot, or even stabbed. Looking into his brother's eyes, however, red-rimmed and puffy from crying, he noticed the same kind of fear and confusion he'd witnessed when one of his *comaradas* lay dying in the street.

"I'll *kill* the fuckin' Lobo who done this to you," he told him. He reached out and fingered some of the dried blood on Luis' forehead. "You got a big bump on your head, man. What'd they hit you with?" Luis didn't answer. King sensed Luis wasn't ready for any questions yet, but he wasn't gonna let him remain silent much longer. He felt like a snarling dog tethered to a chain. King helped Luis get to his feet and half-carried him to the bed, propping him against the pillows before hurrying to the refrigerator for that last beer his mother wanted. King pulled back the pop-top, took a large swig, and offered the can to his little brother.

"You ready to talk about it?" he asked.

Luis accepted the beer with a shaky hand and drank a large amount before speaking. "Juice... Juice is dead."

"*Juice?*" King responded. "What happened? The Diablos kill him?" With a vacant stare, Luis shifted his glassy eyes slowly upward, meeting King's angry gaze. "He wasn't *killed* by anybody, man," he said in a soft voice. "He just *died*. I saw him grab his chest and just... die." King exploded. "*What the fuck do you mean, 'he just died'? Tell me, God damn it! And what happened to you?*"

Luis bit his lower lip and squinted before taking another swig from the can. His eyes shifted to the floor as he started to speak. "We was gonna jack somebody at that new club on First Street. Juice knew someone who worked in the kitchen there. He said some rich *hueros* stay real late every Sunday night drinkin' wine and playin' poker with the owner. Juice told me he could use some reinforcement. He was gonna teach me some shit. So I went over to his house about 11:00. We hung out for awhile and watched some t.v. Then we talked about the way things would go down."

Ψ Ψ Ψ

` "My friend tells me about all those rich, *pinchi hueros* walkin' back to their Benz, or their shiny SUV's, all drunk and laughin', and shit," Juice said, throwing his head back in an imitation. "Those white assholes ain't got a care in the world." Grinning, he added, "They gonna taste real life tonight, man."

Luis smiled. "Where we gonna hide?"

"They got some big-ass bushes around the parking lot," Juice told him, waving his hand in a circle. Darker than shit around there, man. Ain't nobody gonna see us."

"So what am I gonna do?"

"It's all about force, man," Juice replied. "Two guns are better than one. You and me'll both be packin' tonight. You all right with that, *cholito*?"

"Fuck you, Juice!" Luis roared. "I ain't little no more. I'm a *cholo*, man!"

Juice laughed. "King's learnin' you right, little brother. You growin' big *cajones*." He reached into his pocket. "I wanna show ya somethin'. Juice got balls, too, *vato*!"

He pulled out a large Rolex watch. "Got me this off some old man today," he told him. "Broke into the fucker's house when he was supposed to be gone, you know?" He shook his head. "If the stupid ass hadn't gone and given me a hard time I mighta let him live." As the two of them admired the new jewelry, with the gold face and diamond settings representing every number, Juice placed the shiny steel and gold band around his wrist. "We'll leave at two-fifteen," he said.

"Why so late?" Luis asked.

"My friend says they do their bullshit every Sunday night 'til about three. I promised him a take of whatever we get." Juice's tone turned serious. "You always go after the bitches. A man gives up his money real fast that way."

When they arrived, they hid behind the thick-leafed shrubbery of the parking lot. Luis felt the nervous excitement of a hunter readying himself for the kill. Juice's friend got it right. The remaining two cars were expensive ones, a black Escalade SUV and a gold four-door Lexus.

"We need one of 'em to split before the other one," Juice said. "Can't take no chance one of 'em escapes and calls the police."

After a long wait, they heard the approaching sound of loud, festive talk. "What time is it?" Luis whispered.

Bringing his watch close to his face, Juice muttered, "It's about fuckin' time they showed up. It's goddamn three-forty."

They peered through an opening in the bushes. Two couples, white, young and rich looking, moved toward their cars. Forced to watch and wait, Luis thought of what Juice said earlier and hoped they wouldn't leave together. The disappointment hit him hard when both couples got into their cars and started their engines.

"Shit," Juice whispered under his breath. "Fuck it, Luis, it don't look like..."

Their luck changed in an instant when the Escalade drove away while the Lexus owner popped open his trunk and stepped out of his car.

"Yeah, baby, oh yeah," Juice whispered.

"*This is it!*" Luis said to himself.

"Remember, show the bitch your tool, like I told you," Juice instructed, making sure Luis kept his gun pointed at the woman. With a quick nod of his head, Juice gave the signal and the two of them rushed from the bushes.

"*Motherfucker, don't move! Don't fuckin' move!*" Juice shouted, pointing his gun at the man as he stood by his trunk.

"*Get out, get outta the fuckin' car!*" Luis hollered at the woman, approaching her from the passenger seat side. But the woman disobeyed, lunging toward her door and locking it instead. Luis froze in confusion.

"She locked the door!" he yelled.

Keeping the gun pointed at his victim, Juice darted over to the open driver side door, overpowering the panicky woman desperate to close it. "*Get out huera bitch or I'll blow his fuckin' head off!*"

"Don't shoot, don't shoot! Please!" the woman pleaded, exiting the car.

"Give him your fuckin' keys!" Juice commanded, nodding his head towards Luis.

"Don't hurt us! I...I don't want to die!"

"Shut up, bitch!" Juice shouted. "Where's your purse?"

"On the seat!"

Luis grabbed the small, black evening bag and held it up for Juice to see.

"Take the money out," he told him.

Luis opened the bag and found the cash inside a zippered compartment. "I got it!" he declared, waving the bills like a flag before securing them inside his pants pocket.

Juice directed his attention back to the man, pointing the gun at his head. "Now give me your fuckin' wal...*Aah! Aaaahh!*" Still holding his gun, Juice dropped to his knees and grabbed his chest.

Luis stood paralyzed in disbelief. Not knowing what else to do, he aimed his gun at the couple. "You better fuckin' stay right there!"

Looking pale and unsteady, Juice rose to his feet. "*Why's it so fuckin' cold?*" he hollered. His shivering intensified into a strange kind of shaking. He looked to his left, then his right. "*Who said that?*" With an awkward lurch forward, Juice stuck the gun in the man's face. "What the *fuck* are you sayin'?"

"No, please!" the trembling man pleaded, closing his eyes and turning his head away. "I didn't say anything!"

In numb panic, Luis determined Juice must be on some crazy drug making him hear voices. He seemed involved in a conversation with someone, sometimes yelling, like those loony homeless dudes walking down the street.

"*You're talkin' crazy, asshole!*" Juice roared. "*Shut the fuck up! Where are you?*"

With the gun in his left hand, Juice flung his right hand over the side of his face. "*My eye! What the fuck? I can't see! I can't see! I'll kill your ass, God damn it!*" Stumbling in awkward circles, Juice seemed as if he was close to collapsing.

"*I'll kill you, man! You don't scare me, you ass... Ohhh! Aaaahh!*" Juice dropped his gun and grabbed his chest with both hands, collapsing in a heap on the ground.

"*JUICE!*" Luis shouted. Ignoring the couple, he hurried over to help his downed friend. He dropped to his knees, then reared back in horror at the sight of Juice's swollen right eye, covered in a sickening puss-like crust. Under the overhead parking light, the eye appeared colorless, or maybe even slightly blue. Fighting back nausea, Luis continued shaking Juice's limp body in several futile attempts at reviving him, and for a moment, he thought he saw Juice's head turn upwards. He placed his hand just above his friend's mouth to check for breathing, and felt the momentary encouragement of some air. When he touched Juice's face, however, his hopes for a recovery vanished in the shock of his ice-cold skin. Turning his gaze to avoid the freakish, protruding eye, he caught a glimpse of the diamonds on Juice's Rolex, glittering under the parking lot light. Without a reason for noticing, his mind still noted the time: 3:50.

Luis didn't care about the man and woman anymore. He started to rise to his feet, preparing to give them their keys from his sweatshirt pocket, but was unexpectedly tackled from behind and knocked forward. He extended an arm to break his fall but his forehead struck the unforgiving surface of the parking lot and the pain flared like a blowtorch. Hands and knees held him down as other hands tugged at his sweatshirt. When he finally staggered to his feet, unsure how long he'd been down and feeling blood trickling down his face, he realized the *hueros* had taken their keys and driven away.

An unsettling noise startled him from behind. When he spun around, he stood transfixed in terror. Masses of black rats, too numerous to count, ran across the empty parking lot from the same bushes where he'd hidden earlier, leaping onto Juice's body and smothering every inch. The scene reminded him of ants attacking a dead bug, swarming the carcass until you could barely see any part of it. Luis vomited in violent waves over and over again until he thought he might faint. What the squealing rats were doing to his friend was too terrible to watch.

He screamed at the sudden feel of something warm crawling down his leg. Jumping in panic, Luis started beating his leg with his hand. Feeling the wetness, he realized the warm sensation had been his own urine. He knew at that moment he had to leave Juice and get out of there in a hurry. Looking around, frantic at the thought the rats might attack him, he ran as fast as he could. Through his pain and fright, the only thing he wanted to do was just...

"...find my way home, Miguel. I didn't want no Diablos or police to see me, so I hid in bushes. And behind walls." Luis choked back a sob. "I was scared I wouldn't make it back." Tears welled up in his eyes again. "I don't fuckin' understand what happened to Juice," he said. "That last time, when he fell on the ground for good, he didn't make a sound, but... he... turned his head like he was listening to somebody. But not me, you know? Somebody else. I thought I could shake him awake, but I felt his face and he was like... like fuckin' ice, man. And his eye! It was all big and disgusting. It was sick! And the *rats*! All those fuckin' rats!" Luis shook his head wildly several times, as if he could loosen the image from his mind. "Never seen nothin' like that. Never." Luis grew quiet, returning the can of beer to his lips.

ᴛᴊᴛ ᴛᴊᴛ ᴛᴊᴛ

King wasn't aware at what point in Luis' story that he rose from the bed and walked over to the window. But there he stood, a caged lion staring out from behind the bars, wanting to rip someone's head off. But who? What was the answer? He felt confused, more than he could ever recall, and he hated this feeling of helplessness. Of *weakness*. He was *King*, God damn it! He lived for payback. *Chingasos*, man. Kicking some ass. Living the crazy life. *Mi vida loca*. But what was this shit? WHAT WAS THIS SHIT?

"*FUCK!*" King yelled. He needed something, anything, to release his anger. He walked, stiff and brooding, over to the coffee cup his mother had used. Staring with destructive intent at the blue and white mug, as if delivering a telepathic reading of its last rites, King lunged at the cup like a live grenade, hurling it with all his might. As the fragile ceramic pieces exploded like fireworks, leaving brown streams bleeding down the wall, King stood transfixed in his frustration, barely hearing the renewed sobs of his brother filtering through from the bed.

King regained his senses enough to ask Luis a question. "Hey, you got the Rolex?"

"Covered with fuckin' rats, Miguel," he answered.

"*Shit!*" King growled.

Reaching deep intohis pants pocket, Luis pulled out several crinkled bills. "I still got the money," he said. "Got me two hundred twenty-three dollars." With his voice trailing off, he added, "I was gonna split it... with Juice."

King walked over to the bed, counted the money, and placed an affectionate hand behind his brother's head. "You did real fine, *hermanito*," he said. "Juice would be proud of you, man. Real, fuckin' proud." King recounted the money. "Mama said we ain't got nothin' to eat or drink, so she'll be happy, okay? We'll get some food and beer for the house and me and you will use the rest for other shit. Mama knows not to ask no questions. When she comes home, tell her you never made it to school.

85

You got jumped and hurt your head. Got it?"

Luis nodded and took a deep breath. "Whatever you say, Miguel," he said, offering a tiny smile. "You always know best."

FOURTEEN

KEVIN APPLIED ADDED PRESSURE TO the scouring pad, attempting to scrape the burnt spaghetti sauce off the pan. That's what happens when you're cooking and not paying attention to the time, when you're mind is so clogged up with shit that it's impossible to keep a clear head. He figured the double scotch he tossed back after work would relieve his frustration from the chastising he received at work, but the alcohol functioned more like gasoline to a fire.

His boss specialized in speeches about "deadline failures and disappointing attitude," and Kevin found himself on the receiving end earlier that day. He kept his mouth shut during his boss' reprimand, but inspired by that scotch, he imagined all the things he yearned to say. "*Cut me some slack, damn it!...*" *Big deal if I was late with some articles, it's not the end of the world...*" "*Yeah, I missed an important meeting, but was it my fault my hair-trigger nephew went off on one of the Mexican kids the same day?...*" "*He has no friends anymore. Who else was going to pick him up?...*" "*Put yourself in my shoes!*"

Kevin's anger at the day's events prevented him from discussing the idea of a tutor, a *Mexican-American* tutor, to Seth. He felt tempted to lash out at him, telling him how his rebellious attitude sucked, but he didn't need another confrontation so he kept quiet. He poured his after-dinner drink and heard the television turn on in the other room. Poking his head through the kitchen door he asked, "Don't you have any homework to do, Seth?"

"I did it at school," he replied, his eyes remaining glued to the television.

"Any tests coming up?"

"Nope."

Seth's backpack sat leaning against the back of a chair. Kevin realized that he hadn't seen any weekly planners from Seth's teacher in awhile, and he wondered if there was one inside the bag. *"Should I look?"* he asked himself. Kevin stared at the backpack, unsure whether to rummage through Seth's things without his knowledge. He gazed into his scotch, as if searching for the answer inside the copper-colored liquor. He brought his lips to the glass, inhaled the aroma, and swished some around the inside of his mouth before swallowing. *I'll be damned if I'm going to stand by passively and let Warren's kid do poorly in school.*

Kevin removed the familiar blue-framed Clearpoint newsletter and then discovered another one, folded in half, tucked away at the bottom. He reached down, plucked it out, and proceeded to read the contents. Before he finished the final sentence, he was already on his way to talk with Seth.

"Why didn't you show me this note from Mrs. Fisher? he asked. "It's from last Friday."

"Where'd you get that?" "From your backpack."

Seth, who had been sprawled on the couch, jumped to his feet. "You can't look through my stuff! That backpack's mine!"

Kevin read the note out loud. *"Dear Mr. Palmer: I am asking for your help in trying to get Seth to understand the importance of putting in the necessary work at school. There has been a general lack of effort in all of his subjects and his grades are suffering as a consequence. Please sign the bottom of this letter and return it to me next week. I suggest that we arrange a meeting in the near future. Sincerely, Eloise Fisher."*

Kevin took a large swig from his glass. "You weren't going to show this to me, were you?"

"I don't know!" Seth blurted. "Yeah... maybe."

Kevin took several steps toward Seth. "Don't you understand you might to fail if you don't straighten up? Can't you *see* that?"

Seth's eyes moistened and his face turned red. "I don't care!" he screamed.

"What do you mean you don't care? How will you feel when all of your friends go into seventh grade and you have to stay behind. How will you feel then?"

Seth turned away. "I don't have any friends, okay?"

Kevin stared at his nephew. "You've got to start thinking about school again. You need to..."

"No! You can't make me! You can't! I don't have to listen to you!"

"Oh yes, you do, young man!"

"Why should I? You're not my father! You're just... just..."

"Just what Seth? Just your uncle?"

Seth's eyes opened wide, a fire raging inside them. "*You're just a drunk!*"

"*What*? How dare you say that!"

Kevin watched Seth run into his room and slam the door. He remained in that spot for several minutes, feeling his anger ease with each further swig of Scotch. He wondered if a kid Seth's age knew what a drunk really was. Kevin just needed a temporary crutch to survive these dark times. He'd stop when things got better.

Kevin contemplated his options. Should he demand an apology tonight, or let things simmer down and discuss the matter tomorrow? He rubbed his face several times and walked across the room to tap on Seth's door.

"Seth? Seth? Can we talk?"

Silence.

Kevin knocked again. "Come on, Seth. I want to talk with you about something. Dr. Hobart's given me an idea about helping you with your grades. You said he's a nice guy. He knows someone he thinks could help you."

After another round of silence, Kevin thought of another angle.

"Remember, Seth, if your grades improve you'll start getting more television time back again."

The muted response ended a few moments later.

"Go on," he said. "I'm listening."

"There's a woman who runs the day care center at the clinic but she's also a tutor. Dr. Hobart told me she's helped some of the other kids in your "Care and Share" class."

"Big deal," the voice on the other side of the door said. "I don't *care* about school."

"Seth, can we please talk face to face? You're too young to get a job and the law says you have to go to school. Come on out."

He stood there until he heard the turning of he knob. Seth looked at Kevin's hands as soon as he poked his head through the door, leaving Kevin thankful that he'd left his glass on the table.

"Let's go over to the couch," he said.

When they sat, Kevin continued. "Failing isn't an option, Seth. The situation will be worse if the kids in your class pass you by and you're stuck repeating a grade."

"Isn't there somewhere else I could go?" he asked.

"Any school would demand the same things," Kevin said.

"Then it doesn't matter what school I go to, right?"

"But why start over at a new school with kids you don't know?"

Seth's mouth tightened as he stared at Kevin. "'Cause maybe another school wouldn't have *Mexicans*."

Kevin had a sudden urge to rain more scotch down his throat. "You know I don't like hearing that kind of talk from you," he said.

Seth remained unapologetic.

"Do the Mexican girls bother you, too?"

Seth's head tilted a bit to the side, as if the question caught him by surprise. After a long silence, he answered, "I don't know."

"Have any of the Mexican girls at school ever talked to you?"

"Just school stuff," he said. "Like when we're doing things in class."

"Did that go okay?"

"I guess so."

"Then if I'm hearing you right, your feelings toward Mexican girls isn't the same as the boys. There seems to be a difference."

Seth shrugged his shoulders. "I don't know."

The moment of truth had arrived. "The tutor Dr. Hobart's recommending is a Mexican-American woman."

"*What?*"

"She can help you, Seth," Kevin exclaimed. That's all that matters!"

Seth's eyes narrowed. He stood up, put his hands in his pockets, and turned his back on Kevin. He held his position for a long while before turning around to make eye contact.

"Okay," he said. "But if that tutor's like other Mexicans I'm not going back."

FIFTEEN

KEVIN SAT AT A CORNER table for two, away from the early morning patrons at Philippe's, the popular downtown eatery. Lieutenant Atkinson had called him the day before asking for a meeting at the restaurant. Kevin appreciated the few moments alone. His hangover left him feeling shaky, and his focus as scattered as the sawdust on the floor.

"Sorry I'm late, Kevin," the husky, baritone voice said.

Kevin offered a tired smile. "You're just in time, Carl," he replied. "I'm ready to think about something other than myself."

Atkinson placed his coffee on the table before perching his sizable backside onto the round wooden stool. "If you don't mind me saying so, Kevin, you look like shit. And you got your hands wrapped around your coffee cup like it's a damn life preserver."

Kevin placed the cup on the table and rubbed his hands on his face in an attempt to erase the bleariness. "So what do you want to talk about?"

"I need to ask you something about your interviews at Men's County."

"Go ahead."

"Can you recall if any of the gang members mentioned anything about their drugs, like maybe something new on the street?"

"I don't remember anything like that being brought up," he answered. "They just wanted to talk about their exploits and how big and bad their gang was." Kevin raised the cup to his lips. "Why do you ask?"

"With all the shit that's happened between the Diablos and Lobos the last couple of months, the heart attacks and all, we're just trying to cover every base."

"One small step for man, one giant leap for thinning out the herd," he muttered, feeling his head start to clear. "Your inquiry makes sense, though. I'm surprised you didn't ask me earlier."

"The number of heart attacks makes no sense," Atkinson said. "Everyone's in agreement on that. There's so many drugs pushed nowadays, so many illicit lab setups, that anything is possible. The toxicology reports haven't shown a damn thing, but how else do you explain it?"

"If the lab results say nothing's there, you've got no choice, Carl. You have to accept their findings."

"For now, maybe," Atkinson said, looking away. "But final reports leave you with more questions than answers sometimes."

Kevin put his elbows on the table, and leaned forward. "Like what? You can tell me. You should tell me. Look what those assholes have done to my life. And to Seth's." Lowering his voice but not his urgency, he asked, "What are you hiding?"

Atkinson stared at Kevin for several long moments. "How long we known each other?

"Since last September. When I started my interviews."

"That's right," he said. "Almost a year, now. And I've been good to you, wouldn't you agree? Helped you out with introductions, cut through the red tape, right?"

"Why do I get the feeling you're about to cash in on the favor I owe you?"

"Because I need you to *promise* me you won't mention any of this in the newspaper."

"You know damn well I'm not the only reporter that comes around asking questions," Kevin said. "Whatever you're about to tell me, if I've got to go mum on a story, I hope the others fall in line, too."

"We're already under enough pressure to get this damn thing figured out," Atkinson said. "You're one dog I don't need barking his bullshit. But as long as you keep your mouth shut, I'll make an exception and let you in on some things."

"Thank you, Carl," Kevin replied, nodding his head.

"You've paid your dues big time when it comes to the Lobos and Diablos," Atkinson acknowledged. "I respect what you've gone through and how you've taken on the responsibility for your brother's son."

Kevin remained silent, managing a weak smile.

"Just give me your word that what I'm about to tell you remains between us. Once I explain it to you, you'll understand why."

"All right," he said. "I'll keep a lid on it."

Atkinson drank some coffee and glanced around the restaurant before returning his attention to Kevin. "The first reported heart attack was over three months ago. Since that time, there have been *ten* more." He paused a moment, as if wanting that statistic to linger awhile longer. "All of them, *all of them,* were either a Diablo or a Lobo. Nobody else."

"How can you be sure?" Kevin asked. "There's hundreds of gangs all over L.A."

"And not one death from heart attack reported from any other gang unit in the city," Atkinson explained. "Except here. Except us. The Diablos and Lobos. That's it."

Kevin dispensed with a low whistle. "That's really weird."

"Weird?" Atkinson replied, his eyebrows rising. "You want weird?"

Kevin opened his mouth to speak but Atkinson held up his mitt of a left hand.

"The hearts were ice cold, Kevin." Pausing, he added, "Fucking frozen."

Kevin felt his jaw slacken and his vision seemed to glaze over for an instant. He just heard something impossible. *Impossible.*

"Let me guess what's going through your mind right now," Atkinson said. "Probably the same damn thing that went through mine when Captain Dean told me. You think you know what I just said, but not really, like some distant echo that didn't quite register."

Kevin nodded his head, waiting to hear more. *Needing* to hear more.

"I'm going to tell you the same way it was told to me, okay? When someone dies, the temperature of the heart during the early stages is between ninety-seven and one-hundred degrees. By the time most autopsies are performed the heart is generally around room temperature." Atkinson rubbed the back of his neck. "Ten of the eleven victims had hearts between thirty-four and thirty-eight degrees."

"Holy shit," Kevin muttered. "But how do you know they were..."

Atkinson held up his hand again.

"How do we know they were frozen?" It gets a little technical, but after eleven of these things, I'm turning into an expert. Compare the victim's heart to frozen meat. When you freeze meat, the water in the cells expands and the cell walls 'rupture', that's the word the coroner uses. All of the hearts of these dead gang members had ruptured cell walls."

Kevin shook his head, his eyes narrowing as he looked at Atkinson. "Isn't there another explanation for it, Carl? That sounds pretty crazy."

"Crazy?" he replied. "You ain't heard crazy. That eleventh victim, the

93

one whose heart I didn't include with the others? What if I told you his heart had a thin layer of ice around it?"

"Ice?" Kevin whispered, his eyes opening wide.

"Ice," Atkinson repeated. "This kid was in the Lobos. Went by the name of 'Juice', but his real name was Gustavo Robledo. A real piece of work. Spent time behind bars a few times, but never long enough. A man calls the station the other night, sometime after four. Robledo and a second gunman tried to rob this guy and his wife in a parking lot. After he described what happened, it could only have meant one thing. When the officers got there, one of them recognized Robledo. We got lucky with this kid. He had no known family members. We had no obligation to inform anybody first. This gave us a chance to examine the heart as near to the time of death as we'd ever had. That chest was open before five-thirty."

"Before the ice melted, Kevin said.

"There's something else," Atkinson said. "The aorta valves of all the victims have tiny holes in them. Captain Dean compared it to pipes bursting when the water freezes inside. What they're thinking is the blood froze as it left the heart and expanded in the aorta valve. That's how the holes were caused. The aorta burst like a frozen pipe."

"How is that possible?"

"There's more, Kevin," Atkinson said. "Every victim had one of their eyes swell up. And they're covered with some kind of glaze. You can't even see the real color. It winds up looking blue."

"Could that be caused by something internal?" Kevin asked. "Related to the heart's drop in temperature, maybe?"

"You'd think so, yeah," Atkinson said. "But that's another mystery. The lab results show nothing irregular. *Nothing*. It's as if the eye is completely normal."

"I can't believe what I'm hearing," Kevin remarked.

"I'm not finished," Atkinson said. "The victims have multiple scratch marks over their bodies that look like rats got to them. But no hairs or droppings have been found except for one victim. And that includes the ones found inside their bedrooms. How the hell do you explain that?"

"Do you think the rats could have transmitted some kind of disease?"

"It doesn't seem so," Atkinson replied. "The final toxicology results are still pending, but so far nothing outside of your garden variety drugs have been found in their system. And no bite marks."

"No bite marks?" Kevin exclaimed. "Rats do more than just scratch,

Carl."

"I grew up around enough of them," Atkinson said, "so trust me, I know. But there's only been one death where the flesh was visibly eaten. In the old railroad yard east of downtown, a Lobo gang member was found with his face in pretty bad shape. There are plenty of rats around that old yard but he definitely died from heart failure."

"The coroner better come up with some plausible answers soon," Kevin warned. "I don't want anyone else getting a hold of this story before I do."

"Hey!" Atkinson snapped. "You gave me your word..."

This time it was Kevin who held up a hand. "Yes, I did," he said. "And I'll keep quiet, like I told you. But a story this bazaar can't be kept under wraps much longer. If I find out another reporter gets this story out before I do, all bets are off. I'll write about everything I know." Kevin's eyes narrowed as he looked at Atkinson. "You're right about those dues I've paid, Carl. This God damn story is mine."

"Fair enough," Atkinson said. "But if you jump the gun and print any of this, I'll show you first hand what made me an All-City lineman two years running."

"That's one threat I'll take seriously," he replied.

Atkinson nodded before gulping down the rest of his coffee. "Let me tell you something about a *real* threat, Kevin. I was a mean, hard-nosed defensive tackle in my day, but that was nothin' compared to the threat these gangbangers are facing."

SIXTEEN

*H*E DWELLED SOMEWHERE IN TIME between desire and culmination, separation and proximity. Reaching out from his own indiscernible space into the lives of the unsuspecting, he sought to destroy his chosen targets, intent on invasion and the dispensing of justice. He'd been reborn as a lethal antagonist of the Diablos and Lobos, craving their elimination through a spiritual impulse predicated on vengeance. Devoid of color or definition, he inherited a life form no longer dictated by his previous humanity. He heeded his instinctive protection of Seth without reservation, serving as the ever-present danger to their existence, the relentless scraping at their souls. He plagued their lives as a rapidly dividing cell of chaos, capable of invading their thoughts and dreams, intent on intimidation and eradication. He was an affliction depleting their sense of power, a scourge infecting their pursuit of domination. And he couldn't be killed, again.

ᴛᴛ ᴛᴛ ᴛᴛ

Warren Palmer lived and loved as a husband, father, son, and brother. As a young man, his intellect and appreciation of the literary masters created the early framework of the passionate teacher he became. He strove for his students to find pieces of themselves in the books he assigned. *"Each of you will find your life somewhere in these pages,"* he told them. *"Don't fall prey to our decadent and superficial age."* Each year, Professor Palmer, a.k.a. Professor Poemer, remained one of the most popular teachers on campus.

Professor *Poemer*. A student had given him that nickname during his first year, and for every class afterwards he reveled in his reputation.

Edgar Allan Poe was to Warren Palmer what The Beatles were to rock 'n roll fans of their era; an inspiration and a constant source of interest. As a child, his father rented the first scary movie he saw; 'The Pit and the Pendulum'. Vincent Price starred in the film and the next night they watched another Price film entitled, 'The Fall of the House of Usher'. Edgar Allan Poe authored both stories, so when his father told him the man had written a lot more, he asked his parents for an Edgar Allan Poe book. Though some of the tales and poems were difficult to understand at first, one in particular captivated him from the start, and which he reread to a point of near memorization; 'The Tell-Tale Heart'.

Edgar Allan Poe served as the catalyst for Warren's consummation of books, and, eventually, an English Literature major. When his college professor told the class that Warren's recitation of 'The Tell-Tale Heart' was the best he'd ever heard from a student, his determination to commit more of Poe's lurid works to memory grew. He recognized that Poe's fantasies offered something uniquely mesmerizing about fear and the macabre; fantasies, that upon Warren's death, turned into realities.

When Michelle received the news that she had lung cancer, the doctor told her that 10 to 15 percent of those that fall victim are non-smokers, and she turned out to be one of them. Unlike his Vietnam vet father, who chain smoked his way on board a nicotine-filled balloon ride to Cancer Park, Michelle had never touched a cigarette in her life. The year and a half that passed between the biopsy and her death turned Warren into the type of father he never had; someone who could offer genuine displays of love. Warren and Seth relied on each other and functioned as a team. They marketed together, prepared the meals, cleaned the rooms, did the laundry, and catered to Michelle's needs. His love for Seth took on a much greater dimension during her illness, and he came to appreciate how much his son depended on him.

"Look after him," she whispered to Warren, hours before she died. "He's still a young boy. He needs you."

Warren smiled at her, gazing into the diminishing light of her eyes. "These last few months have taught me a valuable lesson," he said. "A son needs his father more than I ever realized. My old man wasn't really there for Kevin or me. But I'm not going to make that mistake with Seth." He grasped her frail hand, offering a gentle squeeze. "I promise, Michelle," he told her, "no matter what, I'll always look after him and protect him. I swear to you."

TᵲᵲT TᵲᵲT TᵲᵲT

When he died, Warren chose a path shaped by a combination of concern for his son and loathing for the perpetrators of his murder. The threads of human emotion still clung to his consciousness as he rejected the light of peace in favor of retribution. He believed Michelle would understand, even condone, his motivations. After all, he had made an oath to her before she died which he had every intention of honoring. Seth had already experienced the grievous loss of his mother. Now he lost his father in a cruel and senseless manner. In death, a wrong could and would be rectified.

He entered a universe where the multitudes of those possessing vindictive thoughts at death gain a foothold and shape their immoral deeds. He delved into an afterlife forged through the allegiance of vengeance and hatred, and he evolved into a contributing spirit. In time, nothing of his conscious remained but awareness of the hurtful link between Seth and the gang members. Another encounter between them couldn't be allowed. The threat must be eliminated. The gangbangers who kill must die.

SEVENTEEN

THE OVERHEAD BULB CAST a harsh light on the solitary figure passing the night in cigarettes and sweat. Too hot to sleep, Eduardo "Slice" Padilla lay in his underwear and damp tank top, blowing smoke rings toward the ceiling above his bed. He wasn't used to sticking around his house at night, preferring to avoid the place as much as possible. But his uncle had died, and his old man drove to Texas for the funeral. Slice was expected to remain here 'cause that old Sanchez lady from across the street got murdered, and the day before his father left, the house down the block was shot up. His mother and two sisters needed protection, but in reality they made a good excuse for the real reason he needed to lay low.

Slice killed a *pisiola* early that morning. A *rata*. A snitch. An ex-Lobo who leaked information to the police. Slice waited for the right time to sneak inside the motherfucker's apartment and drive a knife through his gut, twisting the blade like a goddamn corkscrew before carving up his face as final punishment for betrayal. To any possible future *ratas*, he sent the necessary message.

Slice didn't feel right about the current situation with the Lobos. Too many chicken-shit pussies were leaving the gang, "droppin' the flag," 'cause of all the craziness about the heart attacks. Watching his brothers walk away pained him, and he felt dishonored that so many Lobos showed fear. When your *familia's* under attack, you don't cut and run, you stay together. "*Estar firme*," he whispered to himself, believing that now, more than ever, Lobos needed to remain strong.

Before his father left for Texas, he gave his son a slight nod of the head and an expression that said, "*I expect you to stay*." Raised by the iron-fisted rule of his old man's strict obedience, Slice felt nothing for him.

His father wouldn't say much of anything to anyone for days at a time, and didn't want anyone talking to him without permission. Slice never forgot the time he tried asking a question about fixing a broken chair, and his father hit him hard enough to put him on his ass. "*Shut up!*" he yelled. "*Don't talk to me!*" Even when he did have something to say, he often mocked his son, making him feel, as Slice would say, "like the shit under a Diablo's shoe."

As a child, when Eduardo seeked affection, his father refused, claiming that hugging made boys soft. He used to yell at his son to be tough, 'cause "that's the only way a Mexican man can survive in this *pinchi* gringo world. They'll cut your fuckin' huevos off if you let 'em. Always be ready to cut first." His old man talked a lot of knife talk because that's what he was about, what defined him. As a father he was a piece of shit, but as knife thrower, Slice had to admit he was the *man*.

He never learned how his father got to be so good with a blade, but it was a skill he must have had for a long time. As a kid, Eduardo heard a story about his old man from a neighbor who grew up in the same village of Zacatecas. At first, he didn't believe what he heard, but he came to accept the tale as a stone-cold fact.

In his early twenties, his father won money in a card game against three other players, but one of them accused him of cheating. According to the others at the table, the man was drunk and started yelling insults, but the father walked away. While his back remained turned to the accuser, the drunken fool pulled a gun. Before he could fire, Slice's father drew a hidden knife from his clothes and sent it speeding towards the man's face, splitting his nose in half and leaving him a bloody, screaming mess on the floor. The man he knifed, however, turned out to be the nephew of the local police *capitano*. His father escaped Zacatecas and settled in L.A.

Slice knew better than to ever ask his father about that story. But for as long as he could remember, his old man always carried around a stainless steel switchblade, throwing it at different trees, or fence boards, or rats he'd corner in the house. He observed how others feared his old man and treated him with respect. Young Eduardo didn't understand how a cruel bastard like his father could ever earn respect from anyone. Now Slice understood. Fear, more than anything, earns you respect.

Slice's life changed forever when he came home bloodied, beaten, and robbed of his money by a couple of 'bangers from the Alvarado Street Diablos. His mother washed his cuts and bandaged him up, all the time shouting at him for not being aware of the danger. "*Hijole*, Eduardo!" she yelled. "What are you, crazy? Walking alone in that big park after school?" He flinched as his mother dabbed a cotton ball full of rubbing alcohol on a painful cut above his left eye. "Don't be stupid, okay?" she continued. "Those *pinchi muchachos* are always waiting in that park, looking to hurt boys like you. Understand? *Comprendes?*"

His father didn't say a word. He just stood there staring at him, making Eduardo feel stupid and weak, like *he* was the one to blame for getting the shit kicked out of him. When he spoke, the words wounded him. "I want you to remember how you feel right now," he told him. "Like shit, huh? Like a little girl, huh?" Walking across the room, his father leaned down and studied the bruises on his son's forehead and the cuts around his eyes and nose. Straightening up again, he shook his head back and forth and looked down at Eduardo in disgust. "Never again, you hear me? You're my son. A Padilla! You don't take shit from nobody!" Thirty minutes later, he had his first knife throwing lesson.

Slice enjoyed a deep drag from his cigarette, praising himself on how far he'd come from his endless hours of practice. He blew another smoke ring, imagining the center of the wispy circle as that old paper target he nailed up on the front yard tree; several years, and another lifetime, ago. He recalled the first thing his old man showed him, how a knife makes a half turn every three feet. Using that knowledge, he started out at four feet, always trying to make the knife handle stick straight out, instead of at an upward or downward slant. When he mastered the four foot range, he stepped back five more paces and practiced from there until he hit the center of the target every time, always trying to throw with equal speed and delivery, and finishing with the same follow through.

His father also explained the importance of feeling the weight of the knife on his fingertip before and during the throws. He observed how the angle between his forearm and the floor is a crucial factor for accuracy, and that the pressure of the thumb determines whether the thrown knife flies straight or off center. The hardest part involved the changes in feel of his thumb pressure, squeezing less when the tip of the blade would veer to the left, and increasing the pressure when the blade went to the right. In time, his knowledge of the proper grip seemed as instinctive as touching his own dick.

When his old man felt the moment had come, he gave Eduardo the dagger he had practiced with all those months. Despite the chips along the topside of the blade and the cracked handle, the instant he inherited the knife it turned into the most beautiful thing he had ever seen. His father also gave him something else; advice. Listening to him at that moment, Eduardo realized that the card story was true.

"Your enemy's face is for target practice," he said, his cold intimidation affecting each word. "In a life or death situation, you ain't got time to think, so go for the tip of the nose. That's the bull's eye."

In time, Slice earned a story of his own that opened the door for his invitation to join the North Rampart Lobos. He didn't drink or get stoned, refusing to let anything affect his accuracy with a knife, but on certain nights when some of the other Lobos got high, they asked for a retelling of his famous payback against "*los dos culeros de Los Diablos,*" those two fuckers from the Diablos. He took much pride in that experience, and he relived the thrill all over again with each repeated narration.

ᛃᚱ ᛃᚱ ᛃᚱ

After many months, with the help of destiny and luck, Slice earned his revenge on the two Diablos who shit-kicked him that fateful day. He needed money to buy a couple of Black Butterfly pocket knives he saw at Jaime's Hardware, so Slice signed up to earn twenty-five dollars washing cars for a local carnival raising money for the community library. The organizers stationed him alone in a section of the parking lot across the street, working on the cars in the designated parking spaces meant for a wash. Late in the afternoon, as he cleaned the inside windshield of a Ford truck, he overheard two voices that forced an immediate halt.

"...kick some motherfucker's ass, man. Gotta score some more of this shit."

"*No hay pedo, vato.* There's money at that fuckin' carnival."

"Gimme another hit, *pendejo.*"

"Good shit, huh?"

"Fuck, yeah, man! I'm feelin' *gooood!*"

From a few cars away, the unmistakable, high-pitched laugh, more like a jackal than a person, made Slice's stomach tighten like a fist. Hidden from their view, he looked out from inside the truck and spotted the same two Diablos who beat him up and took his money. The memory of that crazy cackle, echoing in his brain from the day he held Slice's arms while the other one punched his face, seared his soul like a branding iron. He snuck a peak at that fat, bald-headed piece-of-shit sitting in the passenger seat, and his rage ignited an instant desire for revenge.

He had learned his lesson the hard way, never again going anywhere without protection. Armed with the nicked but effective dagger his old man had given him, Slice reached down inside his right sock and felt the reassuring coolness of metal against skin. He gave the knife handle a couple of angry squeezes, and then took a deep breath to calm down. With one knife and two targets, Slice needed to think of a plan.

When he crouched down to listen to their stupid talk, his eyes strayed to a red toolbox under the backseat. He pulled the rectangular case close to him, opened the lid, and spotted a yellow and black handled Phillips screwdriver about ten inches long. Slice now had the extra weapon he needed to carry into the heat of battle. This weapon, however, wouldn't be thrown.

Sliding out from the passenger side door, Slice crawled to the back of the Diablos' car. He removed his dagger and punctured the sidewalls of the two tires, pushing the blade with a full, silent force. As the sound of hissing air whispered its sweet escape, Slice returned to the truck. He watched and waited as they smoked some more dope and downed some beer. He worried that he'd lose his chance if they drove away before the tires lost enough air. Within a few minutes, the demoralizing sound of the engine pierced his hopes.

Slice didn't feel enough time had passed to affect the tires, but the unmistakable flopping greeted their departure. Jerking his car back into park, the Diablo threw his door open and leaped out, running to the back with the speed of a rabid dog.

"*What the FUCK? God damn it! Shit! Look at my fuckin' tires!*"

Slice enjoyed watching the Diablo take his anger out on the hood of the car next to him, slamming his fist down repeatedly and creating a deep, noticeable dent.

"*Shit! Shit! Goddamn motherfuckin'...*"

Slice knew he had to be patient, watching them staring and swearing at his two flat works of art like a couple of stoned dumb-fucks. Now, if the rest of his plan was to succeed, he needed them separated from each other. Slice advanced and then waited three times before darting behind a mini-van parked one car away. When he heard the ringing of a cell phone, he leaned his head beyond the side of the car. He observed that one Diablo sat on the hood of the car, smoking a cigarette and still yelling, as the fat-assed one talked on the phone and paced from one flat tire to the other. He smiled at his good fortune. The two of them had separated, but he'd have to act fast.

Slice placed the dagger in his left hand and held a firm grip on the screwdriver handle with his right. With hushed and skillful quickness, he inched within a few feet of the Diablo sitting on the hood. Popping up like a weapon-wielding jack-in-the-box, he drove most of the screwdriver through the right side of the Diablo's neck, leaving the handle sticking out under the earlobe like a miniature harpoon. The immediate howl of pain caused the other Diablo to look in the direction of the scream, in perfect time to see Slice's dagger hurtling towards his face before he had a chance to react.

"*In a life or death situation, you ain't got time to think, so go for the tip of the nose. That's the bull's eye.*"

The fat Diablo stood paralyzed for the fraction of a second it takes a knife to penetrate flesh. A torrent of blood poured from between his fingers as his clutching hands struggled in a vain attempt to remove the weapon. As he fell to the ground, writhing and wailing in simultaneous agony with his victimized *comarada*, Slice lost track of space and time within the dizzying heights of complete and successful revenge. The noise from the parking lot must have prompted a 9-1-1 call, and when the police came with guns drawn, he hadn't moved, too preoccupied with expressing his own shrill version of hyena-like cackling as he stood in conquest over his two severely injured victims.

Slice considered that day to be the proudest moment of his life. He also believed that was the day he became a man. Despite the fourteen months he served at the correctional facility, nothing could wipe the smile off his face whenever he recalled the memory of those two Diablos staggering and screaming, lost in their own pain and horror. Word of the incident spread throughout the detention camp, and before long he befriended Juice and Money who supported his entry into the Lobos. From that time on, Slice believed that "nobody was gonna fuck with me no more." He was wrong.

TTT TTT TTT

Slice walked to the sink to splash cold water on his sweaty face. His three-day old stubble contrasted with the gleam of his shaven head, glistening from the perspiration beads that shone on his flesh. He looked into the mirror and studied the long sinewy muscles of his tattooed arms, imagining them wrapped around Lucia as he took her from behind. His piercing gaze appeared the same as always: steady and alert, yet retaining the calm of an animal that continues to hunt, despite the smell of danger.

Something beyond the heat and humidity had him on edge but he couldn't pinpoint the cause. He stood still, noting a distant drum-like pounding and wondered where the sound originated. He moved to his window, pressing his ear against the torn screen but that didn't produce a clue. Slice walked to the door and opened it, listening for any noise from somewhere else in the house. His frustration increased as the pounding grew louder and nothing but a dark empty hallway greeted him. He closed the door and returned to his bed. He sat on the edge and glanced at his clock, watching the numbers change to 3:46.

Slice's head started aching, his arms felt numb, and he suddenly had difficulty catching his breath. With the knife still clutched in his right hand, he laid back down for a couple of minutes, hoping he'd feel better. *This is fuckin' weird*, he thought to himself. *I gotta get me some air.*

Slice pushed himself up, feeling a bit slow and unsteady in his movements. Placing his knife on the bed, he picked up the pair of khaki pants off the floor. When he attempted to slip his second leg through the trouser, a nauseating rush of dizziness overwhelmed him, forcing a return to the bed. Taking a cigarette out from the carton, he couldn't help but notice how his hands shook like an old man's as he tried to light a match. Slice felt disgusted with himself. "Fuck this," he grumbled.

"But you should have seen me!"

Slice uttered a breathless cry and grabbed his knife.

"You should have seen how wisely I proceeded."

As sweat poured into his eyes and down his armpits, Slice searched under the bed and in his closet before darting to the bathroom. He spun around, feeling something, *someone*, nearby.

"*Where are you?*" he shouted. "*Motherfu... aahhh!*" Slice dropped his knife as he felt a sudden jolt of pain inside his chest, ripping the air out from his lungs and forcing him to drop to a knee. He wheezed a sincere threat. "I'll... I'll kill... kill you!" he gasped.

"With what caution-with what foresight-with what dissimulation I went to work."

"Fuck... fuck you!" he cried out, weaker than he thought possible. An intense cold surged throughout his body, as if his room had become a meat freezer. His legs started cramping and he couldn't stop shivering. His blurry right eye ached and when he placed his hand over the painful area he recoiled at the pus covering his fingers. He grabbed his knife and struggled to his feet, swaying like a tree in a windstorm. Slice forced himself to assume the knife throwing position, preparing to attack at a moment's notice.

"One of his eyes resembled that of a vulture," the faceless voice whispered. "A pale blue eye, with a film over it."

"I'll cut...cut you up!" he growled. When I find...you, I'll make you blee...bleed, motherfucker!"

"Whenever it fell upon me, my blood ran cold."

"Wha- what the f-fuck are you s-s-sayin?" he whispered between chattering teeth.

"Until at length, a single dim ray, like the thread of a spider, shot out from the crevice and full upon the vulture eye."

Something in the mirror above his sink caught his attention. His legs grew heavy as a quick, frightened sob escaped from his mouth.

"Presently I heard a slight groan, and I knew it was the groan of mortal terror."

He had caught a glimpse of his right eye, seemingly swollen and filled with a weird, jelly-like fluid oozing from the socket. He knew he had to look again, needing to see that his imagination had got the best of him. Slice kept his head down and stared at the floor as he dragged his feet to the sink. He gripped the edge to steady himself. He waited... and waited...and raised his head to see. The voice spoke again as Slice dropped to his knees in fright.

"All a dull blue, with a hideous veil over it that chilled the very marrow in my bones."

Slice knew he needed immediate help and forced himself from the sink to seize his cell phone. He pushed the three numbers that could save his life. When the emergency operator answered, he uttered a muted whimper, falling to the floor in crippling pain as the phone dropped from his hand.

> *"This seemed the signal for a general rush. Forth from the well they hurried in fresh troops. They clung to the wood -they overran it and leaped in hundreds upon my person."*

Slice slammed his one good eye shut as frenzied, scratching rodents entombed him, tugging at his hair, clinging to his neck and face, and burrowing inside his shirt and underwear. Through the intense pain and cold of his suffering, he called out for help but the blanket of rats muted the sound from his mouth. At a point where his mind reached the breaking point, he sensed another strange sensation. The rats had disappeared. He felt himself take a breath…and then another. He was still alive!

He reached for the phone just a few, tantalizing feet from his hand. A paralyzing jolt of pain exploded inside his chest. When he heard the operator asking if anyone was there, he wanted to scream, yet his constricted, swollen throat couldn't form any words. The same couldn't be said of the unknown voice.

> *"The valiant soldier's blood will spill..."*

Through submission and recognition of his fate, Slice listened.
"On red stained lands of sacrifice..."
Perhaps one's appreciation for life is understood most in his final moment.

> *"Beware the heart as cold as ice."*

The operator later reported receiving a call at 3:55 a.m., followed soon after by what appeared to be the dropping of the phone. While trying in vain to reestablish contact, a four minute period of strange, high-pitched squealing continued until ending in abrupt silence at 3:59.

EIGHTEEN

*K*EVIN SAT ALONGSIDE SETH in the waiting room of the day care center, reading a *Parent* magazine. Flipping through the pages helped him turn his attention away from Seth's silence and overall cold demeanor. As the time arrived for their scheduled five p.m. appointment, Kevin heard the clicking of heels from the other side of the closed door. Looking up from his chair, he found himself staring at a strikingly attractive Latina woman who appeared to be in her mid to late twenties. When she smiled, she radiated warmth as comfortable as cashmere. Any uneasiness he previously felt soon disappeared.

"Hello," she said, first looking at Seth. "My name's Veronica."

Seth remained in his chair. "Hi."

Kevin stood and extended his hand. "I'm Kevin Palmer. This is my nephew, Seth."

Kevin scanned her curvaceous body, enhanced by her lightweight skirt and buttoned down silk blouse. Veronica walked over to Seth and sat in the chair next to him.

"What grade are you in, Seth?"

"Sixth."

"That's good," she told him. "I've tutored other sixth grade kids before, so maybe I can help you, too." Veronica looked at the backpack next to his chair. "Are your books in there?"

"Yeah."

"What subjects do you need help in the most?"

"Judging by the talk I had with his teacher," Kevin said, "Math and English are giving him the most trouble. But Science and History aren't far behind."

"I've found that every subject has its own little secrets for success," she said, continuing her eye contact on Seth. "But if we're going to make this work, you'll need to study at home, too, okay?"

Seth glanced at her for a moment before redirecting his attention to the floor.

"Well, what do you say, Seth?" Kevin asked, feeling a bit irritated by his nephew's silence.

Seth continued to look down, saying nothing.

"I know school work's not a lot of fun sometimes," Veronica said, "but I never would have been able to make a better life for myself if I didn't work hard. Believe me, not many things come easy in this life. The smarter you are the better your chances of something good happening."

Seth remained silent a few moments more before turning his eyes upward toward hers.

"I'll try, okay?"

"Thank you," she said.

Veronica looked at Kevin. He felt a momentary sense of embarrassment in his inability to tear his gaze away from her soft brown eyes.

"Dr. Hobart allows me to use an empty office down the hall," she explained. "You're welcome to stay in here if you like."

"No, that's all right," he told her. "I have an errand I need to run. Just show me where you'll be."

Veronica motioned for them to follow her through the door. "What's nice about the office I tutor in is the large desk that lets us spread the books and papers out. It's real quiet, too. All you can hear is the sound of the aquarium."

"You got an aquarium in there?" Seth asked, showing a rare flash of enthusiasm. "Cool."

When they entered the office, Veronica turned the lights on and Seth headed straight for the fish. Kevin offered Veronica his hand again and took advantage of the chance to look into those beautiful eyes once more before leaving.

"Nice to meet you, Veronica," he said, smiling.

"Same here, Mr. Palmer," she replied. "We'll be finished at 6:30."

"Please call me Kevin," he told her.

He had noticed a bar on his way to the appointment and made a mental note of its location. He arrived there happy in the knowledge that he had an hour to kill. *That gives me plenty of time to savor some scotch*, he thought to himself. The first sip was long and deliberate, rolling around the inside of his mouth like a kid with a milkshake. He took another swallow and cherished the deep rich texture of the golden nectar as it swan dived from the back of his tongue into his belly. *"Finally feeling better,"* he whispered to himself, staring into the liquid magic of his glass. *"That kid's like nails to a chalkboard."* Looking up, he observed a man who appeared to be staring at him. The man's eyes drooped a bit, giving him the appearance of someone a drink or two ahead of him.

"Do I know you?" Kevin asked.

"I think so," he said. "Did you ever work for *The Daily News?*"

Kevin smiled as he clutched his glass. "It's been a few years, but yes I did. Were you there, too?"

"No, nothing like that," the man replied. "I was a volunteer for Dianne Feinstein's 2006 reelection campaign. You used to hang around headquarters a lot. I remember your face. You were always asking questions."

Kevin smiled at the recollection of that young, eager reporter. "Public's right to know is what drives us on, my friend." He finished his drink in one large gulp before leaning over a couple of stools in order to shake the man's hand. "My name's Kevin Palmer," he said.

"Don Cassidy," the man replied.

Kevin enjoyed taking that memory lane stroll back to his *Daily News* days. His outlook on life hadn't yet been poisoned by events such as his dad's cancer, or terrorists flying airplanes into buildings or gang problems spiraling out of control.

Or Warren's murder.

"How 'bout another round, Don?" Kevin asked. "It's on me."

Kevin removed the cell phone from his pocket and turned on the silent mode. *"I know where Seth is,"* he said to himself. *"Now I'm going to make sure I enjoy some uninterrupted Kevin time."*

The two men talked and drank, discussing politics, the economy, their jobs, and what the Lakers and Dodgers need to improve. Don offered Kevin a temporary respite from the manic whirlwind his life had become; a person devoid of any connection to his problems. And for the moment, that's all Kevin cared about. He just wanted a chance to drink and be himself and forget about everything. He even forgot about the time.

NINETEEN

"**I**'M SURE HE'LL BE HERE soon, Seth," Veronica said. "Why don't you try calling him again."

Seth dialed his uncle's cell phone number and heard the recording for the third time. Unlike the previous two calls, he hung up without leaving a message. His stomach hurt from hunger, he felt tired, and he wanted to leave. He figured Veronica wanted to go home, too, but she told him she'd wait until his uncle arrived. He appreciated that. He had found her to be different from a normal Mexican. She wasn't bossy and didn't talk loud. She smiled a lot and made him feel comfortable as they worked together. He couldn't believe how smart she was, and how she made studying and remembering things seem easier.

"Sorry, Veronica," he said, hanging up the phone. "I wish he'd get here, already. I'm hungry."

"There's a snack machine in the lobby, Seth. How about some cookies or potato chips?"

"I don't have any money," he told her.

"But I do," she said, rising from her chair. "Chips or cookies?"

"I don't care," he said. "Whatever."

"I'll be right back."

The clock on the wall showed 7:30 and Seth's concern had intensified. Maybe he got in an accident. Seth just knew something bad must have happened. Look what happened to his mom and dad. Why not his uncle, too? He loved his grandma but could he really live with her every day? He didn't care much for his uncle but he liked having a house and his own room. His thoughts ended with the ringing of the desk phone. Seth hesitated a moment, unsure whether to answer. It was Uncle Kevin.

"*Why aren't you here yet?*" he shouted, anger now overtaking relief. "*I called you three times!*"

"I'm really sorry, Seth, but I accidentally locked my keys in the car and my cell phone's in the glove compartment. I've got a locksmith taking care of it now, so I'll be there soon. I had to borrow a man's phone to call you. And then I had to track you down through the front desk. Where's Veronica? Is she still there? Let me talk to her."

"She went to get me some food from the machine."

"Please tell her I'm very sorry and I'll pay for the extra time."

Veronica returned with the cookies and potato chips. "Is that your uncle?" she asked.

Seth nodded. "Just hurry, okay?"

Seth hung up and explained what happened as they shared the food.

"He's not the first person to lock their keys in the car," she told him. "I'm just glad that's all it was."

Seth swallowed the last of his cookie, put a finger to his mouth and began chewing on a nail. "Me, too," he replied, his voice a notch above a whisper. His eyes started to tear. He didn't want Veronica to notice so he got up and walked to the aquarium. But the urge to cry overtook him. Within a few moments she appeared by his side.

"What's the matter, Seth?"

"Nothing," he murmured.

Veronica stood in front of him. "Come on," she said. "We've been friends for a whole one and a half hours. You sure you don't want to talk about it? Were you worried about your Uncle Kevin?"

Seth remained silent for a few moments, trying to regain his composure. "I thought... maybe I'd lose him, too."

"I don't understand."

Seth glanced into her eyes before returning his gaze to the aquarium.

"I don't mean to be nosy," she said. "I'm sorry."

Seth stared into the tank. "My mom and dad are dead."

Veronica put her hand on his shoulder. "I'm so sorry, Seth. I didn't know."

The gurgling sound of the aquarium filtered through the silence in the room. In a way he couldn't quite understand, Seth felt better, as if sharing this information with Veronica unloaded a heavy weight from his shoulders. He decided to tell her everything.

"My mom died of cancer last year. My dad..." Seth's shoulders drooped as he took a deep breath in order to continue. "My dad was killed by Mexican gangbangers in April. He was trying to save me and they..." He swallowed hard. "They shot him."

Seth heard Veronica's reaction. Something seemed unusual in her tone of voice.

"*Oh, no! No! Oh, my God.*"

She asked Seth a question that startled him. "In the parking lot of a market? Alfredo's Market?"

He turned and looked at her. "Yeah."

Veronica stared at him awhile longer before walking back to sit. Seth followed her and did the same. "I had no idea it was you," she said. "It's hard to believe you're here with me like this."

"I don't understand."

"I know that market," she said. "When your father was killed I saw the news on t.v. I remember wondering how in the world... I'm so sorry."

"I feel bad for you, Veronica."

"Me?" she asked, looking surprised. "Why?"

"Cause you're a Mexican and you have to be around Mexican men."

Veronica looked like that didn't bother her. "You shouldn't think that way, Seth. There's plenty of nice Mexican men who aren't like those gangs at all. As for me, I'm a Mexican-*American*, but I'm proud of my Mexican heritage."

"But you're different," he said. "You're not like those other ones. They're nothing but bullies and creeps." Closing his eyes, he flashed back to the moment his father died in his arms. "And they kill people."

Veronica leaned forward in her chair. "I read something interesting the other day about 9/11. Do you know what that is?"

"Yeah, sure," he said. "That's when the planes flew into those buildings."

"Do you know who did it?"

"Some Arab people."

"That's right. And do you know what a hate crime is?"

"No."

"It's when people are attacked for no other reason than someone not liking their religion, or the color of their skin. Things like that. The article explained that the year before 9/11 there were three hate crimes against Arabs in the United States. But the next year, after 9/11, there were over seventy."

"Did they have something to do with the planes?"

"No, not at all," she said. They were attacked simply because people thought they looked and talked like the people who *did* have something to do with the planes. That's unfair, right?"

Seth nodded his head in agreement.

"The same thing applies to your feelings about Mexican men. Just because they may look and sound like those gangbangers doesn't mean you should think of them the same way."

Veronica rose from her chair and walked towards the aquarium. "Come here, Seth."

Seth walked over and stood next to her, staring into the tank.

"There's several kinds of fish living together in there," she said. "Different sizes, shapes, and colors. We're the same way, aren't we? You, me, and everyone else. We're different but living together. As long as we're here, we may as well make the best of it." Veronica pointed towards the fish. "Just like them."

"Here I am!" a voice called out. "Sorry, Veronica."

They looked towards the door at his smiling Uncle Kevin. Seth resented that he appeared so happy after forcing them to wait around like he did, but at least they'd have dinner soon. He wished Veronica could join them but that would mean having his uncle around at the same time. He looked forward to seeing her alone next week.

TWENTY

FACE CONTINUED PUSHING THE BUTTONS of the remote, trying to find a distraction to take his mind off the depressing real-life drama playing in his head. Under normal circumstances, surviving to see another birthday called for a reason to party all night. These were dangerous times, however, and the circumstances far from normal. As an increasing number of his gang brothers died, Face's mood grew darker. The respect he used to reap from neighborhood families had turned into bitterness and obvious disgust. There had been too many funerals, too many tears, and too many unforgiving parents. They knew who he was, that he was a central player in the Diablos, and they held him responsible for their sons' deaths. Some of the parents were real assholes, destined to rot beside his old man in hell, but others loved their kids and tried everything in their power to keep them from jumping into a gang. They just couldn't compete with the street.

Five more dead in just the last few weeks, including two of his closest *comaradas*, Cherry and Player. Stoner and Tick were both shot down the week before, and for that, the Diablos aimed to spill more Lobos blood. But nobody questioned gunshots. What happened to Cherry and Player, however, added to the same confusing craziness. Heart attacks? That's what the police continued claiming, but they say lots of unbelievable shit.

In the ten years since jumping into the Diablos, Face had survived the wars. At twelve-years-old, he got educated fast and without mercy. He proved a quick learner, and soon he started delivering the punishment instead. An eye for an eye-that's just the way life is in the jungle. The last couple of months, however, instilled within him another fact of life; he'd grown tired of the jungle.

Face understood the impossibility of controlling a lot of shit that went down in the Diablos, including recruiting thirteen and fourteen-year-old wannabes. Anxious to prove themselves, some of these kids didn't make it to their next birthday. During those ten months at the correctional facility, lying on his cot in the darkness, Face had plenty of time to think about those dead kids and how lucky he'd been so far. For him, a tough, street-wise gangbanger raised in a war zone, a truce needed declaring between his present life and future dreams. The time to leave the gang approached, but not until meting out retaliation for Stoner and Tick, and getting satisfying answers about the deaths of Cherry and Player.

His mother walking out from the kitchen interrupted his gloomy thoughts.

"I'm cooking *menudo*," she said. "Your favorite. Are you hungry?"

Keeping his eyes on the t.v. screen, Face muttered, "Yeah, I can eat."

"Are you going out tonight?" she asked.

"Yeah, don't know how long,"

Face turned his head to look at his mother as she headed back into the kitchen, his emotions as drab as a morning fog. She made him wanna puke whenever he thought about the beatings he took from his father, and how she sniveled in the corner, too afraid to say or do anything. He couldn't ever forgive her for not being there when he needed her the most.

Before he drank himself to death, his old man pissed away any money he had on booze, bitches, and gambling. When his luck went south, the usual direction, he took his frustrations out on Face. His sister escaped most of that shit because she was smart and went to school and got good grades, unlike her "stupid shit of a brother." That's who and what he was to the old man: "a stupid shit" of a brother. And "a stupid shit" of a son. "*I'm gonna kick your ass, you stupid shit!*" he shouted. "*Don't waste your time helping that stupid shit.*" "*Don't talk to your mother like that, you stupid shit.*" When Face argued with his mother, his father defended her and came after him, but his mother didn't escape his father's outbursts either. Sometimes he slapped her so hard he heard the smacking sound from the other room. He detested his mother's weakness. Her few, pitiful attempts to protect him from the beatings remained in his memory like a foul, lingering odor, and although his father died a couple of years ago, Face's resentment towards his mother remained strong.

When his sister tried to intervene to stop their father from hitting him, she got hurt, too. Face never forgot how she dared to protect her little brother during those years, and he vowed to return the favor as long as he lived. But after his first incarceration, he returned home too late. The damage had been done.

When his father died, Face had to admit he detected a certain change for the better in his mother. She seemed more outgoing, and made friends with other women in the neighborhood, something his old man had discouraged. He also acknowledged his mother's attempts to reach out to him, unlike before, but he compared these late efforts to someone trying to start an unused engine. He wasn't sure there was a spark left in the battery.

With all his resentment, however, Face possessed something for which he gave her complete credit: His *gift*. Without that, he knew for damn sure he'd never be here today on his twenty-second birthday. His mother passed something on from her family genes and blessed him with the extraordinary ability to foresee approaching danger. The first time he experienced the *vision*, he had no idea what it meant.

ᛏᛁᛏ ᛏᛁᛏ ᛏᛁᛏ

He was nine-year Alejandro, playing soccer with the next-door neighbor and trying to smash his face in with the hardest kick of his life. He wanted to give that mama's boy a going-away present to remember him by before the kid moved. But the ball sailed wide of the mark, past the "For Lease" sign in the boy's front yard, and into the street. Alejandro realized that if he lost the boy's ball and his father bought him a new one, he'd make Alejandro pay the price with a beating. He fantasized rolling away like the escaping soccer ball, rushing further and further into the distance as he searched for a place to hide.

"My ball!" the boy screamed in pursuit. "I'm gonna lose my ball!"

Alejandro straggled behind, pausing to admire the longest kick he'd ever achieved-until the image of his angry father got him going. He lived halfway up a hill, so there wasn't a chance they'd retrieve the ball until it flattened out at the road below. He felt relieved as he watched the ball lodge near the back tire of a white pickup truck parked across the street.

"You're an asshole, Alejandro!" the neighbor shouted, trying to catch his breath at the corner, his hands on his knees.

"Shut up, you idiot! You'll get your ball back."

"Fuck you!" he screamed, his middle finger waving in the air.

Alejandro looked on as the boy waited for several cars to pass before stepping off the curb. *"I'm glad you're movin' away, you stupid ass,"* he muttered. As he looked back to see how far they'd run, Alejandro felt a sudden lightheadedness that made his legs wobble and his eyes burn. Trying to blink the odd sensation away, he visualized a strange and powerful image of a red Thunderbird speeding towards the boy. Nearby noises from the neighborhood dissolved into the unmistakable screech of tires echoing between his ears.

Alejandro broke into an uncertain jog, coming to a halt at the curb. He gazed at his surroundings but saw nothing unusual as the boy approached the back of the pickup, crouching low with his hand outstretched. In the next instant the truck started up and zoomed off like a bullet, forcing him to straighten and leap back into the street as a red Thunderbird emerged, barreling around the corner straight towards him. Alejandro knew he had to act fast. He sprinted towards the boy and crashed into him like a linebacker, sending the two of them tumbling onto the sidewalk. Alejandro turned his head in time to see the car speed past the spot where they'd been seconds before. The high-pitched sound of burning rubber signaled the car's *adiós*. As he lay his head back to ponder what had just happened, the moment alerted him to another type of sound.

"Aaah shit! Shit! I'm hurt! Aaah aaah!..." Alejandro stared in astonishment as the boy rolled on the ground, covering his face with his hands. Blood seeped through his fingers and down his arm.

"I'll get you back for this, you fuckin' asshole!"

"That car was gonna hit you!"

"Bullshit! *Aaah aaah!*" The boy tried to sit up, but couldn't rise further than halfway, forced to lie flat again.

Alejandro whipped off his tee shirt and handed it to him to help with the bleeding. A woman who observed what had happened ran out to help. She asked who to call, but the bleeding boy didn't know where to locate either parent. Alejandro knew his father had gone somewhere with the car, but at least his mother was home and she'd know what to do. She arrived with her friend, Mrs. Ortega, who drove them to the *clinica* in her own car.

Alejandro's father didn't have to buy a new soccer ball after all, but the neighbor's angry mother told them, "they better pay every fuckin' cent" of the money she dished out for stitches and medicine. His father didn't argue, believing his son completely responsible. "You're a lying, stupid shit!" he shouted when Alejandro explained what happened.

As his mother wept and his sister tried without success to shield him, Alejandro remained on his bedroom floor, bruised and whimpering, for much of the night.

The next incident occurred later that summer, when Alejandro accompanied his mother to the market.

"Go get me two onions, Alex," she told him. "They're near the back."

"What do you want 'em for?" he asked, preferring to look through the cereal section instead.

"*Hijole*, boy, I need them for dinner tonight. *Burritos con carne y queso*. Your father likes lots of onions with his meat and cheese. Now go."

Alejandro turned the corner towards the section with vegetables and fruit, then stopped and stared as a man and woman stood kissing and rubbing their hands over each other's bodies near the onion bin. Two little kids ran around their legs in circles, laughing and pointing. As he waited for them to leave, the woman looked at the children, smiled, and resumed kissing the man. Alejandro hesitated, unsure what to do. Out of nowhere, a similar sensation to the one he experienced when he saved his neighbor from the speeding car overtook him, and an alarming, bloody image of a man shooting the people in front of him appeared like a movie in his mind. Hearing loud screams and gunshots in his head, he hurried back, frightened, to his mother.

"Mama, something bad's gonna happen!" he shouted. "I saw it!"

Alejandro's mother stared at her son in silence. Leaning down, she whispered into his ear, "Quiet down. What did you see? Tell me quick."

Lowering his voice, he looked into her troubled eyes. "I saw people over there getting shot at. There was lots of blood, too. And I heard screaming."

Abandoning the food in her cart, his mother grabbed his hand, pulling him hard as they rushed out. Walking at a speedy pace through the parking lot and across the street, Alejandro spotted a man running from a parked car into the market. They had gone halfway up the block when gunshots reverberated in the distance, followed by a lady's scream that brought Alejandro's mother to tears. "Hurry!" she shouted, tightening her grip.

By the time they arrived home, the wail of sirens had already sounded and stopped. His mother turned on the television, found a news station, and told Alejandro to sit. The eventual announcement of a special report led to a reporter interviewing a grocery clerk explaining with great difficulty how a man ran into the market and started shouting at the woman before shooting her and the man she was with. He broke down as he described the scene with "blood everywhere." Alejandro and his mother watched in silence as crying customers, police cars, and ambulances appeared on the screen. When the reporter concluded his story, she turned off the television and looked at Alejandro.

"I want to ask you something," she said. "What you saw in the market, was it like the day with the car? Did you see something that wasn't happening yet?" Alejandro nodded. Making the sign of the cross, she said, "Now I know for sure."

Alejandro didn't understand. "Know what?" he asked.

As her eyes filled with tears, she looked more serious than he could ever remember. "Before I tell you anything, promise me, *promise me*, that you'll keep this secret between you and me. Your sister doesn't need to know and your father will only get angry, do you understand?"

"I understand, Mama," he replied, as confused as he could remember.

She smiled and paused a bit before continuing. "You were born with something special," she said. "In my family, a boy from every other generation has been blessed with this gift." Reaching for his hand, she added, "That means you, Alejandro."

"What gift?" he asked.

"You never knew your grandfather, but he also saw things like you do. My mother told me in the Mexican village where he lived, he was respected and known by everybody. Miners would give him money to go with them, to make sure they'd be able to escape trouble."

"You mean he could see what was gonna happen?"

"He knew when danger was coming," she replied. "More than once he saw the mine collapsing before it really did." Lowering her head and closing her eyes for several moments, she took a long, slow breath before looking up at him. "That's why you saw the car. And the shootings."

Alejandro blinked back tears. "I don't like seeing all those scary things, Mama. Make it stop."

She leaned forward and placed his hand in hers. "I can't," she told him. "But as you grow older you'll learn to live with the power and use it to help you. Just like your grandfather."

In the ensuing years, their shared secret did nothing to lessen his animosity toward his mother. Her bullshit about his father having once been a decent man didn't mean a damn thing because he'd only known a different reality. On Face's fifteenth birthday, however, a new, permanent reality emerged. When his sister and mother presented him with a chocolate cake after dinner, his old man, drunk as usual, flipped the cake high into the air, causing it to land in a flattened mess on the floor. His laughter and sneer of superiority shattered Face's control, causing years of pent-up anger and pain to unleash itself in a flurry of punches, breaking his nose, blackening his eye, and bloodying his face. At six feet tall, possessing a body made tough and muscular by conscious effort and a street fighter's education, Face sent an unmistakable message of contempt notifying his father that the days of fucking with his son were over.

TWENTY-ONE

*L*IEUTENANT ATKINSON SAT ON THE chair outside Captain Dean's office and placed the two sheets of paper on the nearby table. Moments later, he picked them up again to evaluate something else. In the next few minutes he'd show Dean his findings, and he wanted to make sure the information contained no inaccuracies or overlooked data. Here they were, the updated names and dates of death of all the North Rampart Lobos and Alvarado Street Diablos who had died since the first reported heart attack a little over four months ago. Something about the impersonal finality of the dead from a computer printout made the situation seem even gloomier. One column contained the list of victims murdered through the usual fashion; guns, knives, and various types of beatings. The other included gang members dead from heart failure.

Having compiled all the names, Atkinson counted and recounted them for the same reason a driver slows down to look at a car wreck: perverse fascination with tragedy. The total of thirty still caused the same numbing sensation from the night before when he made his discovery after cross-referencing the deaths with their respective dates. The "murdered" column listed thirteen dead gang members. The "heart failure" column recorded seventeen names. But in actuality, as Atkinson now realized, the numbers from both columns equaled each other. That brought a whole new light to the heart attacks.

"Come in, Carl," Dean said, opening the door. "Sorry for the delay, but the Mayor kept me on the phone to praise me for the kick-ass job he thinks I'm doing."

Atkinson heard the sarcasm in Dean's voice and decided to skip right to the point. "I've pieced something together you might find interesting, Captain," he said. "Take a look at this."

Atkinson handed him the first of the two sheets. Dean sat in his chair and studied the information, tilting his head in a slight, almost imperceptible manner while using his finger to guide his eyesight along the two columns.

"Thirteen gang members murdered and thirteen heart attacks occurring the day after," he said. Doesn't take an Einstein to see when this guy strikes. But there've been a total of seventeen heart attacks, not thirteen. If we're looking for a tit for tat, that discrepancy puzzles me."

"I think I have the answer on this other page," Atkinson said, handing him the paper. "Maybe the murder victim doesn't have to be a gang member for the heart attacks to occur."

"There's four names on this list," Dean said, scanning the sheet. "Are you telling me these deaths are linked to those four extra heart attacks?"

"Yes, sir."

Dean read the names out loud. "Warren Palmer, April 28th. Alfredo Valenzuela, May 1st. Gregorio Plata, June 24th. Reynaldo Cisneros, July 14th." He shook his head. "Palmer's murder seems like an eternity ago. Killed in the parking lot of the same store on the same night Alfredo Valenzuela was shot. Palmer died in two minutes, Valenzuela in two days." He recited the other two names. "Reynaldo Cisneros. Gregorio Plata. If there's a relationship there, I don't know what it is."

Atkinson stared over Dean's shoulder at the names. "I don't believe there has to be a relationship, Captain. These two men were a couple of innocent victims, like Mr. Palmer and Mr. Valenzuela, and they were killed in the same neighborhood."

"And there's our fifty-fifty split," Dean said, nodding like a bobble-head doll. "An eye for an eye all the way down the line."

Atkinson took the first sheet from Dean's desk, reviewing several of the names and dates. "You'd think that at least a few of these street smart gangbangers could have escaped their fate, or at least delayed it," he said. "When I first put this list together, I had no idea what these dates would come to mean. I started off with the earliest one and went from there. Warren Palmer, shot and killed on April 28th. On April 29th, just a few hours afterwards, Rafael Carranza died of a heart attack. Alfredo Valenzuela, shot on April 29th, died on May 1st. The next day, May 2nd, a member of the North Rampart Lobos, Jose Leyva, died of a heart attack. On May 29th, another Lobo, Omar Rodriguez, was shot and killed. On May 30th, a member of the Alvarado Street Diablos, Rodolfo Crespo, died of a heart attack."

"So now you had three killings and three heart attacks, each pair within twenty-four hours of each other," Dean said. "Is that when the alarm bells went off?"

"Not yet," he answered. "My thoughts centered more on the whole question of why gang members were suddenly getting heart attacks."

"Fair enough," Dean replied.

"The next one opened my eyes to a possible pattern developing," Atkinson said. "Come the fifth one, I knew I'd stumbled onto something. It suddenly became very clear."

Dean leaned back in his chair and looked up over his shoulder at Atkinson. "How'd you work the other two innocents into this?"

"I had the same question you had about the discrepancy in the numbers," he replied. "Why did four more gang members die of heart attacks when the back and forth pattern was so exact otherwise? That's when I did some research on murders in the same neighborhood areas over that period of time. After I found the first match, the other one didn't take long."

Atkinson retrieved the second paper from Dean's desk. "On June 24th, a vagrant by the name of Gregorio Plata was shot and killed. The following day, June 25th, a Lobo named Francisco Martinez died of a heart attack. The other victim, Reynaldo Ciscneros, was an ex-Lobo who had turned his life around. He'd become a community activist working with kids. He was knifed and killed in his home on July 14th. His face looked like a damn tic-tac-toe board from all the slashing. The next day, a Lobo named Eduardo Padilla died of a heart attack in his bedroom."

"I must be getting old," Dean said, narrowing his eyes as he studied the second sheet. "I should have recognized some of this myself. Maybe I was too preoccupied with the uncanny consistency of the four a.m. time."

Atkinson looked away from the paper into the eyes of Dean. "I didn't know the time of death still centered on four o'clock for all these guys," he said.

Dean motioned to the chair in front of his desk. "Sit down."

Leaning on his elbows with his hands clasped under his chin, Dean stared at Atkinson. "Of the seventeen heart attacks, we're pretty sure that the actual time of death in six of the cases was four a.m. The other eleven could very well have happened at the same time according to the coroner."

"Four a.m?" Atkinson repeated. "I remember that was the suspected time frame in the first few cases but that was it. I didn't know about the rest."

"Just another, 'how does he do it?' question for us to wrestle with, Carl."

"Why do you think those six you mentioned were all four a.m.?" Atkinson asked.

Dean offered a slight smile. "Logical question," he said. "A lot of these bangers are night owls, not home in bed like most of us. It wasn't hard to find witnesses in five of the cases. When someone's screaming out on a quiet night, waking you up out of a sound sleep, what's the first thing you do? You look at the clock. Each witness stated they were awakened a few minutes before four a.m. And after four o'clock?" Dean paused before answering his own question. "Silence. No more screaming."

Atkinson whistled in astonishment.

"The one other case was that kid found in the old railroad yard. At that point we didn't think much of it, but when he died, or was about to die, he apparently fell on the tracks and broke his watch. Do I need to tell you what time it showed when it stopped?"

Atkinson shook his head. "I've never imagined this kind of calculated ability to kill was possible," he said. "Unbelievable."

Dean settled back in his chair. "Fucking frightening is what it is, Carl. I can't prove it, and I sure as hell can't explain it, but if I was a betting man I'd lay odds the victims of these heart attacks lost their lives because of a murder they committed the day before. Based on the consistency of the twenty-four hour periods between deaths, what else could it mean? Just don't expect me to go tell the Mayor this shit."

"Has he been told anything about what's going on?"

"I've talked with him a couple of times," Dean said, "but he didn't seem too concerned. Now he's getting pressured from some of the family members to conduct an investigation of our department. That's what the phone call was about a few minutes ago. You know the way it is, Carl. Bad cops are always suspect, right?"

"We can't be blamed for this one," Atkinson muttered.

"I've tried to make him understand how difficult this case has been," he said. "Maybe get him to allocate more money for extra men."

"What did he say?"

"Let's put it this way," Dean said. "If these heart attacks were happening to his Westside or Valley constituents, we'd have every man on the force working this case. But all we've got is two murderous Latino gangs from a poor section of town. He suspects these heart attacks are drug related, so his sympathy gauge isn't too high right now."

"Thirty deaths in four months?" Atkinson said, frustration coating his voice. "And seventeen of them heart attacks? How many more will it take for him to finally respond?"

"One," Dean answered.

Atkinson's head angled in confusion. "One?"

"Yeah, one," Dean repeated. "From another gang. Not a Lobo or a Diablo, but another gang. If and when that happens, we have a possible epidemic and that's when the Mayor wants to be told."

"So, just like that, we're supposed to sweep seventeen heart attacks under the rug?" Atkinson said, his voice rising. "As if that kind of thing is normal?"

Dean gestured for Atkinson to calm down. "We're not sweeping anything under the rug, Carl," he replied. "I don't give a damn what the Mayor's take on this thing is, okay? In fact, I'm thrilled he's leaving us alone 'cause I got enough fuckin' pressure. We got ourselves a serial killer. One like nobody's ever seen. But as long as these deaths stay confined to the Lobos and Diablos, I plan on handling it without any outside interference."

The perfect two-day symmetry of seventeen pairs of deaths had all the earmarks of purposeful planning. The thought scared the shit out of Atkinson.

"If we're forced to deal with a serial killer, why couldn't it be a gun? Or a knife?" he said, as much to himself as to Dean. "I want something I can understand. Frozen hearts? Precise dates? I'm twisted up inside. Four months of this shit and we're still at square one."

Dean bolted up in his chair, his eyes showing a sudden spark. "Hold it, Carl," he blurted, slapping his fist on the desk. "You just said something. 'Precise dates'. Yeah, maybe..." Dean closed his eyes, covering his face with his hands.

"You gonna let me in on it, Captain?" Atkinson asked.

Dean lowered his hands, revealing a surprising smile. "Maybe we can't understand *how* the killings occur, but we do know *when* they occur, don't we?"

Atkinson observed the familiar signs of the Captain's mind at work. He gum chewing doubled in speed and his eyes narrowed, tick-tocking back and forth. "Have I ever asked you to do the impossible before, Carl?"

"Often, sir, yes."

"Good, then I've broken you in," Dean replied with a wink.

"Broken me in or broken me down," Atkinson told him. "Depends on which side of the desk we're talking about."

Dean's demeanor darkened. "You've worked in gang programs. You know some of those guys, right?"

"I deal with members from different gangs," he answered. "The North Rampart Lobos and Alvarado Street Diablos are just a couple of them."

"And you headed the peace talks between two big Valley gangs, right?"

"The Pacoima 13 and the Blythe Street gang. Homicides dropped 60% that year."

"Let's go back to what you said about 'precise dates'," Dean said. "Remember the old schoolyard riddle about the tree falling in the forest? If no one's around when it happens, can you say it really fell? Maybe the eye for an eye pattern you discovered can be thought of like the tree question." Dean stared at Atkinson, methodically stroking his Adam's apple. "If there isn't another murder between the Lobos and Diablos, can you still say there's an active serial killer out there?"

Captain Dean's speculation considered the impossible. Unfortunately, Atkinson knew Mission Impossible involved him. "You want me to work a truce, is that what you're saying? To arrange peace talks?" Rubbing his hand along the top of his shiny head, he looked warily at Dean. "That's a tall order, sir. Whose next, the Bloods and Crips?"

Rising from his chair, Captain Dean walked over to the window. "We have to start somewhere, Carl," he said, gazing outside. "Someone out there is tracking these guys like a freaking satellite." Dean turned back to face him. "My wife's whore-loving step brother manages a sports club on Riverside Drive. He owes me a favor from a sticky situation he found himself in." Dean smiled and paused for a moment. "They've got a gym for basketball and volleyball games. I'll get him to close early one night so we can hold the meeting in there."

"We'll shuttle them over?" Atkinson asked.

"Exactly," Dean answered. "Two gangs, two pick-up spots. I'll be with you, but you run the show. We need to talk to the leaders of these gangs, guys with influence. Keep it down to five or six from each side. I'll have men patrolling the area but we don't want too many of those dogs sniffing each other out."

Atkinson nibbled on his lip, thinking about the daunting task that lay ahead. "With all due respect, Captain, there's a big difference between the Valley peace talks and this one. Pacoima 13 and Blythe Street were killing and dying the old fashioned way. What am I supposed to tell these guys? That they'll suffer a heart attack if they don't make nice?"

Chewing his gum in a slow, rhythmic motion, Dean turned back to stare out the window in momentary silence. "In another couple of months," he said, "the Liquidambar trees out there are going to be beautiful. But when those orange, and red, and yellow leaves fall, they hide thorny little balls that hurt like hell if you step on them. Maybe one day you and I won't be stepping on so many goddamn thorns, Carl. Maybe one day we'll just have those beautiful leaves." Dean looked back at Atkinson, a surprising expression of calm on his face. "Tell them the truth, Lieutenant. State the facts. Get them to understand that for once in their lives, they're on the same side of a deadly war."

TWENTY-TWO

"*WHAT THE FUCK YOU TALKIN' 'BOUT, DROPPIN' THE FLAG?*" King shouted. "*You ain't leavin' the gang, Luis! Don't gimme that shit!*"

"Sorry, Miguel," Luis said, "but I can't get that night with Juice outta my head. I hear a lot of Lobos died the same way. I'm scared."

"*Ooooh, I'm scared,*" King repeated in a mocking tone. "You embarrass me, little boy. Fuck you!"

"Leave him alone, Miguel," his mother said. "He's decided he doesn't want to be part of that shit. You should just respect that, alright?"

Miguel pounded his fist on the dinner table, causing the dishes to rattle. "Part of that *shit*? Is that what you call it, Mama? Where the fuck do you think this meal came from, huh? And this beer? You think it came from you, Mama? You were fired, remember? I'm supporting this goddamn family now. You should be warnin' Luis he better pull his fuckin' weight around here by listenin' to me and doin' what's right!"

"The unemployment checks help, okay?" she replied. "And I'll be findin' me another job as soon as somethin' comes along."

"Those checks don't buy near the shit I get for us," King snarled. "One good night and I bring home food and beer for a week. When Luis starts in, we'll be sittin' real pretty, you know what I'm sayin?" He turned his attention back to Luis. "You drop the flag, you ain't just pissin' *me* off, you're tellin' every Lobo to go fuck off." He leaned in closer, making sure he had Luis' full attention. "I don't think that's gonna go down too good."

Luis looked at King, then his mother. She'd grown quiet, looking back and forth at her two sons as if she'd decided to let them make the final decision. Luis lowered his head, eating his chicken in silence. King knew he had won his mother over; Luis wasn't going anywhere because he couldn't.

King left after dinner for an important gathering at Lafayette Park. He had been contacted by Horse, an ex-Lobo who dropped the flag and now acted as one of those pussy community activists for peace. He couldn't believe what he'd been told; that Detective Atkinson had arranged for ex-Lobo and ex-Diablo gang members to hit the streets and contact key players from both sides, urging them to attend a meeting. Atkinson didn't want anyone but specific members from each gang. Horse told him they'd talk about the whole heart attack situation and that six Lobos had been asked to attend: King, Snapper, Fame, Ram, Tower, and Big Nasty.

Within the expanding shadows of the giant Ash trees, King grabbed his crotch and spit a beer-induced gob of saliva on the grass. "*No me anden vacilando!*" he yelled, telling the other five that he didn't like being messed with. "A fuckin' meeting? With the Diablos and the cops? Do I look goddamn stupid or somethin'? Fuck that shit, man."

"What are you thinkin', homeboy?" King asked Ram. "Some fuckin' joke?"

Guzzling the rest of his beer, Ram crushed the aluminum can and flung it toward the bushes. "I don't know, man," he said. "Sounds crazy, but we ain't got no fuckin' answers for all the shit, you know? Brothers are dyin'. Maybe Atkinson got somethin' to say."

"That *pinchi mayate* ain't gonna tell us shit," King growled. "You trust that motherfuckin' cop? He's the enemy, man."

"He ain't as fucked up as some of the others," Ram replied. "Never gone and beat my ass for no reason."

"They'll be pattin' us down, man," Colt said. "Don't like havin' no protection."

"We ain't leavin' ourselves open for destruction, man," Ram replied. "The homeboys'll stay close, just in case."

Tower lit another cigarette, the bright glowing light from the match resembling a lighthouse from his six foot, three inch skinny frame. "My mother ain't been the same since Leopoldo dropped dead," he said. "If the cops got somethin' to say, I wanna hear it."

"Never thought I'd look at a Diablo without a fuckin' gun in my hand," Colt remarked.

"Piss on the Diablos," King said, guzzling another beer. "Ain't nobody gonna get me in a room with those assholes." He spit on the ground again. "I'm a Lobo, man. Until my dyin' fuckin' day. I ain't gonna go livin' in shame like the rest of you motherfuckers at that meeting." King looked at Snapper. "*Cabron, qué hubole?*" he asked. "You goin' for this shit, too?"

Snapper took several large swigs from his beer and squeezed the can, crushing it with his beefy right fist. In silence, he shook his head and stared at King with an angry expression. "Don't gimme that crap, King," he muttered. "You ain't the only one here with pride, man. We're all Lobos, right? *Verdad?* But you gonna tell me the fun times ain't gone? Bullshit! You ain't noticed what's been happenin'? Things have fuckin' changed, man. They ain't what they used to be. We ain't recruitin' like before. Lobos are leavin'. Droppin' the flag. You know why? 'Cause the word's out, man. Stay away."

"Any motherfuckin' Lobo who drops the flag ain't worth the fuckin' water I shit in," King said, his voice rising with emotion. "All I care about's the *familia* that stays and fights until the end. Everyone else can go fuck themselves!"

"We've lost too much goddamn *familia*, King!" Snapper shouted. "What the fuck you doin' about it?" Turning towards the others, Snapper continued. "We don't know what the fuck's goin' on, man. We all knew the rules checkin' into the gang. You get killed by a *pinchi* Diablo, that's the chance you take. It's war. If you die, you die with respect. But this... this *shit!*" Snapper spit on the ground. "God *damn*, man!" he yelled. "We owe it to Leopoldo, and Slice, and Juice, and Popper. Fuckin' everybody, man. We gotta know. We gotta *understand*." Snapper looked back at King. "There ain't no shame in findin' out *somethin'*. I'm goin' to that meeting, man. You wanna give me shit? Fuck you!"

Everyone stared at King as his eyes zeroed in on Snapper's. A part of him wanted to fight to the death over Snapper dissin' him like that in front of his *comaradas*. Torrents of heat pulsated in an escalating sequence through his body yet he stood there, holding his position. In tense silence, he acknowledged his own confusion over this unexplainable string of deaths, especially the morning Luis returned after witnessing what happened to Juice. He conceded he had no answers, and the survival of the North Rampart Lobos mattered more than anything.

"I'll fuckin' go, man, but any shit goes down at that meeting, it ain't gonna be on my head." King stalked off towards the other end of the park. If Snapper ever dissed him again, he'd kill him.

King suckled his beer as he stood under the cover of the trees, acting as giant black umbrellas protecting him from the bullshit. The thought of sitting in the same room as the Diablos, forced to breathe their stink and look at their ugly faces, made him sick. But the rumors about Diablos also having heart attacks turned out to be true, and without them to blame, his one-way compass of hatred had veered off into an unknown direction. Despising and destroying any Diablo had always defined his entire being, the sum of his identity, but did his beloved North Rampart Lobos now face a common enemy? He wondered if the Diablo he swore vengeance on for ordering Viper's death still lived and if he'd be forced to coexist with him in this new battle. The possibility made him want to puke.

King thought back to the deaths of Hazard and Steel. They were two of the toughest motherfuckers, *chingones,* in the North Rampart Lobos, yet they died within a week of each other. Both bodies had been found slumped on the ground without any signs of blood or a weapon. The police claimed no poison had been found, but he knew Hazard and Steel as too damn tough to be caught and murdered without any sign of a battle. *Don't gimme that shit about heart attacks*, he thought to himself. King liked the feeling of control, dictating the rules of combat, but the puzzling murders of his homeboys had him rattled. He and the rest of the Lobos had never faced such a crisis before.

He attempted to clear his troubling thoughts by reflecting on something that went *right*. His mind returned to that Halloween night with Viper and the hot *puta* bitch inside the van. A perfect plan. A perfect night. Almost two years had passed since it happened and he still remembered *everything*. If he ever got the chance at her ass again, he'd... well, she was broken in good now. She'd want him even more next time, knowing what a real man can do. For a few moments, King felt better. He grabbed his crotch and held on to his aroused dick, rubbing it like a magic lamp and wishing for another chance at her. Finishing his Bud, he hurled the can away and lit a cigarette. Taking a long, pleasing drag, King turned back to rejoin the others.

TWENTY-THREE

FACE COULDN'T SLEEP, ATTENTIVE TO the filtered shadows clinging to his room and his thoughts. The claustrophobic grip on the Alvarado Street Diablos had affected them like fingers tightening on their collective throats. From the time he started bangin', death had been an unavoidable part of his surroundings, but nothing compared to the current state of affairs he'd witnessed. So many brothers had died in such a short period of time that he now received news of another fallen *comarada* as more of an expectation than a bombshell. Loving each other means dying for each other if necessary. Taking a bullet, or a beating, or a knife in the gut for your gang is noble and right. But a fucking heart attack ain't no sacrifice. Ain't nothing noble about it when there's nobody to plot against and attack.

Heart attacks had taken the Lobos down, too, and that changed everything. Without them to blame, nobody knew where to point the finger anymore. Looking back, he sensed all the trouble starting the night of Apache's anniversary, when that kid's old man got killed in the drive-by. Something about that circumstance triggered a strange chain of events that had culminated in many deaths, starting with Swat. Face remained the last surviving Diablo from the drive-by car and wondered if his own death approached. The death of that kid's father hung tight like an evil curse, sticking to his psyche like crusted blood to a knife. Face threw back his sheets and walked to the refrigerator for a beer. He needed to sit in the dark and think. He wanted to feel good again. He revisited a triumphant moment, when love and revenge bonded together in a common cause, a united passion, for the sake of the person who meant more to him than anybody in the world: his sister.

ᛏᛁᚱ ᛏᛁᚱ ᛏᛁᚱ

Assault with a deadly weapon. That's what the judge called it when he sent nineteen-year old Alejandro "Face" Torres to a correctional facility up in Stockton, far away from Alvarado Street, for the near fatal beating of a North Rampart Lobo. For six months he followed their rules and dressed in the clothes they gave him, counting the days until his release. But the time he served meant nothing compared to the ass-kicking he handed out to the drug dealer who got his little cousin hooked on crank in exchange for sex. That attitude changed, however, when he heard the news about his sister. Those final eight weeks catapulted him into moments of maddening turmoil and sleepless nights. Guilt and agony replaced the hands of the clock, turning each hour into a painful, crushing reminder that when people who depend on you for protection are left alone, any minute away could bring tragedy. The animals that hunger for their own pleasures take advantage when the smell of blood is fresh.

He continued to replay the conversation about his sister in his mind. Trap, a newly-arrived Diablo, approached him before dinner looking concerned.

"Hear anything from home, Face?"

"Four fuckin' months away, what do I know, cabron? You tell me. *Qué pasa?*"

"Nothin' about your sister, man? She okay?"

"What the fuck you talkin' about, Trap?"

"You mean... oh, shit, man, I thought you knew."

Face squeezed Trap's arm like a pair of pliers. "Know what? *What?* Fuckin' tell me, God damn it!"

A supervisor looked up from a table nearby. "Hey, you two, split up and get over at separate tables. Move it!"

Face wheeled around. "Gimme another minute, man!"

"Who do you think you're talking to, Torres?" the supervisor shouted. "I said, now!"

Face looked back at Trap, eyes burning. "Spit it out, motherfucker!"

"Your sister, man, she was...*raped!*"

The word spread through Face like a frenzied virus. His mind went numb. Time seemed to stop, and for a moment he forgot where he was. He didn't want to believe what he'd just heard. He seized Trap's shoulders, shaking him like a cigarette machine that doesn't give back the change. "*Who told you that?*"

"Hawk!" Trap answered with a rush. "He was buyin' some weed. Dude told him he heard a Lobo braggin' about it at a party. Name was Viper."

"Viper?" he repeated, searing the name into his brain like a branding iron. "I'll *kill* him!"

"There was another one," Trap said. "*Pinchi* Lobo was sayin' somebody else was with him. Hawk didn't get his name."

The angered supervisor approached, stopping within one foot of Face and Trap. "I said split up and go to separate tables! You've got five goddamn seconds to move!"

Face wanted to tear the punk into small pieces. Had this been anywhere else outside of probation camp, he would have hurt him in a big way. But Trap's news made any desire to kick the supervisor's ass meaningless. He only had three weeks to go, so he wasn't about to blow it now. Payback couldn't come soon enough. Viper was a dead man. And when he found who the other one was, he'd be dead, too.

Face returned home intent on grilling his sister about everything that went down that night, but his tearful mother begged him not to say anything. "She made me promise not to tell you," his mother said. "She knew you'd do something crazy."

Face shouted in anger at his mother's reaction, knowing her to be nothing but a weak-willed woman who put everything in God's hands.

"The first few days..." Shaking her head and making the sign of the cross, his mother continued. "She just stayed in bed. Didn't eat or speak much. But she's all right, thank God."

Face stormed past his mother, almost knocking her down. "I wanna talk to her. She's gotta tell me everything that happened."

"No, Alex, please. If she wants to talk about it, let her do it. She's so close to graduating. Don't make her go through it again."

"And pretend nothin' happened when I was away? Fuck that shit, Ma!"

"She's like you, you know that? Determined. Strong. She's the one acting like nothing ever happened. She goes to her job, comes home and studies. This is her chance to do something good with her life. Don't you want that for her?"

His mother's reasoning made him reevaluate his thinking. His sister deserved a better life than what this death trap of a neighborhood had to offer; a chance to escape the jungle of city streets and the vicious animals that roamed them. But he remained a part of these streets, shaped and represented by the laws of the 'hood, and nothing was gonna stop him from payback.

Face had been obsessed with the image of Viper dying a slow, painful death at his feet. But the news he received from Hawk three weeks later wasn't good. "God damn it!" Face shouted. "Viper's at Eagle Mountain?"

"*Es verdad*, Face," Hawk replied. "Been there over a month. Asshole couldn't even jack a fuckin' car without shootin' someone's ass."

Face almost took his anger out on Hawk, turning away before his anger got the best of him. What the hell was he supposed to do now? Eagle Mountain Community Correctional Facility was miles away in Riverside County. Hell, that Lobo *culero* may as well have been on the moon.

By a stroke of luck, however, the moon got a lot closer a few weeks later.

Leticia Chavez was Cherry's older sister. She also belonged to Tank, a beefy, thick-chested member of the Diablos. Everyone considered Leticia a part of the Diablo *familia*, and before Tank, she'd been another homegirl who had a sexual history with Face. Tank and Leticia wanted to get married one day, but Face remained close to her, sometimes reminiscing about their wild times together. He felt saddened when Leticia told him about Tank's arrest for drug dealing, but when he heard where they sent him, his sympathy transformed into an inspiration.

"We was gonna go to Vegas," she told him. "Get married, you know? Stay in a fancy hotel." Sitting on the curb with Face in front of her apartment, Leticia lowered her head and cried. "He was only gonna sell that shit one more time. He messed up."

"What the fuck happened?" Face asked.

"Undercover," she said in a quiet voice. "The stupid *cabron* sold crank to a cop."

Face closed his eyes, aware of the consequences for Tank. "That's three fuckin' strikes, Leticia," he said. "He ain't comin' out no more."

Leticia's tears turned into sobs. "I... I know."

Face remained silent, taking Leticia into his arms as she buried her head in his chest.

"Where's he at now?"

At first she struggled to answer. "Eagle Mountain," she whimpered.

Face's body stiffened. Leticia pulled away. "What's the matter?" she asked.

"*Eagle Mountain?*"

"Yeah, Face. What's wrong?"

His mind raced as his eyes lasered into hers, searching for a reason to believe. And hope.

"I can't help Tank, Leticia," he said, "but he'll always be a Diablo, *verdad?*"

"*Por supuesto*, of course."

Face held his silence. After a few moments he asked, "You hear what happened to my sister?"

Leticia looked down into the street. "Yeah, I heard. I'm real sorry, Face. How's she doin'?

Face ignored the question. "Sorry enough to help me do somethin' about it?"

"What do you mean?"

"The Lobo piece-of-shit who did it, he's where Tank's at."

Her eyes opened wide. "*Sí?* Eagle Mountain?"

"Yeah," he muttered. "For a long time. Like Tank. You understand what I'm sayin'?"

Leticia nodded her head. "Tank likes your sister. Thinks she's real classy."

"He's known her a long time," Face said.

"He knows what happened to her," Leticia told him. She reached out for Face's hand. "Broke his heart."

"I need his help, Leticia."

"You can't go see him," she said. "You got a record."

"Yeah, I know that," he replied. "When you gonna see him next?"

"Couple days. What do you want me to tell him?"

A tired smile appeared on his face. "I knew you'd help me, Leticia. *Gracias.*"

Leticia stroked his face with her hand. "We got your back, Face. What do you want Tank to do?"

"I want him to kill a Lobo named Viper," he answered. "That's the one who..." Face paused a moment before continuing. "It was him and somebody else."

"*Viper,*" she repeated.

Face peered into Leticia's eyes, wanting to make sure she'd remember his final message. "Tell Tank to do the right thing," he said. "Tell him it's a chance to honor my classy sister."

Face drove to Leticia's house when she returned from Eagle Mountain. She had called him that evening, telling him she had a message from Tank that needed to be told in person. Sitting in the parked car, she said that Tank would take care of Viper, but he first wanted a favor in return.

"You know that pawn shop near the freeway?" she asked. "Across from the park?"

"What about it?"

"Tank borrowed his mother's necklace and pawned it there. Been in the family a long time. She got it from her own mother. It's a gold crucifix with red and yellow stones on it. That's how he got the money for the meth."

Face shook his head in disbelief. "What do you mean, he 'borrowed' it? He fuckin' stole it."

"No, that ain't it," she exclaimed. "We was gonna get it back after we won some money in Vegas. His old lady wasn't gonna know ever. Shit, she only wore it for special days. Now she ain't even talkin' to him."

"He wants me to get it back, right?"

"Yeah. He told me to tell you when you take care of his mother's neck, he'll take care of Viper's."

"What if it ain't there no more?"

"Tank got the man to promise him he'd hold it for three weeks," she explained. "We was gonna give him the money he asked for and everything would be cool."

Face understood how much she depended on him. His feelings were no different; he depended on Tank.

"I'll figure somethin' out," he said.

She smiled at Face. "Tank told me to give you another message."

She leaned over, placing her head against the side of his, allowing her lips to feather his ear. Reaching down between his legs, she started stroking his genitals. "Tank knows I'm a hot-blooded woman," she whispered. "So do you. I gotta have it sometimes, baby. *Real* bad." The gentle caressing turned into feverish rubbing. "He says to keep me happy." Staring at Face with eyes looking dreamy and half-closed, she murmured, "C'mon, Face, make me happy."

The rapid swelling in his crotch gave Leticia the answer she wanted. Lowering her head, she unbuckled his pants and stoked the fire in his penis with her tongue and fingertips. Face leaned back in his seat, surrendering to the ecstasy of the moment. As he raised his hips, Leticia slipped his pants and underwear down to his ankles, maneuvering her way back up to his mouth, kissing him with a passion that excited him even more. Easing her way on top of his lap, she lifted her dress, inviting Face to gaze upon the furry nakedness of her sex. Gripping his stone-hard erection, he slipped in easily through the velvety liquid of her warm flesh, allowing his excitement to build through her moans and whispers. Within moments after what must have been her second or third orgasm, Face came, too, ushering in the gradual ebb of rapid breathing inside the cramped confines of the front seat. A fleeting escape, of the kind that make pleasures of the flesh unique and unavoidable, provided the comfort they sought, and consoled them for the moment from their own feelings of despair.

ᛟᚱ ᛟᚱ ᛟᚱ

As a true *mamacita*, Leticia radiated sexuality, and Face intended to use her kind of persuasion to their advantage. He instructed her to go inside the pawnshop and work her magic while he waited in the park across the street. He figured unless the man was a *maricon* and liked men, an *arrangement* could be made. Leticia knew the game and said she would do it for Tank. After pacing along the perimeter of the park several times, Face watched as she left the store and crossed the street. As she approached him, he saw by her disappointed expression that she didn't get the necklace.

"You don't got it?" he asked.

"No," she answered, her eyes full of anger. "I don't fuckin' got it."

"Was it still there?"

"Yeah. He showed it to me. It's in a wood box up on a shelf."

Face breathed a quiet sigh of relief. "You see a camera?" he asked, having instructed her to look for one just in case.

She nodded. "It's up in the corner. Behind the counter where the jewelry is."

"Tell me what happened."

"I did just like you wanted me to," she said. "Told him my ex-boyfriend stole the crucifix from my mother and she was real sad. I leaned forward a lot, just like this." Face stared at the generous exposure of Leticia's sizable breasts. "He was checkin' 'em out real good," she said. "Just like you, baby."

Face smiled, keeping his eyes on the prize. "You got great tits, *chica*."

Leticia looked down at her cleavage. "Yeah, well, they didn't get me anywhere today."

"Did you try comin' on?"

Leticia leaned over to Face, allowing the upper part of her tank top to reveal her nipples. "*Please, mister, I ain't got the money. Can't I do somethin' to get it back?*" Straightening up, she said in a low voice, "*No. Just bring me the money.*"

"How come the necklace ain't bein' shown with the other shit?" he asked.

"I guess he's still holding it for Tank," she said. "Three weeks, remember?"

"How long we got?"

Leticia's expression darkened. "Two more days."

"*Two fuckin' days*? Face shook his head in frustration. "How much money does he want for it?"

She looked at him with a pained expression. "Seven hundred dollars."

Face realized he had two choices, each presenting a distinct dilemma. He could attempt to steal the necklace, knowing he'd be recognized and sent away again if caught on camera, or he could take seven hundred dollars of the almost nine-hundred fifty he'd earned from his neighborhood car repairs; the same money he'd saved towards an eventual down payment for an auto repair shop. The two-sided coin of his decision offered either risk or pain. He needed time to think.

He continued wrestling with the answer as he sat on his bed in the sticky heat of a late, airless night. Above all else he wanted Viper dead, but if he stole the jewelry he'd face the likelihood of another stay at a correctional facility, or maybe jail. As a brother and a man, however, his spirit already felt imprisoned by his inability to exact revenge for what happened to his sister. As long as he knew Viper's corpse wasn't rotting with the maggots, he'd have no peace of mind. But what if he failed in his attempt and got sent away without retrieving the necklace? Tank might decide killing Viper wasn't worth the trouble.

The other option he weighed involved his hard earned savings. The thought of sacrificing his money to buy back the jewelry pained him, knowing the long hours he'd worked for that ticket to a better life. He wouldn't be much past where he started, delaying his plans to leave the gang and neighborhood behind. One other thought, however, had him worried and feeling pressured for time; what if Viper or Tank got transferred to another prison?

Deep in the silence of that early morning hour, when past sleeps caused any previous observation to go undetected, Face noticed a dim light appear under the doorway of his sister's room. He thought of what his mother had told him, how she studied at all hours of the night, working for her degree. He reflected on earlier times, how she came to his defense when his father talked shit to him, or how she tried to protect him from the inevitable beatings. His decision didn't seem difficult anymore. He owed her big time, even at the loss of his money and dreams.

As he neared the store the following day, Face told Leticia what he expected of Tank after he returned the necklace. "Let him know I took care of my part of the deal," he said. "Tell him I'm waitin'."

"I ain't gonna ask you where you got the money, okay?" Leticia said, her eyes watering as she looked into his. "I'm just happy you got it. Tank will take care of you now. You'll see."

"My sister's the only one in the whole fuckin' world I'd do this for," he said, more to himself than Leticia. The next moment, Face bolted up in his seat in disbelief. "*Oh shit!*" he shouted. "*What the FUCK?*"

Leticia spun around to look through the car window at the store. The roll-away bars just inside the door remained visible in their locked position. Nothing but darkness showed from inside. The "Closed" sign confronted them like a rude challenge.

"He ain't supposed to be closed!" Leticia yelled. "It ain't Sunday. He told me he's only closed on fuckin' Sunday!"

Face pulled over to the curb, threw his door open and hurried to the window, hoping to see someone inside. He fought the urge to kick his foot through the glass, disappointment scraping at his gut like sandpaper. He grabbed his cell phone from his jacket pocket, calling the number written on the window. No answer. No message.

"*Where the fuck is this asshole?*" he said to himself, straining to peer through the window. He lurched backwards and turned to face Leticia. "Fuck this shit!" he yelled. "We'll wait for him in the park!" Their time across the street proved fruitless. The shop never opened.

The following Friday, after three more days of unsuccessful attempts, Leticia contacted the owner. Offering no explanation for the store's closure, he told her that he had returned to the store and would be there that day during normal business hours. Face's anxiety lessened when he saw the open door of the shop as they arrived. "Let's get this fuckin' thing over with," he muttered.

Face walked in and observed the owner's reaction to his presence from behind the counter. The look of surprise, then visible concern, offered nothing unusual to a 'banger like Face. In a neighborhood with gangs and trouble, everyone remained on guard 24/7. Today, however, there'd be no problems. Face had the cash.

Remaining behind the counter, the owner looked at Letica. "May I help you, young lady?"

"I came for my necklace," she said, pointing towards the wooden box, still occupying the same spot. "I was here on Monday, remember?"

The owner studied her for a moment before glancing at Face. Taking a couple of steps closer to the camera, he reached out and flipped a switch on the wall. Within a few moments Face saw himself on the camera screen situated above the owner's head. He felt irritated by the little man's obvious paranoia; he just wanted to take care of business and get the hell out of there.

"I'm sorry," the owner said. "I already have another buyer offering a lot more than you."

"*What?*" Face and Letica screamed, in shocked unison.

The troubled expression returned to the owner's face. "I told you two more days, right?" he said, continuing to direct his attention towards Leticia. "You were here on Monday. May I remind you, today's Saturday."

"You weren't here!" she shouted. Looking at Face, she pointed towards the shelf. "The box is still there!"

"So what?" the owner replied, looking smug. "It's mine, now. I can sell it to anyone I want."

Complete clarity of the owner's scheme hit Face like a sucker's punch to the gut. The little prick purposely stayed away from his store until the end of the two remaining days. He never intended to sell the necklace back to Leticia. Face's eyes burned and his muscles tensed as he struggled to maintain his composure. He reached into his pocket for the cash. Looking at the owner, he caught the look of nervousness on his face.

"I got your seven hundred dollars!" he growled. Approaching the counter, Face prepared to drop the crinkled bills on the glass top when the owner held up his hand and shook his head, rejecting Face's attempt at payment.

"It'll take a lot more than seven hundred dollars, young man," he told him. "I did some research and discovered those are valuable fire opals on that cross. That necklace is worth more than I make in a month."

Face's hourglass of patience trickled down to its final few grains. "Take my money and give me the fuckin' necklace!" he demanded. "*Now!*"

Taking several quick steps backwards, the owner brought his hand to his waist and pulled out a gun. Face held his position as Leticia stood behind him.

"Get out of my store!" he yelled. "If you don't I'll call the police."

The street fighter governing his psyche could no longer be contained. With a sudden mobility that caught the owner unprepared, Face leaped over the glass counter, knocking the gun from his hand as the sound of shattering glass echoed from the misfired bullet. Blood soon gushed from the man's eyes and nose as the relentless force of Face's piston-like punches ignored the diminishing resistance of his helpless victim. He wanted to punish this lying asshole, make him pay for what he tried to do and for what he didn't understand, but the sound of Leticia's voice broke through the concentrated focus of his fury.

"Face, stop!" she screamed. "You'll kill him! *Stop!*"

With his right hand hovering over the red-spattered face of the groaning shop owner, Face's thoughts reeled back to the matter at hand. Needing to steal the film from the camera before they left, he jumped on top of the counter thinking he could reach it, but his hand fell several feet short. His eyes scanned the store looking for something knock it down, but the high-pitched wail of police sirens sounded in the distance. He darted over to the jewelry box, removed it from the shelf, and handed it to Leticia.

"Is that it?" he asked, eyes still wild.

"Yeah!" she shouted.

Face grabbed her arm. "Let's go!"

Despite their escape in his car, he recognized his fate. The cops knew him well, the camera proved his guilt, and he couldn't disprove the shop owner's explanation of the events. Leticia, however, had no record or known face, so they might not come after her. No matter what happened to him, she needed to get that necklace back to Tank's mother.

"They'll be comin' for me, not you," he told her. "I gotta drive ya to Tank's before they find me."

Leticia didn't answer for a few moments. "What'cha gonna do, Face?"

"There ain't nothin' I *can* do," he said. "The rest is up to you. And Tank. Go see him fast as you can. It's *his* turn now."

ᛏᛏᛏ ᛏᛏᛏ ᛏᛏᛏ

Downing the last of his beer, Face recalled that day with pride, as it ultimately led to Tank honoring his sister the only way possible. Knowing Viper had been killed made every moment of his ten months away tolerable. But Viper had said he wasn't alone that night and Face's determination to finish off that second Lobo remained as strong as ever. If he wasn't dead already, Face planned to send that *culero* to the grave as soon as possible. Envisioning an end to his banging, he'd leave the Diablos in peace, knowing his work was complete.

He thought back to Apache's anniversary again, and how the Diablos and Lobos started dropping from heart attacks. Was there a connection? Something indescribable had occurred that had no explanation and maybe no end in sight. Along with the other Diablos who'd been contacted, Rocket, Thorn, Root, Zoom, and Haze, tomorrow's meeting not only created added suspicion about the police, but disgust over sharing the same room with the North Rampart Lobos. But what else could they do? They needed answers and tomorrow offered them their best chance.

Face wondered if they'd have to change somehow and turn away from what they represented. In the quiet of the blackened room, as the invasive ticking of a kitchen clock reminded him that time might be running out, he started to think the unthinkable. The Alvarado Street Diablos and the North Rampart Lobos, deadly rivals for as long as he could remember, were now united by a common enemy.

TWENTY-FOUR

*L*IKE STRATEGIC POSITIONS ON a war map, four officers dressed in civilian attire sat in four unmarked police cars on the north, south, east and west side boundaries of the sports club. Forty-five minutes earlier, two of the cars parked a block away from Lafayette Park on the corner of Marathon Street and Rampart Boulevard, the designated pick-up area for the six North Rampart Lobos. Concurrently, several blocks away on the corner of Reservoir Street and North Alvarado Boulevard, the initiation of the same plan occurred with six members of the Alvarado Street Diablos. Along the entrance off Riverside Drive, yellow caution tape cordoned off any access to the entrance, while large white signs announcing the gym's closure for the day appeared on the doors.

All twelve selected members of the Alvarado Street Diablos and North Rampart Lobos attended. When they had first been informed of the gathering, each was told to expect a search for weapons, and that cell phones and pagers weren't allowed. Two policemen, both dressed as sanitation workers, conducted a separate frisking of the gang members before going outside to wait in the truck. At the conclusion of the meeting, their orders involved escorting the gangs in opposite directions towards the parked shuttles that brought them there.

Within the aging confines of the indoor facility, a barbed climate surrounded the room as Captain Dean sat on a folding chair between the two benches separating each gang. Lieutenant Atkinson sat several feet in front of them, the point of the triangle, facing the entire group. From his vantage point, under the bright glare of the metallic mushroom-shaped lights descending from the ceiling, Atkinson diagnosed their darting eyes and slumped shoulders as telltale signs of mistrust and anxiety. He rose to his feet, cleared his throat, and addressed the gathering.

"Thank you all for coming," he said. "Some of you may know me from my days in the Community Law Enforcement and Recovery program, or, perhaps, the Jeopardy program, but for those of you who don't, I'm Lieutenant Carl Atkinson of the L.A.P.D. Sitting between you is Captain Sherman Dean."

Atkinson waited for their heads to turn towards Dean and back again before continuing. "The urgency of this meeting cannot be overstated, as it involves each and every member of both gangs, not just the twelve of you here today. When we're finished, I want all of you, I *need* all of you, to spread the word, so that everyone, and I mean everyone, understands the danger that your two gangs face."

He watched as the majority of the gang members squirmed on the benches, smirking and shaking their heads. He knew they would never admit to any problem, but Atkinson interpreted their reaction as indicators of apprehension.

"*What's with the fuckin' heart attacks, man?*" someone yelled out. "*What do you know?*"

"*Yeah, tell us, damn it!*" another shouted.

"*What the hell's goin' down?*"

"*Why don't you fuckin' do somethin', man?*"

"*What are you hidin', Atkinson?*"

"*Tell us, man!*"

"*Tell us!*"

"*Let's hear it!*"

Captain Dean bolted from his chair. "You'll get your damn answers if you let him talk!"

The gang members grew silent.

Dean scanned the different faces, looking back and forth from one group to the next. "Believe me," he said, "you better listen to what Lieutenant Atkinson has to say today." He turned back towards Atkinson. "Continue, Lieutenant."

Atkinson reached into his inside breast pocket and pulled out a folded piece of paper. "I've got something I want to read to you," he said. "This information dates back to the first known heart attack. It happened in the early morning of April 30th, just a few hours after the April 29th death of Warren Palmer. If I need to remind any of you, Mr. Palmer was the man who got killed in a drive-by shooting at Alfredo's Market."

Commencing with the death by heart attack of Rafael Carranzaon April 30th, Atkinson proceeded through a sobering, deliberately slow recitation of each Lobo and Diablo gang member that died from heart failure or a known murder weapon, as well as the dates of their demise. Three weeks had passed since Atkinson met Captain Dean in his office, confronting him with his astonishing report on the facts behind the thirty-four deaths. With the discovery of Marcos Ceniceros' body in the front yard of a neighbor's home three days before the meeting, there now totaled one less North Rampart Lobo and one more victim of heart failure. The death count had reached thirty-eight, and the last four, like all the others, maintained the consistent time separation between each death.

In a further continuation of the pattern, two of the four deaths stemmed from a heart attack, including Ceniceros, who caused two separate 9-1-1 calls to occur shortly before 4 a.m. According to the coroner's report, the other recent victim, a known Alvarado Street Diablo named Gonzalo Rios, died "close" to 4 a.m. Captain Dean and Lieutenant Atkinson were now convinced that "close" wasn't close enough. Rios died *at* 4 a.m.

Atkinson concluded with the details of Marcos Ceniceros before sitting back in his chair. As he refolded the paper, preparing to place the sheet back into his pocket, he wondered if any of this information mattered to these guys. Maybe they didn't believe any of the facts they'd just heard, or that one of them could be next if they took an act of vengeance too far. But as he peered out at the faces, he knew he had reached them. The intensity in their eyes verbalized the concern that their silence could not.

"Let's review some facts here," he said. "With the exception of three murder victims who weren't gang members and who were murdered, presumably, by one of your gangs, it seems that whenever one of you kills someone from the other gang, that person dies by a heart attack the next day at what appears to be the killer's designated time of death: four in the morning."

"Gimme me a fuckin' break, man. That's *bullshit*. People get killed all the time, right? We ain't the only game in town."

Members from both benches nodded their head in agreement.

Atkinson wasn't surprised to hear that type of irksome comment from Miguel Ruiz. The kid had always been a bad seed, an incorrigible by-product of two alcoholic parents dumping their shit on society's doorstep. Atkinson had to wipe his shoes clean from these bad-ass types much too often.

"Let me tell you something," Atkinson replied, directing his gaze at Ruiz. "The Lobos and Diablos are the only ones playing *this* kind of game."

Turning to face the others, he continued. "For every heart attack, a homicide in your neighborhoods occurred the day before. Every... single... time." Atkinson took a step forward, preparing to raise his voice to underscore the next point. "Between your two gangs, there have been thirty-five deaths since the night of Mr. Valenzuela's murder. *Thirty-five*. Those three other killings make a total of thirty-eight. Exactly half of those deaths, nineteen of them, have been from heart failure. And all of them, *all* of them, took place the day after a murder. It may sound crazy, but the facts speak for themselves. You kill somebody one day, you die from a heart attack the next."

Atkinson returned to his chair. After a period of silence, in an atypical softened response, a Lobo announced, "Someone's usin' some fuckin' poison, man. How else you explain it?"

Without giving Atkinson a chance to answer the question, another Lobo had something else to add. "Your numbers don't prove nothin'. We ain't the only ones dyin' from this heart shit. Why you just pointin' the finger at us?"

A strong, unhesitating voice from one of the Diablos responded immediately to the last question.

"Cause there ain't no other gangs havin' heart attacks, right?"

Derisive laughter from the Lobos followed as members from both benches turned towards the Diablo who ventured the last comment. Showing a calm sense of conviction, he stared at Atkinson and repeated his belief. "Ain't that right? Nobody else."

Atkinson had wondered if that idea dawned on any of them. If he had been a betting man, he'd have layed his money on Alejandro Torres as the one to figure out the truth. He knew Alejandro from years back, remembered the problems with his father, and thought of him as a sharp kid. Atkinson felt a slight shame for the sense of pleasure he felt over the opportunity to answer Alejandro's question in such dramatic fashion, but after listening to the gangs' sarcastic laughter and observing their skeptical expressions he felt gratified hitting them with the knockout punch. He had been saving that bit of information for the end, as the final jolt to their psyche.

Atkinson looked at Dean, then back at Alejandro. Pausing briefly, he uttered, "You're right. No other gangs are having heart attacks."

A chorus of chaotic voices followed.
"*What the fuck?*"
"*That's bullshit, man!*"
"*No fuckin' way!*"
"*God damn, man, you're crazy!*"
"*I don't fuckin' believe that shit!*"

Captain Dean rose from his chair as the Lobos and Diablos huddled in two groups around their respective benches.

"Sit down, men!" Dean ordered. "We're not done here yet."

Dean walked over to stand behind Atkinson after the gang members returned to their seats. Picking up where he left off, Dean addressed the gangs in a spirited voice. "The Lieutenant told you what we know so far. I'll you what we *don't* know. We don't know how this person gets to you guys. We've had heart attacks happen in the park, the street, alleys, a deserted railroad yard, and in a number of cases, even the goddamn bedroom. We don't know who the hell the victims were talking to before they died, but witnesses say they were carrying on pretty good. We don't know why no one else has ever been seen during that time. And we can't explain how the killer is able to stick to his timetable with such perfection."

"Like I told you," a Lobo said, "motherfucker's shootin' us up with some poison shit."

"We haven't found any traces of poison," Dean replied.

"What the fuck is he doin' then, man?" Ruiz asked. "What are you hidin'?"

Atkinson rose. Turning towards Captain Dean, he leaned close and whispered, "You told me to tell 'em the truth, Captain. That's what I'll do." Glancing first at Ruiz, Atkinson scanned every face before speaking. All eyes zeroed in on him. "There's one more thing we can't figure out. The findings from all nineteen heart attack victims..." Atkinson paused, realizing this next bit of news would either make or break the effect of the entire meeting. "The findings," he repeated, "the autopsies, show that the hearts had been ...frozen." (Dean later described that moment to Atkinson as being so quiet, "you could hear the fraying of the volleyball net.")

Dean stood and offered a tight-lipped smile to his Lieutenant, signifying a job well done. Doing his best to avoid technical details and medical terminology, Dean went on to explain how the coroner arrived at his findings, and why the heart stopped beating. After answering some questions, Dean moved forward to within a few feet of both gangs. "There's something you men better understand," he said, "and the sooner the better. You're no longer in control. Someone out there has got your number, *comprende?* Thirty-five young men from your two gangs have died in the last six months. If you keep this war going, you'll lose a whole lot more. Maybe some of you here tonight."

"Six months and you ain't got a fuckin' clue, man!" Ruiz shouted. "Maybe that's 'cause you don't give a shit if the Mexicans kill each other. If we was white, you'd be all over it."

"*I don't care what damn color you are!*" Atkinson shouted. "We've got a killer on our hands and we need your help, not your paranoid bullshit."

"Let me remind you of something," Dean said. "Nineteen of the deaths over the last six months had nothing to do with heart failure, and everything to do with the Lobos and Diablos. Seems to me it's you guys who don't give a shit if Mexicans go around killing each other."

"You said somethin' 'bout needin' our help," Alejandro interjected. "What kind of help you talkin' 'bout?"

"You want to answer that, Lieutenant?" Dean asked. As Dean moved to the side, Atkinson left his chair to occupy the same spot where Dean had been standing. "The consistent, next day, four a.m. pattern of the heart attacks leads us to believe it's one person behind all this," he said. "When it comes to multiple killings, precision doesn't work well in pairs. This guy's clever. A real shrewd son-of-a-bitch. But in every case so far, one-hundred percent of the time, he only strikes after someone from one of your gangs commits a murder. Based on that fact alone, we believe if you stop your war, he'll stop his."

Dean walked over to Atkinson. Standing side by side, the two of them faced the twelve representatives who they needed to forge a peace, albeit a cold one.

"The Lieutenant has said all there is to say," Dean stated. "The rest is up to you. Go back and let the others know what we discussed today. This isn't a trick or a joke, men, it's a life or death mystery that should scare the shit out you." Dean searched the expressions on the twelve faces again. "I'll leave you with a famous quote," he said. "It's an ancient one, but as meaningful to your two gangs as when it was first spoken." He stood silent for a brief moment. "*The enemy of my enemy is my friend.*" Dean paused for several more seconds before continuing. "What that means, men, if you haven't figured it out by now, is that you share the same enemy and you're in this together, whether you like it or not. *Together.* Someone out there doesn't seem to want you guys around. Either you start understanding this, and stop the killing, or kiss your macho asses goodbye."

TᵢT TᵢT TᵢT

Alejandro Torres approached Atkinson after the meeting. "You ain't bein' straight with us, man," he said. "Seems to me this could be an inside job. Maybe some cops are havin' their way. Treatin' us like their bitch. Got plenty of my homeboys thinkin' that kind of shit."

"I know that's how a lot of you think, Alejandro, but there's nothing that leads me to believe that."

"There's lots of you out there don't like us, man. You gonna argue with that?"

Atkinson glared at Torres. "No, I won't argue with that at all. In fact, I'll add to it. There's lots of us out there that *hate* you. We hate what you stand for, the fear you bring to the good citizens of our community. The heartbreak you bring to so many families, including your own."

Torres gave a sarcastic laugh. "Our own families? We don't got families, man. We got shit at home. Why you think we found each other in the first place?"

"You've got family, Alejandro. I've met your mother and sister. They're good people. And they care about you." One of Alejandro's homeboys called out to him from the door. "Hey, Face! *Estamos listo.*" Acknowledging him with a nod of his head, he yelled back, "Yeah, I'm ready, too!" Atkinson looked towards the door. "Is that what your homeboys call you, Alejandro? 'Face'?"

"That ain't none of your business, man. I just don't need you tellin' me about my mother and sister."

"You're right," Atkinson said. "You don't. You're smart enough to figure things out for yourself. Hell, you were smart enough to figure out that you're the only two gangs getting heart attacks. Seems like nobody else knew but you. Why don't you take those brains of yours and do something useful? Your father was a rough character but he's not around anymore. He can't bother you now. It's time for you to move on, don't you think?"

'Face' turned away to join the others, glancing back in silence.

157

TWENTY-FIVE

PISSED OFF AT THE POSSIBILITY of peace, and frustrated with the lack of satisfactory answers, King sat brooding for several minutes before heading towards the exit where the Lobos had been instructed to go. Fame, Colt, Tower, and Snapper left right away, but Ram stood blocking the doorway. King noticed him staring at Atkinson talking to some pretty-boy Diablo kiss-ass.

"What the hell you lookin' at man?" he asked with disgust. "C'mon, let's get the fuck outta here."

"*Esperate*, King," Ram replied. "You see that asshole talkin' with Atkinson?"

"Yeah," he muttered, "so fuckin' what?"

"I heard one of his homeboys call him Face. That's fuckin' Face, man."

"'*That's fuckin' Face, man*'," King mimicked. "Who the hell is he?"

Ram turned his gaze away and looked at King. "I'll tell you who he is, man," he said, lowering his voice. "He's the *pinchi* asshole worked it out to kill Viper."

Ram's words hit King like a sledgehammer. "*What?*" he barked, his eyes wide and attentive. "How the hell you know that?"

"I was there when Viper went down, man. At Eagle Mountain."

"You saw him take the knife?" he asked. "From that asshole, Face?"

"Wasn't no Face who did it," Ram said. "Some fat Diablo *culero* snuck a handmade knife into the cafeteria. Nobody saw it comin'. When Viper went down the motherfucker kept yellin' somethin' 'bout, 'a message from Face to honor his sister, Victoria'."

King squinted, leaning his head closer to Ram's. "You mean, *Veronica?*" he asked. "Was the bitch's name Veronica?"

"Yeah, man, maybe that was it. Veronica. Face and Veronica."

King felt a surge of adrenaline barreling through his body, realizing

159

that the Diablo asshole talking to Atkinson was actually his old neighbor, Alejandro Torres. His mind raced from the possibilities. This was the news he needed to boost his sagging spirits, to rejoice in the sudden discovery of unexpected inspiration and a reminder of how good it felt to be a North Rampart Lobo.

"C'mon," he said, prodding Ram through the door. "We gonna kill us a Diablo!"

Ram stood his ground. "God *damn*, man," he blurted. "Ain't you heard what's goin' down? Crazy fuckin' shit."

King brought his face to within an inch of Ram's. "Ain't no fuckin' cop bullshit gonna turn me to no pussy," he growled. "Viper was like my brother, man. I been waitin' a long time for this. That Diablo motherfucker is mine!"

King charged to the outside area where the other Lobos waited. He felt drunk, but on the intoxicating nearness of overdue revenge. The taste seemed even sweeter than cold Bud. How many years had it been since his old man abandoned the family for that bitch whore? He wasn't sure, but that's when they had to leave their house and move to the subsidized piece-of-shit they lived in now. One thing he *was* sure of, though, was that Alejandro Torres, the punk-ass neighbor who kicked his soccer ball down the street and almost got him killed, was now a *pinchi* Diablo. That fuckin' asshole deserved to die back then for what he did to him, and was gonna die now for what he did to Viper. King chuckled to himself. He didn't know it at the time, but the perfect payback had already been carried out on Alejandro's sister, Veronica. Life can be a fuckin' funny thing.

ㅠㅠ ㅠㅠ ㅠㅠ

The name on the same mailbox still read "Torres." King plotted his revenge from the passenger seat as Ram accelerated away from the house.

"We'll stake out his place," he said, "and look for a time to catch that Diablo punk alone." King took a large swig from the Bud they shared. "Too many fuckin' eyes around here. We gotta be smart."

Ram downed the last few swallows before tossing the can out the window. "I still ain't cool with this, man," he complained.

King pounded his fist on the dashboard. "Fuck you, Ram! You were there, God damn it! You watched Viper take a knife and get dissed as he was dyin,' man! You gonna let that shit go unpunished?"

King glared at Ram, watching him rub a hand over his face and the top of his shaved head. The thought of a Diablo taunting Viper as he lay bleeding to death sickened him. But he couldn't pull this off alone. You can't have a drive-by without a driver, and he sensed Ram's reluctance weakening.

"It's about respect, man!" King shouted, banging the dashboard again. "Goddamn respect! For Viper. For the North... Rampart... *Lobos*!" King leaned closer to Ram, lowering his voice to a soft growl. "If we don't take a stand, man, what does that make us? Nothin' but pussies. Little fuckin' pussies." Pounding his heart with his fist, he added, "I got too much fuckin' pride, man. I'm goin' after him."

Ram looked over at King. "I ain't doubtin' your heart, man," he said, in the agreeable tone King wanted. "How you gonna do it? Back at his house?"

King nodded. "Yeah, that's what I'm thinkin,'" he answered. "When I'm finished with that motherfucker he'll have more holes than a Tijuana whorehouse."

Ram laughed. "That's a lot of fuckin' holes, man."

"Don't wanna fuck this one up," King said. "I've waited too long. I need to find some shit out. Does he hang around for dinner? Does he sleep there? Does he got some wheels he leaves in the driveway or the street when he's home?"

Ram shook his head. "You can't hang out there, man. You got Diablos gonna spot your ass. How the fuck you gonna learn them things?"

King smiled. "I ain't no *pendejo*, homie," he said. "I need me another pair of eyes. A spy. I'm gonna recruit me a little wannabe gonna do what I tell him."

"You got somebody?" Ram asked.

"Some cholos from Luis' school been askin' him 'bout bangin' with the Lobos. That school ain't no more than a half mile from the house. Gonna find me one who lives close." He rubbed his hands together. "Some lucky little *cabron* is gonna do King a big favor."

"You think a punk-ass *cholito* can pull it off?"

King rocked back and forth, riding the wave of his adrenalin surge. "If he listens to what I tell him to do," he answered. "That fuckin' Diablo rat piece-of-shit ain't gonna spot the smaller trap, man. They're the hardest ones to see."

Ram remained silent for a long moment. "I know what this means to you, King," he said, his voice quiet but intense. "You wanna pull this shit off, and you need help. I got your back, homie. You don't need me tellin' you what not to fuckin' do." Ram cupped the back of King's head. "I'm down, *vato*," he told him. Just tell me when."

TWENTY-SIX

IN ONE WAY, VERONICA HAD come far. That long, difficult journey of working double shifts as a waitress in order to support her schooling and find a stable job away from the neighborhood ended in success. She'd been hired to manage the day care center at a medical clinic in the Valley, kept up with her car payments, and lived in a safe, spacious North Hollywood apartment. But that can of Mace she kept in her purse symbolized a large part of her current life still chained to the past, and as she sat and stared out the window of her apartment, thinking about Kevin Palmer, that chain seemed as inescapable as ever.

He had seen her walking through the mall a few weeks after Seth's tutoring lessons started and asked her to join him for a cup of coffee. Although her initial reluctance turned into a long, enjoyable conversation, she'd managed to keep the relationship from advancing beyond a couple of more lunches together and occasional phone calls and e-mails. His requests to see her more often had been met with imaginary excuses, but how many more could she offer without seeming obvious about it? If he wanted nothing more than her company, no problem arises, but she anticipated and understood his eventual desire for physical love, leading to her rejection of him, and his resentment. Veronica recognized Kevin as someone who didn't make her feel *threatened* like other men, but as long as she remained a slave to the memory that ensnared her like an unyielding cobweb, she couldn't love any man.

She had convinced herself that any emotions tied to love had died, but something about Kevin made her defenses weaken. Still, she remained incapable of laying down her shield. Her feelings alternated as a constant tug-of-war between desire and dread, passion and repulsion. She needed more time, but would he be willing to wait for her to overcome her fear? Would his drifting hands and probing fingers make her grow tense? Would the brushing of the hair from his arms and legs feel like wispy icicles shocking her skin? Could her body welcome his penetration without turning frigid?

Her roommate's cat, Luna, scaled the side of the couch and curled himself in her lap. As she stroked the round, white spot above his eyes, she noticed its resemblance to a solitary moon amidst the black fur. Veronica wondered if her destiny meant living in as cold and isolated a state as the real moon.

"*These are the fun years, girl,*" her roommate, Kimberly, warned her. "*With your face and that body, you could have any man you wanted wrapped around your little finger. Come on, hon, what are you waiting for?*"

The tears formed and fell from Veronica's eyes as she recounted to herself, again, the night that changed her life forever.

ᛙᛙ ᛙᛙ ᛙᛙ

The Halloween party inside the Park and Recreation Center building had been well attended, despite the cold drizzle that moved in that afternoon and persisted into the night. Veronica was only twenty-three years old but entrusted with organizing the neighborhood affair featuring a face painter for the kids, music, food, soda, and, of course, plenty of candy. A special treat was the "Haunted House," for those young souls brave enough to confront the various scare tactics of four different volunteers hiding in the dark. Judging by the screams heard through the evening, the actors played their part quite well.

Along with the originally planned vampire, ghost, and witch, an unexpected late addition brought them a costumed, unshaven pirate wearing a black patch over his left eye. A few minutes before the event started, he approached her near the food stand.

"Me and you used to be neighbors."

Looking up from filling a large bowl of popcorn, Veronica's eyes widened when she saw a stranger staring at her, dressed from head to toe as a pirate. "We did?" she replied. "What's your name?"

"Miguel Ruiz," he answered. "About twelve years ago I lived next door. You're Veronica. And your brother's Alejandro, right?"

Veronica stared at him a few moments before a smile of recognition appeared. "Yes, that's right," she said. "I remember you now. How've you been, Miguel?"

"Good," he said. "What's Alejandro doin' now?"

"He's... working. As a mechanic."

"In L.A.?"

"Yeah... L.A.," she answered, wanting to steer the subject away from her brother serving time. "I like your costume."

"I was thinkin' I could help here," he said. "You need a pirate?"

Veronica looked at her watch. The kids would start arriving in under thirty minutes and she still hadn't prepared the whole food table. "I'll tell you what," she said, smiling, "I need a pirate to help me finish with the food and sodas. Okay?"

"How 'bout over there?" he asked, pointing to the makeshift room with the "Haunted House" sign on the door. "I wanna do that."

"The Haunted House?" she asked. "I wonder if there's enough hiding space left in there." Veronica evaluated the idea for several moments. "All right, Miguel. We'll fit you in. We go from six to nine tonight. Can you stay until the end?"

His smile seemed odd, and his one exposed eye appeared bloodshot, but she figured the effect of the costume caused her uneasiness.

"Yeah, I'll stay," he said. "I'll stick around to help you clean up if you want, too."

"*Muchas gracias*, Miguel." Veronica reached under the table and produced two large bags of M&M's. "Help me put some more candy in the bowls," she said. "Then we'll find you a place to hide."

When the event ended, Veronica felt tired but gratified with her efforts for the neighborhood children. Patricia, Felix, Liz, and Miguel remained behind to help her bag the trash and fold the chairs and tables. Felix teased Miguel about keeping his eye patch on, but Miguel claimed he wanted to leave his costume untouched for another party.

As everyone strolled outside to leave, they stood in a group underneath the overhang. "It's dark, Veronica," Miguel said. "I'll walk you to your car."

"Better a young pirate than an old, wet vampire," Felix quipped, pointing to the faded remnants of his makeup.

"That's not necessary, Miguel," Veronica replied. "I'll be fine."

Without saying goodbye, Miguel seemed to give her a hostile look before spitting on the ground and stalking off towards his van. Everyone stared at him in silence.

"What's he so pissed off about?" Patricia asked. "You hurt his macho pride or something?"

"He gave me the creeps, Veronica," Liz told her. "I'm glad he left."

"I don't know what the big deal was," Veronica said, watching as Miguel drove away. "That was really nice of him to help out, but I just want to lock up here, get in my car and go home. It's been a long day."

Veronica hugged them goodbye and watched as they walked towards their cars. After locking the doors, she placed the recreation keys back in her purse, removed her car keys, and opened her umbrella before heading towards the parking lot. She gave a final wave to the others as they drove away. Veronica felt a deep sense of satisfaction for the success of the event, yet the hours of planning and executing left her drained. She looked forward to getting home and unwinding in a hot bath. Arriving at her car, Veronica unlocked the door, hurriedly sat in the driver's seat and locked the doors again. She tossed the umbrella on the passenger side floor, put the key in the ignition, and *screamed*.

A gun pushed hard against her temple and an angry hand clamped down on her mouth.

"You wanna die, bitch? Huh? You wanna die?" She felt the hot breath from the threatening voice a few inches from her ear. The distinct aroma of liquor infiltrated the close space between them. Her body seemed paralyzed with fright, yet she realized she needed to respond to his question in some way. With her eyes shut tight, she shook her head, indicating her answer.

"That's right, bitch, you don't wanna die," he said. "You're gonna shut up and do what I say." Squeezing his hand tighter over her mouth, continuing to keep the end of his gun pressed against the side of her head, he yelled, "*Right?*"

Veronica clenched her teeth. With small, almost imperceptible motions, she nodded. He slid the barrel down to rest against her neck. "Start the car." Veronica did as she was told. "Now turn your headlights on." After she followed his second command, he continued his instructions. "Listen to me, bitch. I'm gonna take my hand off your mouth." With a sudden rapid movement, he gripped her hair and pulled it from behind. "You try somethin' stupid, bitch, I'll put a hole through that pretty little head of yours."

Removing his hand from her hair, he slid the barrel of his gun along the back of her scalp. "You got beautiful hair, Veronica. That's your name, right? That's what it said on your little badge at the restaurant I seen you workin' at. They dress you old, like a fuckin' *vieja*, but I didn't care. You wasn't no old lady under those clothes. I could tell what you got. You can't hide that gold from Viper."

He kept the gun close to her head as he climbed into the front seat. He lunged over the top of her body, causing her to lean against the door and shut her eyes in fear. Feeling him slide back off, she realized that he'd grabbed her safety belt to lock her in. "Don't want you tryin' somethin' stupid, do we, Veronica?"

She opened her eyes but kept them straight ahead.

"Got an old man waitin' to fuck ya, bitch? Who you live with?"

"Just... my mother."

"Your sweet old mother, huh?" Viper grabbed her purse and dropped it on her lap. "Got a phone in there?" he asked.

"Yes," she answered.

"Call her. Tell her you're goin' to a party. You ain't gonna be home until real late. Don't wait up."

Veronica took the phone from her bag. Viper leaned in close with the gun against the side of her head. "You fuck with me, bitch, you won't be talkin' to nobody no more." Viper circled the end of the gun around the inside of her ear. "You understand me?"

As she made the call she glanced to her right through the darkness. She could see the gun in his hand. Veronica gathered the courage to look his way again. She noticed a cap pulled down over what appeared to be a shaved head, but the illumination from the parking lot lights allowed her to distinguish certain physical characteristics. His abundance of body hair, evident in a plentiful display through his sleeveless tee shirt, made her feel even more vulnerable. He seemed a big man, requiring a lot of space in the seat. Thick, pointed eyebrows framed the fleshy folds of his forehead, and his flattened nose revealed black, angular nostrils that resembled two spiders running from each other. She turned her head in terror when he slid his eyes up and down in a depraved sexual examination.

"What... what are you going to do?"

"Have me some fun," he whispered. "Now start drivin'. I'll tell you where to go."

Veronica accidentally shifted into neutral and depressed the accelerator pedal. The gunning engine startled not only her, but apparently him as well.

"*Hey, what the fuck!*" he yelled, grabbing her by the throat with one hand and wielding his gun with the other.

"I'm sorry! I'm sorry! I didn't mean it!" she shouted back, shutting her tearful eyes in fear once again. "I'm... I'm scared."

Removing his hand from her neck, he brought his face close to hers. "You wanna live to see tomorrow, bitch? Do ya?"

Veronica nodded her head. "Yes."

"Of course you do. That's why you're gonna listen to me." He rubbed her cheek with his fingers. "If you're good to Viper, he'll let you go. You gonna be good to Viper?"

Veronica knew nothing acceptable could be said except one word. "Yes."

Viper directed her from one dark side street to another. She couldn't help but notice that somebody seemed to be following them. A sense of dread iced her gut as she wondered at the possibility that more than one person was involved. The realization of her fear soon revealed itself when she turned and started driving up a darkened hill. The trailing car continued to remain behind. Within moments, its lights flashed.

"Slow down and let him pass." Viper ordered. "Then follow him."

Veronica felt like she'd been sucker-punched when the van passed her. She now understood. Miguel had set her up. A moment later they arrived at an isolated area behind a bank of large trees. Viper ordered her to stop but keep her headlights on. She watched as Miguel walked to the back of his van and peeled off what appeared to be a blank magnetized strip that companies use to advertise on their cars. When he stepped aside, she gazed in horror at the large, painted face of a snarling wolf, a *lobo*, covering most of the two doors. Miguel pounded his heart and pointed at the doors.

"He wanted you to see it," Viper said, smiling. "Ain't it beautiful?"

In silent desperation, Veronica watched Miguel turn the handle to the back of the van. As the doors opened, the head of the wolf seemed to split in two, exposing a large mattress that filled the entire area of the inside except the front seats. Terrified, Veronica understood. She was about to enter the belly of the beast.

"Turn the lights off and get outta the car," Viper instructed, his voice calmer than before.

Following his orders, Veronica considered running away but fear of being killed turned her legs to jelly. Blackness enveloped her like a straitjacket. Miguel switched the interior car lights on and returned to the open door at the back of the van, a can of beer in his hand. "Hey bitch," he said, snickering, "me and you used to be neighbors."

Veronica shook with fright, dropping to her knees and asking God for help. "Get in the van!" Viper shouted, yanking her to her feet. "It's fuckin' wet out here!"

Viper wrapped his arm around her neck and forced her inside. He pushed her down on the mattress as Miguel followed them in and closed the doors. Viper tore Veronica's jacket and shirt away, leaving her shivering in her bra. "Get up!" Viper yelled, grasping her shoulder and forcing her into a sitting position. Veronica tried to cover herself but Viper wrenched her arms back. He took a switchblade knife and flipped it open. "Don't move," he warned her, "or you're gonna get hurt."

Viper slipped behind Veronica and placed the blade under the left shoulder strap. When he cut it, he brought the knife over to the right strap and repeated the same thing. "You ready, King?" he asked with a slight laugh. Veronica caught a glimpse of Miguel's face. His expression was crazed and his eyes... the wild stare... leering at her chest... his hand over his... she couldn't stand to look. Her eyes closed tight when Viper severed the strap across her back, causing the bra to drop away.

"*Mamacita*," Miguel said, his voice a loud, ugly whisper. "Look at those tits! Oh...fuck! Look at 'em!"

Both men forced her down as they began grabbing her breasts, squeezing them and pinching her nipples. She kept her eyes shut, refusing to look. One of them started kissing her, hard and furious, sticking his tongue into her throat. The other one licked her chest and rubbed her genitals over her jeans.

"Get the bottle, King," Viper said, laughing. "Veronica wants to party!"

She tried to scream, but Viper clamped down hard on her mouth. "*Bitch*, shut the fuck up!"

Veronica winced when Viper removed his cap, exposing the tattooed letters, L-O-B-O on his shaved head. She could see that the 'L' appeared in the shape of a snake. When Viper removed his hand, Miguel shoved a bottle of whiskey in her face. "Drink this, bitch!" he yelled.

"Please. Don't do this, Miguel," she pleaded. "I beg you. Let me go."

Grabbing her hair with his left hand, he made a fist with his right, held it against her cheek, and peered down at her face. "Call me King, God damn it! *King!*"

Though the interior car light was dim, the closeness of his face allowed a clear view of the ugly scar where the eye patch had been. As she tried to turn away from the repulsive sight, Viper grabbed her by the neck and pulled her head up. King shoved the bottle in her face and clamped his fingers against her cheeks like a vice, forcing her mouth open to pour the whiskey down her throat. She coughed hard.

"I think she wants some more, King" Viper said, laughing as he pawed at her breasts.

"No... no more," she said, still coughing. "Please... don't."

Viper laughed again. "You hear what she said, King?" he asked, sounding surprised. "Bitch said no."

Viper put his face next to Veronica's and nibbled her ear. "Don't you know what you done?" he whispered. Grabbing her hand, he forced her to feel the stiff outline of his erection. "Feel that? You got me too hot to stop now, baby."

Viper pulled away and looked at King. "You can't take a man this far and say 'no', right, King? No means yes. Veronica understands now."

Miguel put his face a few inches from hers. "This party's our little secret, you got that? You don't want nothin' to happen to Alejandro, do ya? Or Patricia? Me and my homies could fuck her real good, all goddamn night. What a great ass that bitch has. I'd take her like a goddamn dog. It's up to you, Veronica. You snitch, there's gonna be trouble. Understand?"

With a great amount of effort, Veronica whispered, "yes."

"We're wastin' fuckin' time," Viper said.

Veronica hoped her surrender would satisfy them enough to let her go. She submitted to their demands and continued drinking from the bottle, welcoming the mind numbing state of intoxication as her only form of escape. Still, she remained conscious enough to know everything they did. For awhile, they took turns putting their genitals into her mouth but it didn't seem long before she felt her pants and underwear stripped off, fingers poking inside of her, and her legs spread open and held. Despite her incoherence, she couldn't ignore the pain of one, then the other, back and forth, eventually turning her over and taking her that way. Like a dog. Like a... *bitch*. She remembered their shouts. Their laughter. And their unforgettable howling sounds as they ejaculated inside of her. Like wolves. Like *Lobos*.

She didn't know how many times, or how long the ordeal lasted, but when it was finally over, she lay in a semi-conscious state in her car, naked and bleeding, with her clothes heaped in the back seat. As dawn broke, a sudden flash of recognition reminded her of where she was, her nakedness, and the unspeakable experience she had endured. In panic, Veronica lunged for the door locks, but the brutal cramping and burning pain from her violation struck without warning, causing her to collapse against the seat.

Veronica opened the door and vomited to a point of near unconsciousness. She cried with relief when she saw her keys still dangling from the ignition and her clothes crumpled in the back seat. Struggling to dress, she couldn't avoid looking at the caked blood on her inner thighs. Desperate to find her way out of the isolated canyon, she drove along unknown stretches of road until she somehow approached the familiar streets leading to her home. The tears fell heavier at the sight of her driveway, but the loud sobs erupted as violent and sudden as an earthquake when she entered the house.

TₜT TₜT TₜT

For her brother's protection, Veronica persuaded her mother to refrain from telling him anything. She knew that Alex wouldn't rest until he accomplished his own form of justice, and that he would either kill or be killed. She intended to protect him from dying, either at the hands of the Lobos or the hands of the law.

Veronica also refused to let her mother take her to the emergency hospital. She took Miguel's threats seriously and knew the doctor would recognize what happened and inform the police. She had her mother purchase two home pregnancy tests, one for each week it took to recover. When the tests showed a pregnancy hadn't occurred, that made her hopeful, but the confirmation from her next period removed any uncertainty. When she regained enough strength to leave the house, she went straight to the hospital for an HIV test. Upon hearing the results as negative, she broke down from the final, lingering fear of the real-life nightmare that had plagued her every waking moment. She emerged a changed woman, losing confidence in her own judgment and her previous faith in God. With a heart cloaked in doubt and cautiousness, her life now centered on the one goal of earning her degree and leaving the neighborhood behind forever.

TWENTY-SEVEN

KEVIN PALMER IS ON VACATION. That's how the announcement read at the bottom of the second page of Monday's *Los Angeles Times.* Truth be told, he'd been suspended for a week, justified by accusations such as "exhibiting shoddy professionalism" and "a disturbing lack of respect for his job." One more screw-up and the only thing he'd be writing is a resume.

Kevin quit his previous job at *The Daily News* before his impending termination, when the importance of his drinking superseded his deadlines. He wondered if that same path confronted him again. Each evening, between the time Seth went to bed and the completion of his articles, he consumed the required amount of alcohol to prevail through another night. In his attempt at balancing work and inebriation, he attempted changing his routine by writing during the day, but he scrapped that unlikable idea and returned to his original practice of working at night, convinced he could make the combination manageable.

He believed his firing an imminent reality when his boss summoned him into the office, so he took the news of the suspension with a certain amount of relief. With valid indictments hanging over his head, he knew better than to let pride interfere with the person who held the noose with one hand and the lever to the trap door in the other. His biggest concern over this entire scenario concerned the possible investigation by the Department of Child and Family Services. The court documents showed him to be Seth's legal guardian, but those people wouldn't look too kindly upon a guardian with a suspected drinking problem.

His frustration over Veronica anchored his emotions further. Seth's association with her seemed beneficial, contributing towards a healthier attitude towards school, but Kevin's own relationship with Veronica remained stuck in neutral. From the day they had that first coffee together at the mall, he thought of little else but her. Meeting Veronica for other lunches left him hopeful, yet nothing more had transpired. Phone calls and e-mails, sometimes nonsensical, other times heartfelt, had become an enjoyable routine between the two of them, but in person her demeanor seemed reserved much of the time, as if she was a different woman. In those few instances when Veronica appeared outgoing and laughed freely, she provided a calming effect on his psyche, and his spirits would lift, albeit temporarily.

Kevin desired her more than any woman he'd ever known, but Veronica's curvaceous body continued to form nothing more than a shapely question mark. The impenetrable wall around her needed to be removed and he believed he now understood the reason for her hesitancy; he was white and she was a Latina. Veronica's unwillingness to take the plunge from the safety net of friendship to the mysterious excitement of a love affair proved disheartening, but Kevin was determined to pierce that social armor.

Until then, however, without Veronica or assurances of a future together, Kevin consoled himself at bedtime with the only substitute available to him. He made love to his scotch.

ᛏᛈᛏ ᛏᛈᛏ ᛏᛈᛏ

As Veronica entered the lobby of the day care center, Kevin rose from his chair and approached her. "I need to talk with you," he said.

"Can it wait?" she asked. "I have to get back to work right now."

"Then I'll come back when you're finished," he replied, an unintended tone of urgency to his voice.

"Alright," she said. "Sounds like it's important. I'll be done at 4:30."

When he returned to his car, he sat for a while, seeking to calm his anxiety. Checking the time, he realized he had over two hours. Without any work to do, he decided to go to a hamburger joint where he and Seth had eaten before. On his way there, Kevin called him at home.

"Can I eat the leftovers in the fridge?" Seth asked. "I'm hungry."

"Sure, go ahead," he said. "I called to let you know I have a meeting with Veronica at 4:30. I'm not sure how long it'll take."

A lengthy pause followed. "Is it about me?"

"No," Kevin answered. "This time it's about me."

"You?"

"Yeah, me. And her, too."

174

A familiar Eric Clapton guitar lick blared over the speakers as Kevin walked through the doors of the restaurant. He plucked a *Newsweek* magazine from a rack near the hostess counter, ordered a cheeseburger and fries, and started thumbing through the pages of the magazine. An article on Latino gangs in America's southern states and the alarming rise in violence drew his attention. The region's most violent gang was MS-13, *Mara Salva Trucha*. The *Times* had also written about this gang in the past, and Kevin still remembered several disturbing facts: They were a group of thirty to fifty thousand strong in at least a half a dozen countries, including an approximate ten thousand membership in the United States. MS-13 first formed in Los Angeles in the 1980's, originating from the guerrillas and refugees escaping the civil war in El Salvador. Now they were spreading through the south like a noxious virus, to places like Fairfax County, Virginia, Gwinnett County, Georgia, and Charlotte, North Carolina. The article made Kevin realize how much he'd changed, that his past rationalizations about poverty and lack of education as causes for the gang culture, what Warren always labeled as "excuse-making bullshit," was just that; excuse-making bullshit. MS-13? The North Rampart Lobos? The Alvarado Street Diablos? There was no justifying the type of individuals they were. These sick-minded, violent thugs didn't possess an ounce of human decency.

Kevin tossed the magazine aside when his lunch arrived, contemplating, once again, how he'd approach the sensitive subject of race. "*I understand the importance of culture and family history,*" he would say. "*I never want to deprive you of who you are and what you stand for.*" He closed his eyes, picturing the unpleasant scene, an unhappy ending based on her upbringing and racial divisions. "*I'm sorry, but I can't,*" she would tell him. "*I care for you as a friend but we could never be lovers.*" He couldn't let that happen. Kevin feared his burgeoning apprehension might cause him to do or say the wrong thing. He felt too wound up and needed a drink.

Spotting the waitress, he waved his hand to get her attention.

"What can I getcha?" she asked.

"Tell the bartender I want your finest scotch, please," he said.

Returning several minutes later, the waitress set the auburn-colored glass on Kevin's table. Looking at his watch he replied, "I may want another one."

Ten minutes later Kevin ordered a second scotch. Halfway through that one, his confidence level had increased. He pictured a different scene in Veronica's office, culminating in an embrace and passionate kiss. He left the restaurant feeling a sweet sense of optimism surging inside of him. He entered his car and realized he'd forgotten his breath mints, but was that really such a big deal? Everything was going to be all right. Driving with extra caution, he arrived at 4:30, took a deep breath, and made his approach towards the dawn of a new life with the woman he loved.

TTT TTT TTT

Kevin sauntered into the day care center and watched as a frail, red-haired boy gave Veronica a big hug. "See you next time," he told her.

"Don't forget your poetry, Jimmy," she replied, cupping the back of his head with her hand. "I want to read it."

"For sure," he answered.

Looking towards Kevin, Veronica smiled. "You're not the only writer in this room, Mr. Palmer," she said.

Kevin looked at Jimmy. "I'm sure you got me beat in the poetry department, kiddo. Roses are red, violets are blue, but I can't rhyme as well as you."

Veronica gave Kevin a quizzical look and turned towards the woman standing with the young boy. "I'll see Jimmy in two weeks, Lynn," she said.

Kevin winked at Veronica as she escorted them into the lobby. When she returned, she looked at Kevin with a slight tilt of her head. "You're sure acting a lot different," she said, displeasure in her voice. "You sounded so serious before, you had me worried."

Smiling, Kevin held his hand up in a defensive gesture.

"Don't be."

"All right," she said, seeming unconvinced. "What is it?"

Rising from his chair, Kevin took a couple of steps closer. "I like a story with a happy ending," he said. "That's what I hope this will be."

Veronica backed up a step, squinted her eyes, and stared at Kevin with an unmistakable seriousness.

"Something wrong?" he asked.

"Now I understand the change in your behavior," she said angrily. "You've been drinking, haven't you? I can smell it on your breath."

Kevin attempted his best disarming smile. "Guilty as charged," he said.

"In the middle of the day?"

He motioned with his hand towards a couple of chairs. "Do you mind if we sit down?"

"Let's talk in the office where I tutor Seth," she said. "Dr. Hobart asked me to file some papers before I go home."

Veronica walked ahead of Kevin. As he followed behind her, his eyes luxuriated in a slow, vertical journey up the back of her legs, like two ascending bubbles in a lava lamp. He visualized her naked bronze skin under the blue cotton sweater and black skirt. Kevin took a deep, inaudible breath, and reminded himself to stay cool and remember what he was there for. As they entered the room, Veronica sat at the desk as Kevin walked to the couch near the aquarium. He sat and looked at her while she shuffled through papers.

"Veronica," he said, pointing to the couch, "I need you to be here."

Picking up a stack with each hand, she looked discouraged. "See all this? Are you sure?"

"Quite sure," he replied. Scooting over across the couch, Kevin patted the open cushion. "Please. Sit down."

With a slight shrug of her shoulders, Veronica placed the papers back on her desk and advanced towards him. Remaining standing, she looked at Kevin with an annoyed expression.

"First tell me why you got drunk."

"I'm not drunk," he countered.

"Then tell me this," she said. "Are you sober?"

Kevin looked away for a few uncomfortable moments. "No, I guess not," he muttered. Fixing his eyes on her again he added, "So I had a drink. Is it really so important to know why?"

"To me it is, yes," she replied without hesitation.

Kevin patted the open seat of the couch again. "Sit down first, okay?" he asked.

After some apparent misgiving, she relented. "Okay, I'm sitting. Your turn."

"The truth? I was nervous about talking with you. I had a couple of drinks after lunch to calm down."

"A *couple* of drinks?" she asked, her eyes widening. "Since when have a couple of drinks been necessary to talk with me, Kevin? That makes me feel uncomfortable."

Kevin reached out for her hand. "The last thing in the world I want to do is make you feel uncomfortable," he told her. "Just hear me out, okay?"

"Well?" she said, her eyebrows narrowing. "You've got my attention."

"Veronica," he said, pausing again to take a quick breath, "when it comes to us, you've asked me to wait, to be patient. I think I've done a pretty good job. You and I... we both want the best for Seth, of course, but we need to think of ourselves, too. I know it's a cliche, but life's too short, you know what I mean? What I'm trying to say is... I think you know how much I care for you. I think about you all the time. But I want more. You won't even let me kiss you. I'm afraid to put my arm around you. I've wondered about it, trying to figure it all out. And I think I know what the problem is. And it shouldn't *be* a problem. What I need to ask you is... are you against having a relationship with me because... I'm white?"

Veronica gasped, staring at him in silence. Kevin didn't know what to think, recognizing that his comments hung suspended like a flapping kite stuck in a tree. He couldn't tell whether he should say something more or wait for an answer. He felt dejected and skeptical, figuring the longer she took to reply, the more likely she didn't share his feelings. Rising from the couch, Kevin walked towards the aquarium, grateful for the excuse to keep his back turned and his attention diverted.

From somewhere beyond the world of his own thoughts, an unexpected noise infiltrated his consciousness. Kevin lifted his gaze and realized that Veronica elicited a suppressed, breathy kind of sound that he interpreted as laughter. He wheeled around, prepared to defend the integrity of his honesty and courage. But with her face engulfed in trembling hands, Veronica sat sobbing on the couch, rocking back and forth like a holy person in prayer. Kevin went to her side and placed a tentative hand on her arm.

"Sshhh, everything will be fine," he whispered, not knowing what else to say. "Calm down, Veronica. Calm down."

The violent sobs subsided into an eventual silence. With a few deep breaths Veronica looked at Kevin. Her eyes had turned red and puffy, and her mouth quivered as she spoke.

"Is that what you think, Kevin?" she asked in a hoarse whisper. "I couldn't love you because you're white?"

"I'm sorry, maybe I was wrong, but..."

"*You're so wrong!*" she blurted, tears reappearing in her eyes. "*You have no idea! No idea! You don't know!*"

"Know what?" he asked, taking her hand and offering a gentle squeeze. "Please, Veronica, tell me. What don't I know?"

Several strands of hair had fallen across her face as she stared straight ahead, as if under a hypnotic spell. Her thoughts seemed centered on something agonizing and far away. Kevin asked the same question again.

"What don't I know, Veronica?"

She turned to face him. Several more strands of hair had fallen over her bloodshot eyes. Wanting to see her face, *needing* to see her face, Kevin reached out to brush the hair back, drawing a defensive lurch backwards.

"I only wanted to brush the hair back from your face," he said. "I'm sorry."

"It's not you," she said, wiping her eyes. "I'm the one who's sorry." The tears spilled again. "I'm sorry for everything."

"I thought I had it all figured out," he said. "Whatever it is, I feel so stupid. I just didn't know what to think."

"I'm... afraid," she said in a near whisper.

"Afraid?" he repeated. "Of what? Me?"

"Of love," she said. "I'm afraid... to love you."

"But why?" he asked, his eyes clinging to hers. "I don't understand."

"It's like you said before, Kevin. I haven't even let you kiss me. If you only knew how much I want to kiss you. But I'm afraid to be... to be..."

"Afraid to be what, Veronica? What?"

"*To be touched by a man!*" she wailed. "*By... you!*"

Kevin watched in silence as Veronica turned away, staring at the floor. "How can I forget that night?" she asked aloud, her voice sounding cold and measured. "They *forced* me. I was so afraid! So much... *pain*." Veronica covered her face and broke down again.

"Tell me everything that happened, Veronica," he said, dread spreading in his gut. "I want to know."

Veronica swallowed hard. Grabbing his hand, she squeezed with enough force to cause the tips of his fingers to go red. "They raped me." She looked into his eyes, laboring to continue. "Their names were Viper... and Miguel. *King*. That's what Miguel told me to call him after he hit me. *King*." Kevin kept his eyes on hers, his sadness struggling to suppress his rage. "They made me drink... and do things, she said, trembling. "That's why I was angry with you when you came back here. The alcohol on your breath. I was reminded of..."

Kevin held up his hand to stop her. He knew what she was going to say; he just couldn't bear to hear her say it.

"Can you ever forgive me?" he asked in a quiet voice. "I promise I'll quit. I would never do anything to hurt you. You know that, don't you?"

She nodded her head.

"I know I'm telling you something you already know, but there are places for rape victims to go for help."

"I couldn't talk about it," she answered, her voice little more than a hoarse whisper. "I was so ashamed. I just wanted to graduate from school. Move away and find a job somewhere. I couldn't even say the word."

"So you never went to the police?"

Veronica closed her eyes, shaking her head back and forth. "They said if I ever told anyone they'd hurt Alex. And they'd do something terrible to my friend, Patricia. My mother is the only person who knows." She looked deep into his eyes. "I grew up in a rough neighborhood, Kevin. Where I come from, revenge is a way of life. Alex was raised on those beliefs. If I had told him, he wouldn't have stopped until he found them and killed them both. Nothing else would have been good enough. And I don't want my brother going to prison. Or worse. That's why I don't want him to know."

"Is Alex in a gang?" he asked.

Veronica took a long, slow breath. Avoiding his eyes, she looked down at the floor again. "Yes," she answered. "The Alvarado Street Diablos."

Kevin closed his eyes. He loved her too much to turn back now.

"Small world," he replied, his voice low and tight.

"If you leave right now and never come back, I'll understand," she told him.

Kevin placed his hands on each side of Veronica's head. Bringing his face to hers, he kissed her forehead. "I'm not going anywhere," he replied. "You mean more to me than any woman I've ever known. The single thing I'm in a rush to do is make you happy. I'll do whatever it takes, as long as it takes. I want to be the man that teaches you how to trust again. I want to be the man you learn to love."

He reached out for her, and she, in turn, wrapped her arms around his back with her head pressed against his chest. They held that position for a long while, soothed in silence, as he gazed out the window with a new found purpose. As the dimming light signaled the end of another day, Kevin saw the sparkling prospects of a new horizon.

But storms can strike without warning.

TWENTY-EIGHT

KING COULDN'T BELIEVE HIS GOOD luck. A few days before, his depression gripped him by the balls, leaving him angry and without hope. Those feelings seemed far away now. He had been overdue for a change in fortune, and now Lady Luck seemed to be stroking his dick more and more each day. Fate started to turn his way when he finally discovered the one responsible for arranging Viper's death. Killing Alejandro Torres would not only honor Viper's memory, but also deliver payback from the time that asshole tackled him on the sidewalk and left him with the wrinkled scar drooping over his left eye. Now, sitting on the couch in King's apartment, a gang-banger wannabe named Javier presented him with the perfect news about his old neighbor.

"I live a block from Alejandro's house," he said to King. "My mother talks with his sometimes. She told her he's always fixin' up cars in his driveway. He fixed my mother's, too."

King stared at Javier in silence, sizing him up. "You lookin' to bang with the Lobos, little man?"

Javier nodded. "Yeah," he replied. "That's what I been tellin' Luis."

"How old are you?"

"Thirteen," he answered. "But I'm not too young, man. I'm tough. I don't take shit. I'm ready to be a Lobo."

King laughed. "A bad-ass dude, huh? You wanna beer, bad-ass dude?"

Javier smiled and looked over at Luis, sitting on King's bed. "You're right, Luis. Your brother's cool."

Luis returned with three cold Budweisers, handing cans to Javier and King and keeping one for himself. King downed almost half of his before resuming his conversation. "Understand somethin'," he said, speaking with an intensity he didn't show earlier. "It doesn't matter how fuckin'

Keith Steinbaum

old you are. A thirteen-year-old bangin' with the Lobos gotta be ready to fight to the death, *si es necessaria*. Are you tough enough, Javier? To be jumped into the gang?"

Javier gave King a puzzled look. "What's 'jumped into the gang' mean?"

"You gotta be tested, man," King snapped. "Beat on, you understand? You got the *cojones*, Javier? You think your thirteen-year old balls are big enough to deal with that shit?"

Javier nibbled on his lower lip, glancing at Luis before looking back at King. "Yeah, man. I'm down."

King smiled. "You gonna do what I ask?"

Javier cradled the beer can with both hands. Without saying anything at first, he took a few swallows and then wiped his mouth with his sleeve. "I wanna be a Lobo," he said. "What do you want me to do?"

King figured what Javier lacked in street cred, he made up for in his desire to please. And he lived near Torres. That crucial part of the plan meant King had found the small trap he needed. The time had come to catch the rat. Then he'd blow him away.

"You know anything about cars, Javier? How to fix somethin'?"

"I helped my mom change a tire once," he said.

"You ever talk to Torres?"

"No," he replied. "But I met him the day my mom got her car back."

King rubbed his hands together. Swigging the rest of his beer, he belched and brought his face close to Javier's. "Listen to me good, goddammit" he said. "If you do what I tell you, give me the fuckin' information I need, you'll be bangin' with the Lobos real soon. But if you fuck up, man, you better run the other way any time you see one of us comin'. You understand the game, Javier?"

Javier took another sip of beer before giving King a slow nod of his head.

"Good," King said. "Now listen to me. Go to their house. Ask Torres to teach you 'bout fixin' cars and shit. Offer to fetch his tools, or clean 'em, whatever the fuck it takes to stick around. Just get him to trust you, got it?"

"Is that it?" Javier asked.

"Shut up, asshole, I ain't finished," King snapped. "When you become his little assistant, you'll report back to me every fuckin' time you know he's workin' on a car."

"What are you gonna do?" Javier asked.

"That ain't your fuckin' business, you little punk! Don't go askin' me shit, understand? You wanna be a North Rampart Lobo or no? Huh? *Huh?*"

Javier looked down, avoiding King's stare. "I'm sorry, King. Don't be mad, okay?"

King glared at Javier. "I gotta know if you're serious 'bout becomin' a Lobo, man. This is fuckin' important to me. You gonna represent or what?"

"Fuck, yeah," Javier replied, a rapid nod of his head. "I'll do whatever you want, King."

"Goddamn good answer, little man," King said, breaking into a smile. "Time for another beer."

King told Ram about Javier later that day.

"Little shit's gonna do everything I tell him to do," he said. "Our time's comin', man. Gonna be some sweet fireworks when I start shootin' that Diablo's ass."

"That's cool, King," Ram said, his voice subdued.

"What the fuck's the matter with you, man? Fun and games are almost here again and you sound like you don't give a shit."

"There's talk of a truce with the Diablos, he told him. "Until this shit blows over."

"*Truce, my ass!*" King roared. "I don't wanna hear that shit from you, man! Not when we're so close!"

"Some of us are wonderin' what's the point, you know? Some motherfucker wants both gangs dead and we're just helpin' him get there faster."

King's anger made him want to reach through the phone and wrap his hands around Ram's neck. "You gave me your goddamn word, Ram! Don't back down now! I need you at the wheel of that fuckin' drive-by, you understand me?"

Ram remained silent for several moments. "All right," he said. "I told you I would so I'll be there."

"Gracias, *vato*, "King replied, his tone calm again. "You ain't the only one gave his word, okay? I promised Viper payback when he died, man. Shouted it to the goddamn skies. This whole time he's been up there waitin' for his homeboy to do right." King took a deep breath. "He's waited long enough."

TWENTY-NINE

"JAVIER, YOU REMEMBER WHAT THE filter wrench looks like?"

"The one with the loop on the end, right?"

"Yeah. Bring it over here. I'll show you how to change the oil."

Three weeks had passed since Javier first approached Face as he worked on a car in his driveway. "You're Alejandro Torres, right?" he said. "My name's Javier Ramos. You worked on my mom's car. Olivia Ramos, remember?"

"Yeah, I remember," he replied, glancing at Javier from the open hood before resuming his inspection of the engine. "Transmission flush. New drive belt. Why? More problems?"

"No, no, nothin' like that," Javier said, taking a couple of steps closer. "I was just wondering if you could show me how to fix cars like you do."

"You gonna pay me?" Alejandro asked, his gaze still fixed on the engine.

"I ain't got no money, man," Javier replied. "But I could be your helper."

"I don't need no fuckin' helper."

"Look at your tools," Javier said. "You got 'em all over your driveway. I could fetch 'em for you when you need 'em. Clean 'em too, if you want."

The kid's offer got Face's attention, and as he rolled the idea around in his head, he turned away from the engine, reached up to close the hood, and grabbed the remains of a torn tee shirt. He stared at Javier, unsure about the idea of having the kid ask a million questions as he worked.

"I get paid for workin' on these cars," he said, wiping the grease from his hands. "I ain't got time to waste teachin' you shit."

"But I could save you time, right?" Javier said. "I've seen you work before. You're always lookin' around on the ground, trying to find somethin'. I could help you go faster."

"Come back tomorrow," he told him. "I'll try you for a day and then I'll decide."

"What time you want me?"

"Eleven o'clock. We'll go over tools. I'll tell you what they're for. Then you'll clean 'em."

On the third weekend working with Javier, Face taught him something new.

"Before we get under the car, I'll explain about changing oil." Face held the filter wrench in one hand and a drain pan in the other. "Under the car there's a drain plug you gotta unscrew to let all the old sludge out." Extending his arm so Javier could get a better view of the drain pan, he continued. "You use this to catch the shit. When that's done, you loosen the oil filter with the filter wrench. When it's real loose, unscrew the rest with your hand."

Javier seemed distracted. Face had observed him looking up and down the street several times that day, showing an apparent lack of interest in anything he said. When Javier's attention returned to the filter wrench, he looked like he couldn't give a shit. "Yeah, okay," he answered.

"Hey, you gonna listen to me or not, man? If you're bored go home."

"No, no, really, I wanna learn," Javier replied, snapping back to attention. "Sorry."

Face stared at Javier. The kid's behavior seemed unusual. "We're gonna get under the car now," he said. "I'll explain the rest when we're..." In an instant, Face went silent and his body stiffened. A dizzying array of flashing lights caused him to shut his eyes and grapple with a momentary loss of balance. He suddenly visualized two people driving towards him in a brown Impala convertible and a semi-automatic pointing out the window. In his head he heard the distinctive sound of bullets tearing through the air coupled with a fiery light exploding outward. But he saw the shooting occurring somewhere else, with the Impala just a few feet away and some fat kid standing in front of the car in danger of getting hit. He recognized the area as someplace in the neighborhood, but a drive-by headed towards his house and he had to act fast.

Face looked up the street and spotted the Impala making a slow turn from around a corner two blocks to the west. He couldn't run inside the house and put his mother in harm's way from spraying bullets so he snatched the car keys out of his pocket preparing to drive away.

"Javier!" he shouted, seizing his arm. "Run home! Hurry!"

The boy ignored Face's plea as he scanned the street again. Pulling away from his grasp, Javier backed away, a revealing smile appearing on his face. "Lobos gonna kick your ass, man!" he yelled.

Face realized the little punk had set him up for this. With a swift lurch forward, he grabbed Javier by the hair and yanked his head down as his knee came up, catching the boy square on the nose and causing him to drop to the ground, screaming in pain. As he ran towards his Firebird, the advancing car accelerated, accompanied by the full throttled sound of its engine. Jamming the key into the ignition, the car didn't start on the first attempt, but ignoring his dwindling chances of survival, Face's second attempt got the engine roaring its intention.

He shifted into drive and slammed his right foot on the accelerator just as the Impala knocked against the side of his back bumper. Losing control for a brief moment, he regained command and sped down Council Street. Hoping to catch them off guard, he made a sharp right turn at the Dawson Street alley but two misplaced trash cans blocked his path. Having no time to consider their weight, he scattered them like two oversized bowling pins. He sped off, but those several seconds of decreased speed allowed the Impala to close the gap. Face glanced in his rearview mirror and caught sight of the MAC-90 assault rifle directed towards his car. His ability to increase his distance on these small, narrow streets seemed doubtful, so he decided to try for the safety of the freeway. If he escaped from the alley he could take Rockwood Street to Belmont, north to Temple, east to Glendale Boulevard, and get on the 101.

Nearing Rockwood, Face tightened his grip when he saw some boys playing soccer at the end of the alley. He leaned on his horn to force them out of the way, but as he prepared to make a right turn he hit the breaks when a fat kid, *the fat kid*, darted out from behind a large bush into the middle of the alley and froze in apparent terror at the sight of the onrushing cars. Face now recognized the same area he had visualized a few minutes before. The pursuing driver increased his speed, trying to force his way along the driver's side of the Firebird, but Face spun his wheel to the far left and stepped on the accelerator, blocking the path of the Impala and preventing the boy from getting hit. As the front left bumper of Face's car made contact, the Lobos skidded to a halt, allowing the fat kid to escape unharmed. Face caught a split-second glimpse of the Lobo holding the MAC-90. He had a hairless, fleshy scar where much of the eyebrow should have been, and Face had the fleeting thought that he had seen the shooter before. The Lobo brought the rifle up to take aim.

Swerving back to the right in an attempt to escape the bullets, Face heard the blast of gunfire and exploding glass a split-second before a detonation of severe pain throughout his entire left arm. The fire-like sensation surged and spread, leaving his arm dangling like a cracked twig. He felt the blood dampening his shirt, but couldn't tell how much he was losing or how fast. He gripped the wheel with his right hand as the pulsating blasts of pain threatened to overtake his ability to drive. Kicking hard on the accelerator, Face hurried into the street towards Belmont knowing they intended to finish him off. The eastbound traffic on Temple Street forced him to stop at several points as the Lobos remained on his tail, weaving through other cars to maintain a close presence. He wondered if they'd follow him onto the freeway. The unrelenting throbbing grew tougher to ignore, his dilemma harder to solve.

The break he needed appeared in the form of a large eighteen-wheeler heading north on Glendale Boulevard. The driver of the truck had stopped at the light with his left blinker flashing, signaling his intention to turn west on Temple. Face slowed to a stop at his green light, shifted into park, and gunned his engine several times, pretending to have mechanical trouble. As a multitude of horns blared around him and the green light changed to red, Face concentrated on the truck now easing forward into the middle of the street starting his turn. Waiting until the last possible second, Face punched hard on the accelerator while veering left in front of the truck, avoiding a collision with the startled driver by a few feet. Streaking up Glendale Boulevard to Bellevue Avenue, he looked back and saw the truck completing its turn, blocking the path of the Impala and preventing it from advancing any further. Less than half a minute later, as he sped onto the 101 North entrance of the Hollywood Freeway, he knew he'd overcome one problem while another had reached the breaking point.

Face needed immediate attention, but driving himself to an ER meant talking with authorities he wanted to keep away from. He trusted one person to get him to a doctor and avoid dealing with the police, but his cell phone sat at the bottom of his left pocket -the same side where he'd been hit. Unable to use his left arm, he hoped to make it to her street, pull over to the side, and rip off the pocket with his right hand in order to reach his phone. The cars on the freeway sped along like normal, but reaching each off-ramp seemed a more arduous task than the one before. Face gritted his teeth and focused through the pain and sudden lightheadedness, determined to endure every necessary struggle to reach his sister, Veronica.

THIRTY

"**I** SWEAR, VERONICA, I NEVER *EVER* WANT to see James again!"

Veronica tried to pay attention and offer compassion to her heartbroken roommate, but she'd heard this all before. Right now she needed to leave for Kevin's house, where she planned to meet his mother for the first time.

"Kimberly, you're my best friend," she said, gathering her purse and car keys. "I'll always be there for you, but right now I've got to go. I guess you'll be spending more time here again so we'll have plenty of chances to talk, I promise."

On her way towards the garage, Veronica thought about her own relationship. With all of Kevin's attributes, his greatest gift to her remained his continued patience about anything sexual, maintaining his promise to take as much time as she required. Kevin's understanding exceeded her expectations over anything she thought possible for a man. She had learned to *trust* him, and maybe, just maybe, a transformation had started. That impenetrable wall, which once seemed so encompassing and protective, was, she sensed, dismantling brick by brick. Perhaps one day she'd be ready.

Arriving at her car, Veronica placed a container of homemade enchiladas on the passenger seat. She grew dismayed at the sight of the clock on the dashboard showing 2 p.m. "*I should have been there by now,*" she scolded herself. As the security gate opened, Veronica spotted a green Firebird parked across the street that looked identical to Alex's car, with the same colored flames on the side. Pulling out from the garage, she realized the open window on the driver's side had been shattered, with only small shards of glass still clinging to the frame. A sudden, escalating wave of panic overtook her. Veronica jerked the wheel to make a u-turn

189

and parked behind the Firebird. She rushed from her car and looked through the open window. Her hand muffled the sound of her scream when she saw Alex lying on the front seat with his shirt darkened by fresh blood.

Veronica leaned into the car. "Alex!" she shouted. "Alex! Can you hear me?"

Her brother rolled his head upward to look at her. "Veronica," he whispered, "need... your help."

She nodded. "You'll have to sit up. Do you understand? Do you think you can sit up?"

"Don't know," he murmured. "I'll... try."

Veronica looked at her wounded brother, hoping she hadn't found him too late. She ran to her car and waited for a chance to maneuver alongside his door before turning her hazard lights on and getting out. She heard a harsh yell that froze her in her tracks. Alex had achieved an upright position, taking deep, labored breaths.

"Alex, can you get out?" He closed his eyes and nodded, his pain obvious. She opened her passenger door and turned back. "Alright, Alex," she said, fighting back panic. "Come on!" Trying her best to support his weight, Veronica held him by the waist and summoned all her strength to help him into the car. She eased him in and put her face close to his. "I have to move your car where nobody can see it," she told him. "Do you think you can hang on?"

Alex closed his eyes and nodded. Veronica rushed into the Firebird and drove the car to the visitor parking spaces in the back lot of her apartment building. She slammed the door shut and ran back to the street, relieved to see Alex's eyes open and looking at her. Within moments she headed for the emergency room of the same hospital where she worked as the day care center director. She understood the hospital's obligation to report a shooting incident, but she couldn't take the chance of Alex talking with the police. Veronica hesitated as she reached for her phone, uncertain if she placed her job and reputation at risk by the call she needed to make.

"Stephen, I need your help!" she cried out.

"Veronica?" Dr. Hobart replied. "What's the matter?"

"My brother's been shot."

"*Shot?*" he echoed. "Oh my God. What's his condition?"

"I don't know. His shirt's full of blood. I'm really worried."

"Where are you now?"

"On my way to the hospital," she said, her voice cracking. "That's why I called you. I need your help."

"What do you want me to do?"

"Call them for me, Stephen. Tell them *not* to call the police. Please. It's very important."

"I don't know if I can do that," he told her. "There are regulations that have to be followed with any gunshot."

"Stephen, *please*. I can't have the police talking to my brother. Not yet."

"I'll ask them for you but they may not listen to me," he said. "What happened with your brother?"

"I'll explain everything later, I promise," she answered. "But right now I just want to get to the ER as fast as possible."

"I certainly hope he's going to recover," Hobart said. "But if the police aren't called in now they'll definitely question you if he doesn't make it. Do you understand?"

"Yes," she said quietly. "Of course."

"I don't like being in the dark on this, Veronica," he said, his discontent obvious. "It goes against my better judgment. But knowing you as I do, I'll see what can be done."

Glancing over at the sight of her wounded, moaning brother, Veronica hoped what she had always hoped for from the time he was a little boy: that he would be all right.

TTr TTr TTr

He had cleaned the house, returned from the market, chopped the vegetables and prepared the marinade for the chicken. Kevin should have now had his ear pressed against the kitchen door, listening in on the conversation between his mother and Veronica. But he had no clue where she was, and her roommate had informed him she left in a rush over an hour before. Calling her cell phone had proven fruitless up to that point, but he continued to leave messages each time, including a few minutes ago.

Kevin returned to the front room where Seth sat playing a video game and his mother worked on a crossword puzzle. "I don't know what to say other than, 'I'm sorry, Mom'," he said. "I called her again and left another message."

"Do you think she's okay?" Seth asked.

"At this point, I don't know what to think," Kevin replied.

"It's possible that something came up and she can't answer her phone," his mother said, looking up from the paper.

"Maybe you're right," he said. "But there must be a good reason why she hasn't called. She looked forward to meeting you."

The phone rang.

"Kevin!" Veronica was crying.

"Veronica! What's wrong? Where are you?"

"The hospital."

"*What?* What happened? Are you hurt?"

"It's not me," she answered softly. "I'm fine."

He exhaled with relief. "Then why are you there?"

"Alex," she said, her voice soft and raspy. "He was shot."

"Oh, no. How bad is it?"

"He lost a lot of blood, but..." Kevin could hear Veronica's muffled sobs. He turned back to Seth and his mother and mouthed, "*She's okay.*"

Veronica continued, sounding more under control. "They removed a bullet from deep in his shoulder. The doctor said he was lucky. A few more inches and he may not have survived."

"How long will he have to stay there?"

"They'll keep him overnight for observation. He's still pretty weak but if there are no complications they think he'll be able to leave about noon. I'm going to stay here with him."

"Would you like some company?" he asked. "You could probably use a hand to hold right now."

"Thanks, but not now, okay? I have to think about what to do with Alex. The doctor said he wants to see him next week and that he'll need at least ten days of care before he can start doing things on his own."

"Why can't he go home?" Kevin asked. "Your mother could give him the attention he'll need."

"Alex wasn't able to talk much, but he told me the Lobos came after him at the house. I'm sure they'll be looking for him. If he goes back too soon, they'll probably try something again. That could put my mother's life in danger, too."

"Will she be all right?"

"She's probably safer without him there. Maybe if they don't see his car for awhile, they'll move on to someone else."

The two pair of eyes in the room continued to look at him. He walked with the phone away from earshot. "Do you think the Lobos know where he is now?"

"I asked him the same question," she said. "He's certain he lost them. They don't leave their neighborhood much so Alex is safe here."

"Are you *sure* about that?"

"Yes," she replied. "If he'd been followed he'd be dead right now. I found him half-conscious and bleeding badly in his car. He wouldn't have been able to defend himself. That tells me he escaped."

"So he'll stay with you?" Kevin asked.

"That's not going to work either," she told him. "My roommate broke up with her boyfriend again, so she's going to be around for awhile. If I bring him home she'll start asking questions I don't want answered. I've never told her about my brother and the Diablos. I don't like anyone knowing about that part of my life."

"You're right," he said. "That's none of her business. How about renting a motel room until Alex is able to return home? If you need my help for any reason, you could stay at the Ramada Inn down the street from here."

"That would get expensive," she said. "And I can't afford to take time off from my job, so Alex would be left alone a lot."

"I'll help you with the money," he said.

"I won't have you paying for my problem, Kevin. And the thought of him being stuck in bed inside a motel room doesn't make me feel right."

"I love you, okay? That means your problem is my problem. That's the way I see things now."

"You don't know how much I appreciate that," she replied. "But whatever I decide has to come from me and me alone. The thing is, I don't have much time. I'll need a place by tomorrow and I'm not leaving here until he's released."

"I'm just trying to find something I can do," he said.

"I know," she said, the weariness in her voice apparent. "Right now I just need to sit down with a cup of coffee and decide what's best."

"Is Alex really going to be stuck in bed like you say?"

"The doctor told me he's going to feel very weak for awhile and to expect him to spend most of the next few days taking pain pills and drifting in and out of sleep."

"I have an idea, Veronica, but if Seth finds out it could ruin everything."

"I'm listening," she said.

"There's an add-on attached to my garage. The owner built it as a guest room when he lived here. I'm using it to store some of Warren's old things. It's got everything you'll need if we're only talking about you staying a few days. There's a bed for Alex, a couch you can sleep on, and a small bathroom with a tiny but workable shower. There's no refrigerator so you'll be on your own for food. Hopefully Alex will be released tomorrow at the time the doctor said he'd be. Seth will still be at school."

Veronica remained silent.

"Well?" Kevin asked.

"I can't believe you'd do that for me," she said. "Your emotions over my brother's gang are tied up in this, too."

"I'd be lying to you if I said I can't believe it, myself," he replied. "Maybe I don't know what I'm getting myself into. But remember, Veronica, you can only stay for a few days. The Department of Child and Family Services still checks up on me once in awhile, and I don't think they'd approve. And, of course, there's Seth. I'd hate to see what his reaction would be if he found out there was an Alvarado Street Diablo hanging out in the room by the garage."

"You're really something, Mr. Palmer," she said. "I guess I have some planning to do. It's a deal. I'll call you later."

Kevin hung up and stared into the receiver. *"What have I just done?"* he asked himself. *"Am I that selfish putting my desires to please Veronica over the health of Warren's son? What would Seth think if he knew I was doing a favor for an Alvarado Street Diablo? What kind of uncle am I? What kind of brother?"*

194

THIRTY-ONE

*F*ACE FELT LIKE SHIT, RECEIVING limited relief from the pain pills he'd taken every four hours since yesterday. Escorted outside by an attendant pushing his wheelchair, he took a deep breath of the cool, late October air. The Lobo who almost killed him, the one with a scar substituting for an eyebrow, remained as vivid as a photograph inside his head. But desire for payback needed to wait until he healed from his admittedly weakened state. Toiling through spasms of pain as he worked his way into Veronica's front seat, Face settled on the best possible position for minimizing his discomfort.

He stared out the window in silence at the landscaped green lawns and colorful flowers that continued from one block to the next. He contrasted the scenery before him with the cement and blacktop that dominated his own neighborhood, imagining what other differences existed away from the only life he'd ever known. Maybe he could open an auto shop somewhere in the Valley, finally dropping the flag to leave the warring world of the Diablos and Lobos behind. Veronica had escaped to start a new life, so why not him?

The car's front right tire rolled over a pothole and the sudden jerk intensified the grinding pain under his bandages. An audible groan escaped from his lips.

Veronica placed her hand on his knee. "I'm sorry," she said, "I didn't see that coming. Are you all right?"

"Yeah," he answered, teeth clenched against the pain.

"Are those pain pills working at all?"

"Don't know." Face glanced over at his sister and noticed her troubled expression. "*Qué pasa?*"

Veronica took a deep breath. "I have to tell you something," she said.

195

"We won't be staying at my apartment."

Face squirmed in his seat, trying to find a tolerable position. "You sendin' me back home?" he mumbled.

Veronica shook her head. "You know you have to stay away from there for awhile," she told him. "And my place won't work either. I don't want my roommate thinking you might be in a gang."

"They got fuckin' gangs everywhere," he muttered. "Welcome to my world, *chica.*"

Veronica glared at Face. "No, Alex," she told him, "welcome to *my* world. My *new* world. Where I got friends who aren't in gangs. And a great job. And a nice apartment in a safe neighborhood. I left *your* world behind to start a new life. You can't mess it up. You needed me to help you and I did. Now I need you to help me."

Face realized Veronica was right. He *had* needed her, forced his way into her life, and might have died without her help. She had rescued him in a big way, even pulling some strings to keep the police away.

"Okay," he said. "Where we goin'?"

"I've been seeing a man for awhile. A wonderful man. He lives with his nephew in a house that has a room next to the garage. It's got everything we need. A bathroom, a bed for you, and a couch I can sleep on. We can stay there for a few days until I find another place."

"Why ain't you afraid about him findin' out the truth? Like your roommate?"

"He already knows about you," she said, "but to him your name is Alex, not Face. Face has never come up in conversation, alright?"

"Ain't nobody can stop me from bein' who I am."

"*Oh, yeah?*" she yelled. "Is that right, *Face?*" Veronica moved over to the side of the road. "This isn't going to work," she said, wiping a tear away with the back of her hand. "If I can't stop *Face* from being who he is, then why don't I just drive *Face* back to his car. If he's so damn tough, he should go find the bangers who shot him and get his precious payback!"

"Be cool, Veronica," he said, to weak to argue. "That ain't what I meant. I'll be a perfect fuckin' angel."

Veronica stared at him for a long while before pulling back into the street. "There's something else you have to remember," she said. "His nephew also lives in the house, and he *doesn't* know about you." Veronica placed her hand on Face's knee again, giving him a meaningful glance. "He's not going to find out, Alex. He's not even going to know we're there. When he's home you can't leave the room."

Face offered Veronica a small smile of reassurance before turning back towards the window. "Don't wanna lay no 'hood shit on some suburban kid, huh?"

"It's too late for that," she replied. "Seth is the boy whose father got killed in that drive-by at Alfredo's Market."

Face's head swung around again.

"Do you remember?" she asked. "Warren Palmer was his name. The man I'm seeing is Warren's brother, Kevin. That's where we're going."

He stared at Veronica in silence. The same kid whose father got killed that night? How the hell did this happen? Was this more than just a crazy coincidence?

"I don't wanna talk right now," he said.

Face closed his eyes. He thought back again to the failed drive-by, and how he prevented Swat from firing in the direction of the kid. For some reason the police didn't come down hard like he expected them to do. Maybe they found out Swat did the killin', so what did it matter after he died? Atkinson told them Swat's heart attack turned out to be the first one -in his sleep that same night. The little *huero* kid represented the beginning of all the heart attack shit and now they'd be in the same house? Maybe Veronica should be told everything so she'd understand the craziness in his head right now. If he told her the truth she'd realize why they should stay somewhere else.

"Veronica?"

She looked at him and smiled. "Yes?"

Face looked into her eyes and saw the same familiar expression that provided comfort and reassurance after another one of his old man's beatings. He turned back to the window, his eyes anchored to the road. "Forget it," he mumbled.

ᛏᛃᛏ ᛏᛃᛏ ᛏᛃᛏ

After helping Veronica and Alex get settled, Kevin felt relieved when he closed the door, leaving them alone in the room. He'd received grudging permission to work at home that day and a read-between-the-lines suggestion to produce positive results on his article about L.A.'s Vietnamese community; another in a series highlighting the city's expanding cultures. As he started to write, however, he thought about the time that had passed since he last talked with Carl Atkinson. During their meeting at Phillipe's he had told Kevin he'd keep him updated about the situation with the North Rampart Lobos and the Alvarado Street Diablos, but they had only spoken once since that time. Kevin had moved on from his series of reports about L.A.'s Latino gang problem, but he hadn't lost any of his hunger for the latest developments involving the two gangs responsible for Warren's death. If the killer remained out there, he wanted him brought to justice. He also wanted to know if any answers had been uncovered in the strange riddle of the heart attacks -a story as unique as any he could recall, even by L.A.'s standards.

After leaving Atkinson a message, the telephone rang an hour later.

"Haven't heard from you in awhile, Carl," he said. "Let me guess. All this peace on earth, goodwill towards men shit has you spending your time on the golf course?"

Atkinson laughed. "Some things never change, Kevin. War in the world, violence in the streets, and your stupid sarcasm."

"Perhaps you're right," he said, "but I'm serious about wanting to be kept up to date about the heart attacks. Got anything new to tell me?"

"Do you remember the last time we spoke?" Atkinson asked. "About the meeting Captain Dean and I had with the gang members?"

Kevin reached for a pen and paper. "Yes," he said.

"I put it out there the best I could that day. Broke down every death from heart attack. Read off all the names. How one always follows another murder. And the four a.m. connection."

"What four a.m. connection?"

"Shit, I didn't tell you?" Atkinson kept silent for a moment before continuing. "Kevin, I swear, if I see any of this in print I'll come over there and..."

"Show me first hand what made you an All-City lineman two years running, right?"

"Right. So listen to this. You could set your watch to these heart attacks. The ability of the murderer to kill the victim at the same time, every time, is mind-boggling to say the least. We can't prove every one of them occurred at exactly four a.m., but we know a lot of them have. The others are very possibly the same time. Or damn close to it. My hunch is they're all four a.m."

A quiet whistle escaped Kevin's lips. Jotting down '4 a.m.' on the notepad, Kevin drew a large heart around it. "How can you be so sure?"

"Autopsies. Witnesses. Hell, after nineteen heart attacks, the pattern becomes obvious."

"Multiple murders? Same time of death? Move over, Son of Sam. Make room, Ted Bundy. You got company, fellas."

"They won't have company until he's caught," Atkinson remarked. "But you get the picture."

"After that meeting with the gang members, you told me you felt like you made a breakthrough," Kevin said. "Like they actually might have listened to you. It's been about a month and a half since we last talked, Carl. Any difference?"

"Like night and day," he answered. "Captain Dean and I have met each week since then to review the situation and as far as we know, there hasn't been one murder that can be attributed to the Lobos or Diablos. And as you might have guessed, not one heart attack." Atkinson chuckled. "Still no time for golf, though."

Kevin shook his head. "So let me get this straight. As long as the Lobos and Diablos stop killing each other, whoever's causing the heart attacks seems to have lost his desire. And this is where the story ends, and they all lived happily ever after?"

"That's not Kevin Palmer being sarcastic again, is it?"

"Shit, Carl, I can't help myself. This whole thing is so sad and ridiculous."

"In my line of work I've got to take the positive and run with it whenever I can," Atkinson said. "This last month and a half has been paradise compared to all the months before, so you better believe I'm happy. Or as the saying goes, 'cautiously optimistic'. In the meantime, we've still got a killer out there we have to find. And I'm keeping my fingers crossed the two gangs stick to their truce."

"Their *truce*? Is that what this is?"

"Well, there's no damn signatures on a peace treaty, okay?" Atkinson replied. "But if you look at all the years of violence between those gangs, what else would you call it?"

"Is there anything else you can tell me?" Kevin asked.

"No, nothing else," Atkinson answered.

"No fingerprints? Hair samples?"

"Sorry, Sherlock," Atkinson remarked. "This killer's incredibly shrewd. He hasn't made a mistake as far as we can tell. In all my years on the force, I've never faced off with anyone like this." Kevin heard the frustration in Carl's voice and decided to back off the subject. For now.

"Thanks, Carl," he said. "Don't forget about me, alright? Something's got to crack on this thing and I'll be waiting."

"How are things with Seth?"

"Better," he replied. "No *Hallmark* moments yet, but we'll see."

When Kevin placed the phone back on the cradle, he pretended the conversation still continued.

"*So what do you think of this, Carl?*" he said. "*My girlfriend's Alvarado Street Diablo brother was shot trying to escape another gang, no doubt our friends from the North Rampart Lobos. He's hiding out in my back room right now. As we speak. My own actual gangbanger houseguest. Am I as stupid as I sound?*"

Kevin jumped to his feet and went into his room, closing the door behind him. He removed the flask of scotch from his pocket and guzzled some down. He'd been a man of his word until the realization of his offer to Veronica struck home. "Just think of it as a concession towards my mental health, Veronica," he said softly, enjoying the warmth of his long lost friend. Walking into his bathroom and staring into the mirror, he recoiled at the eyes of guilt staring back at him. "*How could I have offered to let this guy stay?*" he asked himself. "*He's a goddamn Alvarado Street Diablo!*"

Kevin wondered if he'd ever be able to turn the page and give Veronica's brother a chance. "Turn the page?" he muttered. "There's not a book thick enough to ever bring Warren back." He took another large swig before placing the flask back into his pocket. After brushing his teeth (making sure to use a large dab of toothpaste), he deposited a couple of mints into his mouth and walked back into the front room. "*Just for awhile, Veronica,*" he said softly.

Kevin picked up the notepad and whistled softly as he stared at his drawing of the heart encircling the '4 a.m.' "*This guy's good,*" he whispered.

THIRTY-TWO

"**I**'M FUCKIN' GOIN' CRAZY IN HERE!" Face complained. "What's it been, four days? How long we gotta stick around this place?"

"Not much longer, Alex," Veronica replied, reapplying the ointment and bandages. "You need a couple of more days here, okay?"

"I'd rather hang at someone else's crib."

"Well, I wouldn't," she said. "All I'm asking is a little more time to make sure you're all right."

"You give Ma a story?"

"Yes," she answered. "I told her that you ran into an old friend who invited you up to Oxnard."

"Cool," he replied. "Thanks for coverin' for me."

"She's going to talk to you about breaking that boy's nose. His mother came to the house looking for you. Mama told me she was really angry."

"*Fuck* that asshole," Face muttered. "I told you he set me up. He's lucky I didn't kill him!"

"And you're lucky they didn't kill you."

"How you been sneakin' off to work without the kid findin' out?"

"There's a side door in the garage that leads to the trash cans. I slip through the gate and go around the corner where my car's parked. I don't like hiding in here either, Alex, but Kevin's offer was exactly what we needed."

"I'm feelin' better," Face told her. "Maybe I'll get me some fresh air. The kid's at school, right?"

"I heard the bus this morning so I know he's gone," she said. "But I don't know what time he comes home, okay? If Seth ever sees you..."

"I know," he said. "The kid'll shit."

201

"You're still not well yet, Alex. The wound still looks bad. Be careful."

Veronica looked at her watch. "I've got to go," she told him, helping him on with his shirt.

"Thanks for the new clothes," he said.

"Just some things from *Target*, but they ought to hold you over." Veronica grabbed her purse. "I can trust you to be smart, right?"

"Got the t.v. you brought me, some food and my cell phone," he told her. "I'm cool."

The door closed and Face stared at it, knowing it was his ticket to a little bit of freedom. Just walking out to the street would be paradise compared to the last few days but he first needed to make an important phone call, his first one since the attempt on his life. He dialed Hawk's number.

"*Qué pasa, cabron?*" he said.

"Face?" Hawk replied, sounding like he'd been sleeping. "Where the fuck you been, man? You ain't returned my calls or nothin'."

"Had me some trouble, *vato*, he said. "Couple of *pinchi* Lobos. Took a bullet but I'm all right."

"What the *fuck*? There ain't been no goddamn killings since that meeting with Atkinson. You ain't gonna let them get away with that shit are you, Face?"

"That's why I'm callin' your ass," he said. "You got your drug connections, your gun connections, hell, you deal with 'em more than anybody I know. Those assholes sell to everybody. Find out if they know 'bout a Lobo motherfucker got a big scar 'round his left eye. You got that, *vato*?"

"Yeah, I got it. You gonna answer the fuckin' phone if I call you this time?"

"Not yet," he told him. "I'm gonna lay low where I'm at a little longer. I'll call you in a few days."

"I don't want you dead, Face. Good to know you're okay."

"One more thing," he said. "Send some eyes to my house. My mother's alone now, understand?"

"We'll be watchin'," he answered.

Face tossed the phone on the bed and headed towards the door. At the right time he'd find the motherfucking Lobo who shot him and mess him up real good. *Maatalo*, killing him, wasn't an option. He wasn't taking chances with his healthy heart.

"Did you put the 'No Pick-Up' sign where the bus driver could see it?" Uncle Kevin asked.

"Yeah," Seth answered, preparing to shovel another spoonful of cereal into his mouth. "I looked through the window and saw the bus pull up and then drive away."

"Good. We'll leave in a few minutes."

"How come Mrs. Fisher's seeing you this morning? I thought parent-teacher meetings were done after school?"

"She's doing me a favor," he said. "My job doesn't let me commit to specific times, especially in the afternoon."

Seth rose from his chair and walked towards the sink with his bowl.

"I'm going to go brush my teeth and then we'll go," his uncle told him. "The trash bag's full. Please take it outside before we leave."

"Can't I do it later?" he grumbled.

"Just do it, okay?"

The garbage spilled over, making the top ends difficult to fasten. Seth thought the knot might come undone so he carried the bag with one hand on top and the other supporting the bottom. He felt what seemed like a large bottle at the bottom of the bag. *Why didn't Uncle Kevin use the recycle container?* he wondered. *He's always telling me to do it.* Seth suddenly had a sinking feeling that required an immediate answer. Stepping outside the door leading from the laundry room, he placed the bag on the ground next to the large black trash container that stood side by side with the blue recycling one. He kneeled down, turned the bag over, and tore open a small hole on the bottom. Reaching his hand inside, he removed an empty bottle of scotch. He stared in anger at the only proof he needed that his uncle had lied to Grandma and him and Veronica about quitting drinking. *Maybe I should bring it back into the kitchen and embarrass him,* he thought. *Or hide it until the next time Grandma comes over and watch him squirm.*

Seth rose to his feet and deposited the trash bag with the rest of the garbage. He picked the bottle up from the ground and clutched it from the neck, debating whether to try and sneak it into his room before they left for school, or bury it in the recycle container for now. "I want Grandma to see this," he whispered to himself. The sudden sound of the side door opening from the garage startled him. He realized he didn't have time to hide the bottle so he darted behind the blue and black trash bins and crouched down, peeking through the skinny space between them. Expecting to see his uncle, Seth felt an immediate shock and fear when an unknown *Mexican* walked outside.

He knew the man must be a burglar. His heart slammed repeatedly against his chest as he gripped the scotch bottle with his right hand, petrified but ready to defend himself. He wondered if the Mexican had been inside the house. Was his uncle all right? Did he even know? Was he *dead*? Seth's eyes followed the man's every move. As he neared the gate, he ascertained that something must be wrong with him. He seemed hurt. A slight bulge protruded from inside the left shoulder area of his shirt and he hunched over towards that side. Seth was afraid, but somewhere inside his fright he gained strength from the promise he had made himself after his father was murdered. *Nobody's gonna bully me again.* Seth slid around the side of the trash container and waited for the Mexican to reach for the latch on the gate, figuring the man would be in the most defenseless position at that moment. But as Seth prepared to attack, something strange happened.

The Mexican wobbled a bit, as if he had lost strength in his legs. He turned away from the gate and leaned against the wall, covering his face with his hands. Seth didn't know what to do. He continued to stare from a safe position, confident that he remained well hidden. He tightened his grip on the bottle's neck, ready to charge at a moment's notice.

"Put the bottle down, kid," the Mexican said.

His back is turned. How does he know I'm here? Seth took a quick breath and held it.

"I ain't gonna hurt you."

I could've sworn he never saw me!

The Mexican approached the gate again. "I just need me some fresh air, man," he said, never looking in Seth's direction. "You ain't supposed to know I'm here, so I don't want no problems."

I'm not supposed to know he's here? Of course I know that, what a stupid thing to say! He wants to rob our house. He thought nobody was home but I caught him. He's bigger than me but I don't care. He's not gonna get away with it! Never again, you Mexican!

Seth waited for the man to reach for the latch. He leaped forward in an attempt to bring the bottle crashing down on his head, but the Mexican spun from the gate and threw his right hand up, catching Seth's wrist. For several moments they started into each other's eyes as the man wrested the bottle from Seth's hand. Seth expected a hard punch to his face, but the realization that he might be cut up or even *killed* strengthened his resolve. He tried to kick the Mexican, twisting at angles to get a better shot at his knees. One of the kicks made solid contact, allowing him to lower his upper body and knock the man against the wall. The Mexican yelled out in pain as he grabbed his left shoulder. Seth wasn't sure what to do, but the image of his dead uncle sent him running into the house. He slammed the door and locked it, taking a quick glance through the window to see if the Mexican was still there. The man hadn't moved.

"*Uncle Kevin!*"

After several moments his uncle rushed into the room.

"*What's the matter?*" he shouted.

"You're alive! Call the police! Hurry!"

"*What the hell is it?*"

"There's a Mexican guy out there and he tried to kill me!"

"*What?*"

His uncle still wasn't dialing.

"*Where?*"

"Just do it!" Seth yelled.

"First tell me where you saw him!"

"Outside! By the trash cans!"

His uncle ran past Seth to look through the window of the laundry room door. "Oh, no," he groaned.

"Why aren't you *doing* anything, Uncle Kevin?" Seth hurried to the window. The Mexican had gotten up and supported himself against the blue container.

"I'll explain everything, Seth," he said, keeping his eyes on the Mexican. "But first tell me what you meant when you said he tried to kill you?"

"He was gonna smash me over the head with a bottle!"

Uncle Kevin glanced back to look at him. "You mean he just came up behind you and you escaped?"

"He had the bottle in his hand but I kicked him and knocked him against the wall. That's when I ran inside."

"So he was hiding when you went out there?"

"Yeah, in the garage. He would've hurt me if he could, for sure. You, too."

"*Damn it!*" his uncle shouted. "I knew I never should have..."

"When he came outside he walked to the gate," Seth explained. "He was going to rob us because he told me I wasn't supposed to know he was there."

"Hold it, Seth," his uncle said, looking surprised. "He *talked* with you?"

"Kind of," he replied. "He was talking out loud, but not at me. I guess he must have known I was hiding behind the trash cans, but he never came over there."

"Now you're telling me *you* were the one that was hiding," his uncle said. "Was he holding the bottle when he walked out of the garage?"

"No, but so what?" Seth replied.

"How did he wind up with a bottle in his hand?"

"I... found one on the ground," he said, wanting to keep his discovery a secret. "He took it from me when we were fighting."

They both directed their gaze at the Mexican again. Seth couldn't understand why the man hadn't tried to escape, preferring instead to stand there looking back at them. Maybe he was more hurt than Seth first thought.

"So let me get this straight," Uncle Kevin said. "You were hiding with a bottle. You felt threatened because you thought he was a robber and you tried to defend yourself." Uncle Kevin gave him a little smile. "You were even trying to defend me. He was walking to the gate when you attacked him and in the process he took the bottle from your hands. Then you knocked him against the wall and ran inside the house."

Seth nodded.

Uncle Kevin closed his eyes and rubbed his face in his hands. "He's right, Seth," he said, removing a box of mints from his pocket and putting one into his mouth. "You weren't supposed to know he was there."

"What do you mean?"

Uncle Kevin looked at his watch. "We can still make it to school on time," he said. "But I need to see if Alex is all right."

"*Alex?* Seth asked. "You know him?"

Uncle Kevin opened the door. "Seth, meet Veronica's brother, Alex."

"*What?*" Seth stared at his uncle open mouthed for a long moment. "*Veronica's brother?*"

Uncle Kevin approached Alex. "Are you all right?"

"Ain't nothin'," he answered.

"Are you sure? Let me look at it."

Uncle Kevin started to move around to Alex's left side but as soon as he touched the shirt Alex spun away in anger. "I said it ain't nothin!" he hollered. "I'm goin' back to the room."

"What room?" Seth asked him.

Alex looked at his Uncle Kevin. "You gonna tell him?" he asked.

"Tell me what?"

"I owe you an explanation, Seth," Uncle Kevin said. "Alex got hurt and needed Veronica to take care of him for a few days. She didn't want to bring him to her apartment because of her roommate and she couldn't afford to stay in a motel. So I offered the room next to my garage."

Seth's eyes narrowed in anger. *"Why didn't you tell me?"*

His uncle took a long, slow breath. "I wasn't sure if you were ready. Do you know what I mean by that?"

Seth stared at Alex. "Yeah, I know what you mean," he said. "And I *don't* like what you did!"

"If that's the way you feel, Seth, then I'll call Veronica today and tell her they have to leave."

Seth looked at his uncle. "Good!" he shouted. He turned away from the both of them and walked towards the garage. "I'll go wait in the car."

He sat brooding in the front seat, thinking about his uncle's explanation. *"Now Veronica's keeping secrets from me, too,"* he said to himself. *"Just like Uncle Kevin and his drinking."* Seth stared at Alex as he walked across the garage. Alex took one step through the door of his room before turning to look back at Seth. He started to approach the car, walking slowly and leaning more to the left than before. *He's coming towards me!* Seth reached over to lock the doors, but realized the front windows were down. He scooted closer to the steering wheel in case he needed to honk the horn. Alex stood by the passenger seat window and lowered his head to look at him.

"You shouldn't be drinkin' that shit, Seth," he said.

"What... what are you talking about?"

"C'mon, man, 'fess up." Seth watched as Alex pulled the empty scotch bottle from the back of his pants. "What do ya call this shit?"

"That's not mine!" Seth hissed.

"Your uncle ain't never gonna find out, okay? Can't say I blame you for needin' to fix your mind up. I know what happened to you. But trust me, man, alcohol ain't the answer for a kid your age. When you go through shit in life you just gotta keep fightin', you understand? Keep believin' there's somethin' better."

Seth stared in confused silence as Alex shuffled back into his room with the bottle and closed the door.

On the way to school his uncle tried to explain again why he allowed Veronica's brother to stay at the house, but Seth didn't pay attention. *"I can't believe he thought that bottle was mine,"* he said to himself. *"I don't want him to think that. What if he tells Veronica? Then Veronica will tell Uncle Kevin and he'll know that I know."*

The school day seemed to drag on longer than usual as Seth's nervousnessincreased. Heneeded to straighten outthemisunderstanding and get that bottle back, but he felt scared. *He knows I tried to hit him with the bottle. He may try to hurt me.* For all he knew, Alex had already broken it somewhere and trying to talk with him would be for nothing.

Seth's other dilemma concerned finding a way to talk to Alex in private. After the school bus dropped him off, his neighbor, Lisa, who Uncle Kevin paid to stay with him each day until he got home from work, greeted him at the door. Seth had devised a plan, and several minutes later he walked into the front room holding a phone to his ear.

"Okay, Uncle Kevin," he replied. "Fifteen minutes? Yeah, I'll tell her." Seth hung up and looked at Lisa. "My uncle will be here in fifteen minutes. He said you could go home now."

Seth reached out to knock on Alex's door but jerked his hand away before making contact. He leaned in close and listened, wondering if Alex was sleeping. Seth didn't hear anything and stepped back, struggling to control his nerves. He looked back to make sure the door leading into the house remained open. *He's hurt,* Seth reminded himself. *I can outrun him if he comes after me.* Seth hesitated for several unsettled moments. *In ten seconds, I'll do it. Ten... nine... eight... seven... six... five... four... three... two... one...* He took a deep breath, closed his eyes, and reached his hand out again.

THIRTY-THREE

THE AFTERNOON PAIN PILLS HELPED a little but Face's steady improvement had suffered a setback by what happened that morning. His vision of Seth leaping out with a bottle from behind the trash containers saved him from a surprise attack, but the unexpected kick to his kneecap caused Face to stumble backwards and smack his wounded shoulder against a sharp corner of the wall. The pain shot through him like an electric shock, forcing him to slump to the ground until he gathered his senses. But Face had gained respect for the kid. The little *huero* showed balls coming after him like he did. That's why Face slipped the bottle down his pants when Seth ran into the house. The kid didn't deserve to get busted by his uncle when all he was doing was showing courage and protecting himself. Face also understood that Seth experienced a kind of pain no doctor could fix.

The accidental meeting that took place turned out to be a good thing. Face had wanted to confront the kid, to look him in the eyes, and find out whether he sensed any kind of link with the heart attacks. Something *revealing*. He would like to have had more time to reach a conclusion but that wasn't gonna happen now. Kevin and Seth wanted them gone. When Veronica returned from work they'd pack up and go to a motel.

Face felt like chillin' for the moment, looking through a car magazine that Veronica found stuffed inside the couch she slept on. He heard a knock on the door and instinctively reached under the pillow where he'd hidden the bottle, making sure he had some protection if necessary. Face remained silent, waiting to see what happened next. The knocking repeated, but this time he heard a voice.

"Alex?"

"Yeah?" he called out, tightening his grip on the bottle.

"Can I come in?"

Face felt an immediate curiosity about the kid's surprise visit. "Alright," he answered, pulling his hand back out again. He watched the door open slowly. Seth remained in a half in, half out position as he looked towards the bed.

"I want to tell you something," Seth said.

"Yeah? What's that?"

Seth hadn't moved. Face looked at the scared face of the kid and figured this offered him another chance to check him out, to see if he detected anything more. "Come in and sit down, man," he said. "I ain't gonna bite."

Seth continued to stand in the doorway, his eyes gazing around the room.

"Look at me," Face told him. "I ain't gettin' off this bed until I leave today. My shoulder hurts like hell every time I move." Face nodded his head towards Seth. "Thanks to you."

Seth took a few hesitant steps into the room. He paused and appeared to be looking at something on the bed.

"Is that my *Motor Trend* magazine?" he asked.

"How do I fuckin' know?" Face answered. He showed the front cover to Seth. "This yours?"

"I lost that a long time ago," he said. "Where'd you find it?"

"Veronica found it in that couch," he said, pointing. "Here, take it."

Seth took a couple of steps closer before wavering again. Face tossed the magazine towards the foot of his bed. "You like cars, man?"

"Yeah," he said, swooping in and plucking it away. Face watched as Seth backpedaled towards the couch.

"So do I," Face told him. "I'd love to work on them sports cars they got in there. Maybe I will one day."

"You a mechanic?" Seth asked.

"Damn right, man. Ain't nobody better."

"You know all about engines and stuff?"

"Hell, yeah," he replied. "I started when I wasn't much older than you. I'm gonna own my own shop one day."

Seth glanced at the front cover and then held it up towards Face. "You see this car?" he asked. "It's a Ferrari Enzo. It costs a million dollars!"

"Are you fuckin' shittin' me?

"It can go from zero to sixty in three and a half seconds! And over two hundred miles per hour!"

Face didn't say a word as Seth sat on the couch and started leafing through the pages. "I want to learn how to fix cars, too," he said.

"Maybe I can show ya some shit."

Seth placed the magazine on the couch and looked at Face with a serious expression. "That wasn't my bottle," he said.

"That's what you told me," Face replied. "What were you doin' with it behind the trash cans?"

"Hiding."

"Yeah, I know, man," he said. "From me."

"No, not really, not at first," Seth told him. "When the door opened I thought you were my uncle."

"Why you hidin' from him for?"

"Because he told me and my grandma that he was gonna quit drinking and he lied. He told Veronica, too. I found the bottle in the trash and I didn't want him to know."

"You afraid to bust him with it? Think he might hurt you?"

"No!" Seth shook his head rapidly back and forth. "He's not that way!"

"I'm glad to hear that," Face said. He slid the bottle out from the pillow. "You still want this?" he asked. He watched as the kid stared at the bottle, looking unsure what to do. Face lobbed it in the same spot he had thrown the magazine. Seth hurried over to grab it and returned to the couch.

"What do you want it so fuckin' bad for?" Face asked.

"To show my grandma."

"Gonna snitch on him, man? You sure you wanna do that?"

"Why not? He always tells me when *I* do something wrong. He doesn't have the right to lie to me like that."

"Veronica don't drink and she don't like liars," Face said. "She ain't gonna like knowin' your uncle's pullin' shit behind her back."

"I guess not," Seth answered, shrugging his shoulders. "But she also keeps secrets from me. She never told me about you staying here." Seth looked away. "She seemed like someone I could trust."

"Give her a fuckin' break, Seth," Face muttered. "Look at the way you were afraid to come in here. How long did it take before you finally sat on the fuckin' couch? You think if Veronica had asked you 'bout me you would've been cool about it? Whatever she was hidin' from you was to help me, but also not to hurt you. You understand?"

Seth nodded his head.

"Your uncle, too, man. He did me and Veronica a big fuckin' favor. If he's lyin' about the drinkin' that ain't cool, but I ain't gonna give him shit 'cause of what he done for us."

Seth gave a small laugh.

"What's so funny, man?" Face asked.

"I've never met anyone who swears as much as you."

Face smiled at the kid. "No shit?"

They both laughed. Face felt a sharp pain and grabbed the back of his shoulder with his opposite hand. Seth grew silent immediately. "Are you okay?" he asked.

Face gnashed his teeth and took several small breaths before he answered. "I'm all right."

"What happened to you?" Seth asked.

"Some asshole shot at me as I was drivin'. Can you believe that shit?"

"Yeah," he replied in a soft voice. "I can believe it."

Face's cell phone suddenly rang. "It's Veronica," he said.

"What time you gonna be here?" he asked her.

"I need another couple of hours," she said. "I'm still at work. Then I have to go to my apartment. After that, I'll go to the motel down the street and get us a room."

"I'll try to figure somethin' out, Veronica," he told her. "I know it's a lot of money."

"*You don't have to go, Alex.*"

Face looked up and saw Seth approaching him. "What?" he asked him.

"Is someone in the room?" Face heard Veronica ask.

"I don't want you to leave," Seth told him. "You're not well enough."

Face stared for several moments into the eyes of the little *huero*. "You sure, Seth?" he asked, smiling.

Seth reached out for Face's phone and took it from his hand. "Hi Veronica," he said. "It's Seth."

Face heard Veronica's surprised response. "*Seth?*"

"You don't have to go to a motel, Veronica. I want you and Alex to stay here until he's all right... yeah, I'm sure... you're welcome, it's okay... no, Uncle Kevin doesn't know yet... Yeah, I remember... okay, I'll see you later."

Seth handed the phone back to Face. "I better start doing my homework," he said. "Veronica's going to test me tomorrow."

Seth grabbed his magazine and bottle off the couch, but as he strode towards the door he stopped, turned around, and walked back to the bed. "Here, Alex," he said, handing him the magazine. "You can keep it for now."

Face watched and waited until the kid reached the door. "Hey, Seth," he called out.

"Yeah?"

"Thanks, man."

Face stared at the closed door for several moments, confident in his conclusion that Seth had nothing to do with the heart attacks.

THIRTY-FOUR

KEVIN SAT ON THE COUCH with Veronica, fascinated by the contradictory scene of a Latino gang member laughing and talking trash with Seth as they competed in a video game. He reflected on the irony of his nephew sitting a few feet from an Alvarado Street Diablo, enjoying himself to the fullest, when his recent past would have considered the present moment to be an impossibility. But in the three days since Seth first visited Alex in his room, logic had been turned on its head and the two of them seemed inseparable. Kevin grew melancholy for a moment, recognizing that Alex would soon be returning to a life of gangs and violence. *We may never see him again after this.*

"Looks like these guys will be busy for awhile," he said to Veronica. "I've delayed looking through Warren's last few boxes long enough. Care to help me?"

"Let's go," she said.

"Anything of mine in there?" Seth asked.

"I'll let you know when I open them," Kevin told him. "The only thing I know for sure is that two of the boxes are filled with your dad's old books."

Veronica helped Kevin carry the five sealed containers from his closet into his office.

"I wasn't ready to open the last of my brother's things," he said. "Especially the books. They were his heart and soul."

"But you're ready now?"

"I have to do it sometime, right?" Kevin smiled. "I'll save the books for last, though."

Close to an hour later, after excavating a blender, a toaster, a paper shredder, several candlesticks, Tupperware containers, three rechargeable flashlights, two cordless telephones, five toner cartridge boxes, two unopened jigsaw puzzles, a globe, three snorkel masks, two pair of fins, a flattened basketball, and other various family items, Kevin and Veronica stared at the remaining boxes marked, 'BOOKS'.

"Were these Warren's personal books or the ones he taught with?" Veronica asked.

"Some of both, I imagine," Kevin said. "There's no way these two boxes were the only ones he owned. Warren read a lot. I'm sure many of the books were left at school, but that's okay. That's where they should be."

Kevin sliced through the tape on the first of the remaining two boxes. When he pulled the side flaps back, a collection of various sized books were revealed in both hard-covered and paperback variety. He grabbed the top two and read the titles aloud. "*The Hunchback of Notre-Dame...Moby Dick.*" Thumbing through some pages, he said, "Warren loved the classics. In his single days he used to seduce the ladies by tossing out flowery quotations." Chuckling, he added, "Maybe he just read them for the pick-up lines."

Kevin counted a total of twenty-three books in the first box, all signifying the types of authors and poets one would expect to find from an English professor. He extracted classic stories by Twain, Austen, Steinbeck, Wilde, and Hemingway as well as poetry books by Browning, Frost, Whitman, Dickinson, Emerson, and Wordsworth.

"I can't believe there's no Edgar Allan Poe books," Kevin said. "He was Warren's favorite writer. Everybody knew it. His students used to call him, 'Professor Poemer', because he'd quote the guy all the time and hold special classes just for him."

"Maybe you'll find some in the other box," Veronica said.

"I'll be shocked if I don't," Kevin replied, sliding the knife.

"Did you find my Tony Hawk shirt?"

Kevin looked up to find Seth and Alex standing in the doorway. "I lost it when I moved here," he said.

Kevin shook his head. "Sorry, Seth, just a lot of odds and ends that were packed away. And these books."

"So who won?" Veronica asked.

Seth tilted his head towards Alex. Nodding his head and flashing a big smile, Alex placed his hand on Seth's shoulder. "I'm the man, Seth. Don't fu... don't mess with the man."

Veronica laughed and clapped her hands. "What do you think of that, Kevin? Somebody finally defeated the champ."

Kevin didn't respond. Reading to himself from a black, hard-covered book, he fell momentarily silent from the discovery he held in his hands.

"Who wrote that one?" Veronica asked.

"You were right, Veronica," he said. "I found a Poe book. But there's something else here I wasn't expecting." He held the time-beaten paper up for everyone to see. "It's a poem my father wrote. It was dedicated to a friend of his from the war who got killed in a hold-up. I remember Warren telling me about it, that he'd found it stuffed inside one of his Poe books." Kevin slowly nodded his head. "Right here at "*The Tell-Tale Heart.*"

"My dad memorized the whole thing," Seth said, sorrow in his voice. "He used to go around reciting lines all the time."

Kevin looked at Veronica. "See, I told you. He never missed a chance."

"I'd like to hear your father's poem, Kevin," Veronica said. "Would you read it?"

"Are you sure?" he asked. "It's pretty much a downer."

"I don't know much about your father," she replied. "I'm interested."

Appearing unsteady, Alex seemed to stagger into the room before sitting on a chair.

"Are you all right?" Veronica asked. "Your face looks red."

"Just dizzy," he mumbled. "Ain't nothin."

"I'll read the poem later," Kevin said.

"Go on, man," Alex said, rubbing his eyes. "Veronica wants to hear your old man's poem."

Kevin surveyed the yellowed notebook paper for a brief moment before commencing.

> *"The valiant soldier's blood will spill*
> *On red-stained lands of sacrifice*
> *The unknown stranger..."*

From the quiet corner where Alex sat, his voice was suddenly heard... "*lies as still...Apart from honor's noble price.*" Kevin stopped, staring in numb disbelief as Alex continued. "*Two victims of a time to kill...*" Alex's eyes narrowed, as if in a trance-like state... "*Beware the heart...*" His eyes opened wide... "*as cold as ice.*"

At that moment, two plus two equaling five made more sense than what had just occurred. Kevin couldn't move. His thoughts turned into a disconnect of frayed wires. His need to speak, to *ask*, felt crippled by a leaden tongue made heavy from the weight of shock. In the odd vacuum of Kevin's office, Veronica's voice filtered through the silence.

"Alex? Where did... Kevin? I thought your father..."

Veronica took the sheet from Kevin's hands. He watched her as she studied the poem, looking up occasionally at her brother still sitting on the chair. Seth, who had remained standing in the doorway, entered the room and sat on the arm of the couch near Alex. Contrary to Kevin's own emotions, Seth seemed infused with excitement over this unexplainable mystery.

"How'd you know the words?" Seth asked, wide-eyed. "You must have seen 'em somewhere, right?"

Alex looked at him without offering an answer. Seth turned his attention to Kevin. "Maybe Grandpa's poem was in a book and he never told you." Kevin didn't answer him either. Seth looked back at Alex. "My teacher told me sometimes we read things and they stick in our heads without us ever knowing. Then one day out of nowhere, the words just come out, like you were reading it or something. Or like when a song comes on you haven't heard in a really long time and you know all the words."

"Maybe you're on to something," Kevin said, convinced otherwise. Placing the scattered books back into the boxes, he rose to his feet and looked at Veronica. He watched as she continued to sift through 'A Victim's Time'. Her mutual bewilderment looked obvious through the intensity of her expression. Like him, she no doubt couldn't fathom the possibility of such a thing. Pure and simple, what Alex did was *impossible*.

Veronica approached Alex with the poem in her hand. "Tell me where you saw this before," she demanded.

He frowned and shook his head. "No *recuerdo*, Veronica."

"You don't remember?" she asked, a dazed expression marking her face. "How could you not..." Veronica took a deep breath. "I'm not going to forget about this," she said, sounding shaken. "Even if Seth's right, and you did see this somewhere, how'd you remember all the words?" She returned the poem to Kevin. "Right now, I don't know what to think."

Alex's manner seemed restrained, giving no clue as to his thinking.

"We gonna eat soon?" Seth asked. "I'm starving."

"I'll go make it now," Kevin said. He looked at Alex. "I still don't understand."

Veronica started to follow Kevin out of the room but stopped and turned to face her brother. "I've never seen you do anything like that in your whole life," she told him. "It makes me feel like you've been hiding something from me."

He looked at her, saying nothing.

THIRTY-FIVE

ETH REMAINED BEHIND, STILL SITTING next to Face. "Veronica's mad at you."

"Don't worry 'bout her," he replied. "She'll be cool."

"I guess my teacher was right," Seth said. "You must have seen the poem somewhere and it just kinda stuck."

Face liked the kid but didn't want to talk about the poem anymore. Though he tried his best to shield his emotions, what had happened a few minutes before unnerved him. Standing in the doorway, as Kevin prepared to read, that sudden lightheadedness and surge of warmth that always preceded another vision struck him, but no image appeared. He remembered that the one other time he felt the effects but didn't see anything occurred moments before Swat killed Seth's father.

The words on the paper turned into his own thoughts, delivered from his mouth as clear and natural as if speaking his name. Like the soccer ball rolling down the hill that day he first discovered his power, the lines from the poem gathered an unstoppable momentum of their own. Within a few moments, he felt normal again.

"You know what I mean?" Seth asked.

Face had stopped listening to Seth. "About what?"

"About what my teacher said. That somebody could read a poem and..."

"I don't wanna talk 'bout it no more, man."

Seth shrugged his shoulders and leaned over to look at Face's watch. "That's really cool. Where'd you get it?"

Face looked down at his watch, recalling his genuine disbelief when his mother gave him the gift. "A birthday present from my mother." Moving his left arm over to his right one in slow motion, he touched the watch with his left hand. "I'm gettin' better. I put the watch on today.

Couldn't yesterday."

Seth pointed to the design under the round encasing. "You got two flags in there," he said. "The American one and the green and red one. What country is that?"

"Mexico, man," he answered, tilting his head in surprise. "You didn't know?"

Leaning back, Seth shook his head. "No, I didn't. You're not mad, are you?"

"Nah. I'm not mad."

Face noticed Seth looking at him, as if he was thinking about something. "*Qué pasó*, Seth?" he asked. "What's on your mind?"

"I just want you to know..." he said, hesitating, "you're the first... *Mexican* guy I'm friends with. The other ones... they kinda scare me sometimes."

Seth's admission struck Face like a head butt. He didn't have to ask where the kid's fear originated, and why the scars remained big time.

"Where I'm from, Seth, I ain't friends with any white guys, okay? They scare the shit outta me, too."

Seth laughed, his eyes opening wide. "They don't really, do they?"

"Well, let's just say I don't trust most of 'em. But I ain't talkin' 'bout you. You're okay. So's your uncle. He's been good to me. He treats my sister right, too. She seems real happy."

"I hope they get married," Seth said. "I really like Veronica. I want her to stay here forever."

Face smiled. "You got good taste in women, my man."

Seth smiled back. "Thanks."

"So you got Mexican kids at your school?"

"Yeah, but like I said, I'm not friends with any of them." Seth looked away for several moments. "Sometimes they tried to pick on me but I wouldn't let them."

"You fight 'em?

"I had to."

Face balled his right fist. "You done right, Seth. Can't let nobody diss you and get away with it."

"I got in trouble for fighting, but things are better now. We kinda leave each other alone. Anyway, if I get in another fight they could kick me out of school."

"I sucked in school, but that don't mean learnin' ain't important. Look at Veronica. She worked hard and done real good for herself."

"Yeah, she's really smart."

"Next time some shit's about to go down," Face said, "and you're not sure how to deal with it, get away for awhile. Find a place where you can chill by yourself and think about what you wanna do."

Face pushed himself up with his right arm and leaned forward. "I got a place like that," he said, lowering his voice. "I just found it one day. My old man wanted to kick my ass. I had a feeling... no, I *knew* he was gonna come after me. So I snuck outta the house and kept walkin'. Didn't think 'bout where I was goin'. Then I saw me a street called 'Casa Place' that goes up and curves around so you can't see where it ends."

"And you went up there?"

"All the way to the top, man. I see a house up there on a big hill. But before you get there you got one of those see-through fences behind some bushes. You can't hardly see it unless you're close, you know? I bent me down a part of it and climbed over. They got a dirt trail leads to some big 'ol trees." Face smiled. "Can't nobody see you inside all those leaves and branches, man. You're like *gone*, you know what I mean? I like that."

"Wow," Seth whispered. "That sounds cool. Anybody else ever seen it?"

"Don't know. Ain't never seen nobody there."

"How 'bout your friends? Or Veronica? Do they know?"

Face shook his head. "Nobody knows." He stared at Seth and leaned closer, lowering his voice to a whisper. "'Cept you, now." He stroked his finger across his closed mouth, signaling for him to keep quiet. "Promise me, Seth. *Swear* to me. You'll keep my place secret. Don't tell nobody."

Holding Face's stare, Seth nodded his head, his expression matching the seriousness of the occasion. "For sure, Alex," he replied in a quiet voice. "I'll never tell anybody. I swear."

THIRTY-SIX

KEVIN AND VERONICA PREPARED DINNER in silence, immersed in their own world of disbelief. Kevin had called his mother several minutes before, inquiring about the remote chance that his father's work had, indeed, been published somewhere, but her answer confirmed what he'd already suspected; his father never submitted anything for publication. When Kevin hung up the phone and looked at Veronica, their eyes relayed the same message: Alex had never seen that poem in his life.

Veronica alternated between feelings of confusion and disillusionment. Alex hadn't done anything *wrong*, but her bewilderment over something as unexplainable as his amazing feat left her with the awkward feeling of alienation. Their difficult years growing up together had created an inseparable bond between them. So who was that Alex look-alike reciting profound, personal phrases he'd never seen? In a type of language she had never heard him use?

Veronica motioned for Alex to follow her into Kevin's office after dinner.

"First thing I want to tell you is that Kevin's arranged to get your car window replaced. They'll also try to repair your fender."

"Where?"

"A place called Marco's Autobody. Kevin knows the guy. He sent Marco to my place so he could look at your car. If we bring it in tomorrow, Marco thinks he can have it ready by Monday afternoon."

"How much will it cost me?"

"Marco's returning a favor, so we'll see. Kevin mentioned him in an article he once wrote and it helped him get more customers."

"I appreciate what the *huero* did," Alex replied.

"Just thank him sometime, alright? And make sure you call Mama. I talked to her today and she told me she hasn't heard from you. She wants to know when you're coming back."

"You heard the doc today. He figures what?... Tuesday or Wednesday?"

"I'll be glad when you're home again, Alex. I don't like Mama being alone in that house for too long."

"Don't worry," he told her. "I called somebody. Ma's protected."

"You didn't give out this address to anyone, did you?"

"Hell no," he exclaimed. "I ain't gonna fuck up your little fiesta."

Veronica stared into her brother's eyes, needing to understand. "Alex, how did you know that poem?"

Several uncomfortable moments passed, but he returned Veronica's gaze, holding his eyes on hers as he spoke. "I ain't never kept no secrets from you, Veronica. 'Cept one. Since I was a kid."

Remaining quiet, she waited for Alex to continue.

"I see things sometimes. Things that are gonna happen. I see the shit before it goes down."

"You mean... like *visions*?"

Alex nodded. "I hear shit, too."

"Since you were a *kid*?"

"Nine years old," he replied in a quiet voice.

"What kind of things do you see?"

Alex offered a tiny smile. "Remember when you'd always tell me how lucky I was for comin' home after the old man had already passed out? That he was lookin' for me earlier, ready to kick my ass?"

"I remember," she answered.

"I saw 'em comin'," he said. "So I stayed away."

"You *saw* Papa hitting you?" she asked, wide-eyed. "Before it happened?"

"Yeah. I knew all about the shit before the shit went down. But the thing is, I only see things when I'm in danger. First I get dizzy and then my eyes feel warm and the light flashes real fast. Then everything gets as clear as fuckin' TV. I woulda been dead if I hadn't seen that drive-by comin' to the house. I drove away just in time. I've also saved my ass bangin' on the streets a few times, too."

"Do any of the Diablos know about this?"

"No," he answered, smiling at her. "They just think I go through one of those seizures or somethin'. I've saved my homeboys from a world of hurt, but they never knew. I'd just persuade 'em to change their plans a bit, you know? Like takin' a different street or maybe waitin' a little more."

"Have you ever told anybody?"

"Not until now," he said. "But Ma knows about it. She told me before I had a fuckin' clue."

Veronica felt like an outsider from her own family. "How did she know?"

"Remember a long time ago, when some pissed off asshole blew away his old lady and her boyfriend at the market Ma used to go to?"

In a daze, Veronica inched her head up and down.

"We were there right before it happened. I saw everything. Saw 'em get smoked. Heard the screamin'. I told Ma and we got our asses outta there." Alex paused, his eyes half-closed as if in reflection. "When we got home, she explained it to me. How every other generation in her family has a boy who gets the ability. That day in the market, she knew."

"Was that the first time you remember seeing visions?"

"The first time was with that stupid kid who used to live next to us. I saw a car headin' straight for him. If it wasn't for me he woulda been dead."

For several moments, Veronica felt woozy. "You mean... Miguel?"

"Yeah," he answered. "Miguel."

Veronica sat back in the chair and closed her eyes, trying to absorb everything she'd been told and how she wished she possessed Alex's power the night she was raped.

"What you've told me still doesn't explain about the poem," she said. "How did you know the words? And what's that got to do with danger? And seeing things?"

"Feelin' like I did, my eyes gettin' warm, the flashin' lights... when that shit happens I see things. But nothin' went down. That ain't happened to me before." Looking away for a moment, he said quietly, "'Cept one time."

"One other time?" she asked. "Did anything happen?"

"Somebody got shot."

"And you were feeling that way again when Kevin was about to read the poem, right?"

"*Sí*. Next thing I know, I had all these words comin' outta me. I wasn't even thinkin' 'bout it. They just happened."

"But you didn't see anything," she said. "And nothing bad happened."

Veronica displayed a tiny smile for her brother. "I can't believe I'm saying this, but maybe this ability of yours lets you read minds, too. The words were in Kevin's head and you picked up on them."

Alex shook his head. "No, that ain't it. There's somethin' in that poem of his. A connection I can't figure out."

THIRTY-SEVEN

FACE RELAXED IN A CHAIR, watching TV with Veronica and Kevin. Seth walked into the room and picked up a notepad lying on the table.

"What's this on the paper, Uncle Kevin?" he asked. "There's a drawing of a heart with 'four a.m.' in the middle of it."

"*What?*" Face whispered, turning his attention from Seth to Kevin.

"It's nothing," Kevin replied. "Just some doodling I was doing."

"You know what it reminds me of? *The Tell-Tale Heart,*" Seth told them. "There's the part where the guy hides the heart under the floor and says, 'it was four o'clock, still dark as midnight'. That's one of the lines I remember."

"You're that newspaper reporter, ain't you?" Face asked.

"I write for the *L.A. Times,* Alex."

"The one who wrote those stories, right? At Men's County. Atkinson set you up. Got you some interviews."

"That's enough, Alex," Veronica said, glancing at Kevin.

Face looked at Seth, who still held the notepad. "I'll tell you what that drawing means," he said, hostility in his voice. "A lot of my homeboys been cut down by heart attacks. All dyin' at four a.m. You get it?" Nodding his head towards Kevin, he added, "Ask your uncle. He'll tell you I'm talkin' straight."

"We don't like to talk about gangs in this house," Kevin said.

"I understand, man. But I lost a lot of brothers, you know? I just wanna make sure you ain't hidin' nothin' from me."

Seth walked over to Face with his hands in his pockets and stopped a few feet from where he sat. Face studied the kid's expression. He didn't think he saw sadness or anger. Rather, a fierce type of *seriousness.*

"Are you in a gang, Alex?"

He nodded. "Yeah, Seth. We're still friends though, ain't we?"

"I *hate* gangs," he snapped. "They killed my dad!"

"I know, man. I'm really sorry. That never shoulda happened."

"Well, it *did* happen!" Seth shouted. "My dad was trying to save me from a gang and another gang shot 'em!"

He approached Face until he stood over him. "I thought we were friends, Alex," he said, his voice rising. "I thought you were different. Not like... *them*!" Balling his fists, he shouted, "*I never want to see you again!*" Seth rushed to his bedroom and slammed the door.

Face looked up from his chair, staring into the empty space that held his young friend a few moments before.

"I didn't know," he said quietly. "How was I supposed to know?"

"Didn't I tell you not to say anything?" Veronica said angrily. "Of course you should have known he'd react like that!"

"That's not what I'm talkin' about," he replied, continuing to stare ahead. "I didn't know Seth was that kid. Or about his father."

"What about his father?" Kevin asked. "What do you mean?"

"It was the anniversary of Apache's murder. We was just lookin' for some payback."

"Who the hell's *Apache*?" Kevin hissed. "What does he have to do with my brother?"

"I'm wonderin' now if somethin' was up. Why that feelin' came over me like I was in danger or somethin'."

Kevin looked at Veronica. "Is he making any sense to you?"

"Alex," she said, "do you know who killed Kevin's brother?"

"Everything was gonna be cool," he said, his voice as soft as a church confessional. "But it all fucked up. Lobos started runnin' everywhere. But I didn't see nothin'. I didn't understand, man. I always saw somethin' before. But I heard a loud voice. Real quick, like a scream. Then a gunshot. But nobody got smoked yet. Swat hadn't pulled the trigger. Then the feelin' left me. I saw a Lobo draggin' a kid away. Usin' him for protection. When he got under a light, I saw the kid was white. I don't want no kid gettin' hurt, but if he's a *huero* that's real trouble, man. Cops don't go for that shit."

"Are you telling me you were there when my brother was murdered?"

Face glanced at Kevin before turning his eyes towards the floor. "Swat was scopin' that Lobo with his rifle. I didn't know what the fuck he was gonna do. I yelled at him, 'Not the kid!' I didn't think he was gonna listen to me. We was losin' time, we had to get outta there. Somebody was runnin' towards the Lobo and the kid. It was dark, but when he got near the light, Swat..." Alex looked up at Kevin. "Yeah, man. I was there. We was wrong. Wasn't no Lobo. That was your brother. He was runnin' for Seth."

Face looked at Veronica. "*Seth*. Now I know. That's what that loud voice was sayin' in my head before the gun went off." He got to his feet. Wiping his hand across his face he turned his attention back to Kevin. "There's somethin' else you should know, man. Swat went down with a heart attack that same night. Four a.m. Diablos and Lobos have been dyin' like that ever since. That's what Atkinson told us. Your brother's death started somethin'. I don't know what, but we're still payin' for it."

Kevin leaped off the couch, watery eyes full of anger. "You thought you killed a Lobo that night, but that doesn't excuse a fucking thing! *Nothing*! Murder's still murder, damn it! You can't just go around killing people! Are you telling me Seth lost his father because of some fucking anniversary? I...I lost my brother because your stupid gangbanger friend made a God damn mistake? What gives you the right to take someone's life that way? What kind of mind thinks like that?"

Face looked at Veronica before answering Kevin. "Veronica escaped that shit, but she knows. Maybe she can explain it to you. The laws of the street ain't like yours, man. Where I come from we got our own rules. You ain't never been there, Kevin. How can you tell us what's right and wrong? You don't understand how we operate. You don't know how we think. Killin' someone is a necessary thing sometimes."

"*A necessary thing*? Are you kidding me"? Kevin closed his eyes for several seconds. When he reopened them, Alex looked at two red watery rims staring right back at him. "Here's something I *do* understand, Alex, and the sooner you and your gangbanger friends understand it, the better. Lieutenant Atkinson told me there hasn't been anyone murdered in either gang for a month and a half. Not one. And you know what? No heart attacks. *None*! If I was a betting man, I'd say there's a relationship there, wouldn't you?"

Face stood rigid, staring at Kevin. "Ain't no relationship between us and the Lobos, man. Ain't never gonna happen."

Kevin looked at Veronica. "There's no use trying to talk sense to him," he said. "I'll call the auto shop first thing tomorrow to see if Marco can have Alex's window ready in the morning. That way you can drop him off on your way to work and let him wait for it." Kevin glared at Face. "It's time he went home anyway. He's been here long enough."

Face didn't say a word as he turned to walk away.

"And what the hell is this *feeling* you're talking about?" Kevin yelled. "You think you see things, or hear things, before they happen? You expect me to believe that shit?"

"I don't fuckin' care if you do or don't, man," he replied in a calm tone. "But I know I been seein' things since I was nine years old. Always showin' me when trouble's comin'. That feelin' I had the night your brother was killed? Yeah, I didn't see nothin', but trouble still hit us big time, right? That blind kinda feelin' never happened before or since until you was readin' that poem. Next thing you know I'm tellin' it to you. Do you believe *that* shit?"

"*How can you live with yourself?*" Kevin screamed. "*How could you go around this whole time hiding something like that from Veronica? And then befriending Seth and me as if nothing happened?*"

"We all gotta hide shit sometimes, don't we, man?"

"What the hell's that supposed to mean?"

"Seth knows. He found something of yours."

"I'm not hiding a damn thing!"

"You sure 'bout that?"

Face returned to his room and stood motionless with his hand on the knob. Nodding his head in silent confirmation, he realized his gut feeling had been proven right. He didn't want Kevin to have the upper hand by agreeing with him to his face, but in reality, he saw things the same way. There *was* a relationship between a Diablo or Lobo being killed and the heart attacks. Atkinson had broken it down during the meeting and the effect on the two gangs spoke to the truth. Life in the streets had changed over the last several weeks. No one had been murdered. Not a single 187. In all his years since he checked in as a Diablo, he couldn't remember so much time passing without a killing.

Face called Hawk. The sound of loud music greeted him. "Who's this?" Hawk shouted.

"*Qué pása, vato?*" Face said.

"Face? Is that you, man?" he asked. "Why the fuck ain't you here, homeboy? When you comin' back?"

"*Mañana*, homie."

"*Face'll be back tomorrow!*" Hawk yelled.

A chorus of cheerful screams and cusses followed his remark.

"Leticia's here. Told me she misses you, *vato*. Ooh, she's lookin' so fine tonight. That's a hot *mamacita*, man! You better get your ass over

232

here *pronto*."

Face closed his eyes and smiled. "You find somethin' out?" he asked.

"Yeah," Hawk replied. "Hold on a minute."

The music and voices faded away.

"You still there, Face? Now I can talk."

"Tell me what you know."

"I bought some weed from Cervantes last night. He told me some interesting shit."

"I'm listenin'."

"That *pinchi* scar, man. Cervantes knew just who the motherfucker was. They call him King. Cervantes says he's crazier than hell. Ugly as a fuckin' zit on a rat's dick, too."

"King can kiss my fuckin' ass," Face muttered in bitterness. "I'll deal with that *culero* motherfucker when the time's right."

"*Cuidado*, Face," he warned. "The heart attacks, man. You know what I mean? The gang's layin' low."

Face heard the sound of Veronica crying as she approached the other side of the door. "Anything else, Hawk?"

"Your mother's safe, homeboy. Everything's cool."

"*Gracias, vato*. You done good."

Veronica walked through the door and looked at him teary-eyed.

"You were right, Alex," she said, wiping the back of her hand across her cheek. "Kevin *was* hiding something from me." She placed both hands on the door and slammed it closed. "Just like you were!"

THIRTY-EIGHT

WHEN ALEX RETURNED TO HIS room, Veronica rose to her feet and took Kevin by the arm. "Come on," she said, pulling him up. "Let's go ask Seth what Alex was talking about."

Kevin followed reluctantly, a bad feeling in his gut. Veronica wasted no time when Seth opened his door. "Alex told us you found something that your Uncle Kevin was hiding. Do you have any idea what he means?"

Seth looked at them both, not saying a word. A slow nod of his head followed. He looked at Kevin again and said, "You promised."

"Promised what?" Veronica asked.

"Whatever it is, just *out* with it, okay?" Kevin said angrily.

Seth's eyes narrowed. "Remember when Grandma was here on Labor Day and how mad she got when she found your bottle of scotch?"

"Yes," he answered, his throat drying.

"You promised you were gonna stop drinking, but you *didn't!*" Seth hurried to his bed, reached underneath, and revealed the proof. Kevin heard Veronica's gasp. "You made me the same promise," she said, continuing to eye the bottle. "I suspected something but I didn't want to believe it." She stared down at her feet. "I feel so stupid."

"C'mon, you two," he said. "You're both seeing something that isn't there. I found that bottle in the driveway when I came home from work. I put it in the recycle container, okay?" Kevin chuckled. "I can't believe you really thought it was mine."

"I found it inside the kitchen trash bag, Uncle Kevin."

She wheeled around to face him. "I'd leave right now if it wasn't for Alex," she said, her voice cracking. "We'll both be gone in the morning."

"Veronica, wait! Let me explain."

"Explain what, Kevin?" she asked. "Why you lied to my face?"

"Please forgive me, Veronica. I love you."

"You love me?" she said, her tone filled with bitterness. "Well, I see something you obviously love more, Kevin. It's that empty bottle that Seth found. I can't be around a man who drinks like you do, don't you understand? I've experienced enough pain in my life because of alcohol. I *refuse* to go through it again!"

Kevin watched in silence as Veronica broke into tears and ran from the room. He turned to look at Seth. "*Are you happy now?*"

"No," he replied. "Why should I be happy?"

Kevin wondered if his nephew's answer was a comment about his own relationship with him. "Call me if you need me," he said. "I'm going out."

⊤⫯⊤ ⊤⫯⊤ ⊤⫯⊤

He tried to get drunk, "to forget about life for awhile," as that old Billy Joel song once said, but the scotch couldn't anesthetize his pain and provide a retreat from the reality of his latest failures. He had come full circle from those alcoholic days of his twenties, back to finding easy reasons to drink, working through his alcoholism at work, and losing the love of a wonderful woman. The continual replay in his mind of Veronica running from the room and out of his life destroyed something inside of him. Two scotches later, nothing had changed.

When he first entered the bar, he saw his drinking buddy, Don, sitting at his usual place. They had gotten to know each other well enough through the last couple of months to share personal information, and tonight Kevin needed someone to talk to.

"...and that's when she ran out of the room," he said. "I'm telling you, Don, if looks could kill, Veronica would be held on murder charges tonight."

"Maybe you're overreacting," Don said. "You know the way women are. They're so moody, you don't know which way the wind blows with them half the time. Maybe she'll feel differently tomorrow."

Kevin shook his head. "I blew it," he replied. "She's as solid as they come. I love that woman. I even pictured us getting married one day. Now she doesn't give a damn about me."

Don guzzled some more of his drink and started nodding emphatically. "I can relate to that, Kevin," he said. "Three marriages and three divorces later, I'm on several women's shit list, believe me. And I swear, it all started from my first mother-in-law's promise to haunt me

236

for eternity when she found out I was cheating on her daughter. If there's such a thing as cursing someone from the grave, she sure is keeping her word. I can't keep a wife, can't hold a job, can't get along with my kids..." Don downed his second drink and called for another. "Ready for a trifecta, my friend?"

Kevin looked at his watch. "I better leave," he said. "I've got a kid at home and a job I'm trying to keep."

On the way to his car, Kevin reminded himself that he had a long drive into Orange County's Little Saigon district the next morning. He closed his door and rubbed his face with his hands, trying to clear his mind. The thought of putting on an act for his Vietnamese hosts as if nothing was wrong depressed him even more. *I'm not ready to go home yet.*

Kevin drove his car up Coldwater Canyon Drive towards Mulholland Drive, intent on finding a good lookout spot where he could park and gaze down at the Valley. Staring at all of the twinkling lights from high above had always been a source of tranquility for him, and he believed that's what he needed now. His impatience to get there increased his need for speed, and as he accelerated up the winding hill, he raced past several cars along the way. Jumbled thoughts flashed in and out of his mind like a kaleidoscope. *I'm such an asshole... How could I have blown it like that with Veronica?... It's always one step forward, two steps back with Seth... He resents me more than ever now... How much longer until I'm fired?... My life is nothing without Veronica.*

Kevin made a sharp right turn on Mulholland, working his way back towards the speed he had reached heading up Coldwater Canyon. His windows were down and he reveled in the sensation of the wind blowing against his face. He started driving faster along the winding curves. Forty-five miles an hour. Fifty miles an hour. *I lied to Veronica. I lied to Seth. I lied to Mom. Hell, I even lied to myself. What a fucking loser.* An overwhelming depression seemed to overtake him as he looked out at the lights of the city far below. *Maybe I should just fly off the goddamn cliff and be with Warren again.* "CAN YOU HEAR ME, WARREN?" he cried out. "ARE YOU READY TO SEE YOUR BRO AGAIN?" Kevin laughed a dark laugh. "WE CAN BE LIKE DON'S MOTHER-IN-LAW AND CURSE THE FUCKING GANGBANGERS FROM THE GRAVE TOGETHER. JUST LIKE YOU ONCE TALKED TO ME ABOUT!"

Suddenly an oncoming driver appeared from out of a blind turn, honking furiously. Kevin had veered into the other lane, approaching within a few seconds from slamming into the car. He jerked his steering wheel to the right to avoid a collision, then back to the left in order to stay on the road, but his high speed and sudden movements caused his car to fishtail out of control. The screeching tires echoed in his ears as he closed his eyes and screamed, believing that he was doomed to slide over the edge of the cliff.

The next sound he heard pierced his consciousness as distinctively as a sonic boom. *Silence.* Kevin's eyes fluttered open as his senses concluded that he was, indeed, still here. He looked through the windshield and saw a crystal clear view of the Valley, yet he remained unsure what had happened and where he'd stopped. He got out and stared in disbelief at the front of his car, resting no more than a couple of feet from the long drop into the canyon below. He gazed out at the Valley again. The view had never looked so beautiful. "*I'm alive,*" he whispered in a trembling voice. Through the peaceful stillness of the surrounding darkness, he threw his hands over his face and wept.

⊤⊤⊤ ⊤⊤⊤ ⊤⊤⊤

Kevin drove back down Coldwater Canyon in a daze, shaken by how close he had come to dying, and sickened by the thought that he had momentarily considered suicide. *Seth's already lost his mom and dad,* he told himself. *He doesn't need to lose me, too.* The night had been a long one and he felt exhausted. He thought back to earlier that evening, before all the shit came down, when Seth innocently asked about the meaning of the "4 a.m." notation inside the outline of the heart. Something he had said struck Kevin as thought provoking, although not to be taken seriously, of course. Seth had quoted that line from "*The Tell-Tale Heart*" about the murderer hiding the victim's heart at 4 a.m. That's the kind of silly daydream Warren talked about the morning of his murder. Whoever caused the heart attacks of the gangbangers seemed to have a certain Poe signature to his work, just like Warren fantasized about.

Kevin dissected whatever details he could remember of that conversation. *He was talking about that psychic in New Orleans. She told him he'd be killed, and that he'd get revenge for his death. He talked about gangbangers and what he'd do to them if that psychic turned out to be right. Then he recited Poe lines about 'icy hearts' and 'sick hearts'.* "I should read through that Poe book," he whispered. "Maybe I'll find some clues in there about the murderer." Kevin gazed up through his windshield at the starless sky. "What do you think of that, Warren?" he said. "Looks like you've got someone doing your dirty work for you."

THIRTY-NINE

THE SEALANT FOR ALEX'S NEWLY replaced window needed a little more time to dry, so Veronica opted to sit and wait at the auto shop with Alex. She preferred spending the extra moments with her brother before saying goodbye. He'd be going back home now, and she couldn't be sure if, or when, she'd see him again. She hoped it would be as soon as a few more weeks.

"Will you stick around for Thanksgiving this time?" she asked.

"Yeah," he answered. "The old man's not around to fuck things up anymore."

"Good," she remarked, "I'll see you there."

Veronica's cell phone rang. Grasping it from inside her purse, she read Kevin's name on the caller screen. She hesitated, unsure whether to answer or not. "Hello, Kevin," she said.

"I've got some bad news, Veronica," he said, his voice sounding tense. "I just got off the phone with the principal from Clearpoint School. Some boys attacked Seth awhile ago."

"Oh, *no*," she whispered. "Is he hurt?"

"*What happened?*" Alex asked, leaning closer.

"He was held by some boys as another one grabbed his neck and kneed him in the stomach," Kevin explained. "Then they hit him in the face." Kevin's voice faltered as he continued. "The nurse says they bloodied his lip and his stomach is sore but she doesn't think there's any internal injury." She heard him choke back a quick sob before he continued. "Four boys, Veronica. *Four*! He's lucky a teacher spotted what was going on or else he could've been hurt a lot worse."

"I feel so bad for him, Kevin," she said. "I wonder if he was still upset about last night."

"That had *nothing* to do with it," Kevin grumbled. "The Principal

241

told me Seth was by himself when he was assaulted. He was threatened earlier but didn't strike back. The boys who did it were older friends of some kids who were found smoking in the bathroom. They thought Seth told on them because he was the last one in there before they got caught. But he had nothing to do with it. The teacher who busted those kids told the principal he smelled the cigarettes from the hallway. No one had to tell him anything."

"He can't catch a break," Veronica muttered with disgust.

"Seems that way," he replied. "Seth would have been in his P.E. class but we washed his gym clothes yesterday and he forgot to bring them back. He was sent inside to help a teacher. That's when he went to the bathroom."

"Were the boys Latino?" she asked.

"Yes. One of them was the older brother of a kid that Seth got in a fight with a long time ago. Maybe he used the cigarette thing as an excuse, I don't know."

"Veronica, what the hell happened to Seth?" Alex asked again.

"Wait," she whispered.

"Those boys found him sitting by himself during a recess period. He told the principal he went there 'to think', whatever that means."

"He had a lot on his mind, Kevin."

"I know he did, Veronica, but you're the only one I can turn to right now. Is there any chance you can have your assistant run things at the Day Care Center for a few hours so you could bring him home? I'll leave here now if I have to, but I'm in Orange County on an assignment and it'll take me an hour and a half to get back."

"I'll call over there," she said. "But please hurry back."

"Thank you," he said. "I'd give anything to be at that school right now, looking each of those little punks in the eyes. Principal Lee told me she was going to make them apologize in front of me, but now you'll have the honor, I guess."

"I'm more concerned about Seth than hearing what they have to say."

"Four older boys attacking one younger one," he groused. "That's the kind of bullshit that goes on with gangs, where groups of them attack one person. I've never understood how 'bangers can act so tough when they always have others there to help them. If you can't walk it on your own don't talk like you're the *man*." Veronica heard Kevin respond to someone in the background. "I've got to go," he said. "I'll call the school to let them know you're coming. Tell Seth I'll be home this afternoon."

"I'll be there as soon as I can," she said.

"Veronica?"

"Yes?"

"I really hope we can talk soon."

Alex, who insisted on knowing everything Kevin had told her, questioned Veronica. When she described the part about Seth sitting off by himself to 'think', Alex responded by saying something unusual.

"He did what I advised 'em to do."

"What do you mean?" she asked.

"I told him when the heat's on it's best to get away sometimes. To think about shit, you know? That's what he done." Alex shook his head. "Those little assholes crashed his time alone. That ain't right."

Veronica rose from her chair. "I have to go get Seth," she said.

"Wait," he told her. "I'll follow you."

Veronica shook her head. "Forget it, Alex. Seth's been through enough already."

Alex bolted out of his chair, glaring at Veronica. "And he'll go through a lot more shit if we let it happen," he growled. "He's a young kid gonna get fucked up in the head without some help from me. What happened today ain't gonna do him no good. I'm the one can make him right, you understand?" He placed his hand on her shoulder. "I know what I'm doin'."

"I don't know if it's the right time for him to see you again."

Alex stepped back, his eyes narrowing. "You said everyone's gonna be in that principal's office, right?"

"Right."

"Then trust me," he told her. "It's the *perfect* time to see me again."

TTT TTT TTT

Sitting with his shoulders hunched in Principal Lee's office, Seth cradled and massaged his tender stomach with one hand as he held an ice pack to his swollen lip with the other. He thought about the last time he'd been here. They sent him home after attacking Esteban Medina for throwing a tomato at him. Principal Lee was mad at him that day, but she seemed angrier this time, scolding the four Mexican eighth graders who sat facing her in a row of chairs on the other side of her desk.

They had threatened him earlier, calling him a snitch for telling on their friends who got caught smoking in the bathroom. Even though he hadn't said anything, they didn't believe him, and they came after him later. He would have defended himself, especially against Lorenzo Gonzalez's older brother, Ramiro, who used to warn him about 'kicking his white ass' for fighting with his brother on the playground, but they outnumbered him four to one. Instead, he decided to follow Alex's advice and find a spot to sit alone and figure out how to deal with the situation.

He saw things in a different way from before. He liked to talk with Veronica after she finished her tutoring, and she had told stories about her old neighborhood and some of her old friends. She got him to realize that there were good Mexican people, too, and that they cared about their families like anyone else. But a lot of them lived in poor neighborhoods, like where his dad was killed, and the parents lived in fear for themselves and their children. That idea made a lot of sense to him. He had experienced the fear that they felt, but he didn't have to live there all the time. He felt bad for the people who couldn't escape from those places that had gangs. He thought about Alex. Alex was in a gang -one of the ones responsible for killing his dad. How could that be possible? He hadn't seemed like a gang member, but so what? He could never be friends with him again.

Everyone looked towards the door as the Assistant Principal entered the room.

"Yes, Mrs. Petrovich?" Principal Lee said.

"The woman that Mr. Palmer called us about is here."

"Ask her to sit down, please. I'll be right out."

Principal Lee directed her attention back to the four boys. "We need to go speak with the woman who came for Seth. All of us. I want her to meet the four eighth grade boys who must be so proud of themselves for ganging up on a sixth grader. Each one of you will apologize to Seth in front of her. And I better be convinced that your apologies are sincere, or your punishment will be worse than it is already."

The boys rose and followed her to the door. Ramiro Gonzalez remained in his chair until the other three walked ahead. As he got up, he glanced at Seth and mouthed the words, "Fuck you." As Seth trailed behind, Ramiro held one hand in back of his head, as if he was scratching it. What he really did, however, was give him the finger. Seth's eyes focused on Ramiro's hand, so he didn't understand why the four boys stopped so suddenly, almost banging into one another, as they entered the waiting room. Ramiro's hand flew off his head and back down to his side, as if he had burned his fingers on his hair. Seth just wanted to see Veronica and go home, so he walked around the four boys towards the center of the room. As he looked up, he, too, came to an immediate halt. Glaring at the eighth graders with a look that gave him the shivers, was Alex.

"Hi, Seth," Veronica said, rising from her chair. "Your friend here insisted on coming."

"Are you hurt, Seth?" Alex asked, his eyes remaining fixed on the four boys.

"A little," he replied, regaining his feet and walking towards Veronica.

"I'm Eleanor Lee," she said, extending her hand towards Veronica. "Principal of Clearpoint School."

Veronica introduced herself and then Alex, who finally looked away from the four boys in order to shake Lee's hand.

"As I told Mr. Palmer, I can't express how sorry I am for what happened to Seth today," she said. "These boys have earned the harsh punishment they'll each be receiving. Seth has overcome his own problems from an earlier time and his behavior has been excellent for quite awhile now. His grades have picked up, too." She looked at Seth. "I hope you see this incident for what it was, Seth; a cowardly act of sheer stupidity. Please don't let what happened to you cloud your thinking. We've got a great group of kids at this school. No one's caused you any trouble for a long time. I hope you remember that."

Seth nodded. "Okay."

"Veronica's going to take you home now," she told him. "But these four boys have something to say to you."

Principal Lee turned towards the four eighth graders who hadn't taken more than a few steps further into the room. Seth noticed their eyes shifting from the floor to occasional nervous-looking peeks at Alex. As the Principal called each boy's name, they approached Seth and apologized. Glancing at Alex first, as if *he* was the head of the school, they spoke loud and clear when they said, "I'm sorry."

After the fourth boy, Ramiro, spoke, Veronica thanked Principal Lee and told her Seth would return tomorrow. Lee shook Veronica's hand again to say goodbye, then turned towards Alex.

"It was nice to meet you, too, Alex."

When he shook her hand, he said, "I wanna do somethin' before I leave, okay?"

"What is it, Alex?" Veronica asked, looking worried. "Everything's taken care of."

Staring at the four boys for several moments, Alex redirected his gaze towards Seth as he walked over to him. Removing his watch from his wrist, he said, "I want you to have this."

Seth couldn't believe it. Alex was giving him his really cool watch that he liked so much.

"*Really?*" Seth asked, wide-eyed. "Why, Alex?"

"You wanna know why?" he asked. "You got two flags on it, right? The American flag and what else?"

"Mexico," Seth answered.

"That's right, my man. Mexico. So think of it this way. You're the American flag, I'm the Mexican flag." Alex looked at the eighth grade boys before turning his gaze back to Seth. "Maybe now you're gonna remember. No matter where you are and what time you got, you and me is always together." Alex pulled Seth's arm toward him and tied the watch around his wrist.

"Wow," Seth replied, exhaling the word. "Thanks, Alex."

Alex stepped back and nodded his head at Seth. Turning his attention to the four boys, he said, "You speak Spanish?"

Each of the boys nodded their head and said that they did.

"*Bueno,*" Alex remarked. He walked up to the boys, who fidgeted, looked away, and seemed more nervous than ever. "I didn't do too good in school," he said, "and I've paid for it. But I learned me some things on the street they don't teach here, so remember this: '*Te enceño el camino, porqué yo ya lo caminé*'."

Seth watched as the boys nodded their heads. He looked at Veronica and saw her smiling at Alex.

"What does that mean?" Principal Lee asked.

"The road I'm showing you, I've already passed," Veronica answered.

"Alex has been through a lot in his life, Eleanor. I just think he's trying to talk some sense into these boys."

Lee smiled. "Thank you, Alex."

"Come on, Seth," Veronica said, "it's time to go."

"I'll walk you out, Veronica," said Lee. "You four boys stay right here."

Alex put an arm around Seth's shoulder. "Let's get outta here," he said. As they neared the hallway, Alex looked at him with a look of reassurance. "Ain't nobody gonna hurt you no more, Seth. Not while I'm around."

"Thanks, Alex," he said quietly, wishing he could do the same for his friend -yes, his friend, whose life would always be in danger as long as he was in a gang.

FORTY

"I'M AN ALCOHOLIC, VERONICA," KEVIN admitted, facing her on his couch. "That's what I tell them at the A.A. meetings I'm attending again, that's what I've told Seth, and that's what I'm telling you. I'm lucky to be alive and I'm not going to blow it another time. I love you and I want you back in my life."

Veronica offered a small smile, staring in silence for several moments. "I don't know yet, Kevin," she replied. "I need more time. This last week has been a painful one."

"I thought I was going over the cliff that night," he said. "What a pathetic legacy that would have been. I've changed, Veronica. Just give me a chance to prove it, okay?"

"I want to believe you, Kevin," she said. "But talking about it is the easy part. You lied to me before and it's hard on me to think you might do it again."

"It's up to me to win your trust back," he said. "I know that. The same thing goes for Seth. I want to make things right with the both of you. And I will." Kevin took Veronica's hand and squeezed it. "Thanks for joining us for dinner tonight. I'm not the only one who missed you around here."

"So what's this discovery you wanted to talk to me about?"

"I wanted to get your opinion about some research I've been doing," Kevin explained. "I've been wondering if I should talk to Lieutenant Atkinson about it, but part of me keeps thinking I should keep it to myself."

"What kind of research?"

"I may have found some clues about the heart attacks," he said. "Something about the killer that hits close to home."

"Why would you keep something to yourself if it can help find the

247

killer?"

"You'll understand my reluctance after I explain," he replied. "I've told you about Warren's love of Edgar Allan Poe, but it seems that the person causing the heart attacks has a passion for Poe just like he had, thinks just like he did. It's so identical that it's eerie."

"Like what, for instance?"

"I have to go back to the day Warren was killed. I went to his home that morning to pick up my Dodger ticket. I had fallen behind at work and had a deadline to meet, so I was going to meet them at the game..."

ᴛᵢᴛ ᴛᵢᴛ ᴛᵢᴛ

"Sorry we can't drive to the park together," Kevin said, sipping coffee while his brother sliced bagels. "I have to go over those tapes of the gangbangers I interviewed."

"Nice bunch of guys you've been talking to," Warren replied, rolling his eyes in a manner that suggested he thought otherwise. "They remind me of a line from Poe; 'There was an iciness, a sinking, a sickening of the heart'. That's how they make me feel."

Kevin shook his head. "Man, you sure grab those lines out of the air, don't you? Which one is that from?"

"*The Fall of the House of Usher*," he answered. "I really mean it, Kevin. Those jerks have no conscience whatsoever. You know why they chill me to the bone? Because their hearts are made of ice."

"That's why I wanted to write these articles. People need to be reminded of what's going on."

"They're no better than the rats in '*The Pit and the Pendulum*'. 'They writhed upon my throat; their cold lips sought my own; I was half stifled by their thronging pressure; disgust, for which the world has no name, swelled my bosom, and chilled, with a heavy clamminess, my heart'."

Kevin smiled, enthralled by his brother's instant recollection of anything Poe. "Sick hearts, icy hearts, clammy hearts. Man, you've really got a thing going with the 'ol ticker this morning, don't you?"

"So did Poe, I guess. He brings out the passion in me like no other."

"So who are the Dodgers playing tonight?"

"The Reds," he answered. "Your ticket's in my jacket by the front door."

Kevin walked out of the kitchen, spotted the jacket on a table, and lifted it by the collar. Reaching into the pocket, he removed not only what he came for, but something else that had gotten trapped inside the folded half of the ticket. Looking closer, he perused the predominantly white, nondescript business card containing corny diagrams of stars and moons. "Madame Sibilia, Psychic," he whispered, reading the name on the back. Noticing the New Orleans street address, he recalled that Warren had planned to visit a psychic before he left. Keeping the card in his hand, he reentered the kitchen.

"So what astonishing prognostications did Madame Sibilia come up with?" he asked, showing the card to Warren. The rapid transformation of his brother's expression from tranquil to troubled caught him by surprise. "Man, look at you," Kevin remarked, fighting back a grin. "Let me guess. She told you about that U.S.C. rejection."

Warren didn't answer for several moments, staring at Kevin. "Where'd you find that?" he asked.

"Your jacket pocket. I thought it was the Dodger ticket."

"I guess I haven't opened that pocket since I returned from New Orleans." Warren shook his head. "Call it my way of trying to forget what she told me that night."

"Oh, come on, Warren!" he scolded. "Enough already. How does a bright, educated man like you fall prey to these phonies? You've always taken this stuff way too seriously."

"Didn't we have this talk in New Orleans?" he asked. "The real question should be why *not* believe? There's been too much verification of people, including ones I know, that predict things, *sense* things they couldn't possibly have known, for you to be so adamant about the way you feel."

Kevin smiled. "All right, then. Tell me what the amazing Madame Sibilia said. I'll judge for myself if you're only half nuts or certifiably insane."

"There's nothing funny about this, Kevin. I can only hope that the woman was, as you say, a phony. I can only hope..." His voice trailed off. Warren poured the coffee before continuing. "The main reason I went searching for a reading was to find out about my chances at U.S.C. After rejecting several other psychics that were closer, and for reasons I still don't understand, I ended up at Madame Sibilia's. We did a Tarot card reading. She told me different things, most of them depressing and worth forgetting. But what I'll always remember is her prediction of my death, and how I'd become a kind of ghost, 'wandering' she said, with a 'spiritual restlessness'."

"Your *death?*" Kevin said, his eyes opening wide. "A *ghost?*" He rubbed his hands over his face and looked at his brother, incredulous. "Are you fucking kidding me, Warren? Psychics are supposed to tell you nice, fun stuff, aren't they? Prophecies of romance or money, right?"

"She described choosing a light of some kind," he said. "Different and darker than that bright-light-to-Heaven thing."

"Oh, and now there's another light?" he asked. "And you're going to choose that one? For what reason, may I ask?"

"In her words, 'to violate someone'."

"To *violate* someone? Why would you want to do that?"

"Revenge."

Kevin remained silent, not knowing what to say about something so ridiculous.

"Her prediction made it appear like I'd be killed and have a vendetta of some kind," Warren explained. "I'd be able to control people's minds and do evil deeds. Something like that."

"Did you ask her how this mind control thing works?"

"According to her, a decent person can become villainous in the afterlife by assimilating a memory of something wicked and acting upon it. When she explained that the memory could be from 'reality or imagination', some passages of Edgar Allan Poe crossed my mind.

"I'm not surprised," Kevin said. "Like that story you mentioned earlier?"

"*The Fall of the House of Usher?* That one doesn't capture his creative imagination for torment like *The Pit and the Pendulum*, or for unique acts of violence like *The Tell-Tale Heart,* but now that you mention it, *Usher* does conjure up a tasty twist. The story centers on Roderick Usher's losing struggle against madness."

"So instead of killing someone, you'd drive them mad instead?" Kevin asked, amused.

"Keep in mind that Usher's sanity is just about gone when he dies at the hands of his murdered sister seeking vengeance against him. If I were to stay true to the story, driving someone crazy wouldn't be enough. They'd die in the end."

"This is a really weird conversation we're having, Warren."

"That line I quoted earlier about a 'sickening of the heart' is actually a descriptive phrase about the narrator's dark feelings for the decaying house and surrounding landscape. But when I was talking about your gangbanger friends before, I was referring to the same sense of foreboding

I get when I see them congregating on streets near school. Wouldn't that be sweet vengeance, indeed," he said, "for someone to be able to scare the shit out of those macho assholes? To have somebody sicken *their* hearts for a change?"

Kevin sat there shaking his head. "Did you ever ask Madame Sibilia how the hell a living person knows so much about death? Wouldn't that have been the sensible thing to do instead of getting your balls all tied up in a knot?"

Warren bit his lip and offered a slight nod of his head.

"Yes, I suppose so," he said. "But there was something so... *convincing* about her. She even talked about someone close to me having health problems. She was right, of course. Michelle had gotten cancer and died."

"*Every* family has someone with a health problem, Warren. That's a pretty safe thing to say, if you ask me."

"Remember when I told you that I was going to visit Michelle's parents before I came home? Madame Sibilia mentioned them by their *names*, Kevin. How could she have known that?"

"They all have tricks up their sleeves. And she sounds like she was good at it."

"That's a typical answer that I don't buy at all," Warren said. "If you had been there you wouldn't be so cavalier about the whole thing, trust me. I didn't even let her read me the final card, the one that would supposedly tie everything together. I just wanted to get the hell out of there."

Kevin finished his coffee and walked over to place the cup in the sink. "I'm guessing you won't mind if I take the card?" Kevin asked.

"Hell, no," Warren replied. "I would have ripped it up anyway." He looked puzzled. "Why do you want her card?"

"I figure if I'm ever in New Orleans again, Madam Sibilia will be someone I'd like to look up."

"Yeah, right," Warren replied. "You? Mr. Nonbeliever?"

"I wouldn't be going for a reading, Warren. I'd give her a piece of my mind, okay? I don't happen to like psychics telling my brother he's about to become Casper the Unfriendly Ghost."

Warren smiled. "Well, so far so good. I was walking around feeling paranoid for awhile, but as you can see, I'm still here."

TTr TTr TTr

"That phrase, 'sickening of the heart', comes from one of the stories Warren mentioned," Kevin told Veronica. "*The Fall of the House of Usher*. I read through it to see if I could make any connections." Kevin reached for the book and angled it towards Veronica. "I want to show you something." Turning the pages to the beginning of the story, Kevin's finger moved through the opening few paragraphs until he found the line he was looking for.

"Here it is," he said. "*There was an iciness, a sinking, a sickening of the heart.*" Kevin raised his head and looked at Veronica. "That's the line he quoted when he talked about how gang members make him feel, and how he wished they could be made to feel the same way."

"There *could* be a relationship between Poe and the murders," she said. "But this doesn't prove anything."

"That's why I'm hesitant to discuss this with Lieutenant Atkinson. Either I'm overreacting or I've hit on something that nobody's thought about yet. It's as if the murderer is carrying out Warren's exact wishes."

Kevin removed Madame Sibilia's business card from his pocket and showed it to Veronica. "Unlike my brother, it's hard for me to give credence to people like this," Kevin said. "But she predicted his death, didn't she?"

"Strange that there's no address on the card," Veronica said.

"You want to hear something *really* strange?" he asked. "Atkinson told me to keep this information to myself, but since I'm talking to you about all of this I think you should know the rest." Kevin turned his attention back to the page they were looking at before. "It's the specific phrase, '*there was an iciness*' that I keep coming back to. That's because every autopsy has shown that the hearts froze at one point. Can you believe it? They *froze.*"

"Oh my God," she whispered.

Kevin recited the line again from the book. "'*There was an iciness, a sinking, a sickening of the heart*'. So let me ask you," he said, "could the '*iciness*' from Poe's story have anything to do with the heart attacks? Until I hear an answer that makes sense, which I haven't, I'll say anything is possible."

Veronica shook her head. "This is getting really weird."

"There's one other common thread, but I haven't found a connection yet," he said. "Atkinson told me each victim has been found with a jelly-like material over one of their eyes that makes it look blue."

"Do they know what it is?"

"Last time I talked with him about it he told me the test results show nothing unusual; as if there isn't anything there at all. At this point I'm sure they've put samples of that stuff under every kind of test, but I haven't heard anything different."

Kevin turned back to the table of contents, studying the titles of the various works. "I never read much Edgar Allan Poe so I don't know a lot about his stories," he said. "I want to see if I find any lines about strange looking blue eyes. I'll start with '*The Tell-Tale Heart*', because that was Warren's favorite. *The Fall of the House of Usher* didn't mention anything, but I remember Warren quoting a line from *The Pit and the Pendulum* so that's another possibility."

The sudden sound of an unexpected voice startled them.

"One of his eyes resembled that of a vulture. A pale blue eye, with a film over it."

Kevin and Veronica swung around the instant they heard Seth's voice. The expression on his face appeared serene as he stood in his pajamas, looking at the two of them.

"That's another line from '*The Tell-Tale Heart*'," he explained. "I think my dad's getting his revenge."

FORTY-ONE

THEY WENT INTO THE KITCHEN to drink hot chocolate and talk. Seth told them he had overheard everything, including the news of the frozen hearts.

"You're right about Edgar Allan Poe and the heart attacks, Uncle Kevin. My dad's gettin' back at those guys."

"I admit there's no answers at this point," Kevin said, "but I'm not ready to believe in ghosts yet, Seth."

"But nobody knows anything for sure, right?"

"Your idea's a pretty hard thing to believe, Seth," Veronica told him.

"Well, I *do*!"

"If that's truly what you think," Kevin said, "I can't stop you. But when the police finally catch this guy, maybe you'll think twice about jumping to conclusions."

Seth lowered his head and rubbed his hands across his eyes before looking up. Teardrops seeped over his lower lids as he spoke. "I was with my dad when he died," he said, his voice cracking. "I held his head in my arms. He could barely talk but he really wanted me to hear what he had to say. 'I promised your mom I'd look after you', he said. 'And protect you. I promise you I will. Always'. Seth shot a quick glance towards Kevin and Veronica before looking down again. "I believed him, okay? And I still do."

Kevin stared in silence for several moments. "There was a time I was so caught up in my own guilty feelings that I'd only think of your father when I looked at you," he said. "I couldn't deal with the loss. Now I see you for yourself. You're quite a kid."

Seth blinked several times as he stared back at Kevin. "You're my dad's twin brother, Uncle Kevin. Who do you think I see when I look at you?"

Kevin leaned back against the sink, unnerved that he'd overlooked such an obvious fact. "I can't help the way I look, Seth, but I'll try my best to do anything I can for you. Just like your mom and dad always did."

"Then can I ask you a big favor?"

"What is it?"

"Will you take me to go see the psychic lady my dad saw?"

"*What*?" he blurted. "Madame Sibilia? Absolutely not!"

Seth furrowed his eyebrows in a pleading gesture. "Please, Uncle Kevin!" he said, dropping his shoulders sharply for emphasis. "You said yourself that she predicted my dad would be killed. And that he'd get revenge after he died, right? I want to know what happened to him. And where he is."

"It was just a big coincidence, Seth," Veronica explained, her tone soft and warm. "You don't really believe people can predict that kind of stuff, do you?"

"How can you be so sure?" Seth asked. "Uncle Kevin said that nobody has any answers yet and that anything is possible."

"I admit this whole thing is really strange," she said. "But that doesn't mean you should expect your uncle to get on an airplane and fly to New Orleans in search of this woman. Believe me, Seth, you'll be setting yourself up for a big disappointment."

Veronica looked at Kevin, sitting quietly in his chair. "Isn't that right, Kevin? Seth needs to get that silly idea out of his head. Madame Sibilia is just a phony who takes advantage of people."

"Even if she lived next door I wouldn't want you talking with her," Kevin said. "She told your father some terrible things. I can't trust her that she wouldn't fill your head with thoughts that might scare you. Can you understand that?"

"All I know is we'll never find out now," Seth said, looking rejected. "I don't care what you say. I know it's my dad."

Kevin rose to his feet, sipping from his cup as he looked at his nephew. He walked to the counter near the sink and turned back to face them, leaning against the ledge. "I certainly can't say I'm as sure as you, Seth. But I also can't overlook the fact that Madame Sibilia is where this whole thing began. If there's one thing I've learned as a reporter, it's that questions are best answered by going to the source."

"What are you saying, Kevin?" Veronica asked, her eyes widening. "You're not thinking…"

"I need to ask Madame Sibilia why she said those things to Warren. It's as if she had a roadmap to the future. I remain skeptical, but I want closure on this thing once and for all."

"All right!" Seth shouted.

"More like, 'all wrong'," Veronica said, shaking her head. "Are you really going to go through with this?"

"Maybe she guessed right on a few things," Kevin replied, "but she's a piece of the puzzle I can't ignore, and the sooner I see her, the better. The problem is, it's been months since Warren talked with her. Who knows if she's still there?"

"The phone number's on her business card," Seth said, bolting from his chair. "You left it in the other room. I'll go get it."

Kevin and Veronica watched as Seth rushed from the kitchen. "Didn't you tell Warren how ridiculous you thought he was for believing her?" Veronica asked.

"You bet I did," he exclaimed. "And I still think that…up to a point." His eyes narrowed as he reflected on all that had happened. "I've been mulling this over this for awhile, Veronica, and I admit I'm curious about this woman. Once Seth brought up the idea of seeing her, I realized the time was right."He breathed in deeply before exhaling in a "maybe I'm crazy" resignation. "This trip is going to cost me a few dollars," he said. "I can only hope that its money well spent."

"When will you go?"

"That depends on a couple of things," he told her. "I first have to know that she's still in business and I can find her. I'll also need to ask my mom if she can look after Seth while I'm gone."

"The phone number's right here," Seth said, returning and pointing to the spot on the card. "Call it, Uncle Kevin."

After a single dial tone, a recording answered with a slight French accented voice delivering the following message:

"*I am Madame Sibilia. You will find me in Pirate's Alley, just beyond the high seas. Come tomorrow night.*" The line went dead.

Kevin hung up the phone. "Well, she's still around," he told them, "but the recording doesn't allow a message to be left. It said she'll be there tomorrow night in a place called, 'Pirate's Alley'." Kevin looked at Seth. "Even if I get a ticket on such short notice, I'd still need your grandma to stay with you all day and overnight. That doesn't give her much time. I think it's best to try for next weekend."

"Veronica could stay with me," Seth answered.

Kevin looked at her and rolled his eyes. "Apparently, Seth likes to volunteer other people's time without asking."

Veronica smiled at Seth. "I still think your uncle's crazy for doing this, but it's a date."

"Cool!" Seth shouted.

"Thanks, Veronica," Kevin said. "I owe you one. Admittedly, I'm anxious to get this over with. I'll see if I can book the flight now." Before going online for reservations, Kevin redialed the number on Madame Sibilia's card, hoping to talk to someone. He heard the beginning of the same recording, but decided to wait and see if he'd get a chance to leave a message this time.

"*I am Madame Sibilia. You will find me in Pirate's Alley, just beyond the high seas. Come tomorrow night.*" Before the line went dead, however, he heard something new that hadn't been said before. "*I have been waiting for you.*"

FORTY-TWO

*A*S KEVIN NEARED THE ST. Louis Cathedral, he knew that he'd reached the vicinity of Pirate's Alley. A few minutes later he stared into the entrance, recalling the words to Madame Sibilia's recording. "*You will find me in Pirate's Alley, just beyond the high seas.*" Kevin gazed down the length of both sides, scanning the various shops. "*She's got to be around here somewhere,*" he said to himself.

Kevin didn't feel the necessity to ask anyone if they knew Madame Sibilia. He wasn't sure what made him so confident about locating her but he just had a *feeling*. As Kevin reached the other end, he saw a park with groups of people sitting at individual tables under the lights. Some of them appeared to be psychics. He stopped at each table to establish their names but didn't find her.

As he reentered the alley, he gazed in astonishment at another entranceway on the left that had gone unnoticed earlier. "*How could I have missed that?*" he asked himself. The almost nonexistent lighting didn't help, but Kevin concluded he'd found the proper direction to take. An oddly shaped building approximately fifty yards ahead caught his attention and lured him closer. He soon realized the strange contour wasn't the building itself, but the large slanted awning angling below the roofline, causing much of the front entrance to be hidden, including the door. The place stood dark with no sound coming from inside. Kevin walked past the far side of the awning and headed towards the entrance. In white wooden letters, large enough to still be legible in the near blackness, the name above the door read, 'The High Seas'. "*So this is what she meant,*" he whispered. "*I'm almost there.*"

Kevin veered around a corner, escorted by the silence of the isolated area. He hadn't seen anybody for awhile, but didn't care. He walked with a hop to his step now, sensing the finalization of his search. The scarce moonlight offered him just enough visibility to observe his surroundings. Huge pots with dense, green Ficus trees stood at attention like palace guards on the right and left sides. Slowing his pace, he discovered a semi-shielded passage hidden from clear view by one of the containers and trees. Venturing inside towards a patio entrance, unmistakable from where he stood, a neon sign in a second floor window read, 'Madame Sibilia -Psychic'.

A large white door stood open, ushering Kevin past more potted Ficus and smaller containers with other types of greenery. Colorful squared stones throughout the walkway resembled a huge patchwork quilt. In the center of the courtyard, an old-fashioned gas lamp created a perfect completion to the unique, New Orleans style ambiance. He felt comforted by the flickering flame; offering him enough light to touch the cold, smooth ridges of the lamp's rod-iron post. Keeping his eyes fixed on the sign in the window, as if drawn by a neon magnet, he climbed the steps and knocked on the door. He gazed out from the deck at the shadow-veiled garden and thought about Warren. So much sadness had ensued since his brother stood in this same spot, innocently hoping for some good news about a teaching job. As the door opened, Kevin prepared to introduce himself. That wouldn't be necessary.

"Hello, Mr. Palmer," the pretty black woman said. "I've been expecting you."

He stared at the woman in the maroon-colored gown and headdress. "How'd you know my name?" he asked. "And what do you mean, 'you were expecting me'?"

"I know you have questions," she said. "I will attempt to answer them all for you. Please follow me."

She led Kevin from the small, candlelit entryway through a curtain into a larger room. Another assemblage of candles provided enough visibility to spotlight a bright green sofa with matching chairs. The dim illumination couldn't camouflage their sharp contrast against the dark wooden walls. A square table on the right, covered by a long black cloth, stood about fifteen feet away. Two chairs faced each other on opposite sides. A blue-colored lava lamp provided an eerie glow from a small round stand in the far left corner, and on the right, he saw a doorway filled with beaded strings. The smell of incense seemed to add the final flourish to the mystery of the moment.

"Come sit down," she said, leading him to the table.

After taking his seat, Kevin reached out to lift a portion of a gray handkerchief draped over something unseen. When he spotted the Tarot cards he held his hand there, his mind flashing back to the conversation he had with Warren about Madame Sibilia.

"I know why you came here, Mr. Palmer," she said. "The Tarot cards are not necessary and shall remain covered."

"Have we met before?" he asked. "You knew who I was as soon as you opened the door."

"Knowledge often extends beyond the point of origin," she replied, her unwavering eyes holding his. "Your brother was a vessel through which I could see others. I became aware of your existence."

"I'm sorry, but I find that hard to believe."

"One's view of reality is based on life experience," she said, her tone gentle yet firm. "What must *not* be impossible to you, Mr. Palmer, is accepting that which you do not understand. If you wish to learn about your brother, and perhaps save him, you must accept a reality much different from what you know."

Kevin remained silent for several moments, unsure what to say or how to react.

"All right," he said, "let's move on. Why did you tell Warren all those terrible things?"

"Your brother's fate was determined, yet he couldn't have known of the perilous journey ahead. There was a reason he found his way to me. I was chosen to interpret his future."

"You were chosen?" Kevin asked. "You mean by someone you work for?"

Madame Sibilia's eyes narrowed. "No, Mr. Palmer. Your brother was summoned by a greater power."

"I'm sorry, I don't get what you mean."

"Some people need guidance," she replied. "Your brother was drawn to me. Directed. He needed to understand certain things. As *you* will learn to understand certain things."

Kevin leaned forward, his eyes burrowing in on hers. "What I need to understand is why my nephew thinks his father is somehow still alive. Thanks to all that craziness you told Warren, his son is under that impression. It's unhealthy and I don't like it one bit."

Madame Sibilia waited in silence for several seconds before responding. "Your brother's journey could not be altered, only explained. I am aware that you come here seeking confirmation of an untruth, but you will discover something else entirely. You will have your answer before you leave here."

"Fine," he replied. "You said you were expecting me. Why?"

"You believe you came here on your own volition, but I can tell you most assuredly, you did not. I was here for your brother. I am here for you."

"You're making me uncomfortable with this kind of talk," he said.

"You may find certain answers difficult, Mr. Palmer, but your presence here is necessary."

"Well, you didn't make it easy, that's for sure," he said. "I got your number from the business card Warren gave me, and all I kept getting was that recording about Pirate's Alley and The High Seas. You should put your address on there."

"The card served as our union; a way to connect us in order to help your brother. Its purpose has been achieved."

"You're right," he said, "the purpose of the card *has* been achieved. Now I don't want it anymore. It's a sad reminder." Kevin reached into his jacket pocket and brought out the card. Preparing to place it on the table, his near inattention turned into an open-mouthed stare of disbelief.

"The card's blank!" he exclaimed. He turned it over. "Both sides!"

"The time has come to search outside your reality, Mr. Palmer. But you must first provide the information of your brother's death, and what has happened to cause your nephew's concern."

Kevin stared at the card in silence awhile longer before dropping it on the table. "I didn't expect to talk with you for long, but I've come all this way, so why not?"

Kevin related the details of Warren's murder. He then recounted their conversation from that morning when Warren discussed the Tarot card reading. He told her everything that he remembered: Her prediction of Warren's death. That he would somehow return seeking revenge. That he would have the ability to carry out certain thoughts from his life.

"That's when we talked about some Edgar Allan Poe stories," he said. "Warren knew all of his works inside and out. He fantasized about an afterlife where he could take some of the gruesome ideas and use them on gang members. Unfortunately, my nephew overheard me talking to my girlfriend about all of this. Now he thinks his father must be the reason for all the heart attacks that have killed the gang members since his murder. And why the autopsies have shown their hearts to have actually frozen. After all these months there still aren't any answers. That's why he's harboring these silly thoughts."

Madame Sibilia closed her eyes, as if in deep thought. Nodding her head, she returned her gaze to Kevin. "You say that many have died since your brother's murder. I believe you will find the heart attacks to account for half that total."

Kevin leaned back in his chair, his eyes opening wide. "How'd you know that?"

"Your brother had a strong moral sense of right and wrong," she said. "But his morality has been misdirected. He seeks revenge against those gang members, yes, but only as a reaction to their murderous behavior. Remnants of his moral compass still influence him. He would never initiate a killing, only respond to one committed by another."

Kevin shook his head. "My brother was a big believer in people like you, Madame Sibilia, but I'm not. Don't expect to persuade me that Warren has anything to do with the murders."

"There is still hope your brother's soul can be redeemed," she said, ignoring his cynicism. "His final card was The Judgment card. That represented a new beginning. But the opportunity could end soon. That is the danger he faces."

Kevin studied her concerned expression. She was either a great actress or an actual believer in everything she said. He decided he wanted to hear more. "What kind of danger?"

"Your brother chose another path from the one which was intended. His is an unsettled spirit, reborn from the union of opposite emotions at the time of death. Love for his son. Hate for his killers. The love will last forever, Mr. Palmer, but he must first reconnect with its existence if he is to find peace."

"So what you're saying is that he's still obsessed with the hate for his killers?"

Madame Sibilia looked at him, nodding her head in an almost imperceptible manner.

"The hate," she said, "stands a chance of consuming him forever. When that happens he'll start to mutate, as if in a cocoon spun from evil. He will be helpless to prevent himself from becoming another spiritual force for wickedness in the world."

Kevin remembered Warren using the word, 'convincing', to describe Madame Sibilia. Now he understood why. Was she a phony with a great script? Maybe...maybe not.

"How do you know so much about death?" he asked.

"Before you leave here, Mr. Palmer, you will have your answer. But we must continue."

"I'm going to hold you to that," he muttered. "Can you explain why after months of murders there suddenly hasn't been a killing between these two gangs in weeks? Or any heart attacks?"

"We must hope his is not a pyrrhic victory," she said. "You must seek him out. His own flesh and blood is the one who can redirect him back to the light of peace."

"His own flesh and blood?"

"Seth. He is the lone connection, the one existing root from his seed. He is the one that can make contact."

"*Seth?*" Kevin uttered, his voice rising from the shock. "Are you kidding me? How could that ever be possible?"

"At a time when your brother violates another," she answered. "Seth must be there."

"Oh sure, no problem!" Kevin rubbed his hands over his face in exasperation. "Give me a break! This is all so absurd!"

"You must have faith, Mr. Palmer," she said. "Your brother's course has followed the path of the Tarot. He left here without hearing a reading of the final card. That is what still gives me hope -the significance of the Judgment."

"What's the Judgment?" Kevin asked bitterly.

"The tenth and final card of your brother's Tarot," she answered. "Representing the outcome of the other nine: Reward, renewal, a cleaning of the slate." Madame Sibilia leaned forward, her eyes set on Kevin's. "The offering of a new beginning, Mr. Palmer."

Kevin's head spun in anxiety and confusion. He had heard more than he bargained for. What was he hoping to achieve, anyway? To find some hidden paperwork that Warren filled out informing her of family names? Concealed cameras exposing her as a phony? Admittedly, he couldn't say he'd discovered *proof* that Warren's fantasies were unfounded, and that surprised him. Her speculations seemed unique and interesting, sure, but what was he left with now? A recommendation to hook Seth up with some dying gangbanger at 3:59 in the morning so he could tell his father to go away? Nothing more remained to be said.

"Madame Sibilia," he said, rising from his chair, "thank you for your time." Reaching into his inside pocket for his wallet, Kevin brought out some money.

"That won't be necessary," she said. "Just believe in the Tarot, Mr. Palmer. Do what you must and your brother will find his way back to the light of peace."

"Whatever you say, Madame Sibilia," he replied, uncaring.

"There is one more thing you must remember," she said.

"Yeah?" he muttered, nearing the door. "What's that?"

"Look for a sign from Heaven and Earth. Then you will know he is safe."

Kevin walked out on the deck to take a final look at the grounds below. The fresh air offered a welcome change from the incense, and he felt his head start to clear. Turning around to say goodbye, he saw Madame Sibilia standing just inside the doorway. He started to walk down the steps when he remembered something he wanted to ask her. "I almost forgot," he said. "Tell me how a young woman like you knows so much about death."

For the first time since his arrival, Madame Sibilia smiled. "Remember, Mr. Palmer, there are times you must be willing to search outside your reality. There are those who die, like your brother, who choose to return in order to hurt others. And there are those who choose to return to help souls on the verge of danger; to guide them through the darkness of their fate. Inside, where I stand, my own destiny is secure. There, where you stand..." Kevin stared at Madame Sibilia as she walked towards him. "...I lost my life."

Kevin froze in horror as Madame Sibilia's face and body transformed into that of an old, haggard woman in the time it took her to step outside the door. A face as unlined as a starless sky suddenly possessed a profusion of wrinkles atop sagging black flesh resembling melted wax. The smooth arms and neck changed into the texture of a dried riverbed, and the proud, straight shoulders drooped like a wilted sunflower. "This would have been me in your world today, Mr. Palmer," she said, her voice a raspy wheeze. "Now go. Believe in the Judgment card. And remember to look for a sign from Heaven and Earth."

FORTY-THREE

K EVIN TOOK SEVERAL QUICK STEPS backward before grabbing
the rail and scrambling down the steps into the hushed darkness
of the deserted alley. He followed his instincts around an unlit corner
on the left, striving to remain calm. *"How the hell can people see around
here?"* he whispered aloud. His inability to hear anything exacerbated
his confusion, making his anxiety worsen. He tried to get his bearings
straight as he walked, looking for that place, 'The High Seas'. For some
reason, the lyric from the Barbara Streisand song that his mother liked so
much came into his head: *People who need people are the luckiest people in
the world.* Right now, Kevin needed people.

The breakthrough came in the sudden sound of laughter emerging
from somewhere around the nearby corner, transforming Kevin's unsure
footsteps into an apprehensive jog. He wasn't aware just how long he
ran, but the sight of a college-aged couple standing in front of a building
eased him back to a walking pace. Wiping beads of sweat with the back
of his hand, Kevin approached them to reacquaint himself with normalcy
and take his mind off of Madame Sibilia.

"Is this place any good?" he asked, nodding towards what appeared
to be some kind of bar and grill.

"The High Seas?" the girl in the Tulane sweatshirt replied. "Oh yeah,
for sure. My friends and I come here all the time."

Kevin didn't understand. "The High Seas?" he asked.

His eyes looked upon the name in colorful block letters above the
door. The large cloth awning had disappeared. A white wooden overhang
with a bank of lights across the underside hung in its place. That was
the only wood he saw on an otherwise solid brick building. Yet as far
as he could tell, the structure he saw before had consisted entirely of

wood. And where was the darkened path he took from Pirate's Alley to Madame Sibilia's? A brick wall with a large trash bin stood there now, cutting off any access to the other side. Hadn't he just come from there? "They changed the location of the place, right?" he asked. "It used to be somewhere else around here."

"Nope," the girl replied, shaking her head and smiling. "This is where it's always been."

"My old man used to eat here when he was a kid," the boy said. "It sure looked different then."

"Well, duh," the girl remarked, laughing. "That's because it burned down, dummy." She rolled her eyes and looked back at Kevin. "Now it's brick instead of wood." She pointed towards the wall. "There was an alley on the other side. That's where the entrance used to be."

Kevin stared at the wall, wondering what the hell was going on. "Have you seen a place around here where the awning is falling off? You have to walk around it to get to the door."

The boy uttered a quick laugh. "There was only one place like that, mister, and you're looking at it."

"What do you mean?" Kevin asked.

"That's old school," he replied. "A long time ago 'The High Seas' had something like that. It was real stupid looking. If you go inside they got a picture of the way it was."

Kevin wanted to shout at the top of his voice, "*You're insane! That's the way it looked just a while ago! I saw it with my own eyes!*" He forced himself to take a long, slow breath.

"Where's that picture?" he asked.

"It's hanging on the wall near the bathrooms," she said. "You can't miss it."

Kevin rushed towards the entrance without saying another word. Throwing the door back, he dashed inside, glanced around, and spotted a framed photograph near the bathroom doors. He moved towards the sizable black and white snapshot as if in a trance, barely cognizant of the busy surroundings. When he got to within easy viewing distance, Kevin grew lightheaded. There on the wall, in a silent testimony to his changing reality, hung a picture of *The High Seas* that looked identical to the darkened establishment he had examined earlier. His eyes moved to the inscription on the bottom right corner of the photograph: *The High Seas -early 1960's.*

Kevin's legs felt leaden as he moved towards the exit like a man walking underwater. Disoriented to a point of nausea, he sat on the outside steps trying to regain his composure. His mind felt thick and stretched to the limit, a gum-like wad of brain tissue struggling to think straight. An alluring need for scotch forced him to his feet and away from the temptation that threatened to envelop him. He hurried through a couple of uncertain turns until he found himself back on Royale Street, the boisterous sound of jazz music prevalent once again.

♩♩♩ ♩♩♩ ♩♩♩

Kevin wanted to leave New Orleans as soon as possible and didn't give a damn that he spent extra money changing his flight home to the earliest time available; 5:30 a.m. With sand bags for legs and a brain sustained by an air pump, he approached a taxi stand in the early morning darkness, still dazed from his encounter with Madame Sibilia and operating on zero sleep. The sound of a horn jolted him from his trance. "*God damn trumpet!*" he muttered. He blinked several times, swaying from a loss of focus as he stared at the taxi parked a few feet away. Looking through the windshield he saw a smiling, heavy-set driver with a bright Hawaiian shirt give him a, '*Well, what's it gonna be?*' motion with his raised arms and open palms. Kevin walked over. "The airport, please," he said, sliding into the back seat.

With a thirty minute ride ahead of him, Kevin scrunched down, pressed his back against the corner of the seat, and gazed through the outside blackness attempting to piece together the ramifications of his experience with Madame Sibilia. If she was to be believed, as Kevin now deemed quite possible, Warren might be on his way to altering into some kind of unwitting force for evil. His brother's good intentions for making those two gangs pay the ultimate price had gone awry. But what kind of irony was in play here? His brother had been a loving family man, a principled human being who used to rail at society's ills. When the two of them were kids, complaining about something as unfair, their father always responded with the same retort: "*Whoever said life was fair?*" Kevin now asked himself another question: "*Whoever said death was fair?*"

"So, you have a good time?"

Kevin thought he heard the driver say something. "I'm sorry," he mumbled, snapping back to attention. "What'd you say?"

"Bourbon Street, my man. Did you find your fun?"

"No, not really," he replied. "To be honest with you, I can't wait to get out of here."

"Don't hear that very often," the driver said. "Maybe next time'll be better."

Kevin stared out his window, pleased to see the street crowds thinning by the minute. "You know what's funny?" he said. "I'd been here one other time and looked forward to coming back. Now I don't think I'll ever return."

"If you don't mind me asking," the driver said, "what are you so down about?"

"It's sort of hard to explain."

"Okay," he replied, "so where you from?"

"L.A."

"Never been there," he told him. "Closest I got was Vegas a couple of times. Born and raised in this great city."

"New Orleans born and raised, huh? Well, sorry to rain on the old parade, my friend. I'm sure it's a great city."

"Yes, sir," the driver replied. "Founded in 1718 by Jean Baptiste Le Mayne. Sold in 1803 to the United States by Napolean I as part of the Louisiana Purchase. Orleans was the family name of two royal dynasties of France; Valois-Orleans and Bourbon-Orleans. That's who Bourbon Street's named after. The French Quarter is actually the site of the original city."

Kevin saw the driver looking at him in the rear view mirror.

"Sorry, man, I hope I'm not boring you or nothin'," he said. "I just love talking about the history of this place."

"No, you're not boring me," Kevin replied. "I didn't know those things."

"My wife calls me, 'The New Orleans Know-It-All," he said. "I can tell you anything you want to know about the city. From the old days up to modern times, whatever."

"What's your name?" Kevin asked.

"Sam," he answered. "And you sir, are?"

"Kevin."

"So tell me, Kevin, what happened? You get mugged or somethin'?"

"No, nothing like that," he said. "I had a weird experience with a psychic tonight. I know that must sound stupid, but she got me upset."

"A psychic, huh? Well, most of 'em are as phony as a politician's promise. Don't let it worry you."

"I wish she was a phony, believe me. That's *exactly* what I was hoping for." Kevin looked out at the darkness. "I have a bad feeling she's for real," he said in a quiet voice.

"I know a few of them psychic ladies," Sam replied. "What's her name?"

"Madame Sibilia," he answered somberly, his eyes staying fixed on the window.

Sam remained silent. Kevin glanced back at him through the rearview mirror. "You know her?"

"Kevin," Sam said, hesitancy to his voice, "the only Madame Sibilia I ever heard of was murdered a long time ago. I was still in diapers when it happened but my folks still talked about her when I was older. That was a big story around here."

Kevin squirmed in his seat. "What can I say?" he asked. "That's what she calls herself."

"Believe me," Sam replied, "anyone who grew up around here would do a double take if they saw the name, 'Madame Sibilia'."

"How was she murdered?" Kevin asked.

"Shot by a man named Tobias Wellington III."

"Sounds like money to me."

"The wife had the dough," Sam said. "She owned property all over the city."

"So what happened?"

"The dude was up to his eyeballs in gambling debts. He wound up torching a joint he owned for the insurance money." Sam chuckled. "Can you believe it? Does that trick ever work? They musta got suspicious 'cause he didn't get shit the whole time they were investigating. What a loser."

"The place that burned down, it wasn't called 'The High Seas' was it?"

"Yeah, that's the name," he answered. "'The High Seas'. They rebuilt the place later. Same name, too. Not as much of a restaurant anymore, though. More of a sports bar kind of place."

Kevin rubbed his face in his hands, trying to maintain his senses. "So how does Madame Sibilia figure into all of this?"

"Mrs. Wellington used to go her for readings. She leased the house to her so maybe there was a trade-off. After the murder, she told reporters Madame Sibilia had warned her about her husband; that he was in financial trouble, that he'd set fire to his place, and that he planned to kill her for the money. The whole nine yards. The mistake she made was leaving a 'screw you' letter at the house telling him all about Madame

Sibilia's information. The guy flipped out. He goes and shoots that poor psychic. Then he kills himself."

"He shot her by the front door of her house, right?"

"Yeah," Sam answered. "How'd you know that?"

"Call it a gut feeling," he said quietly.

They spent the remainder of the ride in relative quiet. Kevin had been away from home less than twenty-four hours, but felt exhausted. Still, the thought of an airport with cranky kids and loud people sharing their conversations on cell phones appealed to him a lot more than sitting alone with his thoughts. When Sam pulled up to the curb, Kevin thanked him and removed his wallet. Counting the cash, he handed him the fare plus a generous tip. Sam had earned every extra dollar.

"Keep the change, Sam," he told him, sliding the wallet back into his pants pocket.

Sam looked at the bills in his hand and smiled, his red beefy cheeks looking like half-filled flesh balloons. "Hey, thanks, bro," he answered. "You ever make it back, come find me, okay? The New Orleans Know-It-All will take care of you big time."

"I'll remember that," Kevin said, doubting he'd ever return. He exited the car and started walking away before suddenly remembering something else he needed to know. "Hey, Sam!" he yelled, approaching the taxi again. "Who lives at Madame Sibilia's house now?"

"It ain't there no more," he answered. "Remember, the house was owned by Wellington's wife. She had the place torn down. They got some shops there now. Real close to Saint Louis Cathedral." Sam shook his head and shrugged. "It's too bad. That was the last house left standing in the area."

"That can't be," he said. "I was at her house before you picked me up."

"No way, Kevin," he said. "Maybe *your* Madame Sibilia has a house somewhere, but not the one I know about. Not anymore, at least."

A woman's voice came over his speaker. Sam had another ride waiting.

"Gotta go, Kevin. Come back and give this great city another chance, okay?"

Departure time still had ninety long minutes to go. The relative quiet of the waiting area felt like an isolation chamber, and without the human distractions he expected, Kevin continued to focus on Madame Sibilia and what she said about Warren's fate. Fatigue and depression sandwiched his thoughts and left him feeling mentally drained. For several minutes he stared down the terminal at the bar entrance, debating whether one drink should or shouldn't be permissible just this time. His parched throat grew harder to ignore as he imagined how uplifting the effect of a fine scotch could be on his shaken psyche. "*It's only one drink,*" he told himself. "*Nobody will know. With what I've gone through I deserve something pleasant, don't I?*"

Kevin vaulted out of his chair and increased his pace as he neared the bar. He located the nearest stool and kept the bartender in his sights until the man came over to take his order. "A scotch, please, no ice."

The bartender nodded and turned around to get the bottle. "No... *wait,*" Kevin blurted. "Make it a double."

A grinning Jim Carrey look-alike wearing a green Starbucks apron and Saints cap approached the bar and leaned forward over the counter. "Hey, Seth," he said, his mocking tone followed by the waving of money. "I got Brees and the boys covering the spread, you hear what I'm saying? No way can your wimpy Texans stop us. No freaking way!"

"Sorry to see you lose your hard earned money, my friend," he replied, laughing, as he brought Kevin his drink. "They'll shut him down like a red neck sheriff at a whorehouse."

"*Seth?*" Kevin asked. "Is that really your name?"

"All my life, buddy. Why?"

"I'm reminded of someone with the same name," Kevin said. "And it couldn't have come at a better time." He stared at his glass for a long, contemplative moment. A smile formed on his lips as he rose from his stool and reached into his pocket for his wallet, pulling out a couple of bills. "Keep the change."

"You leaving already?" the bartender asked, looking surprised. "You didn't touch your drink."

"On the contrary, Seth," he said. "That was the best scotch I ever had."

ᛏᛏᛏ ᛏᛏᛏ ᛏᛏᛏ

Kevin closed the Edgar Allan Poe book and looked out at the predawn darkness as the plane ascended. He scrutinized the combination of blackness and bright lights and envisioned the entire panorama as a giant circuit board. He contrasted this observation with the short-circuiting currents running through his own mind and concluded that his jumbled thoughts seemed a long way from the neatly integrated units he visualized below.

Madame Sibilia appeared to possess knowledge of death that no human being could discern, but he still questioned what to make of her. He witnessed her physical transformation with his own eyes, but had she performed some sort of trickery? He wasn't sure what to think when he located her number on his cell phone's recent call list and pressed redial, only to be told by a phone company recording to "please check the number and dial again." When he dialed a second time, slowly and by hand, he received the same result.

He had walked along the brick entranceway lined with potted plants, touched the gas powered lamppost in the courtyard, viewed the multi-colored stones from the light of the flame, grasped the ornate railing leading to the white wooden deck where he stood, and thought about Warren while standing at her door. He had walked inside and sat at a table, Tarot cards in sight, talking about Warren's visit and what had happened afterwards. He had experienced all of these things, witnessed so much, so how could Sam say the house no longer existed? If he was right, and he seemed to be quite sure, then whose place was that? The more Kevin thought about it, the more he resigned himself to the unavoidable answer. He didn't enter Madame Sibilia's house that exists now. He sat inside the one that existed *then*.

Warren could have gone to any of the easy-to-find psychics, yet he wound up with Madame Sibilia. Was it preordained? She told Kevin that she was there to help those on the verge of danger. Was he somehow brought there, transported into another time and place, to learn of the future by entering the past? His reporter's intuition made him sense in Madame Sibilia a genuine sincerity, but the whole episode with her was one of those 'you had to be there' experiences. He decided he'd disclose some of what she said, but he'd omit the part about Warren's possible 'mutation'. Seth, especially, didn't need to hear that. Nor would he divulge her theory about Seth's ability to communicate with Warren. What was the point of telling them that ridiculous scenario? And the final minute on the patio? How do you explain something like that without coming across as a lunatic?

"*Admit it, Kevin,*" he told himself, "*there was no trickery. What you saw, and touched, and heard was real. The one and only Madame Sibilia exists, no matter what Sam says.*"

If he therefore believed in what he saw, and heard, then Warren's continued existence wasn't just a possibility; it was quite probable. Through the simmering upheaval of his thoughts, the one idea he continued to revisit pertained to Madame Sibilia's answers about his brother's fate. She told him Warren's tenth card meant peace and a new beginning, but how could that be an option when he continued to move closer towards becoming, as she said, "another spiritual force for wickedness in the world?" In the unending hourglass of pain and sorrow that measured how long humanity was meant to suffer, Warren would soon be an added grain of sand.

Madame Sibilia pinpointed Seth as the one link remaining to Warren's spirit, the one person who could allow his soul to rest in peace. Even if the truce ended, how could Seth ever communicate with his father when the killings occurred at unknown locations far away from his presence? And what kind of sign from Heaven and Earth was Madame Sibilia talking about? Would the clouds suddenly part like a billowy white curtain, sending a hand down to tap him on the shoulder? Would Warren's face illuminate like a million neon lights somewhere among the constellations? To the battering ram of questions demanding to be let in on some answers, Kevin had none to offer. How could he expect otherwise, knowing the world he lived in, and identified with, was just a stepping stone to something far beyond his understanding?

FORTY-FOUR

"I COULDN'T LIE TO HIM, VERONICA," Kevin said, reaching for the knife to slice another lemon. "I assumed that Madame Sibilia was a big phony, but as I explained to Seth, she was able to connect the dots and reveal so much that I left there thinking she's the real deal."

"I'm surprised," Veronica replied, still trying to decide if she believed this herself. "I wasn't expecting this kind of reaction from you."

"This is just between us, okay? I'm not about to discuss Madame Sibilia's ideas with anyone else." Kevin chuckled. "Can you imagine if I was to go to the police with this information?"

Veronica finished preparing the meat and placed the bowl in her refrigerator. "I'm still amazed that she knew half the deaths were by heart attack," she said. "And this is because Warren supposedly needs a killing to occur first before he goes and kills? Like a back and forth sort of thing?"

Kevin nodded. "Warren's way of giving these guys a chance to shape up, I guess. But once they cross that line..."

"What was Seth's reaction when you told him?"

"I didn't go into complete detail," he said, taking an onion from the plastic bag on the counter, "because she told me some disturbing things. But he was convinced of Warren's involvement before I went to New Orleans, so this only verified his belief. I urged him to keep this to himself for obvious reasons. He promised me he would."

Veronica walked over to Kevin and watched as he started to slice the onion. "Thanks for helping me with the *posole*," she said, stroking the back of his neck. "You're picking Seth up at his friend's house, right?"

"At six o'clock. When I told him you were cooking dinner for us tonight he got excited. Apparently Alex told him you're an awesome cook."

Veronica smiled. "He'll like it," she said. "And so will you."

Kevin gave her a quick kiss on the lips. "I'm sure I will," he replied, turning away to resume cutting.

Veronica stood behind Kevin, staring in silence. The time had come. "Would you kiss me again?" she asked.

Kevin looked back at her with an expression that transformed itself from one of surprise to one of recognition and longing. Placing his hands on the sides of her face, he leaned forward, brushing her lips with his in tentative fleshy strokes, back and forth, between the corners of her mouth. Veronica wrapped her arms around Kevin's neck and kissed him harder, moving her body close to his until they locked in a full embrace. He reached back to remove the pin holding up her hair, causing the soft avalanche to tumble down around her shoulders. Pulling back to search Kevin's eyes, she whispered, "I hope I'm ready, Kevin."

Kevin leaned his forehead against hers. "I haven't changed the way I feel," he said softly. You're the driver of this car, okay? We'll go as far as you take us."

She took a deep, silent breath. "I want you so much."

Veronica reached for his hand and led him into her room. They fell onto the bed in a frenzy of fervent kissing. She felt his warm breath rushing in airy waves behind the delicate sliding of his tongue, traveling from cheekbone to earlobe. She pressed her breasts against his. Grasping the bottom of his shirt, she pulled it up and over his head, tossing it aside. As she stroked the soft hair along his chest, gliding her fingers around his nipples, she leaned forward. "Take my shirt off, Kevin."

Placing his hands on her cheeks, Kevin gave Veronica a long, soft kiss before undoing the top button. As each one came undone, he stopped and kissed the newly exposed flesh, stroking her skin in soothing circular motions, occupying each additional territory with an apparent wonder and delight that turned into added time spent furthering her own pleasures. Veronica watched him through the semi-darkness, trusting the moment, and offering herself to the one man she wanted.

Unfastening the final button, Kevin removed her shirt and gazed, his eyes taking a slow stroll across the unveiled contour of her light brown skin. "You're beautiful," he whispered. Kevin cupped the round fleshy mounds of her breasts, licking and sucking gently on her nipple in wet pulsating tempos as his fingertips teased and brushed the hardened tip of the other. Veronica closed her eyes and gasped as Kevin's tongue traveled southward to her stomach, simultaneously massaging and caressing her breasts. Placing her hands on the back of his head, she held him there.

As every nerve ending seemed to collaborate towards her sexual release, she pulled him close and whispered the only thing that mattered at that precious point in time. "Kevin, please... I need you. Make love to me."

With eyes half-closed, Veronica watched as the top of Kevin's head ventured further down her legs, immersing her in a blood-stirring stimulation of each uncharted area he explored, until her panties were removed like the cloth on an unveiled sculpture. He lifted her ankles and placed them on his shoulders as he maneuvered his head between her legs. Transforming her thighs into a lusty vise, she held his head in place as he continued to lick and fondle, massage and pet, sending her into a state of wicked surrender. "Kevin", 'she murmured', "come here."

When he laid his head on her pillow, Veronica slid her hand down the front of Kevin's body and elicited a soft moan as she massaged his bulging hardness. Within moments, Veronica grasped the waistband of Kevin's pants and pulled them off. He reached down in a furious attempt to rid himself of the last remaining barrier of clothing but Veronica did the deed for him, flinging his underwear aside and falling into the safe harbor of his arms and legs, finally freeing herself to be a complete woman. To be Kevin's *lover*.

Later, in the reflective afterglow of semen and sweat, sweetness and solace, Veronica curled up with Kevin and reveled in the feeling of renewal and second chances; those lurking images of her past haunting her no more.

But peace of mind is a fleeting event when the wolf approaches your door.

FORTY-FIVE

*K*ing growled into his cell phone, disgusted at Ram's casual disregard for such an important moment.

"*Chinga*, motherfucker! Where the hell are you, man?" He sat alone at the wheel of his van inside the 7-11 parking lot, leaving a second message for his *comarada*. "I'm packin' a *pinchi* .45, God damn it! Don't want no motherfuckin' *policía* askin' questions. Hurry, *cabron*!" Tossing the phone on the passenger seat, King stared into the black November sky. Tonight finally arrived as a second chance at payback, and this time he wouldn't fuck up.

He didn't get a clear shot at Torres last time, and the lucky Diablo piece-of-shit drove off and escaped. He had no choice but to make Javier his lookout again, but the little punk didn't see nothing until Monday when Torres' car showed up in the driveway again. Still, he needed a plan that would work this time. On Wednesday he got the news he needed to hear. Torres' old lady saw Javier's old lady at the market and told her that "*Alejandro y Veronica*" would both be there for Thanksgiving, and to come for dessert so that "Alejandro can apologize to your son."

Javier's old lady "didn't want nothin' to do with Alejandro." Not after Torres... *Alejandro,* busted her kid's nose. King, however, had every intention of crashing the party. Alejandro would be the first to get smoked. Then the mother. And Veronica? Well... another night with her is something he wanted real bad.

King got yanked from his fantasies by a loud knocking on the passenger side window. Startled, he spun his head to the right. "Shit, *vato*," he said, his heart still pounding, "where the fuck you been?" King reached over to open the door. "It's gettin' late, man. Hurry up!"

Ram entered and sat, leaving the door partially open. "Don't start the car," he said, reaching out to grip King's arm. "I ain't goin' tonight.

I came to tell ya."

"*What the fuck?*" he howled. "Don't fuck with me, Ram! *No me chinges*! I ain't never put in work like this alone, man!"

"The time ain't right for puttin' in work, King. I ain't ready to start killin' again. It's been a bad motherfuckin' year for the Lobos, man." Ram started counting names from his fingers. "Ghoul, Flex, Hazard, Juice, Rascal, Joker... and Spice... Teazer... Steel...and all the goddamn others, too. What the fuck did it mean? They didn't die for no Lobo pride. Their fuckin' hearts went dead. And for what, man? 'Cause some fuckin' asshole don't want us around!"

"I don't believe I'm hearin' this shit from you," King snarled. "Ain't no one gonna change me, you understand? Ride or die, man." King pulled his shirt sleeve up, pointing to a tattoo. Two faces, one smiling, the other crying, looked out from the message-inked flesh of his forearm. "This is the way it is, man. You gotta live while you're still around. Who the fuck knows when you ain't gonna be?" King pounded his heart with a closed fist. "*Estar firme,*" he said. "For the Lobos."

"Word's out, King. An agreement's been reached. The Lobos and Diablos gonna shut it down for now. Ain't nobody jumpin' back but you."

King slammed his fist against the back of the seat, missing Ram by several inches. "*Get the fuck outta here!*"

Ram stared at King for several moments before sliding from the seat to stand outside. "I understood shit when it was just the Diablos," he said. "War was a beautiful thing. But this heart attack shit... damn!" Ram shook his head. "I ain't gonna die without no good reason, King."

King gnashed his teeth as Ram slammed the door and disappeared into the night. When he turned the key to the ignition, his eyes fell upon three dots tattooed on the back of his hand, signifying *Mi Vida Loca*, My Crazy Life. "Ain't *nobody* gonna fuckin' change King!" he shouted. He looked at his watch and pulled into the street. Seven o'clock and time to rock.

Many years had passed since he lived next door, but he still remembered one particular area that allowed him to sneak into their back yard. He used to play 'Hide and Seek' with Alejandro and Veronica, and a wooden fence separated the two houses. In the corner of the Torres' backyard they had an old tree with roots so big that part of the fence had lifted and split apart. He used to slide between the broken boards and hide on the other side. If that tree was still there, maybe the roots kept the fence from ever getting fixed. He'd sneak along the perimeter of his old house until he reached the spot. From there, he'd slip through into their yard and wait for someone to step outside or leave the door open. He smiled at the thought of playing his own version of 'Hide and Seek'.

King parked his van near a small park less than two blocks from the house. He wanted to remain within walking distance, but far enough away to make sure none of the neighbors spotted him. Checking the back of his van, he readjusted the magnetic covering to make sure the face of the *lobo* stayed hidden. The moment he'd been waiting for had almost arrived. King pulled the hood of his black sweatshirt over his head, and secured the gun inside his jeans. "*Estar firme*, Viper," he whispered, gazing into the starless sky. "Payback's a bitch."

King maneuvered among the shadows of the neighborhood, giving an occasional disinterested glance at the fuzzy figures of people outlined against the iron bars and closed curtains. When he got within eyesight of the Torres' house, he saw Alejandro's Firebird still in the driveway and Veronica's Honda on the street. To his delight, he saw that his old house next door had an empty driveway and no lights on. "*Perfecto*," he whispered. His throat tingled from the need for beer, but revenge was the alcohol of choice for the moment.

Clinging to the patchy darkness of the street, King crossed into his old driveway, gaining an open view of the large tree still looming in the corner shadows. He walked towards the back, knowing the height of the fence kept him from being detected. As he approached the spot, the dim light shining from the Torres' backyard filtered through the split in the dark brown boards. The same space appeared a couple of feet above the tree root, but with a problem he hadn't anticipated: He was a lot bigger now and no longer able to slip through.

As he stared at the unexpected obstacle, he resisted the urge to loosen a couple of planks with some swift, hard kicks. He studied the opening, viewing the space from different angles, trying to find a way to get in. Crouching as low as he could, King peered into the backyard and looked towards the house. He saw a closed door that he remembered led into the kitchen. Further down on the right he recognized a bathroom window, not too high up, that was open a bit with just a screen for protection. If he encountered a locked door, he felt sure he could climb in through the window.

"*I gotta get in that fuckin' yard*," he told himself. He placed his hand between two slats to pull himself up, but the board on the left loosened and moved over on contact. He stared in excitement at a sudden opening he now believed he could wiggle through. King observed the house again, picturing everything he intended to do. "I'm gonna kill your ass, Alejandro," he whispered. "Your mother's, too." He chuckled. "But don't worry 'bout Veronica, motherfucker. King's got other plans for *her* ass."

FORTY-SIX

*F*ACE SAT IN A CHAIR looking for something to watch on TV. He had stuffed himself on turkey, tamales and beer, and his eyes felt heavy. The night had been a welcome escape from the pressure building up inside of him. He had decided the time was right to drop the flag, to quit the Diablos, but the news wouldn't go down too good with his homeboys. He wasn't expecting threats, although that possibility always remained.

He didn't like the idea of leaving unfinished business behind. He had wanted definite answers about the heart attacks, to be able to turn the page on who or what caused so many of his brothers to die. Now for the first time in months, going back to the time they gunned down Seth's old man, no one was dying. Their truce with the Lobos meant something to somebody, and that somebody wasn't killing no more.

Was he supposed to wait around for the war to continue, and then maybe the heart attacks, too? He wasn't no young cholo no more, not like the old days, with plenty of time to figure things out. He'd also stop thinking about payback for now against that motherfucker, King. The word had spread about that ugly asshole. If and when the killings start, he'll be *numero uno* on the Lobo most wanted list. Face had survived the attempt on his life and set his sights to move on as a mechanic, not a Diablo. He wanted to find a steady job, settle outta the 'hood, and maybe get his own shop one day.

The one thing that would keep him connected to homeboys like Hawk or Bleeder was his desire, his *need*, to find that other piece-of-shit *culero* who raped Veronica. If he hadn't died already and the chance ever came, he'd be all over him like buzzards on a corpse. The thought of some Lobo having his way with his sister, and getting away with it, tortured him every day and cut him up inside like jagged glass.

"Alex? Alex?"

He shook his head, trying to wake himself up. "*Qué pasó?*" he asked, rubbing his palms against his eyes.

"I could use a walk before I leave," Veronica told him. "Would you come with me?"

"Yeah, sure," he said, pushing himself up from the chair.

Face grabbed his sweatshirt off the corner of the couch, checked for his phone and keys, and waited for Veronica to put her jacket on.

"Are you sure you don't want to come, Mama?" she asked.

"No, baby, that's all right. You and Alex don't get a chance to be together much. I'll take care of the dishes."

"Make sure you lock the door, Ma," Face said. "I got my key." He looked at Veronica. "How far you wanna go?"

"To the park."

His mother closed the door behind them as they turned away. The night air helped clear his head and he regained his energy by the time they rounded the corner. "How's Seth doin'?" he asked.

"Great," she said. "And by the way, he loves his new watch. Kevin told me he even wears it to bed."

Face smiled. "That's cool. I like hearin' that."

"You scored a lot of points with him that day at school," Veronica said. "Whenever he brings your name up, it's like he's talking about a big brother."

"Seth's my man," Face exclaimed. "I care about the kid."

"Enough to quit the gang?"

Face didn't respond, walking with his head down in a silent conflict between telling Veronica now or later.

"After all that's happened, Kevin wants to give you another chance to become part of us again," she said, matching him stride for stride. "He knows how much I care about you. Seth, too. But nothing's going to happen as long as you're still bangin'."

Face stopped when Veronica placed her hand on his shoulder. "Kevin knows it wasn't you who murdered his brother. He'll never excuse what you were doing that night, but he believes your story and how bad you feel about what happened. He just needs to know Seth won't be hanging out with a gang member."

Face looked at Veronica and smiled. "Let's finish walkin' to the park," he said. "On the way back I'll tell ya what I been thinkin'."

They maintained a brisk pace, talking about their mother and Face's thawing attitude towards her. "Yeah, I don't hate her so much no more," he told her. "But she didn't protect me from the old man when I was a kid. That was chicken-ass bullshit. I ain't never gonna forget that."

Nearing the entrance to the park, Face lit a cigarette while Veronica waited in silence. She stood close enough to a street lamp where he could observe her expression, and he couldn't help but notice the strange look on her face. She stared hard at something, and seemed troubled by what she saw.

"*Qué pasó?*" he asked, turning to look. Face saw four cars at the front of the park. A cargo van, one often used for fuckin', and partyin', caught his attention because the back of it had a white magnetic sheet that didn't say anything. That seemed strange. Face looked back at Veronica, walking away without him. Something was wrong.

"Veronica, stop!"

"Let's get out of here," she said, sounding afraid.

"Tell me what you're lookin' at!" he commanded. "One of those cars? The van?"

She stood there stone silent, nodding her head.

"So what's the fuckin' problem?" he asked, angry with himself for leaving his gun at home. "You seen someone over there just now?"

"Maybe it's nothing," she answered, her voice a loud whisper. "Please, Alex, let's *go*."

"Not until I know what the fuck is scarin' you," he snapped, stalking towards the van.

"Alex, *no!*"

Veronica ran to grab his arm, but Face pulled away from her grasp. Placing his ear against the back of the door, he heard no one inside and stepped back, ripping off the magnetic strip. Veronica uttered a muffled cry as the open-mouthed face of a painted wolf's head stared back at them. Face wheeled around to confront her.

"You seen this *pinchi lobo* before? Tell me! *Tell me, God damn it*!"

"Pleeease, Alex," she whispered, tears filling her eyes. "I'm scared. Let's go home."

Face approached Veronica and placed his hands on her shoulders. He had a sickening suspicion about her fear, and he felt determined to see if he was right. "Don't make me ask you again," he told her, his voice calm, "Have you seen this van before?"

"Yes," she answered, turning her gaze away.

He tried to ignore the cold blade sliding down his stomach, needing to stay focused on his sister.

"Veronica," he said, his voice remaining calm, "I know about the rape. Did this van have somethin' to do with it?"

Veronica shut her eyes tight. Leaning against his chest, he felt her muscles go loose. He had to support her to keep from falling. He heard her swallow hard before she spoke. "I was raped *in* that van, Alex. By two Lobos."

Face's eyes burned as he glanced back at the van. "I know one of them was named, Viper," he said. "He's dead now, been takin' care of. But I never found out who the other one was." He gently pushed her back enough to look into her eyes. "Do you remember the other one's name?"

"The *other* one?" she spat, her tone as ugly and bitter as he'd ever remembered. "How could I ever forget?" Veronica closed her eyes for a moment, shaking her head. "The boy who used to live next door to us? The one you saved from that car? *He* was the other one, Alex. Miguel Ruiz! The Lobo who now calls himself, *King*!"

"WHAT?" Face roared, pulling away from her. He clenched his fists in a rage that needed immediate release but had none to offer. Adrenaline surged through him like a wild river, threatening to carry him away into an uncontrollable fury. "KING?" I'll *kill* him!"

"It's *over*, Alex!" she yelled. "I never wanted you to find out because I knew that's what you'd do!"

Face stormed back to the van with his eyes on the ground, intending to find a rock big enough to smash every window, but a staggering combination of light and heat came from out of nowhere and forced him to a knee. A swirling wooziness dominated the moment like a strange drug, creating images of blurred shadows and garbled voices. The out-of-focus camera that acted as his vision arrived at an eventual clarity, presenting him with the unmistakable image of King grabbing his mother and hitting her across the face with a gun. They were in his bedroom. The sound of King's voice came next. "*Where the fuck are they*! *I'll kill you if you don't tell me, you fucking bitch! Tell me*!"

"Alex! What's wrong? Are you all right? Alex!"

He was clear-headed again, and as his surroundings came back into view, he saw Veronica kneeling next to him. "What happened?" she asked. "Are you all right?"

Face sprung to his feet. "Ma's in danger!" he shouted. Reaching down, Face grabbed Veronica by the arm and pulled her up. "Let's go!

He's in the house!"

"How do you..." Veronica stopped in mid-sentence. In the brief moment before they started running, Face saw the look of recognition, and belief, in his sister's eyes. She had just witnessed the secret he had always kept from her.

T,r T,r T,r

They stood gathering their breath in the darkness, staring at the quiet house.

"We need to call the police," Veronica whispered.

"No fuckin' way," he answered. "Miguel...*King*, he might kill Ma if there's no way out."

"Right know it's just a break-in," she said. "Do you think he'd go that far?"

"He wants *me*," Face explained. "And if he doesn't get what he came for, he'll take it out on her."

"You're right," she said. "He's capable of anything."

"Got your car keys?" he asked.

"They're in my purse near the door." A soft sob escaped from her mouth. "My i.d. is in there, Alex. He's going to find out where I live."

Face reached into his pocket. "Here," he said, handing her his own car keys. "Get in my car and lock it. Maybe there's another Lobo around here. If you think you're in trouble, don't fuckin' wait around. *Leave.*" He handed her his phone. "Now listen," he told her. "When I go inside, gimme five minutes. Then call the goddamn police."

"I'm not going anywhere," she said. "Not until I see you and Mama walk out that door."

Face saw the steely determination in her eyes. "All right," he said, "then you're gonna help me. You know the fuse box on the side of the house?"

"Yes," she answered.

"If King don't come up on me right away, if he stays hidin' or somethin', I'll leave the door open halfway. First thing I'll do is throw your purse out to you if it's still there. Then I'll get my gun. I want him thinkin' you left, so I'll yell, 'goodbye' or somethin'. When the door closes, that's the sign. Gimme me one more minute then run over and pull the main switch. I want it dark in there. I know the house and he don't."

"Where's your gun?" she asked.

"In my room."

"Do you think you can get it?"

"I don't know."

"I can't believe he's back again," she said, her voice breaking.

Face reached out and stroked Veronica's cheek. "I got to thinkin' I might never find out who the other one was that night," he said, offering her a slight smile. "I been waitin' for this."

He hurried to the door. The image of King attacking his mother was something he sensed had already happened. He could be anywhere in the house now, so Face tried to think of the logical places he'd hide. There were closets in all three bedrooms, a bathroom in his mother's room and a bathroom that he and Veronica used to share between their two rooms. There were some corners to hide behind, too. The house was small, so that was about it. He didn't think they'd be in the backyard 'cause that would make it harder for King to sneak up on him. He told Veronica to give him five minutes, but two or three would probably determine if he would kill or be killed. One other thought troubled him, but he couldn't worry about it now.

Face took a deep breath and braced himself for what might be the final minute of his life. He put the key in the lock, opened the door, and readied himself for an immediate attack. Nothing happened. He spotted Veronica's purse on the table by the door, and within seconds heaved it outside.

"*Adiós*, Veronica!" he hollered. Turning the knob all the way to prevent the door from closing, Face slammed the door shut, then silently pulled it open halfway. He wheeled around again. The house remained quiet. "Hey, Ma!" he yelled, "Veronica had to go! She says she'll call you tomorrow!" No movement. No noise. Waiting another few seconds, Face sped towards his room and opened the drawer. At the moment he discovered the gun missing, he heard the door open from the bathroom next to his room. He had no choice but to rush at King full force, but stopped in his tracks by what he saw.

"I'll *kill* her, motherfucker!"

Face stared in angry frustration at the sight of King with his hand squeezed over his mother's mouth and his stolen gun to her head. Her nose and forehead bled and fear colored her eyes.

"Don't fuckin' move!" he ordered. Face stared at King, a wild hatred battering his gut. "Got a fine nine-millimeter here, Alejandro," he said, rubbing the barrel along the side of his mother's face. "The old bitch led me to it, thinkin' she could be some kinda fuckin' hero." He shook his head back and forth. "Stupid, stupid bitch. Now look what you gone and did." King turned his head towards the front door and dragged Face's mother in that direction. Face made a move to grab the gun, but King yanked her back with a violent motion, causing her to cry out in pain. "*You want her dead, asshole?*" he shouted, tilting the gun towards his mother's eye. "I'll blow her goddamn head off! Sit on the floor and don't move!"

Face held still but his thoughts raced. He kept his eyes on King, following his orders and watching his mother pulled like a rag doll towards the front door. "*Payback!*" King snarled, glaring at Face with a crazed fury as he closed the door. "You took Viper from me, man. Some *culero* shoutin' your fuckin' name stuck a knife in his neck! Mother*fucker!*"

King smiled a killer's smile, one that indicated intimidation and intent. "Remember me, Alejandro? Runnin' after that soccer ball when we was neighbors?" King rubbed several fingers over his scar. "Shoulda been *you* leavin' his skin on the sidewalk, you fuckin' asshole." A wild-eyed look appeared on his face. "I told you I'd get you back for that shit. But you know what, *cabron?* You ain't the Torres I went after first."

King licked his lips in a slow, circular motion that made Face's skin crawl. "*Veronica*," he said in a breathy voice. "The *best* fuckin' pussy I ever had." He pushed himself up against Face's mother, humping her from behind. "You know what I'm talkin' 'bout, right, bitch?" he asked, placing his lips against her ear. "*Right?*" King started grinding his crotch faster and harder. "All that hot... *Veronica... Torres... pussy!* Bitch couldn't get enough!" King started moaning in a high-pitched voice. "*Ooooh, ooooh, ooooh, yeah, yeah, more, more, more, don't stop, don't stop!*"

Face wanted to rip King apart piece by piece, to punish him, to make him suffer worse than anybody had ever suffered before, but with the gun pointed at his mother's head, what could he do? To his surprise, the answer came from an unexpected source. With a strength, and *courage*, he never thought she possessed, his mother screamed with a sudden rage while somehow twisting around to grab the gun and push his hand away, causing a bullet to fire. That spark was the last sign of light in the house. Veronica cut the power.

Face bolted up and leaped towards King, knowing he remained in the approximate area. Following the sound of his movement, he seized his shoulders and jumped on his back. Another shot fired. Face wrapped his arm around King's neck with every intention of squeezing the last breath out of him, trying at the same time to wrench his fingers away from the gun, but King's strength made Face hold on like a cowboy on a bull. He rammed against the wall several times while struggling to fend off King's attempts to claw his face.

Face pushed himself from the wall with his feet, forcing King to stumble back. With his arm still looped around King's neck, Face grabbed hold of the gun hand and drove him forward until he smashed against the door, forcing another bullet to fire before dropping the weapon. With both hands now free, King's ferocity increased. He took hold of Face's arm and rolled his shoulder into him, causing Face to lose his balance and be driven back against the TV, knocking it off the stand. Face fell backwards to the sound of breaking glass, stunned for a moment when his head smacked against the wall. King draped his hands around Face's neck, his coiled grip tightening behind the added pressure of his body weight. Face struggled for air as he tried to force his arms upward between King's and pry them apart, ultimately succeeding and causing him to fall forward.

Face grabbed the side of King's head and used it as leverage to turn him around and force his way on top again, but the strain of catching his breath allowed King to take advantage of Face's temporary weakness, tossing him off like a wrestler unable to pin his opponent. King grabbed the side of Face's head, connecting with a hard blow to his cheek before clamping a hand down on his neck again. Face shut his eyes tight as King's hand crawled over his mouth and nose like a hot, clammy spider. He anticipated King's attempt to pluck his eyes out if he didn't do something in the next few seconds.

Sliding his hands down King's arms, Face locked on to his wrist and bent it until King cried out, forcing him to pull away and tumble back into the darkness. Face leaped up in an attack position but the sudden opening of the front door startled him. In those few moments of dull, street lamp visibility, he caught sight of his mother rushing outside. A few seconds later the door slammed shut, but not before he spotted the gun in King's outstretched hand. Face's reaction was immediate as he hurtled through the darkness. As he heard the bullet whiz past him, Face collided with the edge of the couch and kept still, managing to keep his breathing quiet.

"You're *mine*, motherfucker!" King screamed.

Face heard the heavy footsteps moving towards the door. He knew

King needed the streetlight in order to find him, so he slid behind the couch to avoid being seen. As the door opened, King's sudden yelling surprised him. Face looked up and saw him grab Veronica and hurl her to the ground before rubbing his eyes and waving an unsteady gun in her direction. Face realized Veronica had used her pepper spray on him, but if he didn't get to King in time, she'd be killed.

"You fuckin' bitch!" he yelled. "I'll *kill* you, God damn it!"

Standing in front of the open door, King hesitated while scrubbing his eyes with the palm of his hand. Face sprinted at full speed and rammed his head and shoulders into his gut, causing the gun to go off again. As they plummeted from the top step, Face's savage desire for revenge found its opportunity in that fateful airborne moment. He squeezed his left arm around King's waist, making sure he couldn't twist away. With his right arm, he threw a powerful upward thrust under the chin, forcing King's head all the way back before they hit the ground. Face pitched his weight forward to increase the impact, hoping to bust King's head open like an egg. The cracking noise he heard, however, came from the neck and sounded more like the snapping of a tree branch.

Face's momentum caused him to roll forward, but he scrambled back and pounced on King again, ready to finish what he started. With fists raised and his knees on King's chest, he noticed the unusual angle of the twisted head and the pool of blood forming underneath. King didn't move or make a noise of any kind. Face checked for signs of breathing but found nothing. He pushed himself off the limp body and saw Veronica and their mother looking at him. At that moment he remembered the gun firing when he dove at King. Relieved to see Veronica unhurt, he waved her over.

"You know how to find a pulse?" he asked her.

When Veronica lowered King's wrist and looked up at Face, her eyes told him what he already suspected. King was dead.

⊤⊤⊤ ⊤⊤⊤ ⊤⊤⊤

The three of them stood outside together, several feet away from the lifeless body. Veronica had turned the main power switch back on, and Face saw the blood and swelling on his mother's face.

"You okay, Ma?" he asked.

"*Sí*," she said, crying softly.

"She needs a doctor," Veronica said.

The faint call of sirens sounded in the distance. "I never called the police," she said. "I guess one of the neighbors did."

"I gotta get outta here!" he said.

"Why, Alex?" Veronica asked. "This was self-defense. Nothing's going to happen to you."

"Listen to me, Veronica!" he said, clutching her shoulder. "I killed him. You know what that means?"

"Yes, you saved our life. That's what it means."

"No!" he shouted. "Did you forget? I'm a Diablo. King was a Lobo. Don't you remember what's been happening?"

Veronica stared at him open mouthed, her eyes widening in recognition.

"I don't understand," his mother said.

"I gotta go, Ma," he told her. "Veronica can explain."

"But... if something like that happens," Veronica said, "the police can get you medical attention right away."

"Fuck the police!" he shouted. "How do you know they ain't the ones doin' it?" Face shook his head in disgust. "Maybe not all of 'em, Veronica, but it just takes one, you know? One *pinchi* motherfucker with a badge."

"Where will you be?"

"I ain't gonna say. Don't want you knowin' where I am. Cops can't find nothin' out that way."

"What's going to happen at four o'clock?" she asked, her eyes beginning to tear. "How will I know you're all right?"

Face smiled. "Don't worry 'bout me. You just take care of Ma."

"Alex, *please!*"

"I gotta go, Veronica. Gimme my cell phone."

"I'm going call you later to make sure you're okay."

"No fuckin' way, Veronica. You ain't gonna hear from me until I'm ready."

"When will that be?" she asked.

"What do you think?" he answered. "When it's after four and I ain't dead from no heart attack."

"That still doesn't explain why you won't let me call you."

"Where I'm goin', it's real quiet up there. Can't let nobody hear me. My phone'll be on so I can see the time, but I'm cuttin' the ring."

Veronica stared at him with a worried expression. "Your gun's over there," she said, pointing to a spot on the ground near the door. Face didn't remember how the gun got there, but he felt good rushing over to stick it in his pocket. "Mama had taken the gun," Veronica said. "She told me she was about to shoot him when you came running out."

Face looked at his mother with a virgin admiration. "Is that true, Ma?" he asked.

His mother nodded. "I felt the gun on the floor," she said. "*Díos*, please forgive me, but he wasn't gonna hurt my daughter again." The tears refilled her eyes. "*Never... again.*"

The sirens got louder. Face reached out to hug them both. "*Gracias*," he said. "You both done good." He started to run but stopped to turn around. "Tell Seth to be cool, Veronica. And let Kevin know if I ain't dead by tomorrow, my bangin' days are over."

ттr ттr ттr

He didn't need light to find his way to Casa Place. He welcomed the darkness like a friend, aiding him in his need for protection. He figured the cops would do everything to find him, but he needed to stay out of sight until tomorrow. His head ached and he felt dizzy from knocking it against the wall, but he'd be okay. He now had the chance to fuck up somebody's killing schedule and ruin their party. He'd be the first one to outsmart Mr. Heart Attack. Maybe that might be enough to make him stop or move on to somewhere else. Maybe that was the game he was playing. He'd just never been beaten yet.

Face had lived a full life and wasn't afraid of death, but wouldn't go without a fight, that's for damn sure. If his time came, however, he could now die knowing his payback against King had ended just like a little kid's story; happily ever after. Face smiled as he thought about the way things played out. Everybody contributed. Veronica gave him the opening he needed by spraying that asshole with her own special eye drops. She'll always know that she played a part in getting her revenge. He forgave his mother, too. She showed him something he never thought she had: *Huevos*. Balls. Guts.

Now Face had one more battle to fight and Casa Place remained another fifteen minutes away. "*Four a.m. ain't gonna mean shit tonight, motherfucker*," he whispered, increasing his pace. "*How you gonna kill me if you don't know where I am?*"

FORTY-SEVEN

WARREN HAD WAITED TO JOURNEY to the corridor of another evil heart, to incriminate and assign death, but the continual flow of opportunities had ceased. The basic urge behind his existence teetered on the brink of complete deviation. Something unplanned occurred during the long period of inactivity. His spirit started mutating.

There had been no recent cause for retribution, yet no hibernation from his sinister actions. The original focus of his rebirth had stagnated in the lull between gang killings, causing his spirit to sweep away towards the malignant swirl of mankind's other evils. Warren's transformed consciousness headed into unknown regions of pain and sorrow without any discernible patterns. He found himself circulating among human acts of savagery and torture, his altered spirit contributing as an unintentional force that fueled such horrors.

Seth signified the foundation for Warren's emergence, the inspiration behind his afterlife, and thus the link to his power of reprisal. Without that association, as Warren's uncontrollable attendance to other calamities increased, he operated more as a donor of darkness in the tragedies of mankind. He existed as an entity in need of sustenance, and without the empowering call of vengeance for another gang-related murder, he traveled to alternate paths of abhorrence. Without meaning to, he had converted into a virus of evil, an encouraging influence for sadness and inhumanity. For the first time since his rebirth, Warren had lost control.

Through the maze of his alternate destiny, a sudden recognizable purpose besieged his consciousness. Images of abominations flew from his vision like a swarm of locusts until one specter remained. Another gang killing had occurred, but the vividness of the broken neck disturbed him in a way that differentiated from all the other deaths.

He foresaw the demise of the one known as 'King' to be the most deserved of all his exterminations. Warren had already affected his dreams, causing him to awaken in the night, yet he'd been unwilling to complete the deed until the gangbanger committed a murder. That held as the natural order of propriety. But King had been killed and the gang member who carried out the deed would now have to pay the price with his own life.

At four a.m.

FORTY-EIGHT

UNCLE KEVIN HUNG UP THE phone, looking upset. "That was Veronica," he told them. "Her car was stolen."

"On Thanksgiving night of all nights?" Grandma asked. "What's this world coming to?"

"She wants to know if Seth and I can bring her home."

"Seth doesn't have to go," Grandma said. "He'll help me wash the dishes and I'll stay with him until you return."

"She wants her mother to meet the both of us," Uncle Kevin explained. "If that'll make her feel better, then Seth should come with me."

Although Seth felt bad for Veronica, he looked forward to seeing Alex again. When Grandma left, Uncle Kevin asked him to sit down.

"We have to go, but I need to tell you something first," he said, facing him on the couch. "I didn't tell your grandma the truth. Veronica's car wasn't stolen. Someone broke into their house tonight."

"*Really*?" he said, afraid to hear the rest. "Is she okay? Is Alex okay?"

"They're both fine, Seth. But their mother got roughed up and needs some treatment."

"Wow," Seth replied. "That's really scary."

"There's something else I need to tell you. The bastard that broke into their house was the same gangbanger who grabbed you when your father was shot."

For a moment, Seth lost his ability to speak. "*King?*" he whispered.

"Yes," Uncle Kevin answered. "But he's dead now. Alex killed him in self-defense."

Seth closed his eyes for several moments. His lips tightened into a grimace as he realized what would now happen. "Is Alex gonna go to jail?" he asked, tears threatening to fall.

His uncle shook his head. "No way, Seth. Alex is a hero. He saved Veronica's life tonight, and probably their mother's, too. But right now he's hiding somewhere and we have to find him."

"So we can tell him he's not in trouble, right?"

"It's not that simple," he said. "Remember the night you overheard me talking with Veronica about the heart attacks? And I read those lines from Edgar Allan Poe?"

"Yeah," he answered. "That's when I found out it's my dad getting back at 'em."

"Well, *if* that's true," Kevin said, "and it just might be, Alex could be next."

"But he saved Veronica's life!" Seth exclaimed. "You said so yourself!"

"That's right, I did. But the only gang members who have died of heart attacks were the ones who killed somebody first. What Alex did was in self-defense, but we don't know if that matters. He still killed someone. We can't take a chance. We've got to find him before it's too late."

Seth glanced at the watch that Alex gave him. "You mean by four a.m.?"

"That's exactly what I mean," Uncle Kevin said, looking at his own watch as he rose from the couch. "Come on, it's already past ten. When we're in the car, I have something else I need to talk with you about. Something Madame Sibilia explained to me."

"You mean there's more stuff you didn't tell me?"

"She said something about you that night I never thought could happen, something that sounded so impossible I didn't mention it." He looked at Seth with an unusual expression. "I may have been wrong."

♪♪♪ ♪♪♪ ♪♪♪

Seth didn't mind the long car ride because Uncle Kevin had time to tell him about the other things Madame Sibilia said. Now he wanted to think things over. If Madame Sibilia told the truth about him being the one person who could communicate with his father, what would he say to him if he got the chance? His uncle wanted him to ask for Alex's safety, but he didn't think that would be necessary. His father used to always preach the golden rule, telling him to treat others the same way he wished to be treated himself. Why would his father give Alex one of those heart attacks when Seth and Alex were friends now? Alex had even given

300

him his watch as a reminder of their relationship. And he had done him a big favor by coming to school to make sure he'd never be bullied again. His father would like the way Alex treated his son. He was sure of that.

He would also say that he missed him and mom, and that he'd never forget them. But he wanted his father to know things are okay with Uncle Kevin now, and that he might have a real cool substitute mom in his life soon. He knew his father would like Veronica, and he'd be happy that his brother found someone as pretty and nice as her.

There remained one more thing he wanted to tell him. Please stop the killing. Uncle Kevin said that lots of the gang members had died from heart attacks. He knew his father wanted revenge, but the punishment had lasted long enough. He wasn't sure how to explain it, exactly, but he didn't want to be reminded of that night anymore. As long as his father kept doing what he was doing, how could he ever get over it?

Seth didn't understand why his father killed so many others but not King. He was the worst of them all, and if it weren't for him that night, maybe everything would have been all right. Wasn't King the reason his father got shot? Seth reasoned that Alex did his father a favor; a real bad guy like that wasn't around anymore.

Alex was a hero, just like Uncle Kevin said. And heroes don't deserve to get snitched on. He had a strong feeling that Alex went to hide at that special hideout on Casa Place but he wasn't going to say anything. He had made a pledge to Alex that he intended to keep. "*I swore to him I wouldn't tell anyone about that spot,*" he reminded himself. "*And the next time I see Alex, I'll let him know I'm his friend and kept my word. Just like I promised.*"

FORTY-NINE

K EVIN CALLED VERONICA. "We're pulling up now," he said.

Seth had been so quiet, Kevin thought he'd fallen asleep, but his nephew responded to the activity in front of the house as soon as he placed his phone back in his pocket.

"Look at all the police!" he exclaimed. Kevin surveyed the scene. He had witnessed a similar experience months before in the parking lot of Alfredo's Market. The flashing lights of police vehicles, a covered body, and an area cordoned off by tape. He noticed one other similarity from that night: Curious onlookers. When he arrived at the murder site after Warren's murder he felt like screaming at all of those Grim Reaper-like bystanders to go away, but these people tonight were neighbors with a reason to be concerned. There had been a break-in. And a killing.

When he stepped out of his car he saw Veronica hurrying towards them. Seth intercepted her and gave her a hug. When she approached him next, Kevin held her until she let go.

"How's your mom," he asked.

"She's being treated at the hospital," Veronica said. "She's hurt, but I think she'll be okay. They're going to hold her overnight for observation."

"How ya doin', Kevin?"

Before turning around Kevin recognized the voice immediately. "It's no way to spend a Thanksgiving, Lieutenant," he replied. Kevin faced Lieutenant Atkinson and extended his hand. "Good to see you, Carl."

"Next time for a better reason, I hope," Atkinson said. "As I've told Veronica, we have patrol cars searching over a five mile radius for Alex. He had close to a thirty minute head start by the time I got the word out, but we're going to keep looking."

"That's good to hear," Kevin said. "We don't have much time."

Atkinson looked over his shoulder and Kevin followed his gaze. A

303

police photographer had taken pictures of the body and surrounding areas, and now headed back to the house.

"Homicide's almost finished here," he told him. "Let's go inside."

As the four of them neared the front door, Kevin watched Veronica put her arm around Seth and try to guide him past the covered body, but Seth stopped and stared in silence. Atkinson looked at Kevin, then at Seth. "Sorry you have to see this, son," he said.

Seth's jaw tightened and his eyes remained fixed on King. "I'm not," he said, his tone almost trance-like. "He got what he deserved."

"Come on, Seth," Veronica said. Seth studied his subject a few moments longer before turning away and walking towards the house.

Kevin observed indications of the fight that occurred. Multiple fragments of broken glass were scattered around a corner area where a television had been toppled from its stand. Near the door, black scuff marks from shoes streaked the wall near a slanted picture hook. The mirror it once held lay in pieces on the floor. The couch angled in a strange forty-five degree position, and in his line of sight leading to the back wall, a policeman examined a bullet hole. Kevin squeezed Veronica's arm, shaken by the scene but grateful for her survival. Wherever Alex was, he hoped he'd get the chance to thank him.

Veronica and Seth were asked to sit on the floor until the photographer finished taking pictures of the area around the couch and chairs. Atkinson called Kevin over to him. "He got into the house through the window in that bathroom," he explained, pointing towards the spot. "Veronica said her mother likes to leave it open until she goes to bed. I don't think she'll be doing that anymore. He got into the backyard through a small opening in the fence. His footprints lead to the kitchen door first, then the window."

"I'd hate to think what would have happened if it wasn't for Alex," Kevin said.

"I've seen too many of these scenes," Atkinson replied. "Best not to think about it at all."

Kevin looked at Veronica. "Alex didn't say where he was going?"

"He wouldn't tell me. I tried to get him to stay, but there was no convincing him."

"How could he be so damn cavalier about it?" Kevin muttered. "After all that's happened?"

"Alex told Veronica he thinks the killer might be a cop," Atkinson said. "He didn't want her to say anything that could get him killed."

Kevin looked at his watch. "Eleven-fifteen, Carl. Any ideas?"

"Just the same ones we've been working on," he answered. "If Alex was picked up and driven somewhere there's not much we can do. But I don't think that's what happened. He needed to disappear in a hurry, so I don't see him waiting somewhere for a car. I also don't believe he's in a house or apartment around here. That doesn't tie in to what he said to Veronica."

"What do you mean?" Kevin asked.

"He told me not to call because he didn't want anybody to hear him," Veronica answered. "Wherever he is, he said it was 'real quiet up there'. Those are the words he used."

"I have patrol units focusing on the hilly streets around here," Atkinson said. "We've given them a physical description of what he looks like and what he's wearing. There's not much more we can do at this point."

"I don't know why everyone's so worried."

The three of them looked at Seth. He eyed each of them in return. "I mean it," he said. "You really think my dad would want to hurt Alex now? After what he did tonight?"

"Your dad?" Atkinson asked. "I don't understand."

"Forget it," Kevin said, shooting a sharp-eyed glance at Seth. "Just silly talk we've been having about ghosts."

"Ghosts?" Atkinson said, chuckling. "Well, that would help explain the lack of fingerprints, wouldn't it?"

"Come with me, Seth," Veronica said, rising to her feet. "I want to see if I can talk to my mom. I've told her all about you, so maybe you can say hello."

"Okay," he replied, preparing to stand. "But you'll see. Alex is gonna be fine."

FIFTY

THE LUMP ON THE BACK of his head bothered him, but so what? A little pain meant he was still alive, so bring it on. The late November night chilled his body but he felt secure in his personal hiding place. He sat with his back against a big tree, draped by lots of long, bushy branches that hung down to the ground, making him feel well hidden behind a curtain of leaves. He would have preferred a darker night, but the moon was almost full. Then again, maybe that benefited him because he'd be able to spot someone if they tried anything. This is where he'd hide and stay awake past 4 a.m., just in case. After that he'd catch a little sleep before returning home and dealing with all the bullshit. He figured the police were already looking for him and he'd have to answer all their fucking questions.

Face's confidence strengthened knowing he had something special working for him, something nobody else had: The power. The *vision*. If anyone tried messing with him, he'd be ahead of the game by avoiding traps and recognizing how and where they'll attack. He didn't know for sure if a cop was the killer or not, but he wasn't taking chances. Face planned to outsmart *somebody*, whoever he was, and prove that this particular Diablo happened to be the one motherfucker who had the brains and balls to survive through the night. For the moment, he'd keep his hands in his pockets and his hood pulled over his head trying to stay warm.

Now that he made it up here to Casa Place, he realized he wasn't feeling too good. He felt tired and dizzy. The lump on his head seemed bigger and hurt more than before. Maybe he smashed it against the wall harder than he thought when he fell back over the TV. He flipped his cell phone open to see the time. "*Almost midnight*," he whispered. "*I got me some time. Maybe if I rest a little I'll feel better.*" Finding a position that avoided the painful spot, Face leaned his head back against the tree and closed his eyes.

TᵢᵣT TᵢᵣT TᵢᵣT

Veronica placed the phone back on the cradle, looking defeated as she returned to the kitchen table. Her usual erect posture gave way to sagging shoulders as she dropped on the chair and bowed her head, her face hidden by dangling locks of hair. Kevin pulled his chair closer to hers.

"You'll try him again later, all right?"

"He won't answer," she said in a quiet voice. "I've called five times. What's the use?" Veronica raised her head and stared at the clock on the wall. "I can't just sit here anymore," she complained. "We only have a little more than an hour left." She looked back at him, her eyes moist and rimmed with red. "We've got to find him."

Kevin agreed. Lieutenant Atkinson had continued to preach patience, telling them his units were scouring all areas, but 4 a.m. was fast approaching. They all needed to be part of the search at this point. "You're right," he said. "Everybody has to be involved now."

Seth remained asleep on the couch. Kevin opened the door and saw Atkinson talking on the phone in his car. "You wake Seth, Veronica. I'll tell Carl we're leaving." When he approached the car he stood close by and listened, waiting for the conversation to finish.

"I don't want to send a chopper up there blind. Just make sure it's fueled and ready to go... Yeah, yeah, the Captain knows everything... We don't have time to go banging on every fucking door, okay?... Well, check the park again, damn it!... I told you before, I don't think he drove away. I really believe the kid wants to handle this one alone... That's right, four a.m... It might be our best chance to nail this heart attack asshole... Keep working the hills, that makes the most sense... I know there's no lights up there. He might've been thinking that too, right? Okay, I'll tell you when."

As soon as Carl finished, Kevin wasted no time explaining his intention.

"Yeah, go ahead, Kevin," he answered in a tired voice. "Let's face it, we don't have much time. I'll make sure all units are aware of your vehicle searching the areas. Just do me a favor, all right?" The Lieutenant took a notepad and wrote down a phone number. "Here," he said, tearing off the sheet and handing it to Kevin. "If you find him, call me immediately. Just because the fish is hooked doesn't mean you can reel him in."

FIFTY-ONE

FACE LURCHED AWAKE FROM A dream that ended with him trapped in a coffin of ice, able to breathe and hear, yet powerless to escape. The cold seemed unbearable, and the sound of his heartbeat echoed off the frozen walls. The realization that he just dreamed the situation offered momentary relief that soon gave way to a splitting headache and the awareness of the time when he looked at his phone. Face cursed himself for falling asleep, for getting careless and putting himself in a position where twenty minutes later someone could have sneaked up and finished him off like all the others. He didn't want to think about what a stupid ass, what a *pendejo* he would have been, if he'd been killed in his sleep. He also noticed he'd missed five calls, all from his sister. "*Tell ya what, Veronica,*" he said quietly, changing the ringer control from silent to vibrate, "*if you call again I'll answer. Just to let you know I ain't dead.*"

He felt like shit. His head throbbed and the temperature must have dropped another ten degrees. He also felt dizzy enough to think he could puke at any minute. Face figured he'd feel better if he got to his feet and took some deep breaths. When he stood, he needed to hold his arm out against the tree for support. "*This is bullshit,*" he muttered. Within moments he leaned over, throwing up on the other side of the tree. He straightened up, inhaled more fresh air, and decided he felt better. He reached in the pocket of his sweatshirt and took out his phone. "*Sixteen minutes to find me, asshole,*" he whispered. "*This is too fuckin' easy.*"

In the next instant Face dropped to his knees, blinded by blackness. He started to shiver, and sensed a feeling of walls closing in from all sides, surrounding him like... like a coffin. A slurred voice, impossible to understand, somehow led him to recognize that death approached him, stalking him, determined to follow the 4 a.m. timetable for his destruction. Face then heard the same loud heartbeat from his dream, a steady one-two, one-two thumping he feared as his own. The drum-like sound increased, reaching an intensity that hurt his ears and forced him to place his hands over them in a futile attempt at relief.

He saw himself flat on the ground, struggling to overcome a strange, paralyzing cold that left him open to attack. A terrifying image of black rats, their eyes red and wild, overwhelmed him as their crazed squealing penetrated his hideout. Soon, another vision, this one of ice white hands somehow stretching and moving its fingers inside his body, swam through his bloodstream like a great white shark hungry to kill. Face realized he'd soon be in the grasp of a superior power beyond his control and that his ability to foresee danger meant nothing anymore. He'd be dead soon. At 4.a.m.

FIFTY-TWO

UNCLE KEVIN HAD DRIVEN HIS CAR for almost forty minutes. Veronica sat with him in the front, directing him through the hilly streets of the neighborhood. Seth sat in the back, feeling energized by the actual experience of seeing Casa Place. According to his watch, they drove up the street at 3:23. What a cool feeling, knowing Alex hid up there somewhere, and no one else knew but him. At first he felt nervous, wondering if they'd find him. Alex would think Seth told on him and that would ruin everything. Next time he saw Alex, he'd let him know how everybody worried so much. They'd both have a good laugh. Maybe Alex would share other secrets with him after tonight, knowing he could trust him.

Seth felt bad that Veronica seemed so sad and worried. He wished she believed him about his dad, that he wouldn't be angry with Alex, but she'd just have to see for herself. His dad only killed the bad guys, and Alex wasn't one of those anymore. When Veronica told them that Alex decided to stop being a gang member, Seth knew for sure they had nothing to worry about. Why couldn't anybody else see that?

"Try calling him again," Uncle Kevin told her, pulling to the side of the road.

Veronica's voice sounded tired and depressed. "Why?" she asked. "He won't answer."

"You've hung up the phone every time you called," he remarked. "Aren't you able to leave him a message?"

"I know what he's like," she said, "and it won't do any good. Alex is so stubborn and seemed so determined to be left alone. A voice mail message wouldn't mean a thing."

"It's three thirty-five, Veronica. We don't have time to think that

313

way now."

Veronica looked out her side window. Running a hand through her hair, she took a deep breath, exhaling as if she were blowing out candles on a cake. "You're right," she replied, opening the flap to her phone. "I would love nothing more than to have Alex yell at me tomorrow for going against his wishes."

"I have an idea," he said. "Turn your speaker phone on so Seth can talk into it, too. Maybe Alex might respond if he also hears his young friend's voice."

"I don't know, Uncle Kevin. Alex might think I'm bugging him."

"*So what?*" his uncle exclaimed, sounding upset. "We all care about him, right? I'd like the chance to thank him for what he did tonight, and make sure he's all right. Wouldn't you?"

Veronica turned the speaker on so everyone could hear. Seth figured no harm would come from playing along and leaving a message. Maybe it was for the better. Alex would be able to hear for himself how Seth didn't give anything away. Within moments, the quick, high-pitched tones from the speed dial sounded. "Lean in closer, Seth," she said. I'll hold it for you." Seth heard the ringing on the other end of the line. "You'll hear the beep after five rings," she told him. The fourth ring finished. "Get ready to leave..."

Alex's alarmed voice cut her off in mid-sentence. "*Veronica! Is that you?*"

Veronica gasped as she pulled the phone back towards her mouth. "*Alex!* Where... are you all right?"

Alex started talking in a fast, nervous-sounding way that rattled Seth.

"*I saw crazy shit... lots a fuckin' rats all over me... and white hands... fingers like bones... doin' somethin' inside! Couldn't see. Can't figure it out. And I heard a loud beating sound... like a drum. Or a fuckin' heart!*"

"Alex, you need help! Tell us where you are!"

"*I saw myself... dyin'! So cold... I couldn't fuckin' move!*" After a brief moment of silence, Alex yelled into the phone. "*He's here! Someone's here! Can't see...*"

"Alex!" she shouted. "Can you hear me?"

"*Aaahh!*"

Seth listened in disbelief. A scream that sounded as if Alex was in terrible pain ended with a muffled noise that he couldn't figure out. Maybe a hand covered the phone, or it dropped somewhere, or someone threw it so Alex couldn't communicate with anybody. He thought he heard him yelling in the background but couldn't be sure. Veronica tried several more times without success to get Alex to respond.

She choked back a sob. "Kevin, I don't know what to do!"

Neither did Seth. His confusion caused a struggle for breath, as if he had run a long race. Alex seemed to be in terrible danger, but how could that be? No one knew about his hiding place but him. Suddenly another thought entered his thinking, slowly at first, until the possibility became an unbearable certainty. His dad was with Alex…and he was going to kill him! Seth looked at his watch, at the American and Mexican flags side by side, and remembered what Alex said when he gave it to him.

"*No matter where you are and what time you got, you and me is always together.*"

"You're wrong, Alex," he answered back in a whisper. "The time *does* matter. If I don't find you in the next twelve minutes, we'll never be together again."

Seth shouted as if Uncle Kevin and Veronica were a block away. "*Go to Casa Place! That's where he hides! He told me! Behind some trees! Hurry!*"

FIFTY-THREE

ACE WASN'T ALONE. HE DIDN'T know how to put the feeling into words for Veronica, but he just *knew*. He grabbed his gun, readying himself for a chance to shoot, but a brutal pain shot through his chest.

"*Aaahh!*"

Face dropped the phone and staggered behind the tree, his arm stretched out in a set position to fire. The clear sound of a heartbeat, coming from somewhere, echoed in his ears for several moments before fading away. A voice from out of nowhere soon followed.

"He shrieked once-once only."

"WHAT? WHERE ARE YOU?" Face shouted.

The uninvited moonlight entered through the open branches, leaving him exposed. He felt vulnerable to a long-range rifle or a surprise attack. He wasn't sure whether to stay or move somewhere else. He waited, his gun in one hand and the other massaging his chest where the pain had struck. Face remained on guard through the once-broken silence, his eyes and ears alert for any movement.

"Who's there?"

"I kept quite still and said nothing."

Face jumped back and spun in a complete circle, certain this new enemy stood a few feet away. But where? He suddenly realized if the voice seemed that close without anyone in sight, he must have been hiding in the tree. Face pointed his gun upwards and hurriedly scanned every branch, looking for a reason to shoot. With help from the moonlight, he didn't see anybody there, but his right eye had blurred and felt swollen, hurting like a bitch and leaving him less sure of his ability to protect himself. Keeping one hand on his gun, Face dropped to one knee and placed his free hand over the pain. He felt gooey shit on his fingers and couldn't understand how the puffiness had gotten so much worse in such a short time. *"Damn!"* he grumbled. "It was that fuckin' fight tonight."

Face rose to his feet, making sure he didn't get careless. He continued to hear the beating in his head, but now wondered if the big bump and headache had caused all of his problems. He walked over to a section of overhanging branches and peeked out between them, thinking he might see something there, even with one good eye. Lights from the city sparkled below, making everything seem peaceful for the moment.

"I grew furious as I gazed upon it."

Face fell to the ground, clutching his chest and fighting for air. He couldn't stop shaking from the cold. His insides felt covered in snow, but he had proven himself too much of a man to let something like this happen to him. He had to get up and fight. He *had* to! He tried to stand, rising to one knee before another jolt of pain struck him down again. He lay flat on his back now, staring up with his one good eye at the tree branches above. What he saw made him question if... caused him to *pray...* that he was hallucinating. Masses of squealing black rats, like large hairy fruit, appeared out of nowhere, hanging in packs from every branch in sight. He watched in mind-numbing helplessness as the rodent-filled tree limbs swung back and forth above him, lowering inch by inch with each passing second, closing in on his disabled body.

"Down-steadily down it crept."

Face tried to push away, but with each attempt another crippling ache shot through the inside of his chest, causing him to collapse over and over again. He wondered in horror if his dream about an ice coffin would soon come true.

FIFTY-FOUR

KEVIN RACED HIS CAR to the top of the narrow winding road. A lone house sat upon a hill at the end of the darkened street, filled with pre-dawn shadows from a single streetlight and a cold winter moon. When Seth admitted to knowing Alex's hiding place, his emotions ranged from anger to panic. They were now down to six minutes before four. *Six minutes!* He couldn't believe Seth had allowed so much time to lapse but his confession gave them something they didn't have before: *hope.*

Veronica had directed him back to Casa Place, a street they had already passed a good fifteen minutes before. She called Lieutenant Atkinson to let him know where they were heading and why. Atkinson had wanted to send a helicopter, as much for a spotlight as anything else, but Veronica urged him not to for fear of driving Alex away. "I know my brother," she told him. "He won't trust you. He'll run if he can." Kevin could sense Carl's reluctance to oblige her but the light from the moon would have to suffice.

"He's somewhere in there!" Seth yelled, pointing to a wall of bushes on the left. "He said there's a fence."

They hurried out of the car. "*Alex!*" Veronica yelled. "*Alex, are you here?*"

Seth didn't hear anything. "*Where are you, Alex? It's Seth!*"

Seth darted into the bushes. Veronica went to search another area further up the path. Kevin got on his hands and knees, preparing to crawl into a section between the two of them when he heard Seth's shout. "*I found it! It's here!*"

Kevin ran towards Seth, followed by Veronica. He saw the bushes move and heard the rustling of his legs and feet, knowing he attempted to scale the fence. "Seth!" he cried out. "Can you climb it?"

"Yeah... I... almost... hold on... okay, I'm over! Meet me there! I'm gonna go find him!"

"No, wait for us!" Kevin yelled, hearing the fading footsteps of running feet.

Veronica scurried through the bushes and over the fence at a speed that startled Kevin. When he hoisted himself over he saw that she had already run half-way down the dirt path towards a moonlit area where shadowy shapes of trees rose from a f lat patch of ground. He heard the sound of a car approaching from the other side of the bushes where they had just been. Assuming it was the police, perhaps even Carl, he debated for a moment whether he should wait. A quick glance at his watch provided the instant answer of 'no' and propelled him into a sprint towards Seth and Veronica. The time was 3:56.

Seth's urgent plea for help echoed from somewhere in the vicinity of the trees. With about twenty yards to go before he got there, Kevin saw him bolt out from behind some long, leafy branches and place his hands on his knees, visibly shaken. Veronica parted the descending limbs and immediately uttered a gut-wrenching cry, making Kevin fear that Alex was already dead. He entered through another section of the dark green partition and became mesmerized by a horrific scene he could never have imagined. A volley of rats swung from the branches and dropped down like large black hail, swarming Alex's immobile body.

Despite the hideous event occurring before his eyes, Kevin recognized Warren's presence. He had read his book of Edgar Allan Poe stories and felt convinced these rats were sent from Poe's, 'The Pit and the Pendulum'. The same thing happened now as happened with all the other victims, and Alex would receive nothing more than a bad scare and scratch marks; a prelude to his planned death by heart attack. There was still time.

"Seth!" Kevin shouted. "He's here! Your father's here!"

Seth tried to speak, but was obviously frightened and breathing fast. "He's... he's..."

Kevin grabbed him by the shoulders, shaking hard enough to get his attention. "Alex *needs* you, Seth. Remember what Madame Sibilia said. Your father can hear you. He can *hear* you! Talk to him! *Now!*"

A bright light suddenly appeared from close range. Kevin swatted some limbs aside and saw Carl approaching with a flashlight and drawn gun along with a second officer.

"Kevin!" Atkinson shouted. "Is he alright?"

"Please, Carl," he pleaded, "just wait there. If I'm right, we'll know in another couple of minutes."

Kevin glanced at Veronica, her eyes wild with fear and confusion. "He's still alive, Veronica! Seth can save him!"

She stared at Kevin, her eyes questioning his belief.

"It's his *heart* we have to worry about," he exclaimed, "not the rats! Look!"

Like rushing water disappearing into a street sewer, the rodent horde scampered under the other side of the tree branches and vanished into the night. Kevin, Seth, and Veronica hurried over to Alex, crouching down to check on his condition. Veronica lifted his wrist. "His skin's so *cold*!" she said through muffled sobs.

"Can you feel a pulse?" Kevin asked.

"Yes," she answered, "but it's very weak."

The trickling moonlight produced a ghostly pallor to his face, lined with reddened scratches and coupled with the large, misshapen swelling of his eye that couldn't be ignored.

"Hurry, Seth!" Kevin implored. "It's almost time!"

Seth looked at the both of them before staring down at Alex.

"Dad?" he said, his eyes scanning the darkened area. "Dad? It's me. Seth. Can you hear me, Dad? Don't kill Alex, okay? Please don't kill him. He's my friend. My *friend*! No more killing, Dad. I'm all right now." Seth stood up, looking towards the sky. "God? If you can hear me, you gotta help Dad. He needs you, God. He was only trying to help me. He loved me, God. And he loved my mom. Please, God. Please. Help him find her up there." Seth dropped to his knees and held Alex's hand. "Dad? Please. Let Alex live." Tears rolled down Seth's face. "Go find Mom, okay? Okay, Dad? She'll... she'll be in the rose garden."

In the quiet of the lush canopy, another voice was heard. Alex's eyes remained closed, but his lips moved, whispering something. They all leaned close to listen, and in wonderment, Kevin recognized the words in an instant. Why would Alex be speaking them now?

FIFTY-FIVE

WARREN SENT THE RATS AWAY. In '*The Pit and the Pendulum*', they had swarmed around the prisoner, '*wild, bold, ravenous*', gnawing through the viand-scented bandages until he was freed. This gangbanger's struggle would find a different ending through the punishment of death for his murderous actions. This form of vengeance remained forever valid and worth pursuing. In a world where darkness dominated much of life, Seth remained a lone star worth protecting in an otherwise black, oppressive sky.

The designated time loomed; one minute before four o'clock, *still dark as midnight*. The recitation of '*A Victim's Time*' would now be the one privilege bestowed upon this killer before his heart pumped its final beat.

"The valiant soldier's blood will spill..."

"Dad?" Dad? It's me. Seth"

Warren fell silent, unsure of what had just occurred. He prepared to continue, aware that four o'clock fast approached. Maintaining his death grip on this gangbanger's heart, he started to speak the next line.

"On red-stained lands..."

"Can you hear me, Dad? Don't kill Alex, okay? Please don't kill him. He's my friend. My friend!"

Warren's recognition of the voice took several moments to develop, like a desert wanderer's hesitancy to comprehend the sound of a nearby river. But when he spoke again, there was no mistaking Seth's voice. And, of course, Warren listened. He *wanted* to hear what Seth had to say.

"No more killing, Dad. I'm all right now. God? If you can hear me, you gotta help Dad. He needs you, God. He was only trying to help me. He loved

me, God. And he loved my mom. Please, God. Please. Help him find her up there. Dad? Please. Let Alex live. Go find Mom, okay? Okay, Dad? She'll... she'll be in the rose garden."

Warren's grip on the victim's heart eased, but he didn't let go. He felt a strange unsteadiness in his power, and a sudden uncertainty over his existence. His conviction of purpose started receding, like the remains of a wave accelerating back into the ocean. But what was he hearing now? A whispering voice, so unlike Seth's, overran his consciousness and shocked him into another kind of reflection.

"The valiant soldier's blood will spill
On red-stained lands of sacrifice
The unknown stranger lies as still
Apart from honor's noble price
Two victims of a time to kill
Beware the heart as cold as ice."

The words stripped away Warren's final desire for revenge. Whoever this gangbanger was, by reciting the poem at this crucial moment, he showed his understanding between a life worth dying for and dying without a chance at life. Perhaps hope existed after all.

As he released his remaining hold from the heart, something unexplainable began happening around him. The blackness of his surroundings transformed into an enclosure of dazzling colors, encircling him in every hue imaginable. The constancy of the cold, stale air turned into a warm breeze, instilling in him an unusual yet blissful feeling of floating. He felt as if he drifted away from *something*, but he didn't remember what anymore.

Warren's growing awareness of his imminent fate provided an intuitive sense of peace and fulfilled longing. He visualized Seth, comforted in the knowledge that his son's soul would always be connected to his own. He gazed in understanding and acceptance as the sparkling colors melded into the brilliant white light that now shimmered before him. Warren realized he was at the doorstep to Heaven, marking the end of one journey and the beginning of another. Staring at his naked reflection in the resplendent doorway he now faced, he watched in wonder as the image of Michelle appeared, more beautiful than ever, guiding him to her before wrapping herself around his body, reuniting as one, together, forever.

FIFTY-SIX

"DID YOU CALL ALEX?" Kevin asked.

"He wants me to give you a message," Veronica said. "Congratulations on the engagement and finding the perfect brother-in-law."

Kevin laughed. "Well, I don't know about the perfect brother-in-law," he said, "but Marco must think he found the perfect mechanic. Alex has worked there less than a month and Marco told me he's already the best he's got."

"When are we going to the cemetery?" Seth asked.

Kevin glanced at his watch. "Soon," he told him. "I have something I need to do in my office first."

From the moment he typed his first word, Kevin's fingers continued nonstop until he'd said everything there was to say. As he started to read what he'd written, he shook his head from the surreal feeling of events and changes that occurred within the last year.

> *Today marks the one-year anniversary of my brother's murder. With much thanks to the decision makers around here, I've been given the chance to reflect on the previous three hundred sixty-five days and share some experiences with my readers.*
>
> *A year ago I wrote a series of articles about the increasing danger of various Latino gangs throughout our city. Call it the worst of coincidences, but my brother, Warren, was killed in a drive-by shooting between two such gangs during that same period. I became the legal guardian of his son, Seth, who lost his mother to cancer several months before. Seth took quite awhile to overcome*

the trauma from that fateful night. So did I, apparently. I started to drink heavily, comfortably caught in the tentacle-like clutches of alcohol. Concurrently, Seth's nightmarish encounter with the two Mexican-American gangs that killed his father developed into a strong animosity towards all things Latino, including classmates from his own school. Seth didn't much care for me, either. A cold peace settled over our lives, and friction became our permanent houseguest. Times were darkest before the dawn, indeed.

Something special happened that opened our eyes and led us to discover that life is as unpredictable as the final tick of a watch. That analogy is appropriate because for me, time stopped. Not literally, of course, but the kind of weary, joyless time that made each day border on the intolerable, and cause each minute to seem like three. Kevin Palmer, yours truly, fell in love, and last night the woman in my life accepted my marriage proposal. Seth cheered and clapped when we told him. Something I should mention here: My fiancée is a Mexican-American.

Thanks in large part to her, Seth has learned that every nationality, like those of Mexican heritage, has their fair share of good people. And those bad ones? Like land mines, they're also scattered around the ethnic landscape. We just have to try our best to avoid them. Seth has also befriended my fiancée's brother. So have I. Something else I should mention here: Her brother was a long-time gang member, including most of this last year.

Did Seth care? Or me? Of course we did. But through the barbed wire discord and fog of divisiveness, time somehow brought change. And redemption. And love. And respect. Not only in the life of an ex-gang member, but for Seth and me as well.

Moral of the story? I guess life is often more than just a simple case of good and bad, isn't it? Whether we like it or not, we all must learn to deal with that unrelenting gray in our lives that complicate our decision making and prevent us from keeping things simple and neat. Maybe for those of you out there who don't believe in the future of your fellow man, who think we're closer to dividing than uniting, my story might offer a little hope. Who knows? You might be like Seth or me, seeing your life change for the better in the most unlikely of situations, at the most unexpected of times, and in the most unpredictable of circumstances.

ᛏᛁᚱ ᛏᛁᚱ ᛏᛁᚱ

Kevin opened the car door and got out, gazing down at the sloping green knoll inside the cemetery. On a cloudless day, the cheerful sound of chirping birds penetrated the silent histories beneath the headstones. As he turned back to close his door, Seth approached him.

"Uncle Kevin, is it okay if Veronica goes to see my mom and dad with me before you do?"

"Are you sure, Seth?" Veronica asked. "Maybe you'd rather go alone."

"I want to be the one to introduce you, Veronica," Seth told her. "You're gonna be my new mom. I want them to know how happy I am."

Veronica smiled at Seth before looking teary-eyed at Kevin.

"Of course it's all right, Seth," Kevin said. "It's a darn good idea."

Kevin waited in his car until he caught sight of the two of them returning up ahead. Veronica had her arm around Seth's shoulder, and Kevin could see the tears in Seth's eyes as they neared him.

"Are you okay, Seth?" Kevin asked.

He nodded his head, but didn't speak.

"We're going to walk down to the entrance area," Veronica said. "They've got benches we can sit on. We'll wait for you there."

Kevin stood and watched them for awhile before turning away. He strolled along a pathway that angled up along a grassy slope for about fifty feet, veering left past a vacant motorized cart carrying landscape equipment. When he arrived at Warren's grave site, reading his name etched in cold, white stone, the impact of how much he missed him hit sudden and hard. Kevin allowed himself as much time as he needed to wring his tears out, like a wet rag in need of a good squeeze. When he felt ready, he had some thoughts he wanted to express.

"You took a wrong turn somewhere, Warren," he said, his eyes fixed on the grave, "but I think you found your way home. Back to Heaven. And back to Michelle." Kevin's eyes narrowed. "Sorry to tell you," he added, "things haven't changed much down here." Lieutenant Atkinson had informed Kevin that the Diablos and Lobos ended their truce. The 'killer b's' were back; bullets, blades, and beatings. But no heart attacks had occurred, and he knew why.

His eyes shifted one grave over to Michelle's. "Take care of him, honey. I know he's a load, sometimes, but you're the only one I know who could put up with the guy." Kevin smiled, thinking how nice it would be if they could actually hear his words. "I want you both to know Seth is fine. He's a great kid. I've grown to love him as my own son. He's learned to move on, too. He's back with his friends, and he's doing well in school again." Kevin stared at the grave sites a few moments longer before walking away. After a few steps he turned back. "Oh yeah, I almost forgot to ask you," he said. "What do you think of Veronica?" Kevin listened to the silent response. His eyes watered again. "I wish you could've been here to meet her."

As Kevin wiped his hand across his face, trying to clear his blurred vision, he heard a thudding noise in front of him, as if something dropped from above where he stood. He froze, dazing in disbelief at the small, round object he saw on Warren's grave. With tentative, almost fearful footsteps, Kevin got close enough to bend down and grasp the gold-colored baseball in his hand. He took his fingertip and gently rubbed the 'Dodger' logo written between the stitching. He stared up at the sky, then down at Warren's grave, trying to clear his mind and figure out what he was supposed to do with the present Seth had bought for his father the night of his death.

Once he arrived at his idea, he was convinced Warren wanted the same thing. Kevin had observed a plastic trash can in the back of the landscape cart with several long wooden tool handles sticking out from the top. Hoping to find a shovel in there, he hurried back to look. Spotting one standing a foot above a green rake and a cultivating tool, like a grade school photo of the tallest kid in class, he glanced around before grabbing the wooden handle and rushing back to dig a small hole in front of Warren's headstone, setting the baseball inside. After replacing the soil, he got on his knees and patted the area with his hands. "I can't hear you, Warren," he said, "but if you're saying, 'thank you', you're welcome. This will be our little secret."

On the way back to his car, Kevin suddenly recalled what Madame Sibilia told him about looking for a sign from Heaven and Earth. "That's what she must have meant," he whispered to himself. "Warren and his baseball."

Deep in thought, Kevin rounded a wide curve and slowly headed towards the bottom of the driveway. Madame Sibilia, whoever or whatever she was, sure knew what she was talking about, but she missed something.

"Heaven and Earth, huh?" Kevin said, speaking out loud as if she were with him. "Well, I've got news for you, lady. There are two more signs for me to look for. One's name is Seth and the other one is Veronica. You know what I call that?" Kevin smiled at the obvious answer. "Heaven *on* Earth."

THE END

CPSIA information can be obtained at www.ICGtesting.com
Printed in the USA
BVOW05*0037200615

404291BV00002B/7/P

9 781942 296058